MRS HUDSON GOES TO PARIS

by

Susan Knight

Paperback ISBN 978-1-78705-919-1
ePub ISBN 978-1-78705-920-7
PDF ISBN 978-1-78705-921-4

Published by MX Publishing
335 Princess Park Manor,
Royal Drive, London,
N11 3GX
www.mxpublishing.com

Cover design by Brian Belanger

In Memory of John Laher

Chapter One – to Paris

To read Dr. Watson's accounts of Mr. H"s adventures, you might think that I am forever at the beck and call of my lodgers, without a life of my own. Something, I have to say, that is very far from being the case. Of course, I have become very fond of my two gentlemen over the years, and I would not be without them. Even Mr H with all his faults and demands – one must make allowances for genius. Nevertheless, my life, especially recently, has taken off in directions I could never have imagined when I first came here to Baker Street with dear Henry and our two beloved girls. I have already described some of my adventures elsewhere, and in my latter years have discovered quite a taste for travel. Indeed, I soon find myself getting restless if I do not head off somewhere or other once in a while.

I was thus most intrigued earlier this year to receive a letter from my sister Nelly, who lives in the north of England, the same sister, incidentally, who shared in the adventure of the Vanished Man, about which I have written elsewhere. It seemed that her only son, Ralph, a young man of twenty-one, had taken it into his head that he wanted to be an artist, and so had headed forthwith to France, to Paris, which apparently is where anyone aspiring to that calling must go these days. At least, that is what Ralph told his mother.

Since then she had heard little from him – the odd note dashed off from time to time– and she was worried that her little darling might have fallen into bad company; Paris being, as she wrote to me, such an immoral place. A dangerous place, moreover, with, as the newspapers reported it, anarchist bombs going off right, left and centre.

I should add here that Nelly, a couple of years older than myself, has always been a worrier, given to fanciful exaggeration; the sensational novels and scandal sheets to which she is addicted having coloured her perception of the world. In my opinion, moreover, she has spoiled Ralph to excess, indulging him, where a firm hand might have served the youth better. Like myself, sadly, Nelly was widowed quite young and thenceforth focussed all her attentions and affections on her only son; her daughter, Maria, being considerably older than the boy and well-settled.

Now it seemed nothing would content her but to travel to Paris and find out what was the matter with him, her concern for her darling outweighing any perils to herself from immorality or bombs. Since she could not imagine going alone, as she wrote in her letter, she begged for me to accompany her, especially since, as she said, "you speak the language, Martha." I fear Nelly rather overestimated my fluency. It is true that I had enjoyed learning French in school, and later was able to practise it for a period, thanks to a charming young woman from Normandy whom Henry and I employed as a nursemaid when the girls were little. In the years since then, I have tried to keep it up, and have even been known to peruse the occasional story in that mellifluous tongue, enjoying the works of M. Guy de Maupassant in particular. However, without the occasion to speak it, my ability to do so had fallen somewhat by the wayside.

Still, a trip to Paris in early summer was a most tempting prospect, it being a city I had always wished to visit. I put down the letter and picked up my cup of tea. Why not, I thought. There was nothing at home that demanded my special attention at that particular moment, the gentlemen being about to head off away somewhere or other in the West of England, to solve another mystery, no doubt. Should they return unexpectedly, my maid Clara would be more than capable of holding the fort for a week or so.

I replied straightway to Nelly, before I could change my mind, accepting her invitation.

"They aren't really white, are they?" said Nelly, as we stood on the deck of the ferry looking back at the Dover cliffs. "More greyish, I'd say."

That is the trouble with my sister. Something I always forget in her absence and only recall in her presence: her unerring ability to find fault, to judge the world ever falling short of her expectations. She had already, in the two days spent with me in Baker Street, complained of the filth and dust of the city, and the cramped nature of the accommodation I could provide (the best rooms naturally being those of my lodgers). The very first thing, indeed, that my loving sister had told me was that I had got fat, that I looked crabbed and old – I who am barely fifty! I refrained from commenting in turn on her own wasted appearance, which in truth had rather shocked me – her yellowish complexion that

3

spoke of a bilious constitution – except to ask if she was quite well, to which she sharply replied that there was nothing the matter with *her*.

She hastened to inform me, moreover, that I was far too accepting of Mr. H.'s unreasonable behaviour and untidiness.

"Those smelly experiments of his! If he were my tenant, Martha, I'd have given him a piece of my mind long ago." She stated this forcefully to me in private, though in his presence I was amused to notice she became quite tongue-tied and wide-eyed, while he, I fear, barely registered her existence.

As for poor Phoebe, my clumsy and foolish maid, Nelly would, she insisted, have given the girl her marching orders long ago, sending her back where she came from. In vain I explained that Phoebe came from a large and needy family, and that, in addition, I had grown quite fond of her, despite everything. Indeed, that she was much improved from what she used to be, to which remark Nelly gave a meaningful sniff, as if all the more entrenched in her opinion.

She also proved very fussy about her food and got black looks from Clara when she sent back that treasure's speciality, a mock turtle soup, because it contained onions, which, as she claimed, didn't agree with her. She merely toyed with her roast capon, and ate only one spoonful of her Conservative pudding "because, you know, Martha, it is far too rich for my digestion." No wonder, I thought to myself, that you are all skin and bones.

The sights of London in general she compared unfavourably with those of her own northern city, the one exception being almost on my doorstep in Baker Street. The Waxworks Museum of Madame Tussaud thrilled her utterly. It is not a place I myself like to visit. I find the lifelike and yet lifeless statues unnerve me with their pale and damp-looking skin, so many of them indeed, representing dead people. I do not even care to look upon our dear Queen Victoria, who lives yet, thanks be to God, and wondered if she had ever set eyes upon this copy of herself, in all her youth and beauty, her late consort at her side, and what she thought of it. I should certainly not like to see myself set up like that for idlers to gawk at, and cannot help but fear that, someday, likenesses of Mr. H. and even dear Dr. Watson will be found there. I sincerely hope not. Still, I was so happy that at last Nelly had found something to interest her that I refrained from sharing my revulsion.

She was particularly attracted to the Chamber of Horrors, with its life-size representations of murderers, among them the body-snatchers Burke and Hare and that most unnatural woman, Mary Anne Cotton, who poisoned her three husbands and eleven children. Not to mention the death masks of the victims of the French Revolution, poor King Louis and Queen Marie Antoinette set beside a viciously authentic-looking guillotine.

"But imagine, Martha, poor Ralph falling victim to that!"

Nelly, having learnt that the instrument still served in France as a means of execution, had half convinced herself that her son had already been inveigled into a life of crime by various sinister individuals. When I expressed astonishment that she should imagine such a thing, she referred me to a novel she had recently perused in which the dashing hero, falsely accused, had only escaped the guillotine's blade by the skin of his teeth.

"It was quite terrifying, Martha, to read of it. I could hardly bear it."

5

Somewhat exasperated, I suggested to her that she really ought to change the subject matter of her reading material, the yellow press in which she delighted was giving her a distorted view of the world.

"The world is generally not like that, Nelly," I said.

She sniffed.

Little did I know, of course, that what lay ahead of us would come to resemble those very sensational tales in no small fashion. But, forgive me, I anticipate.

To return to our journey. After disembarking from the ferry at the port of Calais, we boarded the train to Paris and soon were speeding through northern France. It had turned into a gloomy day with louring clouds, and, though it felt hot and humid, we had evidently left the sunshine behind us in England. The landscape meanwhile was flat and uninspiring, a dispiriting enough start to our adventure. Nelly, however, was buried in yet another of those hair-raising novels she favoured, and so I was at least spared her judgment on the scene. For myself, I had acquired a Baedeker travel guide to the French capital and was eagerly picking out places to visit, for I was determined to make the most of our stay, never mind what young Ralph might be up to.

We eventually arrived at the Gare du Nord, a great vaulted hall of a place. A motley crowd that included many low-life individuals, was pressing all about us and we were quick to find porters for our bags, holding fast to our reticules meanwhile in case they should be torn from our hands. I was as relieved as Nelly when she spotted Ralph waiting for us. To be honest, I should not have known him. The skinny, awkward lad I remembered from past visits had grown into a tall and slender young man with something of the athletic look of his late father. But while the latter was always well groomed, Ralph's fair hair hung in strings and the meagre little beard he sported on his chin resembled nothing so much as an eruption of rust.

This provoked a cry from Nelly almost before she had greeted him.

"Ralph," she said, "whatever do you look like? You need a visit to the barbers..." and then regarding his attire, "and to the outfitters."

The boy frowned. I imagined he thought he looked quite the bohemian with his beard and smock and beret and ragged scarlet cravat, and I felt a little sorry that his mother had not saved her exclamations at least until after they had exchanged embraces.

He nodded rather curtly at me as if not quite sure who I was.

"Aren't you going to say hello to your Aunt Martha?" asked Nelly, in a tone one might use to chide a small child.

"Hello, Aunt Martha," Ralph replied, parrot-fashion, with a sort of a sneer.

I greeted him back warmly, however, and added that I was delighted to have the opportunity of seeing a city I had always dreamed of visiting.

"Why haven't you come before, then, if you wanted to so much? After all, it's not darkest Africa."

Oh dear, I thought. This confrontational attitude did not bode at all well for our trip.

He had reserved rooms for us in a hotel, near enough, he said, to his studio apartment in Montmartre. We piled into a cab with some difficulty, given our large cases, the driver growling something incomprehensible and spitting. It proved a most uncomfortable journey, rattling over the cobblestones, clinging on for dear life.

Worse was to come. Alighting at place called Pigalle, we found ourselves in a decidedly seedy and run-down neighbourhood, not at all what I had been expecting from my guidebook. None of the broad boulevards of Baron Haussmann here. No elegant architecture, just higgledy-piggledy structures looming over narrow, sunless streets. Ralph led us down one of these to a most unprepossessing-looking establishment. Indeed, I should never have taken it for a hotel, save for the wording in broken letters indicating as much over the door. Hôtel de lube was the name this place graced itself with, though I doubted that the dawn of its name was visible from any of the grimy little windows.

While Ralph spoke in French to a fat and slovenly woman behind a reception desk, Nelly looked about herself with dismay.

"What is this place, Martha?" she whispered. "It doesn't look quite…"

At that moment a stout middle-aged man in a dark suit and hat descended the stairs, giving us a startled look as he passed out into the street. Behind him ambled a young woman in considerable dishabille. Her hair was falling about her face and her lips were smudged with red. She went behind the desk and helped herself to a cigarette.

"Ralph," I said in sharp tones. "This place will not do."

I did not know exactly what my young nephew was up to, though I had my suspicions.

He turned back in some surprise. The concierge and the young woman stared at me as well.

"What?" he said.

"Oh, Martha." Nelly grabbed my arm. "If Ralph thinks it will suit us, then I am sure it must."

"Admittedly it is not the grandest place, mother. I only wished to save you money. Paris is an expensive city, you know."

"Nonetheless," I said. "We are not staying here." I picked up my cases, turned and walked out the door.

Nelly scurried after me.

"Martha," she said, "whatever are you doing?"

"Perhaps your son is unaware that the place is a brothel," I said. "Or perhaps he thinks it is funny to install his mother and aunt in such a place."

"Oh, I am sure..." At that moment, Ralph joined us. "It's not true, is it Ralph?"

"What?" He looked sullen.

"Your Aunt Martha says... Oh, I cannot repeat it."

"We will find somewhere respectable," I said firmly. "In a better part of town." I glared at the boy. "We are not so poor that we have to stay in a house of ill repute."

"Is it? Goodness!" Ralph replied, seeming all innocent. "Oh, aunt, I had no idea. You obviously have more experience of such places than I have...."

I was aghast. Even Nelly was shocked.

"Ralph!" she exclaimed.

He looked rueful at last. "I only meant coming from London," he said. "You must see all sorts of things there."

I decided to let the insult go. There was no point quarrelling at this early stage. It was perfectly clear to me why Ralph was behaving this way: He did not want us here. He was annoyed with his mother for treating him like a child, but in fact was behaving just like one, a spoilt brat, paying her back.

"My Baedeker," I said handing it to him, "recommends some suitable establishments. Perhaps listed here you can find one for us."

His face had turned red. He took the book from me and thumbed through it.

"The Hotel de Provence in Faubourg Montmartre..." he said finally. "It isn't far."

We took a cab – a larger one than before – and this time travelled in relative comfort toward a much more salubrious part of the city. As it turned out the Provence had no free rooms, due perhaps to its mention in Baedeker. However, the friendly concierge was able to direct us to another establishment very nearby, the Hotel Lilas. Again, from the outside I should hardly have taken it for a lodging house but for the sign. It was a narrow building, squashed between similar structures, but rising up on many floors. Inside, the reception hall looked most respectable and clean; rooms, happily, were available, and the price was acceptable too – less, I think than one would pay for similar in London – which again made me suspect Ralph's motives in trying to install us in L'Aube.

Nelly and I were both fatigued after the long journey, but hungry as well. I asked the concierge, in my rather halting French to recommend a nearby restaurant. It seemed to surprise Ralph that I knew anything at all of the language, Nelly being quite ignorant of it. I must explain here, in parenthesis, that, in the following account, I have smoothed over the inadequacies of my command of this most musical of tongues, certainly not to promote myself, but rather to make the exchanges less tortuous for my readers.

The good woman directed us to an establishment in the same street and said that Père Perrot would look after us well, especially if we mentioned that Madame Albert had sent us.

The name of the brasserie was Le Petit Bonhomme, which could equally well have described its owner. Père Perrot was a small round jolly man, bald-pated but with a slick black moustache and a habit of rubbing his hands together exclaiming, "Bon, bon, bon!" He became almost coy on hearing that Madame Albert had recommended him, seating us in as much style as the modest premises could provide. Thereupon he reeled off a list of the dishes on offer, too fast, I confess, for me to follow. However, Ralph, although to my ear speaking French with a very strong Northern English accent, was able to interpret for us, and we enjoyed a delicious repast. At least I did, with my coq au vin and crusty bread to soak up the juices. Nelly, meticulously picking out the onions and various unknowns from her pot-au-feu, pronounced her dish "rather spicy," though I can hardly imagine that it was. It looked like a good plain meat stew to me. Ralph, I noticed, paid rather more attention to the red wine than to his plate of grilled sardines. In fact he drank most of the bottle, even becoming quite convivial, as if he really were most pleased to see us. He proposed a toast, "to Paris, art and good fellowship." We clinked glasses in the time-hallowed manner, and sipped the wine, although Nelly, after tasting it with a grimace, pronounced it "too sour," and laid it aside, in preference to plain water.

Conversation, at first quite lively, on the subject of the city and all it had to offer the visitor, soon became heavy-going, especially since Ralph proved reluctant to talk about himself and his artistic ambitions and achievements to date. As I said, Nelly and I were worn out, so the little wine I imbibed went straight to my head, and soon I could not stop myself from yawning. For Ralph's part, rather than raising his spirits as it did initially, the second bottle of wine seemed to make him ever more morose. That, or perhaps the good humour he had previously displayed was a mask that now slipped away.

It was with general relief, therefore, that we said "bonsoir" to Père Perrot and "goodnight" to Ralph, and adjourned to our hotel, where I quickly slipped into a dreamless sleep between sheets considerably cleaner and well-starched than I imagined we would have enjoyed at L'Aube.

Chapter Two – Montmartre

We had agreed with Ralph that he would come to pick us up on the following morning at about nine of the clock. Madame Albert had already informed us that the hotel did not serve breakfast, and suggested we return to Le Petit Bonhomme, assuring us that she would inform Ralph of our whereabouts when he arrived.

Our concierge – or was she in fact the owner? (I myself am quite touchy on the subject having often been called Mr. H.'s housekeeper, when in fact I am the property-holder and landlady of the Baker Street premises) – was a chatty woman, of about my age and height, and, as Nelly was quick to observe, even fatter, with a ruddy complexion. I suspected from her manner that she was country-born and, when I asked, she was pleased to tell me that yes indeed, she came from Languedoc, but had moved to Paris on her marriage.

"Alas, Monsieur Albert is no more," she told us, shaking her head.

I informed her that Nelly and I were both widows, too, and the good woman pressed my hand with what looked like tears in her eyes. I took the opportunity then to ask if she owned the hotel premises, and she confirmed that this was the case.

"Yes, indeed. It is a great comfort for me to know that my son's future is provided for."

A landlady, then, like myself, and that was how I thought of her from then on.

We made our way to the brasserie. No sign there of our good friend Père Perrot. No doubt he had been late working the night before and so left the morning service to his staff. It was only subsequently that I discovered the waitress to be his daughter, Laure, a young woman as tall and lean as her father was short and stout.

We sat at a table outside on the street – it already being a warm day – and watched the people hurrying by. A colourful crowd, and somehow different, in dress and manner, from the people one might see in London.

"This is most pleasant," I said.

"Well for you, that you can enjoy it, Martha." Nelly pulled a face. "As for me, I have a terrible headache. I don't think I slept a wink all night."

"I am sorry to hear that," I replied. "I slept very well. Like the proverbial log."

"That is not surprising, given the amount of wine you imbibed," Nelly sniffed. I was growing to dislike that sniff intensely. "As for me, the bed was lumpy, and all those street noises would not let me rest. Not to mention the noises inside the hotel. People clumping up and down the stairs at all hours. So very inconsiderate."

"My bed was most comfortable," I told her. "As for noises, inside or out, I heard none to disturb me, and I can assure you it was not because of the wine, of which I had very little."

"Come now, Martha, you and Ralph finished two bottles between you," Nelly insisted, adding just as I opened my mouth

14

to protest, "However, I am not one to argue with you. I know how stubborn you can be… Whatever is this?"

The waitress had laid before each of us a half stick of white bread with a pat of butter, and a soup bowl of what turned out to be a milky chocolate drink. We had requested "le petit dejeuner" and this was what was served. No eggs, no kidneys, no kedgeree. Not even any marmalade!

Somewhat nonplussed, I asked if this were all we were to get and the waitress gabbled something fast. I must have nodded because she then produced a basket containing several crescent-shaped and very buttery warm rolls. I found them delicious, though Nelly complained that the bread was too crusty for her teeth, and the croissants (as I later discovered the rolls to be called) too oily. My patience with her was fast running out.

"Is nothing ever good enough for you, Nelly?" I asked, rather sharply, at which, I regret to say, my sister burst into tears.

"Oh, I'm so sorry, my dear," I said, glancing round to see if we were observed, but the other customers seemed absorbed either in animated conversation or in their morning papers. "I should have realised how very difficult this is for you."

She could hardly have failed to notice Ralph's lack of enthusiasm at our presence. If either of my daughters had treated me in such an off-hand manner I should have been shocked and hurt, but then I knew that they never would. However, it was not my place to criticise her son, especially since I had learnt from bitter experience that it was not a wise move.

At least Nelly pulled herself together to the extent of sipping some of her chocolate drink and admitting that, even if overly sweet, it was not too bad.

15

Then we waited for Ralph to join us. We waited and waited, and still her son did not come. Nelly became ever more anxious, and I feared she might break down again.

"I hope nothing bad has happened to him," she said at regular intervals, while I, I am sorry to admit it, consumed the last of the croissants. But for once Nelly was far too distracted to make a comment.

At last, at near enough ten o'clock, a dishevelled Ralph burst into the restaurant, apologising with something of a bad grace for his tardiness. He claimed to have returned to his studio after leaving us the night before to work on a commission, the which excuse Nelly accepted readily. However, from the bloodshot nature of his eyes and the sour smell of his breath, I judged that he had spent a large part of the night with another bottle or two, whether in his studio or elsewhere I of course could not say.

He swallowed a tiny cup of strong coffee, refused anything to eat, and then asked if we wished to take a cab to see his studio, or to walk up. Since it was a fine day, and since we felt the need to stretch our limbs, we agreed that we should be happy to walk, even though, as Ralph warned us, the path up the hill of Montmartre was very steep.

On the way we passed the back of a fine edifice, which Ralph told us in an offhand manner was Notre Dame de Lorette.

"A Roman Catholic church, I suppose," I asked.

"I suppose so," he answered. "Aren't they all?.. But," he went on, gesturing up the street, "better than any old churches, there's the house where Delacroix lived and worked."

We looked blankly at him.

"Eugene Delacroix!" he exclaimed, "The great Romantic painter. Mother, Aunt Martha, you absolutely must go and see his wonderful pieces in the Louvre museum. *Liberty Guiding the People*. Such power, such energy."

For the first time, the boy had become enthusiastic, and I softened a little in my opinion of him. It seemed he at least had a true love for art.

"*Liberty Guiding the People*," repeated Nelly in worried tones. I guessed what she was thinking. It smacked of dangerous radicalism.

"His use of colour is so inspiring, as you will see," Ralph went on.

Nelly sniffed.

We reached the house indicated, number 58.

"His studio was up there," he said, regarding it with the same awe I might have afforded the altar piece or stained glass windows in the church we had not visited.

The artist's erstwhile residence had, however, been converted into a cabaret, Le Jockey-Club de Montmartre.

"It is a shocking pity," said Ralph. "They haven't even preserved the interior, you know."

We continued on and, although it was most delightful to see more Parisians about their business, their talk accompanied by wild hand gestures, the way did indeed become breathtakingly steep, especially for Nelly, who had to pause, gasping, every few steps, and grasping hold of Ralph's arm.

Finally we reached the top of the hill. Here a huge basilica in white stone was under construction, to be named, as Ralph told us, The Sacred Heart. The name was become familiar to me from a recent visit to Ireland, and it was with some distaste that I recalled that ghastly image so venerated by Roman Catholics: the heart of the Christ bloody from the crown of thorns embedded in it. That said, and, despite the scaffolding that surrounded it, this building, with its high dome looked to be quite splendid, while, from the front of it, there was the most spectacular view out over the city. Ralph pointed to a metal construction far in the distance like an arrow head pointing at the clouds.

"The Eiffel Tower," said Ralph.

"How ugly it is," Nelly remarked.

"It was built I think for the World's Fair and is the tallest building in the world," I said, having gleaned as much from Baedeker. "Am I not right, Ralph?"

"I'm sure you are, aunt."

"You can ride up to the very top, I believe."

"If you want to."

"I certainly don't want to," Nelly said. "Right up there! I'd be afraid I'd fall off."

Ralph laughed. "Mother, you're so funny. Of course, there's a high barrier all around the top, to prevent anyone falling or jumping or being pushed off."

"Ralph!" Nelly exclaimed. "What horrible notions you have."

He laughed some more, delighted to have shocked her.

"Nevertheless," she continued. "You and Aunt Martha can go up there if you so wish, but count me out, if you please."

More to her taste – and to mine, in fact – was the nearer grey stone building of the ancient cathedral, Our Lady of Paris, rising up on an island in the river. Certainly a place to visit, though

Ralph was less enthusiastic. For him, just another old church, perhaps.

We turned then from contemplation of the panoramic view to walk to the nearby Rue Cortot, where Ralph's studio was situated. Up and up – more gasping, more grasping – many rickety flights of stairs which could do with a good scrub-down, finally to reach a poky little space near the top of the building. If nothing else, it became clear why Ralph could not have accommodated even one visitor. His lodgings consisted of a mere single room with a couch which served, apparently, both for sitting and sleeping, since our gallant host rapidly swept away the signs of bedding that lay upon it, before asking us to take the weight off our feet.

We looked around in wonder.

"You work here, too?" I asked, regarding the easel on which a most indifferent sketch of a street scene stood, its outlines seeming to have been slapped on in haphazard fashion.

Ralph nodded.

"But it cannot be healthy," Nelly said. "The air reeks."

"That's linseed oil and turpentine, mother," he told her. "The tools of my trade, you know." He paused. "I like the smell," he added defiantly. "Oh, and mother, don't touch that." Nelly had picked up a bottle of clear liquid. "That's acid."

"Acid!" She put it down in a hurry.

"Yes. I plan to take up etching, you see."

We looked blank.

"Acid is part of the process. It burns the design onto the metal plate... I'm going to take lessons soon."

19

Nelly grumbled that she didn't like to think of him sleeping in a room surrounded by such dangerous substances, but he assured her, rather sharply, that he was always careful.

Then he offered us coffee, which he brewed over a flame of gas. Hardly safe, I thought, given what we had just learnt, but I said nothing, the boy seeming so proud of his newly acquired domesticity. Sadly, the resulting beverage was strong and bitter, and neither Nelly nor I could drink it down, especially without milk of which there was none. Meanwhile Ralph displayed his work for us. The painting on the easel, which I had thought only a beginning, was apparently a finished product, as evidenced by more of the same, stacked around the walls.

Nelly was somewhat lost for words.

"Do people actually pay money for these?" she asked. "They are so... er... Well, I can hardly tell what they are supposed to represent."

Ralph sighed. "Haven't you heard of Impressionism, mother? These days, slavish imitation of reality has been thrown out. I mean, photography does that sort of thing so much better, doesn't it? We Impressionists," he preened himself, "are painting the world as we see it – in flux, you know, not static, not pinned down like a butterfly in a... a..."

"Display cabinet?" I suggested. I have, by the way, always found that particular practice a gratuitously cruel one.

Ralph gestured impatiently.

"Well, it's all rather too modern for me," Nelly said. "I don't understand it at all."

"Your mother asked if you have sold any?" I felt I had to get back to the point.

"Oh, as to that," Ralph waved an exasperated hand, "real artists cannot be expected to keep thinking all the time of the market. They must be true to their muse, you know."

"It's just," I went on, "that last night you spoke of a commission."

"Ah yes." Ralph sounded evasive. "Yes, indeed."

"Is it this one?" I pointed to the piece on the easel.

"Er, no. Not that one."

We waited.

"I am not ashamed of it," he said at last. "Just that," laughing, "I thought you ladies might be shocked."

He pulled out a canvas from where it had been concealed under sacking.

Nelly gasped. I suppose she was not accustomed to seeing young ladies portrayed in their natural state, without any clothes on. But while I myself am no great sophisticate in such matters, I have seen enough nudes in artistic settings to know that they are a favoured subject of the Old Masters.

Nevertheless, I cannot say that Ralph's painting shewed any greater talent than did his street scenes and landscapes. The poor girl's flesh was of a most unlikely shade of salmon pink, hardly enhanced by greenish shadows, her stance awkward and unnatural and her hands and feet mere splodges. As for her profile, I think even I could have done a better job. And for the rest, well, propriety forbids that I venture further details.

"It is for a new cabaret, you know," Ralph explained. "They are commissioning different artists to produce pieces for them to hang about the place."

"It will be on public display?" exclaimed Nelly, quite horrified. "For anyone and everyone to look at?"

"Yes, indeed." He smiled proudly. "Or even to buy. It is not quite finished, you know, but when it is I shall make sure to sign it clearly and in big letters so that patrons may approach me for more work. It is a great opportunity, mother..." His voice faded away in response to Nelly's disapproval, so markedly evident on her frowning face.

"Who is this person, Ralph?" Nelly gestured at the painting. "Is she your... your particular friend?" The "heaven forbid" though not voiced, was clear from her tone.

Ralph laughed. "Poppy! Not at all. She is a professional model and has been painted by many famous artists. Though I doubt," he added sulkily enough, "that you would have heard of any of them."

The air in the room, despite the open window, was quite suffocating, from the vapours emitted by the linseed oil and particularly the turpentine. We were glad therefore when Ralph suggested going for a tour of "the quarter," as he called it.

"Poppy is coming to pose later," he said. (Nelly gave a shudder), "so I shall have to work. I must finish the picture, you know. But meantime I can shew you some of the local sights."

These sights, according to Ralph, were centred on the Place du Tertre. Crowds of idlers were milling around the small square eyeing the scores of artists who sat at their easels, either working on paintings *"en plein air,"* as Ralph said, or trying to entice passers-by have their portraits sketched in charcoal or coloured crayons for a few sous.

"Can they really make a living at this, Ralph?" I asked.

"People manage somehow."

He himself was lucky, or perhaps, in retrospect, unlucky. His late father had left a modest legacy to him, to be held in trust until his twenty-first birthday. No sooner had that day come, some months earlier, than Ralph, as Nelly had previously informed me, had used it to set himself up in Paris, to seek his fortune as an artist. No amount of protests on her part had been able to dissuade him.

Now it seemed the boy was well-known in the area. He was greeted on all sides by the street artists, most of whom called out to him in French, but some in English.

"That fellow is Danish," he told us. "That one Dutch. Him over there, he's an American if you please. It's a veritable tower of Babel up here, you know."

"Where is the cabaret where your painting will be hung?" I asked.

"Oh, it is not open just yet. But if you like I can take you to another one tonight. They are very jolly places and quite respectable."

At the time we took the word "quite" to mean "perfectly," the way I suppose Ralph meant us to take it. And he told no lie, for of course "quite" can also mean a dubious "fairly," which is how it turned out to be. But I am again getting ahead of myself.

"Would you like your portrait done, mother?" Ralph asked her. "Etienne is rather good at that sort of thing. He indicated one of the artists at work, a large, heavily bearded man with a Mediterranean swarthiness.

"Goodness! I don't know," replied Nelly. "I really don't know. What do you think, Martha?"

23

"Cannot you sketch your mother, Ralph?"

"Oh, as to that," he waved a negligent hand, "I am not great at capturing a likeness. Etienne has the knack."

"Maybe another time," said Nelly.

We took a few turns around the square, then, since there seemed nothing else to do, sat ourselves down at a table outside a café. Ralph ordered the same sort of dark brew of coffee he had drunk in his studio and lit up a long cigarette which, as he smoked it, emitted a fragrance markedly absent from the tobacco that Mr. H. was pleased to stuff in his pipe.

"Egyptian, you know," he said in answer to my query. "Would you like one, aunt?"

I smilingly refused while Nelly sat with pursed lips, pointedly waving away the smoke.

The tea served to us was of a most inferior sort, hardly more than faintly coloured water. No milk was brought, and we were obliged to ask for it.

"No one drinks tea here," Ralph told us. "It is a very English thing, you know. I myself have quite lost my taste for it."

"I am not surprised, if this is what they give you," Nelly said. "You should have warned us, Ralph. If only I had known, I could have brought a packet of good black Assam over with me."

As we sat thus, sipping our drinks, several fellows came over from time to time, clapping Ralph on the back and exchanging a gabble of words with him, while one or two passing young women threw him a smile and a "Bonjour." It seemed he was quite the favourite, which pleased me, until I discovered, much later on, that, even among struggling artists, friendships can be bought. Ralph's relative wealth and ability to treat the others

24

meant that he was courted widely, but of true bonds there were none.

"I had better leave you," he said finally after draining his cup. "Unless of course you want to come back with me and meet Poppy."

He was not expecting us to say yes, and we did not. Instead, we stayed at the café for a little while longer, discussing where to go and what to do. I studied my Baedeker, recalling that boat trips on the river were highly recommended. We could hardly walk all the way down to the Seine, as that waterway was called, and decided to take a fiacre, a little horse-drawn carriage, several of which waited at the fringes of the square to transport tourists down the hill. As we went, Nelly, who had been rather silent, asked me what I thought of Ralph's chosen career. I picked my words carefully.

"He is young," I said. "Perhaps the novelty of this life will wear off, or perhaps he will make a great success of it." Something I doubted from having seen his work. "Tell me, Nelly," I continued, "did Ralph display an aptitude for art in his youth?"

She frowned. "Not particularly. In fact, I don't know where this sudden enthusiasm came from, Martha. I believe maybe he read one of my books, *Trilby* you know, and thought the life sounded romantic. He took some lessons before coming here, both in art and in French."

"Well," I said. "That's good. That shews dedication."

"Yes," she said doubtfully. "Only I wish he might have dedicated himself to something more solid."

I will forbear describing in detail the activities of the day, for my aim in writing this account is rather to tell of the frightful events that subsequently unfolded during our visit, and not to promote the wonders of the French capital. I will leave that to the writers of gazetteers. Just to say that the steamer we took from the quayside was arrayed with merry little flags waving in the breeze, the river sparkled, the guide recounted, in both French and broken English, the marvellous and in some cases sorry histories of the buildings we were passing. Not that any of it spoiled our enjoyment. Indeed, on hearing about revolutions and sieges and bloody battles, about kings and queens and aristocrats who'd had their heads chopped off, Nelly cheered up considerably.

After the trip on the river we visited the imposing edifice that we had seen from the hill of Montmartre, the Cathedral of Our Lady of Paris, with its two great towers, its flying buttresses, its three beautifully carved stone entrance-ways. We found it just as impressive within as without, the high vaulted nave, those stupendous rose windows in stained glass, its massive organ and most lovely statue of the Virgin and Child. Nelly was lacking in the energy to climb the tower and wouldn't agree that I should leave her to do so, not even in a sacred place.

"You never know," she said nervously, "what might happen."

"What?" I asked. "What could happen to you here?"

She just shook her head.

Presumably one of those novels she liked had featured a damsel abducted in a house of God, or some similar foolishness. However, I gave way. The tower could wait for another occasion. Meanwhile, we both said a few prayers and I lit a candle at a side altar for Henry's soul, having found this ritual to be one of the more attractive of the Roman church. Leaving the cathedral, we ambled somewhat aimlessly along the quays, once more observing the Parisians at leisure, and soon stumbled upon a most delightful flower market, where I bought a small bunch of sweet scented freesias to put in my room, Nelly declining to do the same, saying they would only make her sneeze.

Having by this means worked up a huge appetite, especially after the short-comings of breakfast, we partook of lunch in a charming riverside restaurant, where even Nelly expressed herself content enough with her chicken and fried potatoes. Following that, we felt we had seen enough sights for one day, and returned to our hotel for a rest before the evening's expedition to a cabaret.

As we entered, Madame Albert came bustling forward to lay our keys upon the desk. Seeing the flowers in my hand, she told me to wait and then, most kindly, hurried back to fetch a vase for me, leaving the door open behind her. It led to a back parlour where two young men could be seen in intense conversation, waving their hands in the air in the animated fashion of continentals.

On her return, Madame Albert, seeing where I was looking, said proudly, "My son. Phillipe." At which, one of them, a strapping youth of about eighteen, ginger-haired and red of complexion like his mother, looked up at us, but without interest. He resumed his tête-à-tête.

I thanked her for the vase, and Nelly and I climbed to our separate, second-floor rooms. We could I suppose have shared a chamber, but I had insisted on this arrangement, knowing I would need a rest from the company of my sister, and willing to pay the difference. Now I felt justified, glad of the brief period of solitude, as doubtless Nelly did as well. Having put my freesias in their vase, inhaling once more their delicate fragrance, I lay down upon my bed, content enough with the day's expedition so far, and wondering what the evening's adventure would hold.

Chapter Three – At the Moulin Rouge

The Red Windmill or, in French, Le Moulin Rouge, was the name of the cabaret we were to visit. Situated at the base of the hill of Montmartre, it indeed featured a genuine windmill, though one that had long ceased its original function. Moreover, I could not imagine that garish red paint would have been its original colour, or that the sails would previously have been decked with coloured lights and topped with a crudely carved crescent moon.

Seeing the premises, seeing the neighbourhood and the sort of people round about, I immediately had misgivings about our evening, shared and voiced by Nelly.

"Is it really a suitable place for us, Ralph, dear?" she asked. "It looks rather… well, rather…"

"Don't worry, mother. The Prince of Wales himself has patronised it, you know."

Now, while this intelligence might appease and indeed impress my sister, it hardly did as much for me, who has heard so many rumours of the perhaps less than impeccable morals of our own Prince Edward. However, we were here now, and I admit I was curious to see what was going on under those scarlet sails, that wooden moon.

We passed through an imposing enough entrance-way and were conducted by a uniformed usher into a vast hall with small tables and chairs set around a central space where people were dancing. We took our seats and Ralph, still buoyant, proposed champagne.

"Goodness," said Nelly, while I was wondering if Ralph intended to treat us. I very much doubted it.

He called over a black-suited waiter who bowed slightly at our order and moved away through the throng.

We sat looking around us. How adequately to describe the scene? The loud voices, the whirling colours, the strong sweet smell of wine and of the smoke from exotic cigarettes quite made my head spin, and I am sure that for Nelly it was the same. Ralph, however, was in his element, pointing out this famous artist, that scandalous woman, the fat man with astonishing whiskers, who ran the place, the decadents.

"Oscar Wilde used to come here," he told us. "Not any more, of course."

Mr Wilde had only very recently been sentenced to hard labour for his scandalous behaviour. Yet, forgive me, but I could not help thinking that the person who wrote that thrilling tale "The Picture of Dorian Gray" or the sparkling comedy, "The Importance of Being Earnest," which I had attended earlier in the year, could not be entirely vicious, and I pitied him greatly. Nelly however pursed her lips at the name. If the Prince of Wales were a patron she could admire, the same certainly did not go for Mr. Oscar Wilde! It was after all partly the same reprobate's connection with Paris that had inspired her with dread as to the pernicious influences that would beset her beloved son in this wickedest of cities, and had driven her hot-foot to follow him to try to persuade him to return home.

Soon a waiter appeared with the promised tray of hot wine – in rather small glasses, let it be said.

"Don't I deserve a bottle?" Etienne asked. "After risking my life."

The waiter bowed. "I'll ask about it," he said.

"It's champagne we're drinking here, my friend. Not this rotgut stuff."

"I will ask M. Zidler."

"Do."

Now more young men and women were clustering round the table, witnesses to Etienne's heroism. Ralph, in something of a pet, did not bother this time to introduce us. I looked across at Nelly. She was pale and drawn, shaken no doubt by the recent events. It was, anyway, late for the both of us, the noise and atmosphere, even in the open at night, oppressive. A nearly full moon, a silver circle set on black velvet, stood high in the sky over its tawdry wooden counterpart. I quietly suggested that we should leave, especially since I did not wish for us to foot the bill for so many.

"But how will we get back to the hotel?" she asked. "I don't think Ralph is ready to go just yet."

"We don't need a chaperon."

"But Martha, what if those two men are still outside?" She shuddered.

"We can take a fiacre."

She followed me through the throng to the way out, after first slipping Ralph some francs from the two of us. He took them but otherwise hardly paid attention to us leaving, he and his companions being well-oiled with the drink. Their voices had got louder, their gestures ever more expansive. I guessed they would stay on until the place closed.

As we reached the doors, a strange little man, coming in, made way for us. He stood no higher than my shoulder, and I am not tall. His body seemed normal sized – his head if anything was larger than average – but his legs were stunted and he walked with a stick. At the same time, he was neatly dressed and sported pince-nez and a bowler hat, the which he raised politely, nodding to us.

"Mesdames!"

"What a freak!" Nelly whispered. I hoped the little man was out of earshot by then. Especially if he understood English.

"It is hardly his fault, Nelly."

"No, but…" She grabbed my hand. "Oh, Martha, what a terrible place this Paris is. Those horrible men. I wish we could go home."

"Already? But Nelly, we have only arrived. And we had a most pleasant time earlier, did we not? The trip on the river and so forth."

"Yes, of course. And, of course, I do not intend to leave until we have tried to persuade Ralph to come with us. Before it's too late, Martha."

"Too late for what?"

"Before he is utterly corrupted, you know."

With this miserable prospect in mind, we mounted one of the fiacres waiting nearby to carry away the revellers. Above us, the nearly round moon stared down coldly, remotely, as it always had and, I suppose, always will, no matter what goes on here below.

Chapter Four – The Morning After

I slept well enough again that second night, except that it took me a while to throw off the multiple impressions of the day and especially of the evening. Although the Moulin Rouge had hardly proved a suitable place for respectable folk, it had, admittedly, all been rather interesting, even if at moments frightening. Ralph's decision to take us there had further confirmed my belief that he was shocking us deliberately, paying back his – in his opinion – overly solicitous mother for dropping in on him out of a blue sky and making him, as he saw it, look like a baby in the eyes of his new friends.

The next morning, Nelly tapped on my door rather earlier than I should have liked or expected. Inevitably she bemoaned the fact that once again she had been unable to get a proper rest and seemed intent on my sharing her fate, for my pocket watch told me that was only a little past six. She plumped herself down on the side of my bed to vent her woes.

"My head was veritably fizzing all night, Martha, with all that noise, the fight, all those scandalous women prancing about and shewing us their undergarments... I cannot believe that such a personage as the Prince of Wales would patronise such an establishment. Can it really be true?"

I yawned. "From what I have heard, my dear, I don't think the Prince's morals are above reproach."

45

"Goodness… well, I have heard the same thing but hoped not to credit it. His poor mother… "

"His poor wife."

"Well, yes of course."

She twittered on, oblivious to my yawns. When I finally insisted that it was far too early for breakfast, she reluctantly agreed to return to her room for a spell and take up her novel, though, as she said, she didn't know what she would do after she had finished it, for she had brought no other and the bookshops here presumably sold works only in French, which she, of course, could not read.

Finally she left me alone, and I turned over to try to fall back to sleep but could not. I lay watching the patterns on the ceiling made by the sunlight filtering through the lacy curtains and listening to Paris getting up, until I gave in and did the same myself.

It was thus still early when we made our way to Père Perrot's establishment to break our fast. The waitress recognised us and, unasked, brought another basket piled high with croissants. I decided not to be quite so greedy this morning and consumed only two, in addition to the hot chocolate drink and the fresh and crusty white bread which seemed to go so well spread with a thick layer of pale Normandy butter. I refused to pay attention to Nelly's reluctance to eat any of it.

"I wonder when Ralph will arrive," Nelly said anxiously after a while, making crumbs of her roll.

"Did he agree to meet us this morning, then?" I asked. "I cannot recall any such arrangement."

"Oh yes, I am quite sure he did… At least…"

"Well, Nelly," I replied. "I have no intention of sitting around waiting for him. Perhaps we should plan to do something by ourselves again. The Louvre museum, perhaps." I reached for my Baedeker.

"Oh no. It would be too terrible if he came and found us gone."

"How terrible could it be? In any case, didn't he say he had work to do on his commission?"

"That was yesterday."

"Yes, but…" I sighed. Nelly face had fixed in a stubborn expression I recognised so well from our girlhood. Seemingly pliant, she could in certain circumstances not be moved for anything. I would not argue with her and instead reached for my third croissant.

A good half-hour passed and still no sign of Ralph. I was starting to think of leaving Nelly where she was and heading off by myself, when she said, "I know, Martha. Let us go to his studio."

I could not think this a good idea but again Nelly was unyielding. At least she was agreeable to us taking a fiacre up the hill.

"Do you remember the address?" I asked her as we mounted the vehicle.

"Surely you do, Martha. You always know that sort of thing."

I sighed again. "I have a rough notion," I said, and told the driver to take us to the rue Cortot.

Once there, I gazed about myself to try and recall which of the ramshackle buildings was house to Ralph. At least it was not a very long street but even so I tried in vain to fix on the place, even asking a passing old woman if she knew where the English artist lived.

She cackled, revealing a mouth in which most of the teeth were lacking: discoloured canines alone stuck out on each side like fangs. Then she waved a skinny arm around herself in a general manner.

"Artists everywhere," she said, and shuffled off still cackling.

"What did she say?" Nelly asked.

"She didn't know," I replied, and looked at my sister. "Well? What now?"

"I thought you would recognise the house," Nelly replied accusingly. As if it were my fault.

An idea came to me.

"Perhaps we might go to that square with all the artists and ask one of Ralph's friends where he lives."

Nelly grumbled to herself.

"Either that," I said, "or we stand here and wait until he himself appears."

But just as we were setting off again, a young woman strode past us, a froth of white petticoats shewing under the skirt of her blue costume, a confection in silk and feathers topping her red hair.

"Poppy!" I said, hoping I was right.

She stopped, puzzled. Did she know us?

"We met you last night, at the cabaret," I explained. "We are looking for Ralph, but can't recall where he lives…This is his mother, by the way."

"Ah, yes." She smiled. What a beautiful girl, I thought again, even if her mouth is too wide to suit conventional tastes.

"Maman. Yes, I remember... The Moulin Rouge. You enjoyed the show, I hope."

"Not the fight," I replied.

"No indeed. Those wild men. My God, I thought they were going to slit each other's throats in front of us." She laughed as if it were all a great joke. "Naughty Ralph, to take maman to such a place."

I could only agree.

"Come," she continued. "I am going up to the studio too."

As I thought. Ralph was working this morning.

Poppy led us to a house indistinguishable from the others, the flaking yellow plaster, the crooked white shutters. I should never have found it by myself.

"I only hope he will be awake," Poppy said. "He likes to lie in, that one."

I did not feel the need to translate for Nelly's benefit, but might as well have done so because, when Poppy burst through Ralph's door, with us right behind her, the young man was indeed still in bed. At the sight of us, he jumped up, yelling an imprecation and grabbing the sheet to cover himself for he did not appear to be wearing any garments whatsoever.

Nelly clutched my arm, gasping in horror. Not, perhaps so much at Ralph's state of undress, but because he was not alone. A girl huddled back on the divan, also naked. I was greatly astonished and somewhat scandalised, less at the spectacle before us – we had after all broken into the man's bedroom and what happens in such places is always best left behind a closed door– but rather because the young person in question was none other than the pretty little Sylvie, the girlfriend of Etienne.

49

If blame for the ensuing delicate situation rested anywhere it was surely with Poppy. She could at least have knocked on the door and warned the lad. Yet, I suspected, from the satisfied grin on her face, that she half-expected what we would find, and thought it would be amusing to shock two strait-laced old biddies

We retreated in some confusion, Poppy now laughing openly, and Ralph babbling some kind of explanation.

"Come, Nelly," I said. "We will go back to that café in the square. Ralph can join us when he has collected himself. And, in the meantime, we'll have a cup of tea."

"Tea!" my sister exclaimed. I was not sure if she meant no more tea after our last sorry experience of that beverage, or if, for once, she needed something considerably stronger. In the event, we each settled on seltzer water, and settled down to wait.

Not for long. Ralph must have rushed to dress himself, for we had barely sipped at our drinks when he rushed up to us. Nelly frowned, pursed her lips and spoke not a word.

"Well, Ralph," I said to break the silence.

"It's all Poppy's fault, aunt. And you never said you were coming, mother…" He looked sulky as if everyone were to blame apart from himself.

"We were under the impression that you would be joining us again." I thought it best to put it that way, for Nelly's sake, to stand together, even though, as I previously indicated, I myself was under no such misapprehension.

"Well, your impression was wrong. I do have work to do, you know." Still sulky.

"You were hardly working when we arrived." I could not help myself. I had to say it.

50

Ralph, eyes down, drummed his fingers on the table.

"But Sylvie," I continued. "Wasn't she with Etienne?" He nodded, ever so slightly. "Really, Ralph. He is supposed to be your friend."

"You saw what he did. She was angry with him. And then he got very drunk last night," Ralph said, looking me in the eye at last. "When he gets drunk he gets nasty, d'you see. Violent. Sylvie was afraid to go home with him, so I said she could stay with me. To be safe, you know."

He looked away, this hero, protector of damsels in distress. I followed his gaze. The artists were out in force as before, seated at their easels around the square, yet there was no sign of Etienne. He must be sleeping it off too, I thought. Lucky for Ralph.

"I was worried about her."

"Most kind of you I'm sure." Nelly broke her pointed silence, her voice oozing sarcasm. "Most... unselfish, Ralph. What a shame you couldn't find any clothes for the hussy. She must be cold, sitting there in the altogether."

"Oh, Mummy, I'm so sorry." His voice trembling with emotion, he leaned across the table to take her hand.

She drew it back.

"Mummy, you must believe me. I'm so very, very sorry. Can you ever forgive me? Please say you can."

Now tears were running down his face. He laid his head on the table and sobbed.

"Oh, Ralph." She was already relenting. "I knew nothing good would come of Paris. My poor little boy."

She patted his fair locks. He looked up then, rueful, shame-faced. This time it was she who took his hand.

51

"I suppose girls like that…" she went on after a while. "They take advantage of your good nature."

"That's it. That's it. I just wanted to help her. I had no intention, believe me… It was her…"

Though not blessed with sons, I have had sufficient dealings with young men to be suspicious of their supposed kindly and considerate natures, especially when it comes to pretty young women, and I am afraid that I could not believe Ralph's protestations. However, Nelly was ready to be appeased, and smiled wanly at her son, shaking her head.

"Oh Ralph, Ralph, Ralph…"

"And Poppy should never…" he started.

"No," said Nelly. "She shouldn't have."

"She is sorry, too," Ralph said. "In fact, you know, she wants to apologise."

"Does she indeed?" I asked. "Where is she then?"

"She's still in the studio. I need to work on the commission today, Mummy. To finish it, you know, and then I'll be free to spend more time with you. But meantime, I have arranged to pay her for a few hours modelling, so…" He slapped the table. "Just come up for a minute and let her tell you herself."

"What about… that girl…?"

"Don't worry about her, Mummy. Sylvie… she's gone."

"I don't know," Nelly said. "What do you think, Martha?"

I thought we should have done what I suggested in the first place, and taken ourselves off for the day, but there was no turning the clock back now.

"Please, Aunt Martha." Ralph turned to me, blinking away more tears, as if to melt my stony heart. He was trying so very hard to look contrite, that I had difficulty keeping a straight face.

"For a moment, maybe," I said. More for Nelly's sake than his or Poppy's.

Again we toiled up those stairs. I could not help but notice that while Nelly had managed them perfectly well earlier, now she clung to Ralph's arm, puffing like a steam engine. For my part, I hoped Poppy still had all her clothes on, and Ralph must have thought the same, for he went in ahead, gesturing for us to wait. We heard a mumble of words, and then, almost immediately, he opened the door for us. All was well. Poppy was as we had seen her before, in her neat blue outfit. She had cleared the bedclothes away and was sitting primly on the divan, a pad of paper in her hand.

She stood up.

"It is all my fault, Mesdames" she said. "I am devastated. I admit, I thought after last night – which went on very late, you know, quite until dawn – Ralph might still be in bed. But of course, I had no idea that he had company. It was a shock for me, too."

Poppy smiled, not looking shocked in the slightest – and if she had been up all night herself, shewed no sign of fatigue. Now she stepped forward and embraced Nelly, who was quite embarrassed at the familiarity of the gesture.

"Very French, I suppose," she said to me later.

While everyone else was apologising and making up, I took the opportunity to poke around a little. A folder lay on the table. I took it up and thumbed through the pencil sketches within. They depicted twisted torsos of men and women, not pretty, but drawn with a sure strong touch.

"Ralph," I exclaimed. "These are really good."

I was most surprised, since nothing else of his that I had seen was of this quality.

"Oh, those things," he said in an offhand manner. "They aren't mine. They're Poppy's."

"You did these?" I turned to the girl.

"I brought them to shew Ralph," she said. "He asked to see them." She smiled. "I am glad you like them, Madame."

There was a slight emphasis on the "you" as if Ralph himself had been less than enthusiastic. Perhaps indeed he was envious, as well he might be.

"I cannot profess to be a great connoisseur," I said. "But they are most powerful."

"Just now, you know, I am working with Jules Bourdain. He is a great sculptor, a great artist. He encourages me."

"Poppy was Bourdain's model," Ralph said. "And now she is his 'assistant.'" He smiled indulgently at her. "Jules has been very kind to you."

I recalled what had been said the night before, that Poppy was the great man's muse. For now, as they said, one of many.

But the young woman rounded on Ralph with some fire.

"He is a great artist. A professional, not a dilettante…" A hit, a palpable hit, I thought. "He wouldn't let me work with him unless he approved of what I did and valued it. These sketches are for a marble relief we are doing together, depicting the Last Judgment. It is so exciting."

Ralph smirked, but said nothing.

54

"You have a true gift, my dear," I said. I hope I did not emphasise the "true" too much, though I caught Ralph giving me a sharp look.

Now she veritably beamed.

"Thank you," she said. "Thank you so much, Madame."

"Well, this is all very lovely." Ralph turned to the easel on which sat Poppy's wretched portrait. "But I really need to get on with this. "Can we meet later, Mummy, for dinner perhaps? I know a charming little place in the quarter. You will like it. Most respectable."

It was agreed, though I suspected that "respectable" in view of our previous experiences out with Ralph. Well, we would see. Nelly and I said our farewells, and prepared to set off and amuse ourselves as best we could.

Poppy suggested we visit Montmartre cemetery at the bottom of the hill.

"Oh Poppy," Ralph had protested. "That's very morbid. Why are you always so obsessed with death and last judgments and things?"

"I'm not obsessed," she replied, laughing. "The cemetery is a peaceful place, and worth a visit just to view the splendid tombstones. I often go there to sketch... And many famous people are buried within its walls, you know, the composers Berlioz and Offenbach, for instance."

Offenbach – hadn't he composed that music for the can-can!

Nonetheless, we agreed that it might be of interest, especially since it was on our way.

It was a short enough walk thither, and all downhill. I waited for Nelly to comment on recent revelations, but at first she just babbled on inconsequentially. How very hot it had become again? Did I think the weather would hold, or did those clouds presage rain? Would I just look at that woman over there! What did I think of her gown? Was the colour not too strong? And that absurd hat! How awkward those cobblestones were to walk upon. One might easily turn one's ankle... Eventually she gave up in view of my monosyllabic replies, and we continued in silence, absorbed in our own thoughts.

The cemetery turned out to be situated in a hollow, beneath the noises of street level, and once we entered it, it was as if we were enclosed in a shawl of quiet. I could understand why Poppy liked the place. Perhaps she had divined that we too needed a period of calm.

A booth stood just inside the entrance manned by a little old goblin of a man, bent and wizened, looking as if he would soon be joining those of whom he was at present the guardian. For a few sous he sold us a sheet map indicating the whereabouts of the tombs of the eminent departed, most of whom, I confess, were unknown to me, and we set off, dutifully passing along paths that resembled the city streets outside, but in miniature. The houses that lined our way, though roofed and set with windows and doors as if their inmates could come and go as they pleased, were mausoleums, true houses of the dead. It was a little unnerving, to be sure. I studied the map to search out those few names with which we were familiar. Or rather, with whom I was. Neither Berlioz nor Offenbach rang any bells for Nelly, though she enjoyed finding the more elaborate memorials, those crowned with bronze or stone sculptures.

"Miecislas Kamienski," Nelly read, in front of one such featuring a reclining young man, and stumbling over the strange name. "Died in 1859 at the Battle of Magenta. The poor boy, Martha. He looks to be no older than Ralph."

Fatigued with the heat, we decided to make our way back, and soon came upon a circle with a low grassy mound at its centre. This mound was topped with neat flower beds in a symmetrical pattern, alternating red and white blooms, a little too regimented for my taste but pleasing enough. Wooden benches stood around it all, and we were pleased to sit for a while to get some respite under the overhanging trees from the glare of the sun. Nelly even removed her gloves and used them to fan her face.

"You know, Martha," she said after a while and as if it took her some effort to speak. "I was of course terribly shocked and hurt this morning by Ralph's immoral behaviour." I waited. There was evidently a "but" coming. "However," she went on, turning to me and grasping my hand, "you know, in some ways I was relieved."

"Relieved?"

"Yes, dear. You see… you see…"

"What is it?"

"Well, he was with a girl."

"Yes, with Sylvie." I still did not understand

"I was so afraid, you see…" her voice sank to a whisper, "oh dear, this is so hard…"

"Nelly!"

"I was so afraid that he might be a… a deviant. Like Mr. Wilde, you know."

I was astonished. "Why ever should you think such a thing?"

Perhaps she detected a slight chuckle in my tone because she pulled back her hand.

"If you had sons, Martha," she said, "you would know that it is the thing mothers dread."

I resented the belittling nature of the remark, but, as usual in my dealings with Nelly, felt it politic to let it pass.

"Paris is a hotbed of vice," she went on. "Particularly unnatural vice, you know."

"No more than any other big city, Nelly." I knew well that London was not exempt from such activities. Even if practised less openly.

"Oh yes, indeed. I recently read a novel set here in Paris, because, you know, I was coming here and wanted to learn what it was like. You really should read it." She gazed at me earnestly.

"Should I?"

"Oh yes. I can't remember who wrote it but it is titled *The Monster of Montparnasse*. You can get it when you return home. It describes everything so vividly, Martha. So shockingly. My God!" She trembled at the recollection. "The Monster, you know, is a vile seducer of both girls and young men. I could not but think of poor Ralph, exposed to that!"

Poor Ralph, indeed!

"Well, now," I replied. "As I have tried to tell you before, Nelly, you shouldn't believe all you read in such books. It is all just cheap sensationalism, with no regard for truth."

She pursed her lips again. I knew she was thinking that I was too argumentative for words. We sat on without speaking, each with her own thoughts. Mine, because I was too tired and hot to worry that Nelly was cross with me, were like the brilliantly coloured butterflies that were dancing before us from bloom to bloom, sucking the sweet nectar. How entrancing they were. It was, as Poppy had said, a peaceful place. Street sounds were muted down here, and all that could otherwise be heard was the buzzing of bees as they collected pollen from the flowers before us.

Idly I wondered then that I heard no birdsong and, suddenly, realised why: the place was overrun with cats. They lurked everywhere: even now a grey one was approaching warily, probably used to being fed by visitors. (I only hoped the cats weren't feeding off the permanent residents.) This particular mangy specimen came right up to us, regarding us with yellow eyes. Nelly leant down to stroke it, but it hissed, reared up and scratched at her ungloved hand.

"Oh," she yelped, and the cat bounded off.

"Let me see," I said.

Two thin lines of blood marked the wound.

"The beast!" she said, "the horrid, horrid beast." She started sobbing then. Not, as I knew well, just because of the cat, but because of everything else as well. "Oh Martha," she added as I hugged her, "I am so very tired. Can we go back to the hotel?"

I could not refuse her, but urged her to wash her hand in carbolic soap at the earliest opportunity.

"You don't want it to get infected."

"It's nothing," she replied, already pulling away from me. "Please don't make a fuss."

Chapter Five – The Anarchist

I left her resting, and, with a sudden sense of liberation, quitted the hotel. By myself, I did not need a plan or goal, but could wander at will. I could turn down any inviting side street, without having to justify my choice, without having my thoughts interrupted by questions, commentaries and judgments. I loved my sister dearly, but this trip had brought home to me how I preferred to love her at a distance.

Soon I found myself ambling down past the splendid building that houses the Opera and along the avenue that bears its name. I soon discovered myself to be again near the Louvre and was tempted to visit that great museum, but, given the fine weather – the ominous clouds that Nelly had remarked on earlier having dissipated, a fresh breeze from the river now moderating the scorching effect of the sun – took a turn instead in the Gardens of the Tuileries up as far as Concorde Square. I recalled the sinister history of the place from our boat trip of the previous day, that this spacious and elegant square had once been, at the time of the Revolution, the site of the notorious guillotine, the walls of the surrounding buildings then echoing to the taunts of the sans-culottes and the terrified cries of the victims. Here it was, indeed, that the King Louis and his Queen were executed. Whatever their misdeeds – and I knew little of them – it was a horrible and shameful end.

Now, instead of the guillotine, a soaring Egyptian obelisk stood in the centre of the square, enigmatic, with its carved hieroglyphs so unlike any recognisable script, but which, I supposed, had signified something to that ancient race of people. It reminded me of our own obelisk, the so-called Cleopatra's Needle standing on the banks of the Thames, though that designation always makes me laugh – as if even that fabled Queen of Egypt could sew with such an object.

Despite the slight breeze, the afternoon sun was relentless, and I returned with some relief to the gardens to walk in the cooler shade of the chestnut trees. Feeling parched, I purchased an ice from an Italian who was selling his sweet treats from a barrow, and then, to better enjoy the confection, took a seat on a bench near a splendid fountain. As I consumed the raspberry-flavoured ice, I was diverted by the motley crowd, people of fashion there to flaunt their style, young lovers with eyes only for each other, the old shuffling along as best they could, nannies with children, some in perambulators, some running free, especially around the fountain, their guardians warning them in sharp tones not to get wet. It was not at all like a London park. Never mind the people, who in their own ways were so very foreign, louder and given to broad gestures, it was the look of the place, the paths of yellow dust, the orderly flower beds, the trees standing to attention, as well as the scores of statues depicting classical figures, all so very different from my own dear Regent's Park.

Sitting beside me was a young man with his nose in a book. It amused me, with nothing else to think about, to wonder what Mr. H. would make of him, and to see if I could follow the detective's imagined deductions. The book was a hefty tome bound in black, and the young man paused from time to time to make a pencil annotation on a page. I decided it could not be a novel, and, from his somewhat shabby apparel and worn shoes, took the young man to be a student. But of what? From where I was sitting I could not espy the subject matter, but the size of the book suggested to me something legal or medical. No doubt Mr. H. would make much more of it all than I possibly could, and would contradict me in my sorry conclusions as he so often did with the poor Doctor.

Remaining idly thus for a while – there was no great hurry, after all – I let my mind drift, wondering at the events of the last days. I could not imagine that Nelly would have any success in persuading Ralph to return home. Indeed, that particular young man would assuredly be only too delighted to see the back of us. Well, we would be leaving soon, mission not accomplished.

With that in mind, and deciding that I really must behave more like a tourist, and see at least some of the sights while I could, I stood to leave. At that point, the young man beside me looked up.

"Excuse me, Madame," he said, "would you be so kind as to tell me the time?"

Clearly he took me for a French woman. I was delighted to be able to inform him in his own language, by consulting my pocket watch, that it was already past two of the clock.

He smiled and thanked me.

Thus emboldened by his friendly demeanour, I asked him if he were a student, the which he confirmed.

"Yes, I am studying at the Sorbonne."

I knew this to be the University of Paris.

"That is a great book you are reading. What is your subject?"

"Theology, Madame. I am going to be a priest."

I had not thought of that.

"It's hard," he said, with a rueful smile, "but I persist."

I nodded, not quite sure what was hard, the vocation or the book, and could not help feeling sad that such a pleasant young person would give himself up to the celibate life of a priest, as the Roman church demands.

I bade him a courteous au revoir, and wished him well with his studies.

He stood up and bowed.

"Au revoir, Madame, and thank you," adding, "You speak French very well," which pleased me greatly, although it seemed my accent was not good enough to let me pass for a native.

I turned my steps again towards the Louvre, a place all cultured visitors to the city must surely visit. Admittedly I felt a pang of guilt going there without Nelly, but doubted from various dismissive remarks she had made that she had any great love of art. In addition, I knew that she would cling to me through the galleries, her constant chatter providing an unwelcome distraction from my appreciation of the exhibits.

The Louvre is huge. I have visited the British Museum on many occasions and that is big enough, but nothing on this Napoleonic scale. One could get quite lost in the maze of galleries. However, I was determined to see the famed jewels of the collection – the Winged Victory of Samothrace, Perrault's Colonnade, the Egyptian and Oriental antiquities and so on – aided by the handy map provided when I purchased my entrance ticket. I confess, however, that I did not linger long amid the mummies and sarcophagi, and soon set about finding the

63

galleries of French paintings where I assumed that the work so admired by Ralph would be on view. To get to them, I traversed those rooms featuring the Dutch school of artists, Rembrandt and his ilk. My eye was particularly caught by a delicate little portrait of a lace maker by an artist signing himself Johannes Vermeer. I would ask Ralph about him, although, if my nephew's taste was for the massive ostentation of the Delacroix, which I soon after discovered covering much of one wall, I suspected he would be dismissive of such a small domestic subject.

I could admire "Liberty Leading the People" for the skill of its execution, without caring for the subject matter very much. It surely harked back to the riotous times of the Revolution, and I was further unsure why Liberty's dress had slipped down below her plump bosoms. Quite possibly there was an artistic reason for this, but for my part it quite escaped me.

Wandering back through the sculpture hall, I was surprised to discover, amid the ancient Greeks and Romans, the Michelangelos and the Donatellos (I had heard of the former but not the latter), a striking work in white marble by none other than Jules Bourdain. A lovely young woman stood naked, and as if transfixed, the label indicating the subject to be "Semele viewing the splendours of Zeus." I could not recall the myth, if indeed I ever knew it, but with a start recognised the model. It was surely Poppy to the life. The sculpture must be newly acquired. I was so intrigued that I enquired of the matter of an attendant in uniform who happened to be standing by the door. He was not as impressed with my halting French as the young man in the Tuileries gardens had been, but eventually I made my query clear enough to him, and he affirmed what I had thought. Yes, indeed, the Bourdain had only recently been installed. Emboldened, I asked him to explain the subject, but he just shrugged and turned away. It was apparently not his business to know such things or at least not to enlighten inquisitive foreign persons on the subject.

By now, well sated with culture, and with an ache in my back from standing so long, I decided to return to the hotel, to find how Nelly was faring, and to have a rest myself.

"Wherever have you been, Martha?" was how she greeted me, frowning deeply. "You have been gone an age. I was starting to think that something terrible had happened to you."

"I am sorry if you were worried, my dear," I replied. "I thought you wished for a good long rest. I went for a walk and then visited the Louvre."

"The Louvre! How could you, without me! You must know I have been dying to see the place."

I knew no such thing, but told her, if that was the case, I would be happy to return there another day since there was so much to see. She had to be satisfied with that.

The little restaurant to which Ralph took us that evening proved indeed as charming as he had reported. Much to my relief, let it be said, since I wished for no further unpleasant surprises. It was situated near Montmartre, though not exactly in it. A rather more salubrious area, I felt, with better kept houses and shops.

The place itself, bearing the strange name, *Au Terrier de Lapin*, had a low ceiling and was bathed in the soft light of gas lamps, the candles on the tables reflected in the many mirrors. It gave the effect more of a magical cave than a rabbit's burrow, which is what the name meant.

We were shewn to a little booth where the stalls were cushioned with velvet the colour of moss. A polished wooden table was set with cutlery, wine glasses and stiffly starched linen napkins of an impeccable whiteness.

"The cuisine here is from Normandy," Ralph told us. "The fish is quite wonderful. I can particularly recommend the mussels."

I saw Nelly recoil. Oh dear, I thought, are we in for another disastrous meal, after all?

In the end, she settled for a creamy soup followed by chicken escalope, the which I partook of as well and found most acceptable, each dish delicately flavoured.

"Not bad," Nelly pronounced at last – high praise indeed from her, and despite the fact that I was sure the soup contained the hated onions. In fact, she ate everything on her plate, while trying to avoid looking at Ralph's choice. He had followed his first course of mussels in their shells with a sausage that smelt like a mucky farmyard, and which, when cut open, seemed to contain worms.

"Andouillette," he said, smacking his lips. "Very traditional, you know." Though I could not help noticing that he left most of it.

It was just as we were ordering our desserts – Ralph had recommended the tarte normande and, after establishing this to be a kind of apple pie, we accepted his suggestion – that a striking figure, tall and excessively thin, dressed to an extreme degree of elegance, entered the restaurant.

"Isn't that Valentin the Boneless?" I exclaimed, recognising that lean profile, that hooked nose. Although I did not quite recall the goatee beard.

Ralph glanced across at the man who was being seated in a booth opposite ours. His face lit up.

"Not at all," he whispered back. "Though I agree he is rather like. No, aunt, that is Felix Fénéon, the famous anarchist, you know."

"Oh heavens!" exclaimed Nelly. "An anarchist! Has he a bomb with him, do you think?"

To her great consternation, she had recently discovered (from Ralph, of course) that, not long before, a revolutionary had left a bomb in a popular Parisian café. It had killed several people. Indeed, the news had almost persuaded her to depart home on the instant, until reassured (by Ralph) that the perpetrator had been caught and executed, and no repetition of such activities was expected. Now she gazed across in horror at the newcomer, who luckily was turned away from us, all unconscious of the emotion he had aroused in at least one of the restaurant's patrons.

"We will keep an eye on him, mother," Ralph said, smiling and patting her hand. "If he suddenly jumps up and leaves, we will immediately run out after him, before the explosion, you know. However, I do not see a suspicious ticking package about his person. If there is a bomb, it must be a very small one."

"It's no joking matter, Ralph. You told me that people died."

"Quite right, mother. It's not a subject for jokes. Although…" and he looked across at us with gleaming eyes, "I have to say I have some sympathy with their cause."

"Ralph!" Nelly was shocked as I am sure he meant her to be.

67

"Of course," he went on, "I don't really agree with blowing people up. Not the 'propaganda of the deed,' you know, as the extremists preach. Though if it is possible to blow up a few buildings without killing people, well then maybe…" Nellie's eyebrows shot up. "But," he continued before she could speak, "the 'propaganda of the word' is quite admirable in its objectives, you know. Anarchists believe in creating a caring society, in which there is no more inequality, no more poverty. Who can argue with that?"

"It's a great aspiration," I replied. "But given human nature, how likely ever to be achieved?"

"You are too cynical, aunt. Probably as a result of living so closely to a detective who must of necessity have a very sour view of his fellows."

"On the contrary. Mr. Holmes's great work has convinced me that, while there are indeed many villains in this world, they are far outnumbered by decent God-fearing people, intent on doing the right thing in a civilised way."

Ralph clearly did not believe me. He shrugged his shoulders in a gesture that was already become quite Gallic.

"Anyway," he went on, "whatever the situation in Britain, here in France, when gentle persuasion has had no effect, some members of the movement have concluded that the only way to change people's minds is to attack the bourgeoisie directly."

"The what?" asked Nelly.

"The bourgeoisie, mother. The middle and upper classes of society whose wealth, you know, is based on the exploitation of the proletariat."

Ralph sat back in satisfaction, and plunged his fork into his sweet.

"This is very tasty," I said, doing the same and wishing to avoid further inflammatory conversation by pandering to Ralph's desire to shake us. "Though it is not quite as I understand an apple tart to be. There's egg custard here, I believe. And toasted almonds. Delicious. I wonder can the chef give me the recipe."

But Nelly was not to be so easily distracted.

"Oh Ralph," she said. "What has happened to you? You must come home, you know, before you are utterly corrupted."

"Corrupted, mother! It is only now my eyes are opening."

"You refuse to return with me, then?" Nelly said sadly.

"I do. My life is here now." He took another luscious mouthful. "Mm, you are right, Aunt Martha. This is very good."

Nelly leaned forward.

"Promise me something, Ralph."

"What now?"

"Promise me you won't join the anarchists and get yourself guillotined."

He laughed. "You can be sure of that, mother. I have no intention of joining the anarchists. They are yesterday's men anyway."

She sighed with some relief.

"I am much more likely to join the Marxists, you know."

Then, of course, we had to be told who they were, which quite put Nelly off from finishing her tart. So Ralph ate it.

I should perhaps add that, just as before, a quantity of wine had been consumed in the course of the meal, most of it, again, by the young man, something which perhaps contributed to his intemperate conversation and increasingly raised voice.

Now he insisted, that we each have a small glass of Calvados, the famous apple brandy of Normandy, before we departed. Nelly declined, but Ralph ordered one for her anyway and drank it himself, as well as his own. I found it pleasant enough, but strong, beneath its sweetness.

At last it was time to go. Ralph, though it was he who had invited us, clearly had no intention of footing the bill, so this time, Nelly being so flustered, I performed the necessary business. Somewhat astonished at the high price, I studied the paper with attention, noticing several extras tacked on to the cost of the dishes, including something called the "couvert." This, as it turned out, was a charge just for sitting down at the table. I was disgusted. However, there was to be no arguing, since Ralph told me it was customary in the better-class establishments, and I meekly paid up.

On our way out, we had to pass the anarchist's table. This individual unexpectedly leant out and caught Ralph's sleeve, and said to him, in French, "You should treat your mother with more respect, young man." It seemed this Fénéon had not only overheard our conversation, but had understood it all. Ralph went quite red and trembly, while I chuckled.

"What did he say?" asked Nelly anxiously as we emerged into the street.

"He told Ralph off for the way he spoke to you," I replied.

"Oh," was all she said. But that little exclamation contained a multitude of meaning. The fellow might be an anarchist but he was also conscious of the respect due to a parent.

70

Chapter Six – The Famous Sculptor

The next morning, finding it unusual that Nelly had not come to wake me as was her wont, I went out into the passageway and knocked on her door, calling her name. A muted "yes" gave me permission to enter. To my astonishment I found her packing her bags.

"Nelly, what is this?" I asked.

She turned a tear-stained face towards me.

"I realise now," she said, "that we have wasted our time coming over here to try to persuade Ralph to return home. He is lost to me, Martha... and I don't want to stay in this horrible place any longer."

This horrible place! Paris!

"But we have hardly arrived, my dear," I said, putting my arms around her. "It is surely too soon to give up."

I did not add that I was by no means willing to leave just yet.

Nelly sat on the bed, weeping quietly.

"Only yesterday," I continued, "you told me of your great desire to see the Louvre."

"Oh, the Louvre," she said in a tone that dismissed that entire cultural monument.

"But we must certainly go and look at that monstrous metal tower, if only to say that we were there," I said. Then observing that this too had no attraction for her, I added, "And I should dearly like to go shopping."

Nelly looked up. "Shopping?"

"I have it in my head to purchase a Parisian gown. And maybe something more. Do you remember those beautiful hats we saw in that shop on the rue de Rivoli, Nelly? Wouldn't it be a treat to wear one of those and amaze the people at home?"

"Shopping," she repeated thoughtfully. "Well, maybe that would be nice."

"Of course it would. And a good luncheon afterwards."

So off we went, trawling through a seemingly endless number of fancy stores where Nelly insisted on a thorough examination of all the wares, pulling out the dresses and discussing each one with me, while an assistant hovered. None that she saw satisfied her, however, and it was I who ended up making a purchase. The gown of cerise silk was rather more ostentatious than anything I would generally wear though it would suit a special occasion. Nelly had to comment that the colour was far too vivid for my complexion and the style too young for my advanced years, the which made me all the more inclined to have it. In the end, she herself bought only a pair of kidskin gloves, after much fussing around, to the clear annoyance of the saleswoman, though Nelly noticed nothing and cared even less. She balked at the price which was indeed steep, and counted out her francs with reluctance, but at least was distracted from the despair of the morning and even seemed to be enjoying herself, in her own way.

I had a new reason for concern, however. While Nelly was occupied in trying on all those pairs of gloves, I could not fail to notice that the scratch she had received from the cat in the cemetery looked to be angrier than ever, the hand itself somewhat swollen. When I called her attention to this, she insisted rather snappily that it was nothing, even though I caught her rubbing the wound from time to time. My sister could be most annoyingly stubborn. Nevertheless, she was happy after our purchases to find a place to eat and we partook of luncheon in an establishment on the Champs Elysées that served a three-course fixed price menu. The choice was limited but the food most acceptable, if plain. A light soup, followed by a plate of beef with separate vegetables, the way they served them in France, and a tart for dessert, that was nothing like as good as the tarte normande of the previous evening, but tasty enough for all that. Nelly ate heartily, expressing delighted amazement at the moderate prices in such a fashionable part of town. I was only pleased there was no separate charge this time for the "couvert."

We sat back finally, each with a cup of coffee, not prepared again to risk the watery tea, and regarded the comings and goings on the busy thoroughfare outside.

"This is all very nice," Nelly conceded, meaning the place as well as the food. "Perhaps you are right, Martha. Perhaps we'll stay on a few more days as we had originally planned."

"Good. Maybe by then Ralph will come round," I said.

She shook her head. "I fear not."

Because I was rather burdened with my packages – I had bought other bits and pieces including a lace collar for dear Clara – and it was too hot to stroll comfortably through the busy streets, we took a fiacre back to the hotel, while deciding what we would do for the afternoon. It seemed that Nelly's enthusiasm for the

Louvre had altogether worn off, for which I admit I was grateful. The mere thought of its enormity was enough to tire me out.

"The Pantheon, perhaps," I said, referring to my Baedeker, "followed by a turn around the Luxemburg Gardens."

It was not to be, for things were about to take a quite different, and, in retrospect, fateful turn. On entering the hotel, I was astonished to observe, through the open door into the parlour behind the reception desk, the model Poppy, in intense conversation with the two young men I had seen there before, Philippe, the son of the landlady, and his friend. One other sat in shadow, with his back to us.

The girl looked up as Madame Albert fetched our keys and seemed as surprised as we were. She rose and came out to us, closing the parlour door behind her.

"Mesdames," she said in French, "whatever are you doing here?"

"We are staying here," I replied, thinking, and what are YOU doing here?

"Oh, I did not know that." For some reason she seemed put out. We stared at each other silently for a moment, then she noticed our bags. "You have been shopping?"

"We cannot come to Paris and not buy something beautiful to take home,"

"That is so very true."

"Ask her," Nelly said, "if she is going to Ralph's studio now."

I did so, though hoped the answer would be in the negative since I had no wish to accompany her thither, up that steep hill, maybe to witness another embarrassing scene.

"No, no, his picture is finished," she said, adding with a saucy smile, "as finished as it will ever be… No, this afternoon I am going to the studio of M. Bourdain."

"Oh, how lucky you are," I exclaimed. "Such a genius. I saw a piece of his work yesterday in the Louvre. In fact, may I ask? Were you not the model for that same sculpture?"

"For Semele, yes, I was." She was clearly delighted with my enthusiasm.

"It is very beautiful."

"But such a sad story. Do you know it?"

I shook my head. "I tried to ask the attendant, but he couldn't, or wouldn't tell me."

"Well, you see," she explained, "Zeus, the king of the gods, is madly in love with this human girl, Semele, and wishes to reward her, so he makes a solemn promise to grant her anything she wants. When she asks to see him in his full immortal glory, he cannot deny her. But the instant he reveals himself to her, it's like an explosion of light – and bam! – she is reduced to ashes." She giggled. "Sad but also stupid."

"Goodness!" I translated the story for Nelly, who had been hopping impatiently the while, though I could tell none of it made much sense to her.

"Jules, you see," Poppy continued, "wanted to depict the girl in that instant of revelation – the split second when she sees and understands everything – before she is destroyed."

A strange and terrifying myth. I wondered at the sculptor's choice.

"Would you like to come with me to his studio?" Poppy asked suddenly. "Just for a quick look. I am working with him on a relief, the Last Judgment, you know. It is such a great honour for me to be permitted to assist him."

"Yes, I heard that. Poppy, I would be delighted, but…" I glanced at Nelly.

"It wouldn't take long. Jules would be so very pleased to meet some English ladies of good taste."

That is how I put it to Nelly. That the very famous sculptor wished to meet her.

She frowned. "Why?" Then her eyes lit up. "Oh, I suppose he admires Ralph's work."

"Possibly," I replied, keeping my own counsel on that particular notion, and then said to Poppy, "We will just leave our bags in our rooms."

Madame Albert, who had been listening to the conversation, smiling the while, said that Philippe would take them up, to save us the effort of climbing the stairs. (She must have overheard Nelly puffing and panting). Poppy then asked her to say goodbye to "the boys" for her, and we set off.

On the way, I asked her how she came to be visiting the Hotel Lilas.

"Oh," she said carelessly. "You see, I grew up in this neighbourhood, and Philippe and I are friends from childhood." She smiled. "Now, Maman," she said to Nelly who couldn't understand her, "I suppose you are coming to the opening of the cabaret where Ralph's picture will hang."

I translated and Nelly looked puzzled.

"He hasn't mentioned it. When is it?"

I asked. "At the end of the week, apparently. Friday."

"We will be going home before then," she replied firmly.

I told Poppy that.

"A pity. I am sure he would have liked you to be there."

I couldn't help wondering if she had so quickly changed the subject for some reason of her own, and rather suspected she had hurried us away from the hotel on purpose, as well. Whatever was going on?

To say that the eminent M. Jules Bourdain was dying to meet two very ordinary English ladies had definitely been an exaggeration. Indeed, I think he sighed rather at the sight of us and indicated that he was waiting for someone else, since he asked Poppy, "Where is she? Always late. It is intolerable."

However, he was courteous enough to lead us round the studio and explain his work. He spoke English, though not accurately and with a very strong French accent. I am not sure how much Nelly understood but at least I was spared having to translate and could regard the art with full concentration. The heroic sculptures which filled much of the space, quite bowled me over. It struck me that some of them resembled their creator, for M. Bourdain was a large and powerful man himself, though well past his prime. I judged him to be at least sixty, with that full grey beard. His intense gaze, through eyes as blue as lapis lazuli, was disconcerting, and I could not help but feel that his polite words and manner masked something deeper and possibly darker in his nature.

Nelly asked him if he were acquainted with the work of her son, but he shook his head and bowed slightly.

"Alas, no, Madame."

She gave a little sniff and looked at me reproachfully, as if I had brought her there on false pretences. But her sense of pique wasn't about to drag me away quite yet.

"So tell me, please, M. Bourdain," I asked, "where is the piece you are working on with Poppy?"

"Poppy?"

I waved across at the young woman who sat, sketch book in hand, perched under an alabaster figure of a male athlete, whose nakedness might raise a blush with the unsophisticated, being rather graphically executed in the Greek style. Not a fig leaf in sight.

"Oh," the sculptor exclaimed. "You mean Gigi!"

I looked askance. The girl herself burst out laughing.

"The artists on the Butte call me Poupée," she explained, "because they think I am their doll, some toy to play with. Your Ralph calls me Poppy, because he misheard the first time. However, my birth name is Garance Germaine, and so to Jules I am Gigi. Who cares? I answer to anything as long as it isn't a bad word."

She jumped down and shewed me her sketchpad. In a few brief seconds, she had captured likenesses of both Nelly and myself.

"Goodness," I said. "That's wonderful, isn't it, Nelly."

"Very good," she replied with a little edge to her voice, as if to intimate that her Ralph could probably have done better.

"You would like to have it?" the girl – I will still call her Poppy – asked me, indicating the sketch of myself.

"I would love it," I said. "Can I buy it from you?"

"Not at all. It is my pleasure." She signed the two sketches GG, tearing the sheets from the pad and rolling them up into a tube.

"Thank you so much." My pleasure was utterly sincere. The picture was charming, and I was thrilled to have it. Nelly accepted hers with less of a good grace but I don't think the girl noticed. "So please shew us the relief?" I said again.

"Over here."

The piece was covered in sacking. Poppy pulled it back to reveal a massive slab of white marble depicting the Last Judgment in its full horror. Souls in torment emerging from the stone, tumbled down into hell. And though the mark of the master was there, I also recognised in the contorted shapes, some of the forms I had seen in Poppy's drawings. She was as much represented here as he was, and I wondered how much credit he would give her.

"Good heavens," was all Nelly could say, rather appositely, while I commented, "It would be enough to turn a heathen to God."

M. Bourdain threw back his head and laughed loudly.

"Very good, Madame. I like it." He translated for Poppy's benefit.

"Jules thinks he *is* God," was all she said.

At that moment we were joined by a dumpy middle-aged woman, who gazed at us balefully.

"I have brought your lunch, Jules," she said gruffly, producing a pot of something steaming.

Was this a servant? She looked like one in her drab dress and stained apron. Yet her manner wasn't servile at all.

"Thank you, *ma chérie*," he said, taking the pot and placing it on a wooden bench.

"Good afternoon, Thérèse," said Poppy, smiling. "That certainly smells tasty."

The smile was not returned. In fact, the woman quite ignored her.

"Be sure to eat it all up, Jules," she said. "It is good soup." Then she turned to us. "You have come to buy something?"

"No, just to look," I said. Whatever did she think we could purchase? It was all on such a huge scale.

"Ah," she said dismissively, turning on her heels and clumping out.

Poppy looked at me and shook her head. "Don't mind her," she said. "It's her way. She is very devoted." She turned to the sculptor. "How long have you been together with Thérèse, Jules?"

He grunted, busy assembling his tools, and paid no more attention to us, or, for that matter, the soup.

Poppy took the hint and told us, "But now I am afraid, Mesdames, we have to work. As you can see, the piece is far from finished."

"Of course. We are so grateful to you for the chance to see this."

M. Bourdain nodded then, but picked up a hammer and chisel, and turned away. We were not to watch him at work, although I should dearly have liked to.

"Are you going straight back to the hotel?" the girl asked.

Again I thought, from something in her tone, that there was more to this remark than a polite question.

"I don't know... We haven't decided."

"Only there is a beautiful park near here. You should certainly visit it. The Parc Monceau. I can give you directions if you like."

I translated the suggestion to Nelly and she agreed that it might prove a pleasant excursion. I again thanked the sculptor, who bowed gravely at us, as we left. But then, just as Poppy was pointing the way down the road to the park, a young woman nearly slammed into us in her eagerness to arrive.

"I am so very sorry to be late," she babbled at Poppy, glancing at us with a vague look.

"Yes, hurry on in. Jules is waiting."

The girl had not seemed to recognise us, but I knew her at once. It was lucky, perhaps, under the circumstances, that Nelly is a little short-sighted, and only found out it was Sylvie when I mentioned the fact after the girl had passed. Of course the last time we had seen her, she was in Ralph's bed in a state of complete undress, coppery ringlets hanging down, so she had looked rather different.

"She is the model?" I asked Poppy.

"Yes, now that I am becoming a sculptor, Jules says that he needs someone else to pose. Sylvie was available."

She didn't look too pleased with the choice. Perhaps she feared that the girl, who was decidedly pretty and whose morals did not appear to be very strict, posed a threat to her position as favourite with the artist. But perhaps I only think of that now, in the light of subsequent events.

Once Poppy had set us on the right path, she returned to the studio with dispatch, while we headed as directed toward the park, chatting about what we had seen. While I was enthusiastic,

81

Nelly opined that there was altogether too much naked flesh on view.

"I can't understand it about these French people. Why they have to keep taking their clothes off. It is most unseemly, Martha, most unseemly."

Chapter Seven – The Plot

Poppy's suggestion was inspired. The park was just what Nelly and I needed to refresh our spirits. We wandered its shaded winding paths, and with delight stumbled upon one folly after another. Nelly was particularly impressed by the classical colonnade, so we sat near it for a while, looking across the lake with its picturesque reflection of the surrounding trees and shrubs. In places, ducks and moorhens pulled trails in their wake, breaking the perfect clarity of the image until the waters settled again to stillness. Sparrows trilled in the branches or hopped hopefully at our feet but we had no crumbs for them, and they soon gave up on us.

It was all so very peaceful under a sun that, as the afternoon wore on, had lost its power to scorch, mellowing into golden light. I closed my eyes and let the softly aromatic breeze waft over me. It seemed to me then that nothing bad could ever happen in this Eden.

"I wonder if Ralph knows this place, Martha," Nelly remarked suddenly. "He could paint some lovely pictures here. Nice landscapes instead of…well… you know…"

"Mm," I replied. "You must mention it to him," dreading to think what frightful daubs he might produce.

On our eventual return to the hotel, we found a note from the boy himself to say that we must excuse him for the evening, for he had to take his painting to be hung in the new cabaret. He would come around the following morning, he wrote. Not too late, I hoped.

There was no sign now of the young men we had seen earlier, only Madame Albert with her warm smile, asking if we had enjoyed the visit to the sculptor's studio. She didn't miss much.

We had decided, for convenience, to take our dinner that evening at Le Petit Bonhomme and proceeded thither after a short rest in our rooms. Père Perrot was as delighted as ever to see us, rubbing his podgy hands and exclaiming "Bon, bon, bon." He recommended the sole meunière, which I ordered, while Nelly settled for a plain omelette.

She was more subdued than usual and not quite herself, the which I put down to the exertions of the day. That she ate little was nothing remarkable. Indeed, she explained that, since she had already partaken of a three-course meal that day, a heavy repast was now beyond her. Unusually, however, she refrained from commenting on how much I was eating – the sole was delicious and I picked the bones quite clean – or that I took a glass of wine with my meal. When I asked if she felt poorly, she simply replied that she was very tired.

The next morning, not finding her up and about, and she not answering my knock, I entered her room to rouse her, only to find her lying in bed, looking at me with wild eyes as if not quite recognising who I was. Her forehead burned with fever and the wounded hand, which lay on the coverlet, was red and more swollen that ever. Much concerned, I ran down to the vestibule and asked Madam Albert to come up and see what was the matter which the good woman did at once.

She too was shocked at the change in my sister, and paid special attention to the infected hand.

"What is this?" she asked and, when I told her that Nelly had been scratched by a wild cat, she threw up her hands in horror.

"My God," she exclaimed. "We must summon a doctor at once. It is doubtless the hydrophobia!"

Such horrifying words. Surely it could not be. My poor, poor sister.

I stayed with Nelly, applying a cool damp cloth to her forehead, while Madame Albert hurried off to send for a local medic, telling me she knew of one in a nearby street. At least Nelly took some water, when I held a glass to her lips. This relieved me somewhat. If it was as Madame had suggested, surely she would refuse the drink, since the very name of the disease suggested a great fear of that blameless liquid.

The doctor arrived promptly. He was a lugubrious young man, pale-skinned, with smooth black hair, and so tall that – evidently to try and offset the effect – he walked with a permanent stoop, the which, led by his long thin nose, made him look forever on the point of toppling forward. Added to this rather off-putting exterior, he had no bedside manner whatsoever. He took one look at Nelly, brusquely examined under her arm, presumably for swollen glands, asked me a few sharp questions, and then pronounced that it was certainly not hydrophobia, but cat scratch disease (he gave it a fancy Latinate name at first and then, with some disdain, simplified it for the benefit of Madame Albert and myself). He added that, with rest, the patient should recover in a few days and prescribed a tincture to reduce the fever, ordering that the wound to be washed regularly with carbolic soap and then painted with gentian violet. Speaking in irritated tones, he expressed exasperation with the patient – and quite unjustly, I thought, with myself – for having neglected the wound.

"We are to return to England in two days," I told him.

"Impossible," he replied, frowning. "Because there is a fever now, there may be complications later due to your initial neglect of the wound, and I should not like to have to answer for the consequences, should anything untoward occur en route."

Goodness, I thought. Even if not hydrophobia, it was bad news. Or was the young man just looking to pocket a larger fee? He certainly took what I offered with alacrity. Oh, how I wished I could consult with the good Dr Watson, but that of course was out of the question.

At the very moment the doctor, Lepine was his name, was taking his leave, Ralph arrived. At the news of his mother's indisposition and the sight of her feverish state and swollen hand, he was full of a sincere concern, the which inclined me to look upon the lad with more favour. Perhaps he was not quite the spoilt and self-centred child I had thought him.

Madame Albert undertaking to collect the necessary medicines from the pharmacy, and Ralph to stay with his mother, I took the opportunity to break my fast for I had become quite hungry. As usual I returned to Le Petit Bonhomme, where the waitress – not the daughter of the house but a bustling little body who had served us once before – welcomed me and asked if the other lady would be joining me. When I explained the matter, observing my distress, she expressed her sympathy and directed me to a quiet booth at the back of the restaurant, which I found most thoughtful of her.

I wish I could say that Nelly's condition put me off my food but I am afraid I indulged as much as ever in the buttery croissants. Once finished eating, over a refill of my cup of chocolate, I started to compose a letter to send to Clara, explaining the reasons for my delay in returning home, hoping that all was well, and asking if my two lodgers had yet returned from their travels, to wonder at my continued absence.

I am not sure when exactly I became aware of the voices in the next booth. The men there could not see me nor I them, but some trick of sound meant that I could overhear their conversation quite clearly. There were two of them, and one was not French but spoke that tongue in a strong accent I took perhaps to be Spanish. The other, in response, replied so slowly and clearly that I could make out exactly what he was saying. At first, however, I could not believe my ears.

How unpredictable and yet relentless is one's fate. If Nelly were not ill, I should never have overheard the conversation in the next booth. Had she not neglected the infection in her hand, she would not have got sick. Had she not stroked the cat in the cemetery of Montmartre, she would not have got scratched. Had Poppy not suggested we go there, had we not met Poppy in the first place… Well, one could go on and on. But the fact remains that every action and happening in the past had brought me to this point, and in retrospect I could not but think it was my destiny. That I was there to listen in with a purpose.

"We need a bold stroke, my friend," I heard the Frenchman say.

"Agreed, but when?" The Spaniard.

"The sooner the better. Tonight."

"Where?"

"The pig leaves the Prefecture regularly at seven in the evening. We will be waiting. I will point him out to you. Then, for the security of the Cause, I will leave you to do the deed alone. You understand."

"Of course. But surely I should not shoot him just there. It is too dangerous. With all the other flics around."

Shoot him! Did I hear correctly? I strained to learn more.

"Not there, of course," the Frenchman said, "you are right, Leon. But you see, Cochot is a man of habit. On a fine evening he likes to stroll along the quays at his leisure. And tonight, my friend, be sure it will be fine." The man laughed. It made me shiver to hear murder discussed with such cold-blooded nonchalance. "He makes the perfect target, so fat and ugly. You will be able to pick him off very easily."

"And if there are other people nearby?"

"All the better to let them see him die like the pig he is. Don't be afraid, my friend. You know how it always is. The public stand transfixed in horror, frozen to the spot, mouths open, allowing you time to run off into the shadows."

"I am not afraid, Maxim. I would die for the Cause if necessary."

"Of course, as would we all, Leon. Like Emil before us. Only let us hope such a sacrifice will not be necessary. The movement needs every one of us to keep ourselves safe."

I sat in horror – not transfixed or frozen, my mouth closed fast, unlike the imagined witnesses of the murderous attack, but spurred to jot down the names, times and place on the sheet of paper that was my letter to Clara.

At that moment, another man passed me and joined the others in the next booth. I only saw him briefly from the back, a long stringy fellow. Was it the anarchist Fénéon I had seen in the restaurant the other night? Was it Valentin the Boneless? Was it someone else? I could not be sure.

I heard the newcomer mutter, though his voice was too low for me to make out what he said. Then one of the others put his head over the top of the booth to look at me. With a slight shock, I recognised him. It was the young man I had seen the previous morning in intense conversation with Philippe Albert and Poppy.

I nodded as carelessly as I could, and said in English, "Good morning, monsewer! Another lovely day."

He stared at me, while I sipped at my hot chocolate (it had in truth gone rather cold). Then he nodded back curtly.

I heard him say something like "stupid English woman." However, I was unable to make out anything further, since they lowered their voices to a murmur.

What was I to do? Who was this Cochot, the target of their murderous plot and how could I warn him?

I called the waitress and paid my bill. Getting up to leave, I was careful not to look at the men in the other booth. I walked out slowly, as if with all the time in the world, and returned to the hotel. As I pushed open the door, I saw, reflected in the window glass, Philippe's friend lurking behind me. Good heavens, I thought, they do not trust me after all. I am being followed.

Careful to display no consciousness of this, I entered the hallway.

Madame Albert flew out talking to me, in French of course, about my sister. Aware of the man outside, I made gestures indicating, I hoped, that I could not understand what she was saying. If the man suspected I was at all fluent in his language, I might be in grave danger. Our landlady looked puzzled, but did not insist – perhaps imagining me to be distraught – and I went up to Nelly's room, where Ralph was sitting, looking glum.

At least, Madame Albert had managed to acquire the necessary medicines. Nelly, as Ralph informed me, had taken the tincture, and now he shewed me her hand, the wound painted purple with gentian violet. She was sleeping, too, which I always think a good sign and one of the best routes to recovery.

I asked Ralph, softly and without explaining why I wanted to know, if he could tell me who was M. Cochot. He shook his head.

"I have no idea, aunt."

"Then where," I asked, "is the Prefecture?"

"The police station? Why do you want to know that?"

Thinking quickly, I said, "Oh, Mr. Holmes asked me to call in as a courtesy, to pay his respects. He has had dealings with the French police in the past, you know." The which, for all I knew, might be true.

Ralph then shewed me where it was on my map. On the island of St-Louis. Surrounded by quays, any one of which might provide a place of ambush.

"Would you mind very much, "I asked, "if I went there right now, leaving you with your mother for a while longer?"

"Right now? Well, you know, aunt, I am very busy today."

I could not imagine with what, but promised to be gone for not more than an hour, and he nodded reluctantly.

"No need," I added, "to tell anyone else where I have gone. In case they should ask, you know."

"Why ever not?"

Why indeed.

"Oh," I replied, "I get the feeling the police aren't very popular round here. People might think, ha ha, that I am reporting on them for some reason. Promise me, Ralph."

The lad must have found this odd – particularly given the urgency of my tone – but nodded to indulge his old aunt, and I left him staring into space.

I managed to slip out of the hotel without encountering Madame Albert. However, once in the street, I felt a tingling sensation and was sure that I was still being watched. It would not do to go straight to the Prefecture. If I were indeed being followed, I must lose my pursuers as soon as possible.

I thought again of Mr. H. and how easily he could don disguises to enable him to move through the city of London inconspicuously. For me it was not so easy. However, there were places a lady could enter where no man alone would go, dress shops for instance. If only she could get out of them again without being seen.

I hailed a fiacre, although was not naïve enough to think that I could not be followed in that. In loud tones, in English, I asked to be taken to the Vivienne Gallery. I knew from my Baedeker that this place formed something of a covered maze of shops, with several entrances, and thus hoped that I could confuse any pursuers enough, or at least have them give up the chase, taking me indeed for a stupid and idle Englishwoman only interested in shopping.

The gallery proved to be truly beautiful, with mosaic floors, arched windows and doorways set between pale yellow pillars, a vaulted glass roof and a glass cupola at the centre of all. The effect was light and airy. Treasures of all sorts filled the elegant stores: tailors, cobblers, a wine shop, a restaurant, a bookstore, a draper's establishment, a confectioner, a print-seller. I hoped to be able to return under happier circumstances and explore at my leisure.

Just now, however, my mind was set on other matters. I forced myself to walk slowly, pausing frequently to look in shop windows as if at the goods on display, but in fact to see if I could recognise anyone behind me. I was not sure. I entered a confectioners and bought some chocolates, ever checking the people outside surreptitiously. At last I concluded that I was not being followed after all. Surely I was being overly cautious.

Another window caught my eye. It artfully displayed a selection of fans opened in various designs. One of those, I thought, would be perfect as a gift for my little maid, Phoebe. She would love a frivolous accoutrement like that: I could just see her waving it in front of her face, considering herself quite the lady of fashion. I entered the shop and, not to waste too much time, swiftly selected one of the least expensive in pastel colours depicting a shepherd and shepherdess in amorous though decorous conversation. It was suitably sentimental for the girl. Then I walked out of the gallery into a different street from the one by which I had entered. I checked my map, and as I did so, out of the corner of my eye, spotted the figure of a man, standing motionless amid the busy throng and turned in my direction. I did not look at him but feared the worst. I was still in danger.

What to do? How to lose him? I should never forgive myself if I failed to warn this M. Cochot in time.

While pondering the matter, I made an elaborate show of opening the box of chocolates (intended for Nelly, but this was a good cause), chose one and ate it. I am sure it was delicious but I hardly tasted it, for an idea had just come to me. A bold idea, to be sure, but necessity demanded extreme measures.

Turning towards my pursuer, I let my face light up in surprised delight, for it was indeed the Frenchman from the café. I walked right up to him – and was pleased to note his discomfiture.

"Oh, bonjour, Monsewer," I said in the worst French accent I could muster, and then spoke in English. "You naughty man." I was still holding the fan I has just purchased, and tapped him playfully on the chest with it. "Have you been following me?" He drew back.

"No, Madame, I assure you." I opened the fan and fluttered it about my face. "Ooh la la, my mother warned me about you naughty Frenchmen… But I am a respectable married woman, you know." Following the words with a wink and another tap on his chest.

"Would you like a chocolate?" I asked. "Do have one?" I thrust the box under his nose.

He shook his head.

"Oh, go on," I said. "You know you want to. They are most delightfully soft, you know. They just melt in the mouth." I took another myself, licking my lips.

I had no idea how much he could understand, though my flirtatious tone and manner surely translated into any language. But what if, heaven forbid, he took me up on my offer! He was half my age but, still, one never knew with continentals.

However, my matronly appearance was unlikely to inspire unbridled lust in any young man and so it turned out. With horror in his eyes, he turned and quite ran away from me. Success! I smiled in satisfaction, only then to catch the eye of a white-haired gentleman of considerable age, nattily dressed, a pink carnation in his lapel, who had evidently been watching the proceedings. With a broad grin on his face, he stepped forward and bowed, about to speak, but I was already off, back through the gallery as fast as decorum permitted and out another door, where I jumped into a fiacre and told the driver to make haste for the Prefecture, assured this time that no one was in pursuit.

I sank back against the cushions, my heart pounding. How lucky, I thought, that I had seen so many of the plays of poor Mr. Wilde. Indeed, I felt as if I had just acted in one. And how very shocked Nelly would have been at my carrying-on. I started to laugh then, but in truth it was no laughing matter. These people, from what I had overheard, were quite ruthless.

Chapter Eight – The Police Commissioner

"No, Madame, it is quite impossible. The Prefect cannot be disturbed."

The official at the front desk, a weaselly little man, provided the usual obstructive barrier to such places, all decked out as he was with a false sense of his own overweening importance. He pursed his lips. He would not be moved.

I had not wished to explain my reasons for seeing M. Cochot except to the man himself. As I have learnt from Mr. H., one never knows whom one can trust. In vain I pleaded the importance of my case and even said that it was a matter of life and death, but to no avail.

"You might speak to Inspector Lambert, Madame."

"Who is he?"

"M. Lambert is one of the officers. But in any case, not today. You must make an appointment."

What to do? It was more than frustrating. Suddenly, I recalled what I had told Ralph about the reason for my visit. It was worth a try.

"I am sure you would not treat my colleague, Mr. Sherlock Holmes, in such a way," I said haughtily.

"Who?"

"Mr. Sherlock Holmes, the great London detective. As I said, he is my colleague. I come from him." (Forgive me, Mr. H., for presuming).

It worked. Instantly, the man's whole demeanour changed.

"You have a connection to… to Him? To Mr. Sherlock Holmes!"

I sighed. "Must I repeat myself? Yes, yes and again yes."

"Wait here, please, Madame." He scurried off.

Well, now, I thought. How useful to know that the mere mention of my lodger's name can work such magic. Open sesame, indeed.

In no time at all, the man was back, now all grovelling smiles.

"This way, Madame, if you please."

I swept through the gate he opened with a bow, and proceeded along a fine corridor, all marble floors and decorative plasterwork. The French police look after themselves, I was thinking, a notion that was confirmed in bushels when I was shewn into the august presence of the Prefect, M. Cochot himself.

This gentleman rose to meet me, imposing in his bemedalled black uniform, or he would have been imposing had it fitted less tightly over his portly frame and not looked, rather comically, as if the gold buttons were about to burst open. Not that I should have dismissed him as "fat and ugly," however, as the plotters had done earlier. Admittedly he had lost most of his hair and his eyes were small and perhaps one might even say piggy, but ugly he was not. Rather the opposite in fact for a man of his years, which I put to be slightly more than my own. M. Cochot was what my mother might have described as "a fine figure of a man," with an added air of alert intelligence. He told me graciously to be seated and then sat back himself in his leather-padded throne. My seat was rather more ordinary.

"Well, Madame... Hudson. I understand you bring a message from my dear friend, Mr. Holmes. And a gift perhaps?"

I was puzzled at this until I realised he was referring to the pretty bag I held on my lap, containing the box of fancy chocolates I had just purchased.

"Ah no," I said. "Not exactly. But please help yourself, Monsieur."

I opened the box, placed it on the big mahogany desk and pushed it towards him. It turned out that M. Cochot had a very sweet tooth indeed, for he popped one confection after another into his mouth. No matter. It was in a good cause, and Nelly would never know what she had missed.

"I am afraid," I said, "that I have come on a very serious matter indeed."

He raised dark eyebrows and helped himself to a praline sprinkled with cocoa powder.

"Please to continue, Madame." He bit off half of the chocolate, not taking his eyes from my face, as he listened to my stumbling account (in French) of what I had overheard.

Before I reached the nub of the matter he held up a meaty hand.

"I am sorry, Madame, but what has Mr. Sherlock Holmes to do with this?"

"Nothing."

"Nothing?"

"I am afraid I just had to get past the desk and speak to you privately... Please let me proceed."

"This is a most serious matter," he said, and put down the cherry enrobed in dark chocolate that he was holding. "Impersonating a colleague of Mr. Holmes! How do I know that you yourself are not a member of this gang of which you speak?"

He actually started to reach for his pistol.

"M. Cochot," I said hastily, "let me assure you that I come in good faith. Mr. Holmes resides in my house in Baker Street as my lodger. And perhaps I might even say, my friend." Hardly that, but by now I was getting desperate.

"Hm." To my relief, he let go his pistol and popped the cherry confection into his mouth instead.

"Go on."

This time I managed to tell the whole of the tale, not omitting the fact that I had been followed part of the way to the Prefecture (though not revealing exactly how I had thrown off my pursuer). I could see that M. Cochot was still highly sceptical, perhaps taking me for some hysterical fantasist. It was not until I mentioned the names of Maxim, Leon and Emil that he sat up.

"Maxim Brandes and Leon Garcia?" he asked. "Emil Henri?

"I don't know their last names," I said. "And I am not sure, but I think Felix Fénéon might have come in to join them."

"You know Fénéon?" Again he twitched with suspicion.

"He was pointed out to me in a restaurant as a dangerous radical. But as I said, I am not sure that it was he."

"But he is very recognisable."

"I only saw this newcomer from the back. Under the circumstances, I didn't want to shew any particular interest in them all."

"No, I understand. And it is true that I have on occasion received death threats from anarchist and other groups... Pray continue."

When I finished my account, he sat for a while, staring at me, drumming his fingers on the desk.

"Well now, if what you say is true, Madame," he said finally, "I owe you the deepest gratitude. Indeed, I may owe you my life. Of course, I cannot take your word for any of this – you may have misheard. Still, counter-measures will assuredly be taken."

I told him that I was most relieved to hear it.

"In the meantime," he went on, "you must realise that you might have put yourself in grave danger. I advise you very strongly to return to England at once, Madame, or at the very least to change your lodgings."

"That is impossible at the moment," I said, and told him about my sister's indisposition.

"Let us hope then, that we manage to round up all the gang. Is anyone else involved, do you suspect, apart from those you have mentioned?"

I thought of Philippe. How it would break Madame Albert's heart if he were to be arrested. In any case, I had no proof he was part of the gang. Neither he nor Poppy, for that matter. They might be all, as she had told me, old friends from childhood. I wanted to believe it.

I shook my head. "No. There's no one else."

Having done my duty, I felt a wave of relief, which soon turned to extreme fatigue. Quickly walking away from the Prefecture in case any of the plotters lurking about, I managed to make my weary way to the park at the end of the larger Island of the City. There I sat for a while on a stone bench under a weeping willow to collect myself. Taking deep breaths, I could not help but wonder how it was that these days I seemed so regularly to get into situations like this. It was never thus when dear Henry was alive, but then I seldom left the environs of Baker Street. When one travels, one must always, I suppose, expect the unexpected.

The vista here in any case soothed me. An occasional barge passed nearby, creating a wash of waves. Families aboard were about their everyday business, the men navigating the craft, the womenfolk with children under their feet, babes tied to their breasts, engaged at the same time in domestic duties, sweeping the deck, peeling vegetables into a bucket, hanging laundry on makeshift lines. I wondered idly how far they might be going and what kind of a life it would be on the move all the time, without roots. And how difficult it would be to keep everything orderly in such a narrow space.

All around me in the park, other children played; some kicked balls that were ever in danger of falling into the river, boys fought each other with wooden swords, girls skipped with ropes, calling out to each other and to their mothers or nurses. It was all most charming to watch. Elegant ladies paraded with parasols against the burn of the sun, for it was yet another hot day. I cooled myself with the fan I had bought for Phoebe, and sat on, unwilling to leave, revelling in the tranquillity, the ordinariness of the scene. Fishermen, who had perched themselves at the edge of the quays, smoking clay pipes, were busy only with waiting, hardly caring, it seemed to me, if they caught anything or not. Yes, it was as if nothing could disturb the peace of the everyday, and yet I could not but think of what M. Cochot had said. If any of the gang realised who had betrayed them, the consequences might indeed prove fatal for me. These were after all ruthless fanatics. But how could I have acted otherwise when a man's life was at stake?

With some reluctance, I dragged myself away at last from the haven of the island, and ambled back through the city. Arriving at the hotel, it was to find, to my dismay, that of Madame Albert there was no sign. Instead, it was large, ginger-haired Philippe Albert who was standing at the desk, and not at all friendly. Was he looking out for me? Had I been wrong to spare him? However, he merely informed me that, because Ralph had not waited for me to return – admittedly I had been gone near enough three hours – his mother was now sitting up with my sister. This must then be the cause of his coolness, that my prolonged absence had forced him to take on desk duty. Another idle and spoilt son, perhaps.

Relieved, at least, to find my initial suspicions misplaced, I went immediately to Nelly's room where Madame Albert sat placidly knitting. She smiled that broad smile of hers and informed me that the patient's fever seemed to have abated somewhat. Nelly stirred at the sound of our voices, hushed though they were, and looked over at us sleepily. She still seemed confused and, despite what Madame had told me, her forehead felt hotter than it ought to be.

The good landlady rose from her seat and nodded at my effusive apologies for discommoding her.

"M. Ralph," she said, "told me he had some important business to attend to, and asked me to stay with his mother. But it is of no account, Madame. I was pleased to do it. And you see, I managed to complete many rows."

She held up the garment, a shawl I supposed, in grey wool.

I took her place, wishing that I too had some knitting, since it was most tedious to sit idly. At least, I was able, finally, to write that letter to Clara, though, having completed it, I realised that a telegraphic wire would reach her much more quickly, and resolved to find a post office as soon as Nelly's improvement was sufficient to allow me to leave her by herself. Dr. Lepine had engaged to visit the following morning to check on his patient and, no doubt, to receive another handful of francs.

I sat thus for the rest of the day, quite glad indeed, under the circumstances, and apart from the enforced idleness, to be confined safely in a hotel room, while the drama unfolded elsewhere in the city. I picked up Nelly's novel – "The Perils of Elsie" – which, I admit, diverted me somewhat, though in my opinion it was very poorly written. Elsie, the silly goose, needed, in my opinion, to pull herself together and not indulge in so many fits of the vapours, even given the seemingly endless series of perils she found herself in.

Towards evening, Madame Albert most kindly brought up a plate of stew for me as well as a light soup for the patient. Nelly would only take a mouthful or two, while I, as usual, cleared my plate, although, to be honest, the dish, which Madame pronounced to be a "cassoulet" and a speciality of her native Languedoc, was too rich and greasy for me to enjoy wholeheartedly. But I was hungry. A disadvantage of being away from home is that one has not unlimited access to a kitchen and is constantly dependent on others for sustenance.

I was prepared to sleep overnight in the room with Nelly, in the armchair. Indeed, I had dozed there earlier and found it comfortable enough. However, Madame Albert assured me that it was not necessary.

"You see how cool she is now, Madame, and you yourself need a proper rest." She turned to my sister. "Is that not so, Madame Nelly?"

The latter had to agree, though in a martyred voice that trembled rather. That decided me. She was clearly overdoing it, sounding just like the vaporous Elsie in the novel.

"I am only next door," I told her briskly. "You can call out if you need me."

Once in the sanctuary of my own room, I checked the time. Ten of the clock. My thoughts again turned to M. Cochot, hoping he had managed to outwit those with designs on his life. I quite fizzed with the worry of that and, of course, of Nelly, too, despite my seemingly hardened heart in her case. However Madame Albert had most thoughtfully provided me with a glass of cognac – the quality a little rough but acceptable enough – and with its help I soon succumbed to sleep. If poor Nelly called out in the night, I am sure I did not hear her.

True to his word, Dr. Lepine put in an appearance early the next morning, as lugubrious as ever. He expressed, without any great pleasure, satisfaction at the improvement in his patient.

"The swelling has gone down, as you can see, and the fever also. However, Madame should remain in bed for the rest of the day. I will call again tomorrow."

"Is it necessary?" I asked. "Since my sister is clearly getting better."

He shook his head.

"There have been cases of a relapse, Madame. I should not like to risk that."

"No, indeed, doctor," said Nelly. I feared she was starting rather to enjoy the attention she was getting. "I do hope dear Ralph will call in again today."

"I expect he will, unless of course he is too busy," I replied. The edge of sarcasm escaped my sister.

"Yes, the new cabaret opens tomorrow night. They might need him there. To arrange things, you know."

I nodded, although reckoning that, since Ralph had presumably already delivered his painting to Le Chien Jaune, there was surely nothing more for him to do in that regard.

Lepine was packing up his bag, while Madame Albert hovered. I think she had a soft spot for the man though I could not imagine why.

"Great goings-on last night, Doctor," she said.

He nodded. "Yes, as I understand it."

"Goings-on?" I asked.

"Oh yes. It is all over the morning papers," the good woman went on. "I can bring one up for you if you would like to see it."

"But what it is it about?" As if I knew nothing of the matter.

"It appears," said Dr. Lepine, "that the police have managed to thwart an anarchist plot to assassinate the Prefect as he left the Prefecture. One of the plotters shot himself rather than be captured." He shook his head and Madame Albert blessed herself. "All very sordid. I thought those anarchists had abandoned their violent tactics."

"The police must have had a tip-off," added our landlady all agog. "I shouldn't like to be in that person's shoes if the revolutionaries find out who they are."

"No, indeed," I said, shuffling a bit uncomfortably. "Did they not round up the whole gang then?"

"Who can know?" Lepine said. "They picked up another man, I believe, but these cells – it is all so secret. Who can tell how large they really are?"

Just one other man, then, presumably Maxim, assuming it was Leon who perished. Yet there were three of them at that table. Perhaps after all it would be wise to leave the country as soon as possible.

"So how soon, doctor, can my sister and I return to England?" I asked as though changing the subject.

Lepine considered his patient.

"Perhaps after the weekend. I will see how she improves."

After the weekend! That meant four more days. I could not stay locked up in my hotel room that long. In any case, it would look most strange.

"Don't be so sad, Madame," our landlady told me. "Go out and enjoy Paris. It is a city for enjoyment."

"Apart, of course, from the occasional shooting," said Lepine.

Chapter Nine: A Fine Dinner

I was quite prepared to spend most of the day sitting quietly with Nelly but our landlady had other ideas.

"Madame Martha," she said. "It is a beautiful day in a beautiful city. You must go out and enjoy it. Victorine can stay with your sister."

Victorine, it seemed, was a niece who came to the hotel sometimes to help with the cleaning and other chores.

"Oh dear," I replied. "I don't know if I should."

My feelings were mixed. Of course, all things being equal, I should much prefer to be out and about, enjoying the city, as Madame Albert had instructed me. However, all things were far from being equal. It was most possible any surviving anarchists would be on the look-out for me, if they had any suspicions of my being the one who betrayed their plot. Nonetheless, I needed at the very least to send a message to Clara, to inform her of my delay in returning.

I smiled at Madame Albert.

"Thank you for the offer. I will go out for a little while."

I nearly changed my mind when Victorine arrived, a sullen, skinny, yellow-complexioned little thing of about eleven years old.

"Shouldn't you be at school?" I asked.

The child shrugged. Perhaps she didn't understand my English accent. She sat herself on the chair I had vacated and stared fixedly, but without any apparent interest, at Nelly, who stared back.

"I won't be long," I called over to my sister. She returned a long-suffering sigh. It wasn't my fault, I thought as I hurried downstairs, that she had got herself scratched by an infected cat.

Madame Albert promised to look in on the pair of them from time to time – "Victorine will let me know if anything is amiss" – and gave me directions to the nearest post office, which was, as it turned out, near the Louvre museum. I left the hotel and looked about myself as if I weren't sure where to go, although of course I did. In truth, I was checking to see if there were any suspicious looking characters nearby. Thank goodness, no one I saw fitted that description – everyone was as usual rushing about with their own affairs – and it was with a lighter heart that I made my way towards the museum and the river. I was becoming very familiar with this route, and almost felt myself an authentic Parisian.

My business speedily completed in the most imposing post office I have ever visited, more like a palace than a place of business, I decided to avail a while longer of the services of Victorine – trying to imagine wryly what possible communication might be taking place between her and Nelly. But the morning was bright – it would assuredly soon get hotter – and there was so much to see. So many new impressions. A short delay could surely do no harm.

I soon found myself wandering through the great glass-roofed structure that comprises the main food market of Paris. I do so love the bustle of such places – and this one didn't disappoint with its wondrous array of food shops, emitting enticing odours. The vendors here had a knack of presenting their produce in the most attractive way. Even the meat looked luscious, fresh and tender, though I pitied the poor skinned rabbits, their flesh as smooth and shiny as marble. Beyond them heaps of bright fruit, gleaming as if polished, beside vegetables that included strangely shaped exotics quite unknown to me. Further on again, rows of cakes and pastries that resembled bejewelled works of art rather than comestibles. I have to admit that the French do this sort of thing much better than the British, perhaps because they value good food more highly than we do. As someone once said, while we in Britain eat to live, in France they live to eat.

I paused in particular admiration over a fish counter, where silvery herring and mackerel lay in decorative patterns on a bed of ice, shimmering in rainbow colours, and surrounded by pink shrimps, prawns and crabs, and that most bizarre of sea creatures, the octopus. Because I lingered so long, the fishmonger finally asked me what I wanted and held up a fine lobster for me to admire. I shook my head, smiling. I could hardly carry a fish around with me, even as a gift for Madame Albert. I was tempted, more, by the cheese shop. Although almost overcome by the sharp, sour odours, I lingered, curious. The place stocked so many varieties of that particular comestible that I had never seen before, some in hard and golden blocks, some soft, oozing from their white or yellow rinds. Offered tastes by the vendor, I found the first far too strong for my taste, but the second was pleasantly creamy, and I purchased a small slice of the "brie," as it was called, to eat back at the hotel later. It occurred to me then that I was hungry, having quite forgotten, in the excitement of the morning, to break my fast. How ever had that happened? It was so unlike me. Outside the market, I found a pleasant little café with tables on the street. For a change, I ordered off the menu a "pain au chocolate," which I found to be like a croissant only with the sweet confection folded inside. I also risked a lemon tea, which, drunk without milk, I found to be pleasantly refreshing.

Somewhat guiltily, I then started back, pausing only to make a couple of further small purchases at the Galeries Lafayette, a great store near to the hotel. In fact, I had been gone only just over an hour, and Madame Albert was quite surprised to see me.

"So soon?" she said. "You should have stayed out longer, Madame." Then she winked at me and gave a sly smile. "But perhaps you hurried back to see what your admirer had sent you?"

"My admirer?"

Whatever did she mean?

From under the counter, like a magician pulling a rabbit out of a hat, she produced a large bouquet of white lilies.

"These arrived soon after you left," she told me.

I was astonished. Indeed, my first evil thought was that my enemies had sent them. After all, lilies are often associated with funerals and death. Perhaps this was a sinister message. However, the blooms were so beautiful, they smelt so good, that I soon discounted that notion. But who else could they be from?

"There is a note," she said, and handed a sealed envelope to me, inscribed with my name.

It turned out to be from none other than the Prefect himself, M. Cochot, yet again expressing his grateful thanks, and hoping that I would join him for dinner that evening. "You can tell me all about your famous lodger, Mr. Sherlock Holmes," he wrote.

Madame Albert studied my face. I am sure she could read nothing in it except mystification. Surely the flowers were enough of a thank you. I was not at all inclined to accept the invitation. Was it even within the bounds of propriety to dine out with a man I barely knew? On the other hand, M. Cochot was a person of eminent respectability and, if the subject of our conversation was to be Mr. H. – who seemed a firm favourite with the French police – it would surely be churlish to refuse. And I was, after all, in Paris.

"I am invited to dinner," I told our landlady. "But I am not sure. My sister..."

The good woman smiled broadly. "Aha, you have made a conquest, Madame Martha. Rest assured, your sister will be properly looked after here."

All well and good, but I wondered what Nelly would say.

"Who is he?" She pulled herself right up in bed and glared at me. "Who is this stranger who invites you to dinner and gives you flowers?"

"Oh, just an associate of Mr. H.," I told her, unwilling to explain further.

"Are you sure of that?" she replied, and tapped the novel she had been re-reading for want of anything else. "Elsie, you know, trusts in the nobility of mind of a pleasing scoundrel, and only escapes the white slavers by the skin of her teeth."

I burst out laughing.

"Oh Nelly, you're incorrigible," I said. "What white slaver would ever want me?"

"That's true enough," she replied, rather too easily, I thought. "I suppose you'll be wearing that scarlet dress you bought."

"The cerise, you mean." I hadn't thought of it, but the expression on her face, God forgive me, decided me.

"What a good idea," I replied.

In fact, things worked out somewhat better than I had feared, for in the afternoon Ralph turned up and undertook to stay with his mother for the evening. Nelly was pleased, of course, though I found the boy much less exuberant than usual, as if something were troubling him. However, when I asked, he dismissed the suggestion.

"Not at all, aunt. I am just worried about my dear mummy."

That pleased Nelly even more, though it failed to convince me. He had a strained look about him, and was nervous and fidgety.

"You know," he said, as if to change the subject, "those anarchists last night…."

"Yes."

"They were here. I saw them. Well, one of them."

"What!" exclaimed Nelly. "Here in the hotel?" She gripped her sheet with whitened knuckles

"I'm sure you are mistaken," I said.

Had the boy no sense? He must know the news would send his mother into a paroxysm of panic.

"No, I assure you. I recognised him from his picture in the paper. Maxim someone…"

"Well anyway, he has been captured," I said firmly.

"Yes, but what of the others? There must be others. The woman downstairs, her son, perhaps…"

"Not at all. Ralph, you are upsetting your mother."

Realisation dawned at last. He glanced at Nelly.

"Ah…Well, maybe I am mistaken," he said. "Yes, it is most probable. A mistake. He just looked somewhat like."

"The Hotel Lilas, a hotbed of sedition," I said. "Madame Albert the head of the gang I suppose."

We all laughed merrily at that, although Nelly still looked thoughtful and I myself was hardly calmed. It was, after all, more than probable that Philippe knew something of the matter, even if he were not a member of the cell himself. Better not to reveal to anyone the identity of my host for the evening.

"I have to tell you, Madame, that tonight you look most enchanting." The Prefect raised a glass and smiled.

I suppose such compliments come easily to French gentlemen, but they make me most uncomfortable. The cerise dress was perhaps to blame, for, if I say so myself, it looked rather good on me, most stylish. Still, I could have wished M. Cochot to be a little less gallant. We had enjoyed a fine meal in a most delightful seafood restaurant, quite near to the Prefecture, I partaking of a juicy lobster, perhaps brother to the one I had seen in the morning. My companion had watched approvingly as I attacked the beast and extracted the sweet meat.

"It is good to see a woman who enjoys her food," he said. "So many of our French ladies only pick and choose, wishing, I suppose, to stay petite and svelte."

No one could accuse me of being that way. Nelly least of all.

112

"My mother always told me never to trust a thin cook," I told him.

He laughed. "Your mother is very wise."

"It's true I like my food, monsieur. Especially when it is as beautifully prepared as this. The sauce is quite delicious."

"Lobster thermidor, made, I believe, with cream and eggs and cognac."

On that basis, I am afraid I shall never be either petite or svelte. But, then, nor will my companion, his rotund corpulence evidence of many a fine dinner before this one. Still, I liked his face. It reminded me just a little of my dear late husband, though Henry's eyes were bigger and he had more hair.

Before this exchange, we had chatted most pleasantly about Mr. H. and the good Dr. Watson.

"Alas, him, the marvellous chronicler, I regret I have never met," M. Cochot told me. "But Sherlock Holmes, now! He is a hero to us. You know perhaps that he was instrumental in helping to capture an arch villain who had eluded the Sûreté for a very long time."

"I am afraid he doesn't discuss his cases with me, Monsieur. I have to read the accounts of them as written by Dr. Watson. So far I don't think he has described that particular one."

"And never will. It has to be kept secret from the general public. The survival of a great house hung in the balance. Were it not for the genius of Mr Holmes in capturing the perpetrator, a terrible scandal would have ensued, that would have shaken the very foundations of our Republic."

"He is indeed a great man," I said sincerely. I was not about to tarnish my lodger's reputation by complaining of his many

113

shortcomings as a tenant, his untidiness, those frightful experiments that left the whole house stinking, his thoughtless custom of playing his violin loudly into the night. These were secrets to be kept between Doctor Watson, Clara and me.

"But you also, Madame," M. Cochot was saying, "you also have given great service to the French police, and in particular to myself. I doubt very much we would be sitting here in this charming restaurant, drinking a good Sancerre, had it not been for your detective skills. You saved my life. To you, Madame Martha Hudson."

He raised his glass and I obligingly clinked mine against his. We drank the toast. One of many that night.

"It was sad, all the same," I said, "that a young man had to die."

He pulled a face. "Ah, no, just one less piece of garbage in the world."

I did not like that. "However misplaced in his beliefs, Monsieur, Leon Garcia proved to be a young man of principle, prepared to kill himself rather than to be captured."

"Then he was stupid as well as bad."

I shook my head.

"You are too soft, Madame. Most assuredly he is better off. Would you rather he rotted his life away in La Santé prison? Or be shipped off to South America?"

"Yes, indeed. Where there is life, after all, there is hope. Hope of salvation."

"Another of your mother's little sayings?"

I shook my head, annoyed. At least, M. Cochot was sensitive enough to perceive this.

114

"Forgive me, Madame. You express a Christian spirit of forgiveness that is most admirable. But you know, this same idealistic young man was quite prepared to send me flying to heaven or to hell, so please forgive me if I am rather less able to mourn his death."

He was right.

"Of course. It was thoughtless of me."

"No, no. Just an example of your womanly compassion and pity."

We might have gone on apologising to each other thus for quite a while, but just then, luckily, our waiter arrived with our food and gave us another topic of conversation altogether.

The restaurant was intimate – perhaps a little too much so for my complete peace of mind, though M. Cochot's behaviour was entirely that of a gentleman. The oak panelled walls featured landscape paintings and mirrors that threw back the candlelight. Our comfortably upholstered armchairs were set in a booth at a small table covered with dark red damask that almost matched my dress. I guessed that the place was expensive, rather beyond my scant resources, but then I was not paying. I thought, too, from the solicitude of the waiters, that they knew M. Cochot rather well.

"You come here often, I think," I asked after the waiter had refilled our glasses.

"Oh, sometimes… Yes it is a favourite of mine."

I paused, thoughtfully, wondering whether to make a point that had just occurred to me. I decided that I would.

"You must know these things better than I do," I said, "but it might be wise to change your pattern of behaviour."

"Whyever do you say that, Madame?"

"Because I overheard Maxim describe you as a man of habit. That might be dangerous if they are still watching you, if there are still men out there that wish you harm."

"Hm." He sat back in his chair and studied me. Was he angry with me for presuming to tell him his business? At last he leaned forward again.

"You are absolutely correct, Madame. I bow to your superior wisdom. I shall vary my customs from now on."

He raised his glass and again clinked it against mine.

I was most glad to be conducted back to the hotel in a fiacre, for my head was rather spinning. M. Cochot had insisted on accompanying me, and I am afraid the wine and cognac (with our after-dinner coffee) had somewhat gone to his head too, for as I prepared to descend from the vehicle, he took my hand and kissed it with an excessive, to my mind, degree of warmth. But perhaps it is just a common French practice, and I should not read anything special into it.

"Madame Hudson," he said. "I enjoyed our evening very much. I hope before you return to London and to Mr. Sherlock Holmes, we can meet again like this."

"Thank you, Monsieur," I replied. "It was all most agreeable. But you know, you are supposed to be varying your habits from now on."

He laughed heartily, as if I had said something very witty. Then gave an order to the driver and sped off into the night. As for me, I stood watching them depart, not quite knowing what to make of it all. Not knowing, indeed, if I wished to see him again, without for one moment suspecting that I should do so under completely different circumstances.

Madame Albert emerged from her parlour as I entered the hotel.

"I think you have had a good time," she said somewhat archly as she handed me my key.

"Indeed," I replied, trying to maintain my dignity, but aware that I was not entirely steady upon my feet. "How is my sister?"

She shook her head and sighed.

"The fever is a little up again, I think. Just a little. And Madame Nelly, she demands a lot."

Somewhat alarmed at this intelligence, I hurried up the stairs and tapped on Nelly's door. A weak "yes" gave me leave to enter and it was with some astonishment that I found Ralph still in attendance, hunched in his chair. Either he was very concerned about his mother or something else caused him to linger. However, I could not think about that just then, and hurried over to feel Nelly's forehead. It was a little hot, though not enough, I judged, to cause concern. Anyway, Dr. Lepine would be visiting the next morning.

Nelly sniffed as I bent over her.

"You have been drinking, Martha," she said.

I bit back a smile. Ever my older sister.

"Just a glass or two of fine French wine with my dinner." No need to mention the cognac. "Can you forgive me for that, my dear?"

"I am most glad that you had a good time."

"Thank you. Yes, I enjoyed the company and the food." I turned to my nephew. "You can go home now, Ralph," I said.

For he seemed inclined to remain, and it was with some reluctance that he got to his feet.

"If you are sure," he said. "I can stay, you know. I don't mind. In fact, I would rather like to."

"No, no." Nelly spoke firmly. "You have been here long enough. I was most relieved to have your company instead of that of the miserable little scrap that was here earlier. Never said a word for hours on end. Just stared. It was quite unnerving, I can tell you." She pursed her lips. "No, no. You head off, Ralph. I am sure you have important things to do, and your aunt is here now. Though I think you should change your dress, Martha. It is hardly suitable under the circumstances for a sick room, and the crinkling sound it makes is most jarring."

"The crinkling sound?"

"The rustling of the silk. Whenever you move."

I looked at Ralph, and he at me. Neither of us could restrain ourselves and we burst out laughing.

"Whatever next, mother?" he said.

"Well anyway," I added, "it is late, and I need to prepare for sleep."

To be quite frank, the unwonted amount I had eaten – having been unable to resist the crème brulée and petits fours that rounded off the meal – had caused my dress to feel rather tighter than before. It would be a relief to remove it.

Ralph lingered while I went to my room to change into my night clothes and robe, only leaving when I returned to my sister. Any hope that she was ready to settle down was not to be. She wished to hear all about my evening. Who this man was and where we went. I parried her questions as best I could, the which she found most unsatisfactory.

"I do not understand, Martha, why you are being so secretive," she complained. "I hope you have not got yourself entangled in something illicit." Her eyes turned again to the book on her counterpane, "The Perils of Elsie".

"Not quite." I decided the only way out of the problem was to feed her addiction for the sensational. "But you know, Nelly, Mr. H. has recently been involved in a case of great sensitivity with the French secret service. It is on that account and that alone that I met with a certain person tonight, and for reasons of state security which I am sure you'll understand, I feel I cannot break my trust even to you, dear sister."

It was only a slight embroidery of the truth.

Nelly stared at me in awe.

"Oh no… I see… Very well… Goodness."

"Maybe one day my lips will be unsealed. But until then…" I shook my head. "Now, would you like a hot drink? Some milk, perhaps. I can ask Madame Albert to prepare it."

"That would be good, thank you."

Feeling slightly guilty at deceiving my sister, I went downstairs to place the order.

"Perhaps I'll add just a little cognac to the milk to help your sister fall sleep. What do you think, Madame?"

"A good idea," I said. "Make me one, too."

Chapter Ten: A Duel

The cognac in the milk did not quite have the required effect. True it was that I fell asleep almost immediately, but then awoke in the early hours, when all was silent, with a terrific thirst upon me. Discovering my water carafe to be empty, I lay for a while hoping to drift again into sleep, but to no avail. I must have a drink. I arose, covered my night attire with my robe, and, clutching my carafe, slipped out into the corridor and down stairs lit dimly by a gas lamp.

With luck, someone would be manning the front desk. After all, the hotel stayed open all night for late-coming guests, those who frequented the many places of nocturnal entertainment offered by the city. However, although the hall was brightly lit, there was no one to be seen. The door to the parlour stood ajar and I waited a moment or two, in case someone should return, but in vain. It was then that I discerned a murmur of voices coming from the kitchen behind the parlour. So they were up at least, and I should not disturb their slumbers with my request.

Forthwith, I crossed behind the desk and into the parlour, a place I had hitherto never entered. Even now, I could not make out much of it in the dark, the only illumination being behind me from the hallway or in front, a thin line under the kitchen door.

I was about to tap on the latter, when I froze in my tracks. Philippe Albert's angry voice was clearly audible.

"I tell you, Maman, Leon did not shoot himself. That would have been the coward's way. No, he was killed by the flics."

"You are sure?" That was indeed Madame Albert.

"Benoit was just behind him, to keep watch. He told me how it was. It was an ambush. The flics were waiting for him. He didn't stand a chance."

"Oh, my God. Poor Leon. His poor mother."

"They shot him down in cold blood, Maman… Someone must have ratted."

"You think so? How frightful. Who? Who was it?"

There was a pause. I trembled.

"I do not know for sure," Philippe finally replied. "But I have my suspicions."

He lowered his voice I couldn't make out what name he uttered, but Madame instantly exclaimed, "Ah, no, Philippe. It could not be she."

She! So was it me he suspected? It had to be. I was in mortal danger now, for I knew these people would not hesitate to take their revenge.

How ever had they discovered me? They had evidently suspected me after I had eavesdropped the plot in the café, but I thought I had convinced them otherwise by my antics. I racked my brains. Perhaps I had been observed coming out of the Prefecture. Or, if there were others out there still following M. Cochot, then they would know that I met him the previous evening, and the rest would be simple to divine. How foolish was I to accept his flowers, his invitation. I backed away from the door, dreading to bump into any furniture and make a noise to

121

alert the others. Happily, I made it safely back to my room, my thirst quite forgotten in the light of all I had heard.

So Philippe and his mother were truly involved – to what extent I of course did not know. It was still possible they were simply acquaintances of the gang. I could not see the kindly Madame Albert condoning murder. Yet during the Revolution women sat knitting by the guillotine. It was all most puzzling and shocking. Then there was the disturbing revelation that M. Cochot had lied to me, letting me think, like everyone else, that Leon had killed himself rather than be captured. Why he should do that, I could not readily explain to myself, except that it made the police look less culpable. All I knew was that they had shot a man down, and I was directly responsible for the loss of his young life. Never mind that the alternative might have been the death of the Prefect. One way or another, my actions had precipitated the fatal outcome of the night.

I sat in the dark and prayed for forgiveness and for the soul of Leon Garcia. I was angry too. Angry with the misplaced idealism of the anarchists, the machinations of the French police, who could easily have arrested the man and not spilt his blood. It would most certainly, I was sure, not have happened so summarily in England. Our police are more restrained, more disciplined. Inspector Lestrade, for instance would not have permitted his men to shoot to kill. He would have taken the wiser course, had the boy arrested and then interrogated to try to find out more about his associates.

While reflecting on this I admit that I was afraid, too. Afraid for myself? Of course I was. Nelly and I must leave this hotel, leave Paris before the plotters had a chance to take their revenge. But it was hardly feasible with my sister still bedridden.

Further sleep seemed impossible as I debated with myself what best to do. All I could think of, however distasteful it was, was to reveal all to M. Cochot as soon as morning came. There would be more arrests but not, I hoped, more deaths.

The flesh is weak, however, and daylight was streaming through my window as a hammering on the door awakened me from the troubled dreams that had after all overcome me. Was I too late then to save myself? Had they come for me so soon?

But no. It was Poppy of all people, who burst in upon me, looking wild and unkempt. I learned afterwards that she had run all the way from the Butte of Montmartre. She was uncustomarily incoherent.

"Aunt Martha," she babbled at last. "Such a terrible thing… You must come at once… Ah, poor Ralph."

"What has happened?"

"Oh, it is so terrible…" She flung herself on to the chair and stared up at me, shaking her head. In fact, she was trembling all over. "My God!"

"Poppy," I said. "Gigi. Tell me."

"It was Etienne…" She gradually calmed down and managed to explain. "Etienne discovered about Ralph and Sylvie… You know… How they were together. Remember, we saw…"

"Yes, yes. And then…?"

"Etienne, you must know, is a nobleman… Oh, I know he doesn't look it. But he is Count something or other, and has the stupid sense of honour of his class…" She broke down. "Oh my God! The blood."

"The blood!" I was horrified. "Poppy, is Ralph dead? Tell me, for God's sake."

She made an effort to calm herself, taking deep breaths.

"What happened was this, Aunt Martha. Etienne challenged Ralph to a duel. With rapiers."

I was utterly astounded. A duel in this day and age! And did Ralph even know how to fence?

"So he is dead, then?"

"No, no. No, aunt. Not dead... But wounded. Badly. You must come right now."

"Is he at the hospital?"

"Oh no. That's not possible."

"Whyever not?"

She looked at me as if I were stupid. "If he goes to the hospital, they will know that he has been fighting in a duel, and then he will be arrested. It is against the law to fight duels here, even though they are common enough."

As she spoke, I was already hastily throwing on my clothes. I did not feel the need to practice modesty in front of this particular young woman.

"Has he seen a doctor at least?"

"I don't think so."

"Who is with him? He is not alone, I hope."

"No, no. He is not alone. He is at my place. My neighbour, Mère Angèle, is with him."

Just then I heard more voices on the stairs. Madame Albert and Dr. Lepine, come to see Nelly.

"Should we ask the doctor to accompany us?" I whispered.

"The doctor?"

124

"M. Lepine. He has been tending Ralph's mother."

"Maurice! Has he indeed." A strange expression crossed her face and I wondered at her use of his Christian name. "Well, perhaps," adding sharply, "if we pay him enough to keep quiet."

I nodded and we went out on to the corridor.

Madame Albert, unusually for her, looked coldly upon us, and I thought again of the danger I could be in. But for the moment that had to be put aside.

"Doctor," I said. "Might we have a word, before you go in to see my sister?"

He started somewhat at the sight of my companion, but soon regained his composure. The landlady, for her part, turned on her heel without a word, still unsmiling, and went away.

I let Poppy explain the matter, which she did more calmly than she had to me. Lepine narrowed his eyes and looked from one of us to the other.

"What a stupid boy," he said at last, and sighed.

"We can pay you well for your trouble," I said.

He sighed again.

"Do I at least have time to look at my patient here?"

"Afterwards, Maurice," Poppy said. "Please come now. It is very urgent."

I could tell at once that Ralph was making more of his wound than it warranted. There was no imminent threat to his life whatsoever, the blade having entered his shoulder. The old crone who had waited with him had done her best to staunch the bleeding with a torn up petticoat belonging to Poppy.

"Oooh," Ralph moaned as the doctor prodded him. "Aaah."

"You will live," Lepine pronounced, as he skilfully applied a bandage. "But I hope not live to fight another day, young man." His long face expressed distaste. "I have genuinely sick people to attend to, you know. Not fools who put themselves in the way of a steel blade for no good reason."

Ralph nodded. He looked up at me, almost reproachfully, and I remembered how much under strain he had appeared the previous evening. How he had asked to be allowed to stay with his mother, I suppose, to hide from his adversary. If he had then confessed the matter, this madness could have been avoided.

"I hope at least," the doctor continued, "you did not kill your rival?"

"No," Ralph replied. "How could I? I have never held a sword in my hand before this morning."

"Perhaps you should have demanded pistols, then," Lepine said, "as was your right as the one challenged."

So the good doctor knew something more of the etiquette of duelling than he had previously made out.

"In my youth," he went on, having decided for some reason to be more expansive, "I too fought a duel. I nearly killed my opponent over a woman." He glanced at Poppy. "Over a nothing… It taught me a lesson, as I hope this has you."

In his youth, he had said. He who was barely over thirty.

I took my purse out of my reticule.

"No," he told me. "I will not take money for this. In fact, I was never here. Now I will return to your sister. You may come with me if you wish, Madame, though I suppose you will prefer to remain here with your nephew."

I nodded and he took his leave, nodding curtly at us.

126

Poppy was astonished.

"It is the first time I have seen that man refuse a fee," she said, and turned to Ralph. "You must have reminded him of his misspent youth.

I had a rather different notion. I had seen the way Lepine had looked at Poppy and suspected he might wish to impress such an attractive young woman, if indeed there was not more than I knew to their relationship. But now was not the time to dwell on that.

"How does Ralph come to be here with you?" I asked.

Poppy looked a little uncomfortable. The boy also looked down.

"Well, you see… I was his second," she said at last.

At first I did not understand. Then, as the saying goes, the penny dropped.

"His second! You, a woman!" I was astonished, for I knew enough of the rules of duelling – from my readings of Samuel Richardson and Sir Walter Scott – that the second was invariably a gentleman friend of the combatant.

"I had no one else to ask. No one I could trust," Ralph whispered, a little pathetically. He who was supposed to have so many friends.

"I dressed as a man," Poppy explained, as if it were the most natural thing in the world. "So that I could run away quicker if the flics turned up."

I paused to digest this information. Poppy, being lean and tall, might at a pinch, pass as a boy, her hair concealed under a cap. But all the same, how extraordinary it all was. For a moment I even wondered if I were still caught up in strange dreams.

"Why did you not try to stop it, this madness?" I said finally, quite angry.

"I tried."

"She did. She really did, Aunt Martha. But, you know, at first I thought it would be a lark... So romantic..."

Romantic! Had he read those dratted novels, too?

"Then I realised that Etienne really wanted to kill me. And by that time it was too late to withdraw honourably."

"If he had wanted to kill you, he would have done so," Poppy remarked coldly. "Etienne is a skilled swordsman, and you hadn't a clue. He could have run you through at any moment. No, Ralph, he just wanted to teach you a lesson."

"Maybe at first. But then... did you see the fire in his eyes, Poppy? As he faced me in the dawn light. In that terrible place." Ralph shivered at the memory. "His blood was up. And afterwards he just walked away. He didn't care if I bled to death."

She conceded the point, or at least humoured him. "True enough. Etienne is a man of strong passion and a deep sense of honour. Yes, Ralph, I think maybe after all you had a lucky escape."

"So where is he?" I asked. "This Etienne?"

Poppy shrugged. "Who knows? There is no danger now anyway. His honour has been satisfied."

"Are you sure?" Ralph moaned, and shifted his position. "Oh, the pain, the pain!"

The girl shook her head in impatience. "You aren't dying. Be grateful for that."

I suspect she was resentful at what this foolish boy had put her through, she imagining him, from his howls of agony, to be at death's door. "I will call a fiacre to take you home."

Ralph looked shocked. "I can't go back there. Not alone. Can't I stay here? Please, Poppy."

"That's my bed you are lying on and I am not about to give it up for you. Nor am I a nurse. No, Ralph, you must leave."

"But those stairs to the studio. I shall never be able to climb them…"

"You can come back with me to the hotel," I said.

"No, I can't. I can't, Aunt Martha. For then mummy will know all about it…" He looked at me slyly. "She will get so upset. And she herself is so ill."

"Perhaps Sylvie could take you in," Poppy suggested. "After all, she is the cause of it all."

"No," Ralph replied. "Impossible. I never want to see Sylvie ever again."

We sat in silence for a few minutes.

"Listen, Ralph," I said finally. "I agree you cannot stay here and you cannot return alone to your lodgings. The only other place to go is the hotel…" He started to object. "Hear me out. We can tell your mother that you were attacked by thieves. She will be upset about your wound, of course she will, but, as for the rest, she need never know about the duel."

Ralph reluctantly agreed, for in truth he had no choice. Poppy went to find a fiacre, and, with nothing else to engage me, Ralph being in a silent sulk, I took time to look at the art work in her room. It seemed every inch of wall space was covered with a drawing or painting, while exquisitely sculpted miniatures stood on the floor and on any spare surface. Again I was struck with the young woman's talent: assured lines in the sketches of figures, such delicacy of tone. And in the paintings a mastery of colour. One in particular caught my eye, a landscape in that unfinished style they call Impressionism which up to now had not – please to excuse the pun – impressed me very highly. In this piece, however, depicting a woodland scene, I could appreciate the technique, the shimmering effect of sunlight on leaves. I felt I might step into the picture and follow the little path as it wound away under the trees.

"It's beautiful," I said. "Don't you agree, Ralph?"

"What?"

"The painting. It's so real somehow."

"Mm."

"Poppy is very gifted."

Silence.

"Don't you agree?"

"Aunt Martha, I'm in pain. I'm not in the mood to go into ecstasies over someone else's paintings."

That was it. He was jealous. Or begrudging, at the least.

When Poppy returned, however, I made sure I praised her work and singled out in particular the woodland scene.

"Thank you" she said, evidently pleased. "Yes, I painted it from memory. It is a place in the Midi I went to once and to which I often long to return. So peaceful. So far from all this." Suddenly she looked sad.

"Maybe you will one day, my dear," I told her.

"Anyway," she said. "Your fiacre is below, waiting. You had better go."

"Thank you for looking after him," I replied since Ralph himself apparently didn't feel the need to express his gratitude, He had that spoilt, sullen look on his face that I had come to know so well. But perhaps I am being unkind. The boy had to be in real pain.

We helped him down the stairs and, as he climbed into the vehicle, Poppy asked, "Will you be able to attend the opening of the new cabaret tomorrow night, Ralph?"

"I hope so," he said, an heroic timbre to his voice. "I'll do my best."

"And you too, Aunt Martha. You must promise to be there too. It will be fun."

I smiled, not about to make promises I might not be able to keep.

"I'll try," I said.

Chapter Eleven: Where is Poppy?

I had, as previously indicated, been planning to make contact with M. Cochot as soon as possible to let him know what I had discovered the night before. However, Madame Albert was so friendly towards me and so sympathetic regarding Ralph, as he hobbled in to the hotel on my arm, that I began to doubt she could possibly consider me the source of the information that had led to the death of Leon Garcia. Philippe too, who was engaged in some repair work to the stairwell, gave me no more than a cursory and uninterested glance. I breathed a little more freely.

"It is lucky for you," Madame Albert was telling Ralph, "that I have a room to spare. M. Aragon left only this morning."

I confess it had never occurred to me that there might not be accommodation for Ralph in the hotel. I was aware of other guests, but only as somewhat ghostly presences: the sounds of footsteps or low voices in the corridor or on the stairs. It was seldom that I actually saw anyone else and even then they flitted by me, almost disembodied. They were there but I suppose I simply wasn't paying attention to them.

"Victorine is cleaning the room just now," Madame Albert said to Ralph. "You can wait down here in the parlour if you wish, monsieur. Or perhaps you would like to go up to your mother."

Since the moment of truth could hardly be delayed for long, he agreed to the second option. However, I judged it best first to precede him, and break the news of his wound to his mother as gently as possible, making little of it.

Just as I was about to ascend the stairs, Madame Albert summoned me back, a knowing smile on her face.

"Oh, my God, I nearly forgot. A telegram came for you this morning, just after you went out. And a letter arrived as well. You are popular, Madame." She gave me the two missives. "I think one may be from your particular friend, no?" She chuckled.

I glanced at the letter in particular. It was sealed down, unopened with my name written upon it in a flowing script. "Thank you," I said.

"No trouble at all."

No, she suspected nothing.

Upstairs at last, I started by asking Nelly about Dr. Lepine. What he had said about her recovery.

"He is not happy. Not happy at all, Martha," she said in long-suffering tones. "You see, my hand is so slow getting over the infection."

She held it out, and indeed, the scratch still looked angry and swollen under the purple of a fresh application of gentian violet.

"He recommends that I stay in bed for another day. Oh, Martha, I am getting so tired of it all. I just want to go home. Can we not just leave?"

"My dear, I should like nothing better," I replied. "But I think we should wait a little longer. To be sure you are up to it. How terrible if something happened on that long journey."

She nodded and emitted a deep sigh.

"Perhaps you will be well enough to come to the cabaret tomorrow night," I went on. "Ralph would like that."

"Oh, the cabaret," she replied, sounding rather less than enthusiastic. "But you know, Martha, we did not enjoy the first one we went to." She shuddered at the memory. "What if there is another fight, like the last time?"

"Well, let us wait and see how you feel," I said. "And by the way, please don't worry, but Ralph has had a little accident."

"What!" She shot up in the bed.

"Nelly, I said not to worry. It's a scratch, that's all. A thief tried to rob him and he ended up with a stab wound in the shoulder. The doctor has already bandaged it up for him and says it is nothing."

"Oh my God! This terrible city! The poor boy. Where is he? I must go to him." She started to get up.

"No need for that. He's here. We thought it best he should stay in this hotel for a day or two until he feels better."

"It's bad enough for that!"

I crossed to the door and opened it, calling out into the corridor, "Ralph, you can come up now."

Making something of a meal of it – it was after all his shoulder, not his leg that was injured – he staggered along the corridor and into his mother's room, over to her bed. Collapsing on to the side of it, he started sobbing and she hugged him back, until the pain of the embrace caused him to cry out. Feeling myself rather too hard-hearted to support this afflicting scene, I made my excuses, leaving them be. Really, they deserved each other, I thought uncharitably.

It was with no little relief that I reached the calm of my own bedroom, where I sat down to read my mail. I opened the telegram first. It was, as I had thought, a reply from Clara. She informed me that all was well in Baker Street, and that my lodgers had not yet returned from their trip. The intelligence eased my mind, for otherwise I might have felt it necessary to hurry back, while – the weight of fear having been removed from me, and despite what I had told Nelly – there was still so much here that I should like to see and do.

I turned to the other letter, inscribed on heavy paper. It was indeed, as Madame Albert had surmised, from my "particular friend." Signing himself "Your ever respectful and devoted servant, Frédéric Cochot," he wrote that he had judged it advisable under the circumstances to leave Paris for the countryside. "Indeed, dear Madame," he went on, "you yourself told me to change my habits. I will be gone for a mere two days and sincerely hope and trust that we can resume our most delightful conversation on my return."

I gazed thoughtfully over at my dressing table where the bouquet of lilies sat in a glass vase. They were as beautiful as ever, and as heavily scented. But did I really want to see the giver again, even should I still be here on his return? To what purpose, except perhaps to provide further information on the plotters? Did I really wish to do that? Should I after all betray Madame Albert to the "flics" as Philippe and Poppy liked to call the police, simply because she had expressed a natural concern at the killing of Leon Garcia, a man dismissed as "garbage" by the Prefect? It seemed so unlikely that our kindly landlady could be mixed up with dangerous anarchists. Maybe, as I had surmised before, she and her son were mere acquaintances of the plotters. So many questions, and I was in no hurry to come to a decision, still angry that the Prefect had lied to me about the circumstances of Leon's death. For now anyway the matter had been taken out of my hands. I decided I would live for the moment, and this particular moment told me that I was very hungry indeed, having yet again missed my breakfast.

Reluctant to face Nelly and Ralph again in case they delayed me, and loth for obvious reasons to return to Le Petit Bonhomme, I decided on an expedition in a direction I had not as yet taken, and soon found myself in a fine square beside a large and imposing church, fronted by a charming park. A café with a pleasant view over the scene provided all I needed in the way of sustenance, a bowl of onion soup, with a round of toasted bread and melting cheese floating rather strangely in it. Despite the surprise of this, it proved most delicious. I could not help but smile to myself thinking of all the new and exotic dishes I might prepare for Mr. H. and the doctor when I returned to London. They had met examples of Irish cooking, following my return from that country, with varying degrees of enthusiasm, so we would see what they would think of onion soup, croque monsieur, coq au vin or even lobster thermidor.

I was curious, after my meal, to explore the nearby church, Catholic of course, but a house of God nonetheless. Although it looked ancient, the Church of the Trinity turned out to have been built only about thirty years earlier. Nonetheless, it was most striking both outside and in. The exterior was decorated with many statues and had a bell tower that soared into a blue sky. Within were more sculptures, though what struck me most was the effect of space, a vast nave illuminated with chandeliers, and surmounted by an ornate vaulted ceiling. I seated myself in a pew to look around myself, to take it all in, the stone columns, the intricate carvings, the richly stained glass of the windows, marvelling as ever at the work of man in praise of his God. As I sat, the mighty organ sounded out. Someone was playing as if just for me. The soaring chords lifted my soul to the very heavens and I was entranced.

Beside me there happened to be a statue of a saint, a Magdalene, her hands together at her breast in prayer, her eyes raised in contemplation of her God. Perhaps it was she who called to mind another female sculpture, recently viewed. I froze in sudden shock, a dark thought interposing itself between me and the glorious music.

Heretofore, I had been entirely wrapped up in the notion that the woman Philippe suspected of betrayal was myself, and had not considered whom else it might be. Now it came to me. It had to be Poppy, Poppy whom I had seen talking as if clandestinely in the hotel's back parlour with Philippe and Maxim Brandes before the planned attack. Poppy who had been in such a hurry to get Nelly and myself away from the hotel that day. Perhaps I was wrong, I hoped I was, but nevertheless, the girl should be warned.

I hurried from the church and was about to call a fiacre. Then again the awareness hit me. Although I had visited her lodgings that very morning, I had no clear idea where to find it again, except that it was somewhere on the Butte. I would have to return first to the hotel and ask Ralph.

"I don't know," he said grumpily. He was lying on the bed of his room and I had awakened him from a sleep

"You must know. Surely, Ralph. You were there."

"So were you, aunt."

"Yes, but I paid no attention."

"Neither did I. As you may remember I had other things on my mind at the time. Like this excruciating wound for instance." His mouth curled into a self-righteous expression that was exactly like his mother's. "I wasn't in the habit of visiting my model at her home, you know, in case you think I was. She always came to my studio."

"Who else might know?"

Ralph shook his head. "No idea..." He scowled. "I suppose you want to go back and buy that picture of hers that you liked so very much."

I was about to deny it, when it occurred to me that it was a far better excuse than any other I could come up with.

"I was thinking of it," I said. "Or one of those exquisite little sculptures."

"I knew it." He looked sulky, jealous no doubt of the girl's talent. I also suddenly guessed where she might be, and if not, could perhaps find out from there.

Apologising for disturbing his rest, I bade him farewell and hurried out of the hotel again. This time I took a fiacre to an address I remembered well. It wasn't far and, once arrived, I knocked on the door. Not getting a response immediately, I hammered more loudly.

"Yes, yes, yes. I'm coming," It was the sour-faced Thérèse, who finally opened it, no more delighted to see me than before.

"Excuse me, Madame," I said. "I am looking for…" what was the girl's real name? "Garance. Garance Germaine."

"Not here." She was about to shut the door on me.

"It's very important I find out where she lives."

She said nothing. Just stared at me. Really, she was excessively plain, poor woman, shapeless of figure, with a sagging face and bad skin of an olive hue. Matted grey hair, pulled back in a straggling bun. She quite clearly made no attempt whatsoever to appear in any way attractive.

"Perhaps your husband…"

"I am not married."

"I apologise. I thought… well, perhaps M. Bourdain might have an address for her."

She slammed the door shut and I could hear her stomp off. Was that it, then? I waited in case, and a good thing too, for a few moments later the door opened again, and she thrust a piece of paper at me, with an address on it so scrawled I could hardly decipher it.

Before I could blurt out my thanks, the door slammed shut again.

The fiacre in which I had arrived was still standing nearby waiting for a new fare. I shewed the driver the destination, he nodded, and we took off again.

Poppy was not at home. The toothless old crone who opened the door to me – the same who had ministered to Ralph – shook her head and, when I asked where Garance might be, babbled something I could not begin to understand. I was about to give up when at last I caught something from the unbroken stream of sounds. Le Chien Jaune. Of course. It was quite possible she might be there, maybe helping to set up the cabaret for the next evening's entertainment.

I had asked the driver of the fiacre to wait, and now instructed him to take me to the cabaret. He shook his head and gave a Gallic shrug.

"I don't know it, Madame."

"It's a new place. Not open yet."

No, that rang no bells.

We could drive around aimlessly, looking, or I could take myself to the Place du Tertre and ask one of the artists. They would doubtless know. But then Poppy might not be there either. She could, in fact, be anywhere, modelling for some artist, perhaps. Suddenly I felt utterly dispirited. I was uncomfortably hot, too, under the blazing afternoon sun, and all I wished to do was to lie down on my bed and rest.

I told the driver to take me back to the hotel. With God's grace, nothing bad would happen to the girl in the meantime.

On opening reluctant eyes, I found – Good heavens! – that I had slept until twilight. My head was throbbing horribly and, although I knew I had dreamed of something troubling, I could not recapture the memory.

It seemed to me that the air had thickened, the scent of the lilies lying heavily upon me. Now I am far from being fanciful, but, in the powdery blue light, those blooms looked to be rearing up in a threatening manner, as if possessed of some demonic spirit. I had a sudden premonition that something terrible was about to happen.

Rising from the bed, I staggered across the room. What was happening to me? I managed to open the window and breathe in the fresher air of the city, and soon came almost to myself again. But yet I could not rid myself of the superstitious notion that the flowers had tried to stifle me. I picked them from the vase with a view to throwing them away, but could not bring myself to do so. They were still beautiful. Instead, I replaced them and carried them downstairs. Madame Albert was dozing in the parlour behind the hallway, her knitting on her lap. She roused herself at the small sounds I made and when I offered her the flowers for the desk, accepted with pleasure.

"The scent is too strong for me, in my small room," I explained. "They will look good here."

"You are very kind, Madame," she replied.

You might not say that if you knew all, I thought. Whence they came.

I then rejoined my sister in her room, she shewing herself yet again to be miffed at my prolonged absence and expressing no sympathy when I told her that I had been tired out, and had not meant to rest for so long.

"I suppose you are off tonight with your fancy man friend," she said.

"Not at all."

In fact, I could hardly bear the thought even of going out for my supper. Madame Albert was providing Nelly with her meals. Perhaps I could order something from Père Perrot in Le Petit Bonhomme to eat with my sister. When I suggested this, my sister looked to be appeased.

"I should like that, Martha," she said, and I felt guilty. It must be horribly tedious for her to be alone all the time.

I descended the stairs again and told Madame Albert what we had decided.

"If you have no objection," I added. "I am too weary to go out again."

"It is not a problem at all, Madame. In fact, I have a lièvre à la cocotte in the oven. There is plenty of it. You are welcome to share."

"Lièvre?" I could not for the moment remember what the word meant.

Madame Albert laughed, put her two hands up on either side of her head and flapped them like ears. Then she hopped around the room. I laughed, too, diverted by the comical sight.

It wasn't rabbit. That I knew was "lapin." I tried to think. Really, my brain was moving very slowly. Then "Hare!" I exclaimed. Yes, that was it.

If I looked uncertain at the prospect of eating one, she reassured me, "It is very delicious, Madame Martha. Cooked in plenty of red wine, cream and good Normandy butter, with vegetables."

"That sounds excellent, if you can spare some."

We had already arranged that we would pay her handsomely for Nelly's meals, a most satisfactory arrangement for her.

"We will of course add this to our bill," I said, and she nodded.

"There is no problem, Madame Martha. You are tired out with all these worries. First your sister and now your nephew… And the heat. Paris is not usually so stifling in June."

If the good woman only knew the extent of my worries. Not the least of them was what Nelly would think of a hare stew. Perhaps she could be persuaded that it was chicken.

On my earlier wanderings, I had stumbled upon a shop that sold a few books in English, albeit without any great choice, as well as another that stocked wool and needles for knitting. Nelly had proved happy enough with the highly sensational novels I had found for her, while for myself I had purchased a work in French that looked elementary enough for me to read, some stories by M. Gustave Flaubert. Just now, however, the tale of the poor unloved servant Félicité was rather beyond my powers of concentration – my head still throbbing, if not as badly – and I gratefully turned to the less cerebral occupation of knitting. So the two of us sat companionably for the evening. Nelly even eating a fair portion of her dinner, while pronouncing it to be somewhat too rich for her taste.

"I shall be glad to return to plain English cooking," she said. "And by the way, what is this meat?"

I told her, biting my tongue, that I was not sure.

"I think it is hare," she pronounced. "You know, Martha, I have always liked a bit of hare."

Well, there you are! My sister can still surprise me.

I felt calmer then, than I had felt for a long time, and laughed to myself at my earlier fancies and premonitions. Just the result of bad dreams and a stuffy room. That is all they were.

I slept well that night, even though I had doubted I would, after such a long doze in the afternoon. The glass of wine with dinner, and the little cognac to finish might have helped. The following evening, of course, would see the grand opening of the cabaret of Le Chien Jaune, and Dr. Lepine, on his morning visit, gave Nelly a grudging permission to attend – she had decided that after all she would like to – as long as she did not stay late and avoided alcoholic beverages.

"Although one glass of hot wine will do no great harm," he conceded.

I was starting to like the young man more. I could see that he was devoted to his calling and that his apparent rapacity was no such thing. He merely wished to keep matters on a business-like level, something I could well appreciate. I have never quite approved of the slapdash way in which Mr. H., for instance, manages his affairs.

"Your sister recovers at last," Dr. Lepine told me as I walked down with him. "I think you may safely return home in a day or two."

News I confess I received with mixed feelings. While Nelly could hardly wait to get back to her humdrum existence, and while I should, naturally, be pleased to do the same in due course, yet there was so much still to see in Paris that I would hope to stay just a little longer.

Be careful what you wish for, as someone once said.

Chapter Twelve: Caught in a Storm

Of course, I was still most anxious to find Poppy, in order to warn her that she might be in danger, hoping that I might, at the same time, convey the message without letting her suspect my part in the business. Or that I even knew what the business was. Or, indeed, that she herself might know anything about it, which was by no means certain. My only evidence, after all, was that I had seen her in conversation with at least one of the plotters, and that Philippe had mentioned a "she" as the informant. It was a quandary. I concluded that my best course was just to say it as it had happened: that I had overheard an exchange between Madame Albert and Philippe talking of betrayal and revenge with regard to some woman they knew. I could even ask her if she could think of such a person. If she knew nothing and took me for a foolish meddler, so be it. Her reaction would depend on how close she was to the conspiracy. As to saying nothing, it wasn't an option for me. I could not stay quiet if a beautiful and talented young woman were to suffer as a result of something I had done. I already felt guilty enough over poor Leon's fate.

It was my intention to quit the hotel as early as possible – ready once more to miss my breakfast in a good cause, planning to take a fiacre again to Poppy's lodgings, hoping to catch her before she herself went out. However, it was not to be so straightforward. First Dr. Lepine arrived to see Nelly, as I have already recounted, and she begged me to stay and hear him out. Then he himself required me to be present when he examined Ralph. That young man's wound, being even more superficial than previously thought, just needed a wash in carbolic and a regular change of dressing. The doctor shewed me how to do it, to save him returning, the which incurred yet a further delay, and Ralph, I might add, moaning throughout in apparent agony. Though no doubt the soap wash stung somewhat, I am afraid neither the doctor nor I could muster any great sympathy for him.

Next Madame Albert appeared with a splendid breakfast of hot rolls and eggs, a choice of coffee or chocolate for all of us, insisting her favourite, Dr. Lepine, stay and partake, and urging everyone sit and eat. I could hardly find an excuse to leave them until all was finished.

Even then, Nelly complained.

"Going out again, Martha! You must have seen everything there is to see in this city by now."

"Perhaps your sister has an assignation," suggested Madame Albert, with a knowing smile. A suggestion hardly likely to appease our patient.

"Aunt Martha is mad to find Poppy," said Ralph. "She wants to buy one of her pictures. She is afraid someone will get there before her, I suppose, and snap it up."

I should have preferred my destination not to be known, for, at Poppy's name, both landlady and doctor gave me searching looks, while Nelly was just disgruntled.

"If you want to buy a picture, I should have thought you would rather support your own nephew," she said.

146

"Well, as to that… I will certainly consider it," I replied, as I hastened to leave.

I could consider all I wanted. That did not mean I would actually buy one of Ralph's daubs, although I feared I might have to.

Of course, by the time I got there, the girl was no longer at home. Again her neighbour, Mère Angèle, appeared, unable to suggest where she might have gone. This time, however, I came prepared, with a sealed note that expressed my anxiety to meet her as soon as possible, on a matter of the gravest urgency, adding that I would be in the Parc Monceau for the remainder of the morning, and, after luncheon, back at the hotel. In the evening I would attend the cabaret grand opening, where at least I could be certain to meet her.

The day had already turned sultry, already become oppressive, as I made my way again to the studio of Jules Bourdain. It was the only aspect of Paris that I should like changed, being unaccustomed to such continuous heat and humidity. Though Madame Albert had assured me that the weather was unusual for the time of year, that knowledge made it no easier to bear. The sky that day wasn't even a clear azure but tended to a sulphurous yellow from which the sun glared as if hostile. Though perhaps, after all, it was my anxiety that was colouring everything in an inauspicious light.

The way seemed longer than before – it always does, I find, when one is in a hurry – but at last I arrived at the studio. This time it was the sculptor himself who opened the door to me, gazing as if into my soul with those disconcertingly penetrating blue eyes. He was all politeness, however, even though no doubt exasperated to be disturbed on such a seemingly trivial matter.

"Alas, Gigi is not here, Madame. I regret it. She may call later, although we have made no such arrangement for today. Her presence is no longer required. Her work here is finished."

That greatly surprised me, but I repeated the details of where I would be for the rest of the day, in case after all she made an appearance. I think he was somewhat bemused by my insistence, but nodded in an abstracted way. Quite probably he forgot my message the minute he closed the door on me.

From the studio, I made my way again towards Park Monceau, somewhat alarmed by the black clouds that were thickening overhead, and hoping that it would not rain since I had not come prepared with an umbrella.

The mood of the park was quite different from that of my previous visit. Gone was the peace and tranquillity of the place. The tall trees were restless, their leaves shivering, agitated by an ominous wind. The waters of the little lake, previously a mirror, were now being tossed into angry peaks by that same wind. No ducks were to be seen on the lake's surface, nor could birdsong be heard. Evidently these creatures could sense, more than any mere human, what was coming. And come it soon did, with a bang. A great flash of lightning shot across the sky, immediately followed by a resounding clap of thunder. After that, it was not long before great droplets started to fall from the heavens, vouchsafing some relief from the heaviness of the atmosphere, but hardly conducive to a leisurely stroll. I was lucky to make it in time to the rotunda at the corner of the park, the which provided shelter for me and the few other people caught off-guard by the sudden change in the weather.

The rain was now rattling down, as if angry gods were shooting arrows at the earth. More lightning and more thunder contributed to the sense of a bombardment. There was even, despite the previous oppressive heat, a new chill in the air. It would be necessary to stay put for the time being, hoping the storm would soon abate, for there was no prospect of leaving the rotunda without getting soaked to the very skin. In fact, the malevolent wind was trying its hardest to blow rain in on top of us poor souls gathered there, forcing us to huddle against the back wall to avoid a drenching.

When one is waiting like that, minutes drag as if hours. Some of our number could bear it no longer, indeed, and made a dash for it when they thought the rain had eased off somewhat. Foolishly, for it soon lashed down even heavier than before. There was, to be sure, something headily elemental in this onslaught: it called to mind Mr. Turner, the artist, who, as I had once learnt, had caused himself to be tied fast to the mast of a boat, so that so that he might experience the full fury of a storm at sea, and then, safe at home, render it in paint. Perhaps, if I were an artist myself, I might have been more sanguine about the present situation, instead of cursing it mightily.

At last the rage of the gods was spent and a fine drizzle filled the air. The clouds cleared and a watery sun, restored benevolence, caused a pale rainbow to arch above the trees. The scene was pretty now, light dancing on wet leaves, as if the previous hour had been nothing but a bad dream. Nevertheless, the park, with all its puddles, was no longer inviting, and instead

149

I betook myself to a café facing it, to sit at a convenient window. Should Poppy arrive, I hoped that I would spot her.

However, two glasses of lemon tea and a pastry later, there was still no sign of her, and reluctantly I made my soggy way back to the hotel. I had no desire at all for Nelly's company just then, and even less for that of Ralph. I presumed in any case they were together, and so, nodding to Madame Albert at the desk behind her splendid lilies – how could I ever have found them sinister? – I climbed up to my room, there to wait in case Poppy should arrive. It was only then that I realised it was not the wisest thing I had ever done, to invite the girl into what might be a lion's den.

Seated by the window, I anxiously looked out for her, intending to rush down and intercept her before she could enter the hotel.

I still had the piece of brie cheese I had bought three days earlier, and on the way home had purchased some crusty bread from a bakery rich with seductive aromas, that tempted me to another little cake as well. In this way I was able to partake of luncheon in my room. The cheese, I have to say, had become quite a degree stronger and more pungent in the meantime, but it was still tasty enough, if of a somewhat liquid consistency. The cake, a tartlet of pear and almond paste, looked almost too pretty to eat, but I managed it somehow – it was as good as it looked – and continued my watch.

None of the young women scurrying down the street proving to be Poppy, I gave up the watch at last, and rejoined my sister and nephew. Nelly's manner was somewhat cold. She shewed no interest in my doings of the morning, and it was Ralph who asked me if I had succeeded in tracking Poppy down. I replied that I had not and when I described my ordeal in the thunderstorm, I am afraid that Nelly's face took on an expression almost of satisfaction.

"I suppose you got very wet, Martha," she said with insincere sympathy, and even looked quite disappointed to learn that I had avoided the worst of it. Though perhaps I am wronging her. Her hand still looked sore, and constant discomfort will surely sour the temper.

Soon conversation turned to a less contentious subject, the forthcoming events of the evening. The grand opening of Le Chien Jaune was to take place at nine of the clock, and would, according to Ralph, be preceded by a spectacular procession. People in costume would carry flaming torches up Rue Lepic to the top of the Butte. Then, from the Place du Tertre, they would make their way down winding streets to the location of the new establishment. Ralph was determined, despite his wound to take part in this, but I demurred on behalf of myself and Nelly. We would wait, I said, in the Place and would join the procession for the short final walk. I only hoped that, after her long confinement, Nelly would be able even for that degree of exertion.

"But Ralph," she said, "would it not be better for you to stay with us? You don't want to re-open your wound."

"Not at all," replied Ralph, the hero. "I'll be just fine, mother."

Nelly then expressed the hope that there would be no more rain, to put a damper on the event. I did not quite trust the candour of her sentiment, however, and suspected that she might wish the weather bad for the evening, to prevent Ralph going off. If that were her hope, however, it seemed unlikely to be fulfilled. The storm had cleared the air, which had become much fresher. I decided again to wear my new cerise gown in honour of the occasion, even while anticipating looks and remarks from my ever-critical sister. My black straw hat with the ribbons would sit well with it. Nelly herself, who only ever wore dull colours, decided on her grey outfit in broadcloth which I should have thought more suitable to church than to a night out on the town.

Food, Ralph told us, would be provided at the club, but we might be wise to have a snack beforehand.

"For, you know, what they serve might be quite spicy, mother."

Nelly and I were happy to leave early and take a fiacre to the Place du Tertre, where we installed ourselves in the same café as before. The quality of the fare was nothing very much, but it served the purpose and staved off the pangs. I again ordered the onion soup, though it was nowhere near the standard of the previous one. Nelly, of course, would not taste that but picked something supposedly with chicken, which contained a deal of potatoes and cornflour (and quite possibly onions, though I said nothing on that particular subject).

We sat then and waited, Nelly drinking plain water, me with a glass of the lemon tea to which I had become most partial.

"How can you abide that, Martha!" Nelly said. "It isn't tea at all. Just coloured water."

"You should try it," I replied. "It is most refreshing."

My sister sniffed.

A large crowd was now gathering in the square, doubtless attracted by the numerous posters on all available wall space, proclaiming the opening of the cabaret. These images featured a startling design of a yellow dog (what else?) – with one decidedly lascivious and un-doglike open eye, the other closed in a wink – being caressed by a flirtatious young lady whose light robe had slipped down over her plump bosoms, just as in the depiction of Liberty by M. Delacroix, though in other ways, of course, not at all similar. This crude image did not reassure as to the nature of the performance we were about to witness. Luckily Nelly didn't seem to have noticed the posters, being, as I have previously mentioned, somewhat short-sighted.

A noise of fife, drums and tambourines preceded the physical arrival of the procession. The first marchers entered the square soon after, to loud applause and cheers. For some reason, those carrying the flaming torches were dressed in medieval costume, as were the musicians. Behind them jostled a crowd of mostly young people, already merry with good spirits. Nelly looked out for Ralph, and I for Poppy. My sister was the more successful. There was still no sign of the young woman, but Ralph marched in the thick of all, surrounded by laughing friends and apparently none the worse for his wound. He did not glance once in our direction.

"He has not seen us," Nelly said, waving.

I doubted this. He was looking everywhere but in our direction, although we had told him where we would be.

"Never mind," I said. "We can meet up with him later. Let us follow the procession to the club."

We paid the somewhat excessive bill for our meal, given its inferior nature, and gathered ourselves to leave. On the way down, at the tag end of the procession, Nelly expressed curiosity as to what we might expect from the evening.

"I am sure it will all be very noisy," she said.

"Undoubtedly," I replied. "Well, we need not stay long."

From what Dr. Lepine had told me, I expected singing and dancing. And, I supposed, lots of drinking. However, never could I have anticipated the fateful events about to take place.

Chapter Thirteen – The Yellow Dog

The walk was longer than we had expected, though downhill all the way, the which made it somewhat easier. However, Nelly felt an increasing need to lean on me for support, and, for such a slight person, she managed to seem unusually heavy. I made no complaint for she seemed to be truly suffering: under the light of the flickering torches she looked pale and strained, and hardly spoke. I was delighted, therefore, when a familiar voice offered assistance. It was Dr. Lepine, of all people.

"You here," I exclaimed. "I should not have thought this was your kind of place."

Though, after all, what did I know of the young man?

"Curiosity," he replied. "And I am very fond of the songs of Yvette Guilbert and Aristide Bruant, who will be performing here tonight."

He had taken hold of Nelly's other arm, so that we were able almost to swing her down the street in the way small children love to go.

"Who are they?" I asked. "I have never heard of them."

"They would hardly be known in England," he replied. "They both go in for a very particular type of street song, in a particular Parisian slang. It is perhaps to be welcomed that you ladies will not understand the words, for they are not always quite respectable."

"Oh dear," I said, and glanced at Nelly, who luckily could not understand our conversation. "But you like them, all the same?"

"They are the true voice of the people."

By now we had arrived at Le Chien Jaune cabaret. There was no mistaking what it was. The undeniably vulgar frontage had walls of a sickly yellow, the doorway crudely painted to resemble the open jaws of a huge dog. Two members of the procession stood with flaming torches, on either side of the portal.

"Goodness gracious," said Nelly.

She cast her eyes around for her son, of whom there was no sign. Ralph must have gone in without us, yet more evidence of the boy's thoughtless neglect, or worse, of his mother. I said nothing, not to distress her further. Nor did the doctor, who shewed himself sensitive to the situation. We were indeed most appreciative of the courteous manner in which he conducted us within, as if it were quite natural that he should do so, even paying for our tickets, while assuring us that we could settle with him later. He led us through the entrance-way into a long hall, with a stage at the far end and tables down the sides, leaving a space between evidently designed for dancing. The walls, painted the same bilious yellow as the outside of the establishment, were hung with scores of paintings – mostly featuring unclad young ladies – among which we searched for sight of Ralph's work, It was not prominently displayed but I spotted it at last in a remote corner. Nelly, who couldn't see it at all, was perhaps more relieved than not at the fact.

The entry fee apparently covered at least one drink on the house, but there was no choice to be had. Glasses of hot wine, of a blueish hue, were set in front of us by a waiter flying between the tables. Nelly eyed hers suspiciously, and rightly so, for the taste proved very rough. Still, we toasted each other in festive anticipation, Dr. Lepine seeming content for the time being at least to stay with us. While grateful for this, I rather wondered at it, since ladies of our vintage are hardly jolly company for young men: maybe he felt it would be ungallant to abandon us. Meanwhile, I had my eyes peeled for any sign of Poppy amid the throng. I stood up to see better and also to try to find Ralph – intending at some point to give that young man a stern piece of my mind – and spotted him at last across the hall in the middle of a high-spirited group that seemed made up of his artist friends. No Etienne, however. And no Poppy. As I looked, the doctor looked, too, and it occurred to me that, knowing I wished to meet with her, he was perhaps hoping the young woman would approach our table of her own accord. What their relationship was, I of course did not know, but it seemed to be more than that of casual acquaintances.

Meanwhile, people continued to flow in, and it was lucky that we had already seated ourselves at a table, for any free places were quickly being filled.

Among the already colourful crowd, a giant of a man stood out. He was wearing the most extraordinary hat, wide-brimmed, and flaunting long yellow feathers, no doubt plucked from the tails of unfortunate birds. His extravagant garb was also yellow and dated from some previous century: A knee-length tunic over tight hose revealed sturdy calves, while a short, cloak trimmed with somewhat mangy-looking gingery fur adorned his shoulders. To complete this eccentric rig-out, a sword in a scabbard hung from his belt. He had to be an actor. Part of the

157

show. Just then he was forcing his way through the crowd, with what sounded like oaths, towards a reserved table near the stage. Accompanying him, I was surprised to spot none other than the sculptor, Jules Bourdain, together with a young woman I took at first glance, by her red hair, to be the elusive Poppy. But no. It was Sylvie, the new favourite, clad in a low-cut gown of emerald green silk. She was clearly delighted with the attention she was getting, not only from the elderly sculptor himself, but also from people who knew her, artists for whom perhaps she had posed, calling to her, and pulling at her lacy sleeves.

Lepine, seeing where I was looking, identified the flamboyant man as no actor but Jean-Auguste Renard, the owner of the club. Renard, I thought, a fox.

"As for the others," he said, "he is a famous sculptor…"

"Yes, we have met M. Bourdain," I interrupted him. "And Mlle. Sylvie as well."

"Then you know more than I do, Madame," Lepine said, a rare smile lighting up his long face. "I am not acquainted with the young woman."

"She is very pretty, is she not?"

He shook his head.

"Eye-catching, but a little too much so, perhaps," he said. "I am surprised at Bourdain. Though perhaps I should not be. He is notorious for his taste in young women."

Goodness, I thought. To be having such a conversation! The doctor seemed to think I was quite the woman of the world.

"He has a… not a wife but…" I did not quite know how to put it. "We also met Thérèse."

"Ah yes, Thérèse…"

"Does he never bring her out with him?"

Lepine actually laughed. It suited him.

"You have seen her?" Now that was less than gentlemanly and I frowned. "Forgive me but you see, Madame Hudson, in France it is very common for a man to have a lady friend, as well as a wife, even a common law wife. As long as it is discreet, no one objects."

"Discreet?" I said, looking across at Sylvie, who was laughing loudly and calling for champagne, while Bourdain smiled benignly.

"Well, in this particular case…"

"What are you saying?" Nelly interrupted. If it was rude to leave her out of the conversation, it was, on the other hand, not a very fitting subject for her fastidious ears.

I translated what Lepine had said about M. Renard, the owner of the club, who was currently going among the crowd pressing hands or, in the case of ladies, raising theirs to his thick red lips.

Nelly sniffed.

"But Martha," she complained, "cannot you find Ralph?"

"He is sitting over there with some artist friends. I am sure he will join us soon." The boy hardly looked as if he had any such intention, but I was trying to appease her.

"I knew we should not have come," she said.

Just then, a fanfare almost burst our eardrums. M. Renard had mounted the stage and gave a speech I found almost unintelligible, though understanding the gist to be that he welcomed so many friends to this auspicious occasion. He waved his arms a lot, and even brandished his sword at one point, giving rise to extreme mirth from the audience.

"He is challenging anyone who isn't enjoying themselves to come on stage and tell him to his face," Lepine explained.

I reported the same to Nelly, and thought how amusing it would be if she took the man up on his challenge, for it was most evident that she wasn't enjoying herself at all.

Eventually Renard stopped his antics and, as Lepine whispered, told how many of his friends would be entertaining us, starting with M. Aristide Bruant.

"One of the singers you mentioned, I think," I said.

"Indeed."

A striking individual now joined Renard on stage. Carrying a thick stick for some reason and wearing a wide brimmed black hat atop a square, clean-shaven face, a scarlet shirt and black jacket, shiny boots up to his knees, the new arrival was met with wild cheers. He said something in a harsh voice to Renard and the crowd almost doubled up in laughter.

"He has been very insulting about the club, but that is his trademark. He loves to offend, especially the bourgeoisie."

That word again.

Renard made as if to plunge his sword into the singer's chest, and the other parried with his stick, and for a couple of minutes they fenced in this way on stage. Then, sweeping his feathered hat off his head to brush the floor, Renard gave a low bow and backed off, in that way ceding the limelight to M. Bruant.

All the time this mock fight was going on, the musicians who had provided the fanfare, with their trumpets, fifes and drums, had stood impassively at the back of the stage. Now they stepped forward to accompany the singer.

Lepine was right. I understood very few of the words of the songs, particularly since so many of them were drowned out with laughter from the audience, including from our companion who gave us sidelong looks from time to time, and shook his head.

Nor were the songs melodious in any way. Discordant rather, and all sounding alike. It was evidently the words that mattered more than the tunes. I felt Nelly shrinking beside me and expected at any moment for her to demand that we leave. However, given the crush, that would have been impossible without a struggle.

Eventually Renard stepped on to the stage again, shouting "Enough! Enough!" the which was received with a chorus of boos from the audience. Not least from a tiny man who had leapt from his seat just below the stage and stood shaking his fist in a mock threat. I recognised him from somewhere, with his strangely huge head and stunted body, and suddenly remembered the polite midget from our first trip to a cabaret. It was certainly the same neat little man.

"That's M. de Toulouse-Lautrec," Lepine told me with some excitement. "He's a very great artist. You must have seen some of his posters."

"Not the one for this place, I hope?"

"Oh no, not that horror. But he has designed bills both for Bruant and Yvette Guilbert, for the Moulin Rouge, you know."

"Ah yes." I faintly remembered some eye-catching images from that night.

"All right, one more song, Aristide," Renard was saying. "But then you must make place for a real artiste."

Before Bruant could threaten him again with his stick, Renard withdrew to cheers. The final song seemed to be about Montmartre itself, for I caught the word several times, though that was the full extent of my understanding. After he had finished, the singer descended the stage and joined the little artist at his table.

"They are great friends," said Lepine. "The posters Lautrec has designed for him... well, you should see them, Madame. Most striking."

He called over a waiter and ordered a bottle of wine. "Something better than this poison," he said, pointing with disgust at the dregs of the complimentary blue wine in our glasses. "Ladies, will you eat something?"

"What is there?" I asked.

"Bread and cheese, perhaps. Sausage... Waiter, bring us a mixed cold plate." He turned back to us. "It is good to eat when you drink."

"Yes, doctor," I said, and smiled. I was getting to like this young man with his long nose more and more. It just goes to shew how mistaken initial impressions can be.

Meanwhile, an upright piano had been wheeled on to the stage and a dapper fellow with whiskers and eye-glasses ambled up beside it. He sat himself down and without a word launched into a strange and exquisite little piece of music.

You wouldn't have thought the rowdy crowd would have kept quiet through such a very different performance, but no one made a sound. Even the waiters paused in mid-flight as it were, and at the end of the piece, everyone burst into loud and appreciative applause.

162

"Whoever is he?" I asked, "And what is that wonderful music?"

"That is M. Erik Satie. He composed the piece himself, I believe."

"It is quite exquisite."

The musician stood and acknowledged the applause with a brief bow, and then gestured to someone waiting in the wings to join him. At that, one of the oddest looking women I have ever seen now appeared: tall and thin as a stick, with a decidedly plain face, orange paint on wide grinning lips, the whole topped by a mop of ginger hair. This unprepossessing apparition was wearing a grubby-looking sleeveless white dress with long black gloves up above the elbows of her skinny white arms. On seeing her, Lepine actually leapt up and joined the ecstatic applause of the audience. She introduced herself as Yvette Guilbert in a harsh voice to an audience which clearly was not in need of any introduction from her. That done, accompanied by M. Satie, she launched herself into a series of songs, and again I had some difficulty following them, even though she enunciated clearly enough. However, she acted out the words in such an amusing way, her face contorting the while into the most comical of expressions that it was impossible not to laugh. Even Nelly was diverted and conceded a smile. For my part, what I did manage to understand quite definitely sounded a long way from the parlour songs we were used to in England.

In the midst of all, the waiter arrived with a huge platter of cold meats and cheeses and crusty bread, as well as a bottle of wine of Bordeaux and three clean glasses. Lepine examined the label, frowning, and tasted the wine.

"If this is the best you have, it will have to do," he said finally. It was certainly an improvement on the hot beverage we had been given earlier. No doubt, my palate regarding wine was not as discriminating as that of the doctor.

Yvette Guilbert was meanwhile entertaining the company further. One song I was able to follow fairly well concerned a certain Madame Arthur who managed to live a lavish lifestyle solely on the basis of her "je ne sais quoi." When Nelly asked me, as she did from time to time, "What's it about?" I just shook my head. Along with our beloved Queen, Nelly would not have been amused.

Mlle Guilbert was followed by other acts, comedy sketches and more songs, which after a while, and mixed with the wine, tended to blend into each other. Finally, however, a familiar sight. The stout queen of Montmartre, La Goulue herself, strutted onto the stage, followed by her inevitable shadow, Valentin le Désossé. If the crowd had lost some of its enthusiasm during recent performances, it recovered it now. Loud cheers welcomed the pair. La Goulue flung kisses into the audience as if they were flowers and soon, accompanied by the band of musicians, launched into a wild cancan, ever circled by her shadow. At a certain point, Valentin leapt from the stage and La Goulue followed, flinging herself into his arms. I admired him for not staggering under the weight. They then continued their dance between the tables, La Goulue pausing from time to time, as was her custom, to seize a sausage or glass of wine and swallow them down in one gulp. If a young man, or even a not so young one caught her eye, she would drag him up with her to dance a few steps. Meanwhile, Valentin did the same with the ladies. After a while, more people started dancing. It seemed the formal part of the evening was over.

And suddenly, there she was. It was as if a magician had conjured her up, for I could have sworn she was nowhere in the hall before that moment.

"Poppy," I said. "Thank God. I have been needing so much to talk to you."

The young woman, however, paid no attention to me. Her eyes were glistening, her pale cheeks were flushed and damp, and she seemed in a heightened state of excitement.

"Maurice," she said, seizing Lepine's hand, "come dance with me. Come…"

He rose as if mesmerised. I could not stop them. Laughing wildly, she pulled him behind her into the throng and soon they were swallowed up, lost to view. Well, I thought, I can wait a little longer. Nothing bad can happen here, can it, not among so many?

"Mesdames, may we join you?"

Of all people Laure Perrot, the waitress from Le Petit Bonhomme, stood in front of us, in the company of a sturdy, red-faced young man.

They sat down without being given permission.

"I am happy you are feeling better," she said in French to Nelly, the which I translated.

Nelly took off her glove to display her hand, and was gratified at the girl's shocked response.

"Oh, my God," she said. "that's very bad. You are lucky, Madame."

When queried as to what on earth was lucky about it, Laure then recounted a lurid tale of an acquaintance of a friend of hers who had received a similar scratch, neglected it, and was dead within a week.

Nelly was of course thrilled at the story, and gave me an accusatory look as if to suggest I had not taken her wound seriously enough. During this exchange, the young man sat with a rather stupid smile on his face. Laure at length remembered him.

"This," she said, "is my good friend, Baptiste. He is eager to practice his English, so when I said "Ah, there are the two English ladies from the brasserie," well, of course, he had to come and meet you."

The young man blushed an even deeper red.

"My English is very bad," he said, and I wondered if he were as eager as all that, since he seemed unwilling to say another word.

However, Nelly and I made an effort to draw him out and soon a kind of conversation started, while Laure sat back, happy enough to hear the unaccustomed sounds of our language. I will not try to reproduce Baptiste's accent or his mistakes. Just to say that he spoke very slowly, and it was quite a task not to jump in and anticipate what he wanted to say. However, Nelly proved happy to converse, so I soon left her to it, looking again among the dancers for Poppy and Lepine. Sometimes, I caught sight of them, she still wild, he, looming over her, tall though she herself was, serious and intense, as if his eyes alone could eat her up.

Laure followed my gaze.

"He likes her," she said. "He likes her a lot."

"Yes, indeed."

"I wonder what his wife would think of that."

"His wife?"

She laughed. "Of course. The good doctor has a sweet little wife and two even sweeter little children."

I was very surprised. I had not thought him a married man, nor yet a father.

"You are shocked. But have no fear for Madame Lepine. Men do not leave their wives for such a one as that."

I had no time to digest the information. With no intention of dancing myself, I was quite astonished when now requested to do so. The gentleman in question, a weasely little fellow, looked somewhat familiar to me, but I could not place him. Thanking him, I shook my head in polite refusal, but this it seemed would not do.

"Madame Hudson," he said. "I insist."

He knew my name, and at last I recognised him too, even without his uniform. It was the policeman from the Prefecture, who had at first attempted to prevent me from seeing M. Cochot and then, having heard of my association with the great English detective, become so ingratiating.

What to do? It was a tricky situation to say the least. If I were to be seen with a "flic," assuming someone recognised him, things might go badly for me. On the other hand, to reject him, might be worse. He might inadvertently say something indiscreet.

Laure was watching closely. I took a deep breath and, to Nelly's evident amazement, accepted the proffered hand, and stepped out on to the crowded dance floor.

"To think," the man said, grinning, "I am dancing with someone who has perhaps danced with the great Sherlock Holmes."

Mr. H. dancing! And with me! The utter absurdity of the notion made me laugh out loud. Anyone watching us would think we were having a wonderful time.

"You know," I said to him, after a few twirls, "I have to be careful. I should not be seen with you."

"Oh," he replied. "Oh… I understand. You are undercover, perhaps."

"That's it. Undercover."

"Of course, if that is the case, I will return you to your friends at once, dear Madame."

But just then that I spotted Poppy and Lepine. They were getting very close to the table at which Bourdain was sitting with Sylvie, those two heads close together, in a world of their own, as the saying goes. For some reason – Poppy's agitation perhaps – I sensed something momentous was about to happen. Now, of course it is for the man to lead in a dance, but curiosity prompted me to try and edge towards them all, in the opposite direction from that which my partner was trying to take me. Nearer the stage and away from my table.

"I need to speak to that young woman urgently," I told my partner, finally, to explain myself.

"I see. Is it part of the… you know…?"

"Yes. The undercover. It is very important."

"Then, of course, Madame…" and he propelled us through the dancers.

Just as we were about to reach the couple, Poppy shot away from Lepine, and rushed to where Sylvie and Bourdain were sitting. By then I was near enough for me to hear what she said, for her voice was loud and sharp.

"You think you have him now." She laughed. "You in your fancy new dress, you with your cheap trinkets, you with your…" There I think, by the accompanying gesture, she must have made an exceedingly crude remark about a part of Sylvie's anatomy. "Ha… he will tire of you soon enough, you know, like all the others…"

She was leaning toward Sylvie in a threatening manner.

"Like you, you mean," the other said. "*Salope*." She laughed.

Poppy slapped Sylvie hard in the face, and the girl recoiled. Bourdain stood up and smashed Poppy with his fist. People gasped as she staggered back and fell to the ground. Blood flowed from her nose down her dress.

"You are drunk, Gigi," Bourdain muttered. "Go and sober up in some filthy alleyway where you belong."

Poppy, however, was not giving up so easily.

"If you want that tramp in your bed, Jules, you can have her," she said, wiping blood from her nose, her voice suddenly soft and menacing. "But what about all I have done for you? Why have you told me not to come to the studio? What about the Last Judgment? What about all my work?"

"Your work," he sneered.

"Yes, my work. Will you at least give me the recognition I deserve?"

He stood, laughing at her.

"Your work! Your hack-work, you mean. No, Gigi, I will never permit you to enter my studio ever again, let alone work with me."

He turned away. Sylvie burst out laughing, and I suspected from the look of triumph she gave Poppy that it was she who had elicited a promise from him to exclude the girl. Poppy spat curses on the two of them and started beating her fists on the sculptor's back. He turned swiftly and grabbed her wrists in one huge hand. With the other he reached for her hair, to pull back her head, an ugly expression on his face. My God, I thought, this man is capable of anything. At that instant, Lepine stepped forward, trying to insert himself between the pair, but looking, despite his height very slight beside the looming figure of the sculptor. Everyone held their breath. What would happen next? A fight? Would the sculptor swat the fly? Astonishingly, it was Valentin le Désossé who now swept forward and scooped the girl up. Then, careless who was in his path, he danced her through the crowd, to the very door, out and away. We all looked after them, frozen in shock. Then Lepine rushed after them. There was no way I could reach Poppy now. She was gone.

Yet, if you think that was the end of the excitement, think again. The circus continued. Now it was Etienne, the rejected lover, who, lo and behold, appeared as if from nowhere. He was very drunk, wild-eyed and belligerent, his thick black hair standing on end. I remembered what Ralph had said, that Etienne could be very nasty when in his cups.

"Poupée is right," he shouted. "You don't belong with that old man. You are my woman, Sylvie. Mine." He seized her arm and started pulling her away.

She squealed in terror and Bourdain stood up again to defend her. However, though the sculptor might easily overpower Poppy, or even Lepine, Etienne, as tall and broad as he, was younger and stronger. Moreover, the latter – and the assembly gasped at the sight – pulled out a knife, the bright lights of the room glinting on the long thin blade. If M. Renard had not intervened at that moment, God only knows what might have happened. The cabaret owner seized Etienne from behind, pinning his arms behind his back. The knife dropped to the floor.

"Now, now, young fellow," he said. "We'll have none of that carry-on here. The young lady can decide for herself whom she wants to be with." He called to a couple of the waiters. "Throw this ruffian out and make sure he doesn't come back. Ever… You're banned, chum. No young pup is going to wreck my party and get away with it."

Amid a stunned silence, Etienne was duly ejected. M. Renard picked up the knife and laid it on the table next to Bourdain, who had sat down, his arm around the weeping Sylvie, comforting her. The flamboyant master of ceremonies exchanged a few words with them, and then waved to the musicians, who had ceased playing, to strike up again. After a short while, things returned, almost, to the way they had been before.

I regarded my partner, whose name I didn't even know. It was a little strange, I thought, that he had not intervened in the unpleasantness, in his official capacity. Perhaps he reckoned M. Renard would deal with it more efficiently, as he indeed had done. The business was, moreover, none of mine. I was just glad no one knew I had been dancing with a policeman.

"I should like to return to my sister," I said, and he nodded, understanding.

"This is no place for you, Madame," he said, before delivering me back to my table. "It has nevertheless been an honour. Might I be permitted to say that you look quite charming tonight. Mr. Holmes is indeed a lucky man."

Whatever did he think my relations with my lodger might be? However, I was not about to enlighten him, just get rid of him as quickly as possible.

I was a little surprised to find Ralph, at last come in search of his mother, now sitting beside her. Laure and Baptiste were smiling broadly, as they stood up to make room for me.

"What a lark!" Laure said with relish. "Never a dull moment in Montmartre and that's a true fact. Come, Baptiste. Let's you and me dance."

He bowed politely. "Good bye, missies and mister."

Before they left, Laure laid a hand on my shoulder and bent down to whisper in my ear, "Madame Hudson, you have interesting friends and you speak French quite well... I think perhaps you understand it even better." With that and a wink she followed her partner on to the dance floor.

I stared after her. What exactly did she mean by that? Disturbed, I turned back to my table.

Ralph had evidently been drinking a fair amount, and now was in a highly excited state.

"She's right, that one. Never a dull moment in Montmartre. My God, I thought someone was bound to get killed. That Etienne..." In satisfaction, he helped himself to some of the left-over meat, using his fingers, which he then licked.

"Ralph," Nelly admonished him. "Manners!"

It was so incongruous a reaction on top of all that had happened that I didn't know whether to laugh or cry.

"I should like to go home now," I said.

"Really!" Nelly raised her eyebrows. "You seemed to be having such a jolly time with Mr…Mr…I didn't catch his name."

I ignored her.

"You may remain if you wish," I said, "but I cannot stay here any longer."

"I have no wish whatsoever to stay. As you know, I didn't want to come in the first place since you, Ralph, clearly had no desire for us to be here."

He started to object.

"No need to pretend. Your new friends clearly mean more to you than your aunt and mother."

"Don't be silly, mummy. I adore you." He kissed her cheek and then helped himself to a piece of cheese, this time rubbing his fingers clean on his shirt.

Nelly sighed.

"Yes, Martha, let us go home, away from this Sodom and Gomorrah."

On the way out, we were accosted by M. Jean-Auguste Renard himself.

"Dear ladies," he said, removing his hat with a flourish. "I sincerely hope you enjoyed your first visit to Le Chien Jaune, and that it will not be your last. The recent events, I can assure you, will not be typical of the entertainments on offer here in the future."

I nodded back at him, not wishing to reveal my nationality through speech.

"Come again, and tell all your friends," he cried gaily after us, as we stepped out in search of a fiacre.

This took some time, because we were in a side street where carriages were not stationed, and we were compelled to walk part way up the Butte again before finding a conveyance. Nelly muttered complaints while I looked out for Poppy. But, of course, she was long gone.

Chapter Fourteen – The Search

Despite my exhaustion, physical and mental, I couldn't easily fall asleep that night. That drunken fight, the raucous mocking voices of the singers, the swirl of the dancers – La Goulue, strutting and posturing, the long thin twisted shadow that was Valentin the Boneless ever behind her – that strange parting remark from Laure, the whole of it tinged with a horrid yellow hue: My poor brain fizzed. Above all, thoughts of Poppy and how I still had not been able to warn her.

A fitful heaviness must at last have overcome me for, when I opened my eyes, a dirty grey light was filtering through the thin curtains. It was still quite early, given the lateness of our return the night before, but I was disinclined to prolong my rest, for rest it was not. As for Nelly, I would not disturb her, in the hope that she, at least, was benefitting from some restorative slumber. Instead, I sat with my knitting. I was making a jacket in white wool for my daughter Judy's little girl, Effie, a favourite of mine, even though I see her so seldom, since they live in Edinburgh. Recollections of that charming family calmed me somewhat, and I could wish myself walking the Royal Mile or ambling through Prince's Street gardens or even, once more, attempting to clamber up Arthur's Seat, a place where another of my adventures had started.

Thus lulled with sweet thoughts, I dozed off where I was sitting, the knitting fallen in my lap. It was only when Nelly knocked on my door that I roused myself again.

"Martha," she said, entering. "You look quite dreadful." Words not likely to make me feel any better.

She herself appeared daisy-fresh, the which was most vexing.

"I suppose," she continued, "that you are trying to recover from the wild night you spent."

"Me?"

She pursed her lips. "Don't pretend you don't know what I mean." She folded her arms across her narrow chest. "It is high time we left this city of iniquity and I don't care what the doctor says. We must leave this very day."

"Today! Oh… But what of Ralph?"

"I wash my hands of him, Martha. I have been thinking about it all night and have decided he must make his own way in the world. If in due course he wishes to return home, then I will of course be glad to welcome him. Until then I cannot waste any more of my energies, not to mention my money, upon the ungrateful wretch. It is just too much."

This was a change, indeed. She must have been very hurt by the indifferent behaviour of her darling.

"He did not return here last night, you know, even though I reserved his room and will have to pay for it, whether or not he slept there. It is most thoughtless of him."

"Certainly."

"This city has changed him, and, I have to add…" Here she looked severely upon me, "my decision to go home is partly driven by concern for you, Martha. I have seen how this city of vice has changed you, also. Not for the better, I might add."

This was just too much. It was as if we were little girls again and she, the elder, chiding me for my naughtiness. But we were grown women of middle-age, with only a year or two between us, and I was not about to be lectured to by her now.

"I do not wish to return home today, Nelly," I said. "I have unfinished business here."

"Have you, indeed? With one of your many gentleman friends, perhaps."

Ah, was there maybe a touch of jealousy mixed in, as well? As if I were turning heads all around me! The notion was laughable.

"No, Nelly. The reason I wish to remain is that I still haven't managed to talk with Poppy, and it is imperative that I do."

"Oh, Poppy, again, is it! I should have thought, after the outrageous show she put on last eve, not to mention the scandalous way she makes her living, that no self-respecting person would wish to have anything to do with her. A slattern like that!"

"Well," I sighed, "let me get dressed and then we can go for breakfast and talk some more about it."

She left me with something of a toss of the head, and I made haste to prepare myself. Really, despite my earlier hankerings for familiar happier places, I could not admit a wish to go home just yet. It was not only because of Poppy. Something extraordinary was going on here and my natural curiosity needed to find out what it was.

Nelly was somewhat taken aback that I did not plan to break my fast, as usual, in Le Petit Bonhomme. The fact was that I rather dreaded encountering Laure again. Instead, on the pretext that it was somewhere she must see, I conducted my sister the short distance to that same elegant square which featured the imposing Church of the Trinity. It was a dull and dreary day, so different from the previous baking sun, but at least the rain was holding off for the present. To be on the safe side, however, I had this time brought with me an umbrella, and had urged Nelly to do likewise.

The breakfast they served in the café – the place I had frequented before and found most acceptable – was almost identical to that chez Père Perrot, with the addition of a pot of apricot jam to go with the crusty bread, and cream to be added, if one so wished, to the hot chocolate. It made the simple meal seem a little more special. Nelly was satisfied, and that was the main thing.

"It is certainly pleasant here," she said, popping a blob of cream on to her drink. "But, you know, Martha, I still wish to go home very soon."

"Soon" at least was not the same as "today," so some progress had already been made.

"On Monday, perhaps," I said, this being Saturday, me thinking I might have achieved something of my plans by then. Or I could at least buy time to put her off some more. "Tomorrow maybe we could go to church, Nelly. That would be nice."

"In there?" she said, looking up dubiously at the great edifice of the Trinity.

"Well, that, of course, is a Roman church," I said. "I myself would not object for once, but you…"

"Good heavens, Martha. You would consort with Papists!"

Nelly, as I knew well, for she often spoke of it, regularly attended a very low church, with no graven images or incense or candles in silver candlesticks, or anything of the sort. Transubstantiation, where the bread and wine are supposed to turn, during the mass, to the actual body and blood of Christ, a belief which I merely found fantastical, filled my sister with horrified disgust, considering it nothing more nor less than the cannibalism practised by primitive tribes.

The previous Sunday we had failed to attend church under the misapprehension that all the places of worship in Paris were of the Roman Catholic variety. Ralph had not seen fit to enlighten us on the subject, though perhaps he knew nothing about it, since, to Nelly's deep chagrin, church going was no part of his life these days. It was Madame Albert of all people who had assured me that yes, indeed, there were several churches that served a Protestant congregation, the nearest being a German one. Since neither Nelly nor I spoke a single word of that language, we could have no interest in going there. Further afield somewhere was an American church as well as an English one, although our good landlady did not know exactly where either was situated.

"We can easily find out," I told Nelly.

"I wonder, though, would it be high Anglican? I should not like that, Martha. I should prefer to get down on my knees in my bedroom. God would understand."

There is no pleasing some people, and I let the matter drop for the moment.

179

Nelly expressing herself sufficiently recovered to go out and about again, we agreed to visit that monstrous metal tower which dominates the Paris skies, and maybe even, despite my sister's fears, take the lift at least a part way up. After all, I could hardly drag her around, looking for Poppy. I just hoped that the young woman, on discovering my message, would at last come to me.

On our return to the hotel, we were accosted by Madame Albert.

"The doctor was here, asking for you," she told us. "And in such a state. I was astonished, Madame Martha. Never have I seen the poor man like that before."

"Do you know where he went?"

"He rushed out, to look for you, I think."

We had not expected him this morning, since Nelly was so much better, and Ralph, too.

I explained this to Madame Albert, telling of our intention to visit the Eiffel Tower. We could hardly change our plans on the off chance that Lepine would return, no matter how urgent the case.

"Well, Madame Martha, if he comes back, I will tell him as much."

In fact, he arrived, in timely fashion, just as we were setting off. A Lepine very different from the sober young doctor we were used to seeing. He appeared to be wearing the same clothes as on the yester eve, his hair tossed, his dark eyes bloodshot, a smear of dirt down his cheek.

"Thank God, I have found you at last, Madame."

"What is it, Doctor? Whatever is the matter?"

180

"I have looked for her all night," he babbled. "I waited outside her rooms, even sleeping on the step. She never came back. She is nowhere to be found, I tell you…"

"Poppy?"

He nodded impatiently. "Garance, yes. Madame." He seized my hand. "In God's name tell me why you wanted so much to talk to her. It was not really to buy a painting, was it?"

I looked at him and judged his desperation. Even if I could not condone this married man's passion for another woman, I felt pity for him.

"Nelly," I said. "I need to discuss something important with Dr. Lepine. Would you mind waiting somewhere for me, please, for just a little while?"

She clearly minded very much. "I will go to my room and read my book," she said, moving towards the stairs with an air of offended dignity, muttering something about people with secrets.

I drew Lepine out into the street, away from the sharp ears of Madame Albert.

"Let us go somewhere quiet to sit," I said.

All I could think of was the place I had just come from. There were stone benches in the park of the square, and, even though it was overcast, it was not cold.

Thither we proceeded and sat ourselves down. The man was actually shaking.

"Calm yourself," I said, and took his hand in a motherly way. "Tell me about it."

"It is madness, I know, Madame, but I cannot help myself. I adore her."

"But you are married, Doctor. It is hardly right."

181

"Right?" He gave a bitter laugh. "If you only knew, Madame, how much I have fought against it... I love my wife, too, very much, but this is different. This... overwhelms me."

He had assured me the last evening that it was acceptable in France for a married man to have a mistress, as long as it was a discreet affair. This passion, however, struck me as quite a different matter. A sickness, even.

"And she?" I asked. "Does she return your feelings?"

"I thought so for a while... But you know, that is of no importance. The main thing is that she be safe... You have been looking for her too."

"Yes," I replied.

"Please tell me why. It might have bearings on her disappearance."

Could I trust him? I did not know.

"Are you sure she has disappeared?" I asked instead. "To spend one night away from home... in her case... is surely not so very surprising."

"You think little of her, Madame."

"I know very little about her except what I have seen. For example, that she and M. Bourdain have had a special friendship. That's a fact, isn't it?"

"That man. That ..." Lepine uttered a word with which I was unacquainted, but which did not seem to reflect well on the sculptor. "All these so-called artists, they think they can amuse themselves with their models and then just cast them aside, like trash. I have seen it so often. It is disgusting. You saw how he behaved to her last night."

He slapped a hand hard on the bench, as if to crush the insect named Bourdain.

"Of course, you are correct, Madame," he continued in somewhat calmer tones. "Garance may have spent the night elsewhere." He jumped up. "Let us return to her rooms and see if she is back. After all, you still wish to find her, even if you are unwilling to tell me why."

"But your wife, doctor, won't she be worried about you? Think of your children."

He drew a hand across his troubled brow.

"Again you are right. I am selfish and worthless. Oh God."

"Let you return home," I said, "and I will go and see if Poppy... if Garance has returned home. You can find me later. I will leave a note for you at the hotel if I am out."

He agreed to that, and to my relief directed his steps towards his home. Before he left, he turned back and told me, "By the way, Madame, this Square of the Trinity is the subject of a charming painting by a certain M. Pierre-Auguste Renoir. Another artist who abuses his models."

I took a fiacre the familiar way up the Butte.

No, the crone informed me, as well as I could understand her, Mlle. Gigi was again not at home. Others had come looking for her. She herself was quite worn out answering the door.

Others? I thought. More than just the doctor? I dreaded to think whom it might be.

Wishing to clear my head, I decided to walk to the hotel, it being pleasantly downhill all the way. Nelly would be displeased at my tardiness, but that was the least of my worries.

In fact Nelly hardly registered my reappearance. She was far too concerned about Ralph, who had staggered back some time after my departure, having evidently, at some point in the night, been in a fight, for his face was bloodied and bruised and his shoulder wound had reopened.

"The doctor is not with you, then?" was all she said to me. "I thought he might have been, since you went off together."

"No, he returned home," I told her.

"Well, he wasn't there when Philippe went to look for him." She wrung her hands. "Oh, what to do? Poor Ralph is very bad."

This time I had to agree. The boy's face was swollen, his nose looked to be broken, and he had the beginnings of a black eye. Blood was oozing from the wound on his shoulder. At least I knew how to deal with that, and set to with the carbolic soap and dressings the doctor had provided for the purpose. Ralph screamed when I started to clean it. Nelly winced.

"Don't hurt him more, Martha," she said.

"It is to stop the wound getting infected. It only stings for a second. You are all right now, Ralph, aren't you?"

He nodded reluctantly.

"What happened?"

"He was set upon by cutpurses."

I stared at the boy in doubt. He looked back at me through his one good eye, and then looked away.

"I see," I said, wondering if it were possible that Etienne still bore a grudge.

Just then, there came a tap on the door. It was Dr. Lepine, looking much cleaner and fresher than before, though purple shadows marred his pale countenance. I shook my head slightly at him to indicate the failure of my mission, whereupon he turned his attention to the patient.

"My goodness, Ralph. Whatever have you been up to?"

"He was attacked by thieves," I told him. "Again."

"Was he indeed? Those thieves must take you for a rich man, for some reason. I trust they didn't relieve you of very much."

I suspected Lepine was as doubting of Ralph's explanation as I was.

"Ask the doctor, will he lose the eye," Nelly said.

I translated.

Lepine laughed.

"Not at all. He will have an ugly bruise for a few days. It will turn yellow as it heals. If Madame Albert has ice, that will help reduce the swelling. On the eye and on the nose."

Otherwise, after examining Ralph thoroughly, the doctor opined that his injuries were largely superficial. He commended me on treating the shoulder wound so efficiently, and assured Nelly that her son would live. He urged the young man to avoid dark alleyways where villains assembled, seeming almost jovial as he said it. No one would have imagined this coolly professional man to have shewn himself so recently to be victim of an obsessive passion.

Before he left, he examined Nelly's hand and pronounced himself fully satisfied.

"You ladies may return home when you will," he said.

I translated this remark, but Nelly retorted, "Good heavens, Martha. I cannot think of leaving poor Ralph when he is so in need of me."

"I will go down and ask for the ice," I said.

185

"Let me accompany you, Madame." Lepine bowed to Nelly, who pressed some francs into his hand. He did not refuse to accept them.

"No sign of Garance yet then?" he asked, as we descended the stairs.

"No, the old woman said others had been round asking for her. I wondered if she just meant you. Or if more people are trying to find her."

"What people?"

I shook my head as if to indicate ignorance, but the searching look he gave me shewed that he did not entirely believe me.

Madame Albert had no ice but suggested asking at Le Petit Bonhomme. Well, I supposed I should have to return there sooner or later. Bidding farewell to Dr. Lepine, who promised to stay in touch, I made my short way to the brasserie. I need not have worried. Laure was not there. It was Père Perrot himself who hurried to provide me with a dish of ice, expressing concern at the news of Ralph's injury.

"The poor young man." He shook his head. "But who knows what these lads get up to? Assuredly he will not tell his mother all. Or his aunt." He smiled at me. "I am blessed. I just have a daughter, a sensible young woman who causes me no anxiety."

"Indeed, I also am blessed with daughters," I told him, looking around. "Laure is not here today, then?"

"No, she has gone to the Bois de Boulogne with her young man. They are to be married soon, you know."

"Ah. Congratulations."

"By the way, Madame, we have something special for luncheon today, if you would wish to return later. Boeuf

Bourguignon, followed by cherry clafoutis." He kissed his fingers to his lips.

"It sounds good." I had no idea what these dishes were, but suddenly realised that I was very hungry.

"Bon, bon, bon. I will reserve a table for you."

"Near the window, if you please."

"Bon."

Nelly took some persuading. She did not wish to leave her son's bedside for a second, but I insisted that she must keep up her strength. Ralph helped me out by saying that he wanted to sleep. Perhaps he did, or perhaps he found her solicitude a little too wearying.

Chapter Fifteen: A Red Rag to a Bull

The luncheon was indeed very tasty. Père Perrot promised to provide me with the recipe for the cherry clafoutis, a kind of solid custard packed with fruit. I resolved to treat Mr. H. and the doctor to the dessert on my return, even though neither gentleman had a particularly sweet tooth. But while I ate up everything on my plate, Nelly picked at her meal without enthusiasm. Her talk was as ever of Ralph and her renewed decision to whisk him away from this cesspool of a city as soon as he was fit enough to travel.

She had no interest now in sight-seeing, but only wished to stay by her son's side.

"I know the doctor said his injuries were not life threatening, but he might have overlooked something. Ralph's chest is paining him. Imagine if his ribs were broken and they punctured his lungs. Just imagine that, Martha."

I replied that I thought it most unlikely, but that, since Lepine had promised to return in the evening to check on the patient, she could make sure then that there were no complications. As for myself, I still kept wondering how exactly the young man had come by his injuries. To trot out the same excuse as before shewed, I felt, a distinct lack of imagination. But then Ralph did not strike me as the imaginative type.

On our return, the patient appeared sullen and uncommunicative, his bruises even uglier than before. Despite

the fact that he seemed indifferent or even resistant to his
mother's presence, she asserted that she would not leave his side
again for the rest of the day. As for me, I was restless. Unwilling
to pursue the heretofore vain search for the missing girl, I decided
instead that I would at last visit M. Eiffel's tower by myself, and
duly made my way thither by tram, a change from the eternal cab,
considerably cheaper and – seated among its denizens as I was –
giving me a better sense of being part of the city. Once arrived, I
found it was daunting enough simply to stand beneath the great
structure, never mind ascend it. Was it quite safe? Nelly would
certainly have said no. Nevertheless, I had not come so far only
to baulk at the last. So it was that, feeling most intrepid, I took
lifts in three stages to the very top, a dizzying enough experience
by itself.

Once up, however, and safely enclosed by the high railing
mentioned by Ralph, I was exhilarated at the thought that I was
quite literally on top of the world, on the tallest edifice ever built
by man. That was indeed something to think about. Moreover, I
was standing where, as a notice informed me, many dignitaries
and celebrities had stood, among them our own Edward, Prince
of Wales, the actress Sarah Bernhardt, as well as a gentleman
named Buffalo Bill Cody, some sort of famed North American
cowboy as I understood it.

From the viewing point, I looked out across the city,
consulting, to get my bearings, a long brass display sign into
which the outline of all notable buildings had been etched. Under
a louring sky, with clouds seeming almost near enough to touch,
the unfinished Basilica of the Sacred Heart, which required such
an effort to reach, on top of the Butte of Montmartre as it was,

from here looked tiny, like a child's toy, as did the twin towers of the Cathedral of Our Lady far below, on their ship-shaped island. Directly facing, across the winding River Seine, stood an imposing structure I discovered to be the Palace of the Trocadero, site, as my Baedeker revealed, of the World Fair of 1878, for which event M. Eiffel had also constructed his tower. Indeed, everything in Paris was visible from here. Everything, that is, except Poppy. I purchased a souvenir card of the tower from the little post office, and wrote it there and then, addressing it to Clara and Phoebe and marking a little cross at the top of the image, beside which I wrote in tiny letters, "I am here", before stamping and posting it. My two girls would be amazed.

As I had travelled up, I had noticed a patisserie on the second level, and could not resist stopping there on the way down. Seating myself at a table with a fine view, I indulged myself in something called a "baba au rhum," which turned out to be a very dark moist sponge, served with a scoop of cream on the side, taking a lemon tea to temper the sweetness of the cake. The enormity of the bill slapped down with the order rather took me aback, but I supposed one paid as much for the setting as for the food. It was pleasant, anyway, to linger there, away, for a time, from all that awaited me below, and hoping against hope that everything, after all, would be well.

Once safely down on God's good earth again, I decided to explore the palace grounds that I had seen from on high, and crossed the river to the formal gardens of the Trocadero. A pool there, as a notice informed me, contained all the fishes of France. Not all of them, surely, I thought, peering into the dark depths to try and catch flashes of quicksilver.

How good it felt, I mused, standing there, to be a simple tourist for a little while longer, and, as the afternoon progressed into evening, I took my time strolling back along the quays. The cloudy sky was becoming ever greyer, and a mist was rising from the river, but nothing daunted the fishermen, still tranquilly smoking their clay pipes, legs dangling over the edge, or the lovers straying close in intimate conversation, or the nannies pushing prams, or the old folk sitting staring into space. It was bitter-sweet, somehow, to think how some things continue the same through generations. How decades before one might have made the same walk, seeing the same, though different, people, and how, when we, who are here now, are all dust, others will walk the same path and see the same, but different, people, too.

Enough of that, Martha Hudson. Perhaps Paris was, as Nelly insisted, getting under my skin. I made my way up through the city, away from the eternally flowing river.

Dr. Lepine looked less in control than he had that morning. His hands were shaking again, his habit in disarray. Had he then neglected his duties, after all, and spent the day in another fruitless search for Poppy? I knew it must be fruitless, for he shook his head at me – something become a secret sign between us.

In answer to Nelly's queries concerning Ralph's condition and whether his ribs might be cracked, he answered in an abstracted way, reassuring her in tones that she did not find at all reassuring.

"Is he sure?" she asked through me. "I do not think he has examined Ralph properly."

191

Lepine repeated his opinion in firmer tones, stating that if ribs were cracked or broken, there would be swelling and more tenderness than was evident. She had to be satisfied with that.

I walked out with him.

"Maybe Garance will go home later," I said, "but do not, I beg you, spend another night encamped on her doorstep. Go home to your wife."

He nodded, but I did not entirely trust him to do as I urged. Instead, he seized my hand.

"You must tell me, Madame Martha. I beg you. Why, why, why are you looking for her?"

It was hard to resist his appeal. Yet Madame Albert was looking inquiringly at us, the which made me most uncomfortable.

"I promise to tell you tomorrow," I whispered, "if she has not returned by then."

The next day dawned with an ominous purple sky. If I were superstitious or fanciful, I should imagine that the weather was reflecting the darkening events surrounding us all. It was Sunday, however, and in an attempt to put aside gloomy thoughts, I was much inclined to find heavenly solace in church. Since Nelly insisted she must remain by the side of her son, in case he took a turn for the worse, and being, furthermore, deeply suspicious that the Roman Church might have tainted the Anglican practice here, she declined to accompany me. I thought at first to make my way alone to one or other of the services in my own language, only to discover that both the English and American churches were on the far side of the city, quite near, as it happened, to where I had been on the previous day. I am afraid I felt too fatigued for another such journey, and instead returned to the now familiar Church of the Trinity, where I attended a mass without, however, partaking of the host. The service was not difficult to follow. I stood when the others did, knelt with them and muttered the responses as best I could. It was the glorious singing of the choir which lifted my spirits the most, and, after lighting a candle for Poppy, felt my soul refreshed as I made my short way back to the hotel. Despite the bad things that might happen on Earth, our Lord God in Heaven would surely in the end make all good for those who truly trusted in Him.

This philosophical frame of mind, however, melted away as soon as I entered the hotel, and found Lepine pacing up and down the small hallway. I have never seen anyone tearing their hair before, though it is a description that occurs in certain sensational novels. However, Lepine was doing exactly that, pulling his dark locks above his scalp as if endeavouring to wrench them from their roots.

"She is nowhere to be found, Madame," he said. "It is as if she has vanished from the face of the Earth. I went to visit her rooms first thing this morning, and now even Mère Angèle is worried. She says Garance would never have abandoned her bird for days like that."

"Her bird?"

Madame Albert, who had been standing at her desk listening to his outburst, went into her parlour and immediately came out again carrying a cage in which a little yellow songbird was hopping about, chirping prettily.

"Here, Madame. Gigi calls it Bijou."

A jewel, then. I looked at the poor caged creature which, to my mind should be flying free somewhere.

"But what is it doing here?" I asked.

"Mère Angèle was feeding it but she says she cannot mind it any longer," Lepine explained. "So Madame Albert has very kindly offered to look after it in case…." his voice broke a little, "until Garance returns."

"That's very kind of you, Madame," I said.

"It is nothing. His singing cheers the place up. Doesn't it, Bijou?" She tapped her finger on the wire of the cage. The bird cocked its head on one side and looked back at her. "What a little darling… I should never have thought of getting such a creature, but now that I have one, I don't think I shall ever be without. I could sit and watch him singing his heart out all day long."

I nodded politely. Perhaps after all, the colourful little creature was better off where it was. Were it to be set free, it would perhaps too soon be pecked to death by its drabber cousins, as I have heard frequently happens to such exotic species.

Uninterested in the landlady's chatter, the doctor now addressed me, "I trust you remember your promise, Madame."

I nodded, sighing. It would have to be done.

First, though, I went to tell Nelly that I would be out for a little while longer. She simply nodded in resignation. She looked utterly miserable.

"How is Ralph?"

We both regarded him, lying in bed, his face as if pressed to the wall. It was impossible to know if he were asleep or not.

"He is very low," she whispered, and gestured to the door. We went out on to the landing, before she continued, "He won't speak about it at all. When I suggested we should inform the police, he became almost violent."

"The doctor thinks all he needs is rest. Nothing is broken."

"Hmm." She was still sceptical.

"Is there anything you would like me to get you, Nelly?"

She shook her head. "Madame Albert brought us up some breakfast." She indicated, through the open doorway, a tray of rolls that looked largely untouched.

"Try and eat something… And try not to worry too much. I promise I will be back soon. Perhaps I can sit with Ralph, while you rest."

She nodded, and I pressed her arm in sympathy.

But ah, promises, promises.

I rejoined the impatient doctor, and we walked out into the city.

"That is truly shocking news!" he exclaimed, staring at me. "You must be mistaken."

We were yet again sitting in the gardens of the Trinity church. It was the most secluded place that could be found nearby, the weather being too bleak for strollers. I had just explained all to him, not omitting my own involvement and sense of guilt regarding the young woman.

"It is impossible to imagine Garance mixed up in anything like that," he continued. "I know her, Madame. She might be angry at the plight of the dispossessed but she would never ever have anything to do with violence."

"I should like very much to believe it, Dr. Lepine, but I tell you again, I saw her at the hotel in earnest conversation with at least one of the plotters," I said. "Philippe Albert must somehow be connected, too. There can be no doubt of it, given the conversation with his mother that I overheard by chance."

"Madame Albert involved in such a business! No! Impossible!" He barked out a laugh at the very thought.

"I did not dream it, Doctor. I know what I heard."

"Still, it doesn't prove their guilt or involvement. Just that they knew Maxim and the others."

"Perhaps. I should like to hope as much."

Lepine sat frowning deeply for a while, rubbing his hands.

Finally he said, "You must go at once to the Prefecture, Madame, and tell them of your fears for Garance. No need to mention Madame Albert, whom I am sure, is also guiltless." He paused. "But perhaps, after all – without being part of it, you understand, for I will never admit that – Garance learnt something of what was afoot, and now the plotters suspect that it was she who betrayed them. Yes. That is indeed quite likely. You must make haste, Madame."

"Why should I go? You yourself could report her disappearance." I was most disinclined for various reasons to set foot in the Prefecture again.

"Believe me, Madame, if I report the disappearance of an artist's model, they will simply laugh at me. For you, given your connections as you have explained them to me, they have respect."

I could not argue further. Lepine agreed to accompany me thither, but not to go in with me. We took a cab to save time.

"If what you suggest is what has really happened," he said despairingly, as we journeyed along, "I fear it is already too late. She is dead."

I have to admit I feared the same myself. "Let us hope and pray not," I replied.

"Madame Hudson! A very good day to you!" It was my dancing partner from the cabaret who again stood behind the reception desk. "To what do I owe this very considerable pleasure?" He smoothed back sparse hair with his hand, and smirked, as if imagining that I had come especially to see him.

"Is M. Cochot back?" I asked.

"Alas, not yet… Tomorrow, I think."

"Ah, well, I am sure you can help me, Monsieur."

"Of course, Madame. And please call me Hubert."

I did not know if that was his first or last name and hoped it was the latter, for otherwise it suggested a degree of intimacy which I certainly did not wish to encourage.

"Well, M. Hubert," I started...

As the doctor had predicted, the policeman was dismissive of the matter.

"Madame Hudson," he said, in a patronising tone. "These girls… their way of life… it's all so very far from your own experience. This Garance is probably tucked away in a love nest – please excuse the freedom of the expression – with some little friend. After all, you know, it is not yet two days since she was last seen."

I insisted, however, and reluctantly he took out a sheet on which he noted the details in a pen that kept leaving blots behind it. Since I did not want to incriminate Poppy through association, or Philippe and his mother either – not trusting the police to act with restraint after the fiasco of Leon – I omitted most of the details about the anarchists. To read my statement, it would seem to be simply the case of a missing girl, who might or might not have been taken for the person who betrayed the plot to kill the Prefect. As a result, M. Hubert was somewhat perplexed at my persistence.

"Well," he said finally. "If there is any news, we will let you know."

"You will do a search for her, then?"

"A search! Madame, if you only knew how many girls of that sort go missing, how many young men as well. The Paris police force has many other more pressing cases to attend to. Robberies, murders...I am sorry."

"This may well turn into a murder case," I snapped. "Then I suppose at last you might be interested."

"The murder of a prostitute!" His eyes narrowed. He had turned back into the officious little door-keeper I had encountered on my first visit. "It is hardly worth the trouble." He relented a little. "I am truly sorry, Madame. But look on the brighter side. From what you have told me it was either her or you. Surely it is better that she should suffer, even if in error, than that you should."

If he thought I was mollified by this, he was sorely mistaken. I was furious and strode out, without another word.

Lepine, waiting across the street, listened to my diatribe impassively.

"I am not really surprised, Madame Martha. But at least you tried."

We sat on the quays for a while, gazing at the restless inky waters of the river, each one of us with our own thoughts. Perhaps he was wondering, as I was, if somewhere down there, the body of an innocent young woman tossed in its endless sleep. I started to wish, God forgive me, that I had left well enough alone. That I had done nothing in the first place, ignoring what I had overheard, and abandoning M. Cochot to his fate.

Suddenly, Lepine stood up.

"Bourdain," he said. "He may at least know something. She may even be with him." He slapped his forehead. "How foolish of me not to think of that before."

He had forgotten how he had previously dismissed the suggestion when it came from me. As for me, contrariwise, I had since come to the conclusion, given what I knew of Poppy's character, that it was most unlikely she would have returned there.

"But doctor," I said. "Remember how he forbade her to come to the studio, how he insulted her. Would she have gone to him after that? She is too proud, I think."

"Yes, Garance is proud. But she is also a passionate woman." He looked stricken. "It is sadly possible that she feels strongly for him." He paused, seeing my sceptical expression. "Forgive me, Madame, you are not in love. You have perhaps forgotten the madness that overwhelms, the obsession, the forgetting of all that is not the beloved."

If I ever knew such feelings, I could not now have forgotten them. Dear Henry and I enjoyed a much more placid romance, none the less deep for all that, and one which I do not regret in the slightest. I regarded the suffering young man as he stood before me, himself consumed by the mania of love. No, I did not envy him his passion.

Yet he could be right, after all. It was at least possible that the scorned young woman had returned to her elderly lover, if only to beg for some recognition of her work. A stronger motive than the other, in my view. We must go and find out.

"No," said Thérèse, finally opening the door a tiny crack. "No. Mlle. Germaine is not here and isn't likely ever to be again. Jules refuses to admit her."

"But, Madame, can we not just talk to M. Bourdain for a moment? It is very important. I cannot exaggerate how much." Lepine's words and tone would surely melt even the hardest of hearts, even that of Thérèse.

"Jules is not here." Her granite face was impassive.

"Where is he?"

"He is out... I am sorry Monsieur, Madame. I cannot help you."

She slammed the door shut with some finality. We looked at each other. What to do?

As we walked off, I glanced back at the house, discerning there a shadowy figure standing at a window, watching us leave. Thérèse? Bourdain himself? It was impossible to tell.

There was nothing else but to go on our way empty-handed. I urged Lepine to busy himself with his medical duties, for to my mind there is nothing that distracts better from worries than keeping busy. He agreed, but sadly. As for myself, I had no duties to occupy me, and yet could not face Nelly and Ralph and the confines of the hotel just then. Bidding farewell to my companion, I walked in a direction not yet taken, and after a good three-quarters of an hour found myself on the edge of the Bois de Boulogne. This, I recalled, was where, as Père Perrot had told me, his daughter, Laure, had, on the yesterday, taken herself off with her beau. It was hardly likely she would have returned now, but even if she did, the park was huge, and, according to Baedeker, full of attractions, so an uncomfortable encounter was most unlikely.

It was anyway time for luncheon and I was hungry. Luckily, the park featured a café where I dined lightly on a ham baguette and a seltzer water. Given the size of the Bois and despite the expense, I was glad thereafter to take a carriage to go about and see the sights in comfort. It was the best thing I could have done, sitting in an open barouche (a reluctant sun was now peeping out from behind the clouds) and traversing the huge expanse. Another lady had proved happy to share the space – and cost – with me. This was a person of about my own age who introduced herself as Madame Ducasse. She seemed respectable enough, and was dressed soberly, apart from a frivolous little feathered hat and rouged cheeks, and from time to time we exchanged chit-chat about nothing very much. It was most agreeable, except that I could make neither head nor tail of what our driver was saying to us, for he had a rough Parisian accent that reminded me of the singer, Aristide Bruant. Luckily, Madame Ducasse was able to put his words into understandable French for me.

In that way we traversed the Bois, which wasn't much of a wood after all, despite its name, past manicured formal gardens, picturesque lakes and waterfalls, a grotto set into the cliff. None of these latter, amazingly, were natural features, but constructs to delight the visitors. We went on, past the zoo, the amusement park, the botanical gardens, the charming little Chateau de la Bagatelle, constructed, as Madame Ducasse informed me with a tinkling laugh, as the result of wager between the brother of Louis XVI and Marie Antoinette.

"Then they all had their heads chopped off."

She did not seem in the slightest degree regretful. Maybe she was a Republican.

At a certain point, our driver turned to us and asked something of which I understood not a word. My companion explained that in the arena nearby, very shortly, a bullfight would take place, featuring of all things a lady toreador.

"Something most unusual," she said. "I have never heard of such a thing before."

Apparently our driver had asked if we would be interested in attending.

A bullfight! I had only the vaguest idea what that entailed. Bulls fighting each other in some way is what I thought in my innocence – a cockfight on a grander scale perhaps – puzzled as to why this should be of any interest. Had I known the true nature of the entertainment in advance, I should never have agreed. At the time, however, I decided to be open to new impressions, and concurred with the plan, especially since Madame Ducasse was most enthusiastic at the prospect, and insisted I would enjoy it.

It was a brutal and horrid spectacle. The poor bull stood no chance whatsoever. The creature was, as I soon understood from the illustrated programme, to be slaughtered before our very eyes by a prancing man, the "matador" as he was called, rigged out in an elaborate, gold-embroidered costume and sporting a bright red cloak. But before it was permitted to be put out of its final misery, the poor beast had to submit to much baiting and torment at the hands of three horseback riders, one of whom was the exceptional female mentioned by Madame Ducasse. This Mlle. Maria Genty was a lean, mannish woman in bloomers and jaunty hat whose activities proved hardly womanly. Leaning from her horse, she repeatedly attempted to stab the bull in the flesh behind its neck with a beribboned lance. Each time she achieved this feat, the crowd roared its approval, while the lances were left sticking up in place like some horrific decoration. Mlle. Genty was undoubtedly a skilled equestrian, for on several occasions, when she and her mount were threatened by the horns of the bull, she nimbly evaded them, to further cheers. What she was doing was undoubtedly dangerous and she was very brave, but in such a perverted cause!

At last, blood pouring down the flanks of the enraged creature, the matador stepped forward, sword in hand. He goaded the bull further by flashing his scarlet cloak before it, encouraging it to charge at him, and swivelling out of the way just before it had a chance to gore him. Each time, there were more cheers and gasps. Loss of blood, however, meant the animal was weakening, and by now it was become an unequal fight with the outcome assured. Soon the bull fell as to its knees, as if it were begging for mercy, and the matador was able to inflict the coup de grace. Standing over the prostrate body which still heaved in its death throes, the hero of the day gallantly beckoned Mlle. Genty to join him. Nothing loath, she thrust her two hands into the bull's still gushing blood, and held them up to shew the crowd, who cheered even louder. None louder than my companion, the feathers on her foolish little hat fluttering violently, her rouged cheeks become even redder.

I excused myself to her, saying that the spectacle was not for me. I stood to leave.

"But Madame, you must wait a little. The matador will be presented with his reward. We must wave white handkerchiefs to indicate that we think he deserves a prize."

"A prize for that?"

"Indeed." She did not hear my tone of disgust for she herself was too excited. "The bull's ear at the very least. Or two ears and even a tail if considered exceptional. Who knows, maybe he will give an ear to the lady. For you know she was very good. As good as any man. "

Thereupon she pulled out a white handkerchief and started waving it wildly, along with many others in the audience. I could not stay to witness yet more barbarism, and pushed my way out, not even bidding Madame Ducasse adieu. To me, the hands that shook those kerchiefs were as bloody as those of Mlle. Genty herself. My hands too, for colluding, albeit unwittingly, in the killing of an innocent creature.

What a perversion of womanhood! Whoever it was had called us the gentle sex must never have set eyes upon this horrific spectacle, must never have seen what even women can be capable of. I was shocked to my very soul.

Thus, the day, which had so briefly pleased and diverted me, was now become ghastly. Even the sun, earlier so coy at shewing itself, was setting into a sack of purple cloud and turning the waters of the lake as red as the blood of the unfortunate bull. I sat for a while, trembling, and wondering what new horrors the next day might bring. For I was sure this could not be the end of it. At last I dragged myself up and walked on until I found a line of carriages. I took the first and ordered the driver to take me back to the hotel. There I informed a startled Nelly that I felt too sick to eat, and fell into bed where images of dying bulls and dead girls occupied my troubled mind, so that it was long into the night before I slept.

Chapter Sixteen – A Visit to the Morgue

The next morning saw rain drilling down from leaden skies. It was not a day for going out, but the prospect of staying locked in my room with my thoughts was not attractive either. As for going home – this was the Monday when we might be supposed to leave Paris at last – of this Nelly mentioned not a word.

Another practical concern of mine was that, since we had stayed so much longer than originally planned, and since there was no apparent end in sight either, the funds I had brought with me were diminishing fast. I should have again to visit the telegraph office and arrange for more to be wired over to me. This at least would be a suitable task for a dull morning and, after breakfasting, I headed out to do the necessary. I was glad to have with me a stout umbrella, not, alas, that which had belonged to dear Henry, for that particular appurtenance had undergone irreparable damage during my previous adventure in Ireland, serving me well in a way for which it had not originally been intended. No, this was a less handsome object, lacking the dog-head handle which had so distinguished Henry's. But it did its duty and kept off the worst of the rain.

My business in the telegraph office finally completed, though at rather greater length and with more bureaucracy than I had envisaged, and the rain shewing no sign of abating, I reluctantly set off back to the hotel. Awaiting me there I was most surprised to find a young and raw-looking officer of the law, kicking his heels in the hallway, while Madame Albert looked on agog as she pointed me out to him. Perhaps she thought my life of crime had finally caught up with me. Certainly the grim demeanour of the officer, and his words too, were likely to reinforce that supposition.

"Madame Hudson, you must accompany me to the Prefecture straight away," he said, refusing to give any further explanation.

"Tell my sister I shall be back soon, if you please," I told Madame Albert, who shook her head as if doubting this very much.

The officer spoke not a word, during our ride back through the city, but kept a severe frown on his face, perhaps intending to intimidate me. To be fair to the lad, I imagine he knew no more of the matter than I did, so was unsure whether to treat me as a suspect or a witness.

Once arrived, I was swept past M. Hubert, who also looked at me strangely, and from there into the august presence of none other than M. Cochot himself, now returned from his break. He too displayed no sign of any prior acquaintanceship with me, and I started to wonder if I had indeed inadvertently broken French law in some unforgiveable way. However, once the officer had saluted and left the room, M. Cochot relaxed, and even pulled out a chair for me to sit upon.

"You may be puzzled, Madame, at the abrupt way in which you were plucked from your hotel." He chuckled. "Believe me, I have no intention of abducting you. Not today, at any rate."

He paused as if expecting me to laugh with him.

"Be so kind as to explain, Monsieur," I said. "It is not pleasant to be brought here in such a way. I am sure the landlady took me for a dangerous criminal."

"I am sorry about that. I shall talk most severely to Officer Chevalier."

"Please do no such thing. I do not think it his fault. I imagine he was given no clear instructions by his superiors."

I was not inclined to be friendly.

"Yes, well… of course…" He picked up a sheet from his desk, which, from the blots visible upon it, I took to be my statement of the day before.

"You reported a young woman missing yesterday." He started briskly, but then his tone softened again. "I was not here, as you know. Taking a break in the Loire valley. A most delightful place. You really must visit it before you leave France, Madame. I can highly recommend an excellent hotel in Amboise."

Would he never come to the point, which must, I thought, concern Poppy?

He tapped the sheet with a chubby finger. "You have, I think, a particular interest in this person."

I told him that was indeed the case, adding that I had not quite revealed all I knew to M. Hubert. The Prefect raised his eyebrows at the familiarity with which I spoke of his subordinate, but listened in silence while I explained that it was a delicate matter, and that I had no desire to implicate people who might be quite innocent of wrongdoing. However, I continued, my greatest concern was for the safety of Poppy… Mlle. Germaine, a charming young woman.

"The anarchists know that someone informed the police about the plot to assassinate you, Monsieur, and, for certain reasons, I worry that they took it to be Mlle. Germaine. In that case, you know, she would have found herself in grave danger of retribution."

He drummed his fingers on the desk, and looked me full in the face. I waited.

At last he gave a great sigh.

"I am afraid I have bad news for you, Madame. A body has been found. The body of a young woman…" he referred to the blotchy sheet, "as you describe her here, slender and with red hair, aged around twenty."

"Oh, my God!"

My worst fears realised. Poppy killed and all my fault!

Now, I am not inclined to faint, but I was glad to be sitting, for suddenly I felt very dizzy, and clutched at my head.

"Madame." He came round to me quickly with a glass of water, which I gulped back.

Water, did I say? There was water present but also a fair amount of spirituous liquid and I was seized by a paroxysm of coughing. M. Cochot patted me on the back, with perhaps a little more enthusiasm than was quite necessary.

"Dear Madame Hudson…"

The fit passed and I gathered myself together. He still stood over me. Too close for comfort.

"Dear Madame, it is a lot to ask, but I wonder would you agree to accompany me to the morgue to view the body. For identification purposes, you understand."

I nodded. It was the least I could do for the poor girl.

"It is not far to walk," he said, "though, given the weather, perhaps we should take a car."

I could not care either way. I was numb with grief. Such a beautiful talented girl, plucked from life just as she was coming into bloom. All my fault. Her blood on my hands.

We took a car but were in it only a few minutes. The morgue was indeed close by, being on the adjacent island, and just behind the Cathedral of Our Lady. I was most astonished to see outside the building vendors of sweetmeats and oranges standing around in the rain, while a small crowd of people purchased the same before entering the premises.

"It is to our advantage that the bad weather has discouraged more sightseers," said M. Cochot.

"Good heavens," I replied. "Do you mean to say that people come here to divert themselves with views of the dead?"

"Oh yes. It is a great attraction. Of course, some come, like yourself, to check if a missing relative or friend is here. But others…well, as you can see, Madame…"

There were families with children, there were foreigners. I even heard English spoken. Some of the tourists who the previous day might have risen with me to the top of M. Eiffel's tower were now disporting themselves among mutilated corpses. It was quite horrible. Between this and the bullfight, I felt myself to be in an alien place indeed.

M. Cochot led me quickly past the rows of bodies that were displayed prone on stone slabs, their heads, when they still had them attached to their necks, slightly raised so that their faces could clearly be seen. All were naked but for cloths covering their modesty, and beside each of them hung their clothes, so as

210

to help, I supposed, with identification when ghastly injuries might make the business less straightforward.

This was, in fact, the case with the body in front of which M. Cochot finally stopped, peremptorily waving off those with their noses stuck to the glass partition.

I gasped in shock. The Prefect took fast hold of me, fearing perhaps that I was about to fall in another faint.

"I can manage, Monsieur," I told him somewhat coldly, and he relinquished his grasp.

I forced myself to look again on the horrid sight. The poor soul in front of me had suffered terribly before death, the features of her face obliterated into a bloody mess.

"Whatever happened to her?"

"Acid," he said. "Flung in her face. Then she was stabbed in the breast several times, to make sure she was quite dead."

I clung to the railing, gazing at what remained of…

"But, Monsieur," I said. "That's not Poppy."

"What?"

"It isn't her… It isn't Mlle. Germaine."

He stared at me.

"However," I continued, "I know who it is."

"Then please be so good as to tell me, Madame."

"Her name is Sylvie."

"How can you be so sure?"

I pointed to the long angry scar on her neck. "I recognise that. I noticed it the first time I met her… She is an artists' model, Monsieur, like Mlle Germaine. And that," I pointed to the emerald green dress hanging beside the body, and now stained horribly, "is what she was wearing the last time I saw her. At the opening of Le Chien Jaune night club."

I burst into tears then, all the pent-up feelings of the last days welling out of me. Perhaps tears of relief were mixed in also. It was a terrible and selfish thing to admit to myself, since this poor girl, too, surely never deserved such an end. Yet the corpse was not Poppy! She had not been killed because of me. Emotion overwhelmed me, and I sank to my knees. I could not care that people were eying me curiously. Doubtless they took me for the mother of the poor girl in front of them. M. Cochot gently raised me up and led me away.

"Do you know her last name, this Sylvie? Where she lives?" he asked.

I shook my head. "Ralph might know." Then I bit my lip. The last thing I wanted to do was to drag my nephew into the sorry business, especially, now that I came to think of it, with all his mysterious injuries.

"Ralph?"

"My sister's son. But there are others, Monsieur, who would know her much better. Etienne…"

It was too late.

"Let us start with Ralph," he said.

The Prefect himself, of course, did not deign to fetch and carry. He expressed the intention of sending M. Hubert back with me to fetch Ralph. M. Hubert Blanchard.

"Since you seem to know my officer so well, Madame," M. Cochot said, an edge to his voice that seemed to me rather unnecessary.

212

"Ralph is not well," I tried to argue. "It would be better to look for Etienne. He's… he used to be her special friend."

I did not inform M. Cochot of Etienne's tendency to jealous rage, as evinced by both the duel with Ralph and the scene with Jules Bourdain at Le Chien Jaune, not wishing to incriminate someone who might be quite innocent. The police would soon find it all out from others, without my help. Indeed, M. Hubert Blanchard himself had been a witness to the confrontation.

"Etienne who? Where can I find him?"

I had to admit I did not know.

"Perhaps in the Place du Tertre," I said. "He sketches there."

M. Cochot gave me a look. "So do fifty other so-called artists," he said. "No, we'll bring your Ralph here first and see what he can tell us."

I dreaded Nelly's reaction and rightly so. She became utterly hysterical at the thought of her son undergoing a police interrogation, for that was how she saw it. In vain I told her he was simply to provide information concerning someone of his acquaintance who had met with a violent death. (I had been warned not to reveal names or circumstances).

"A murder! My Ralph is not involved in murder!"

"Nelly, he will be back soon. It is just routine."

However, I saw the officer looking askance at Ralph's injuries and cursed the unguarded moment I had involved my nephew in the affair. Not without wondering, I must admit, if indeed he might be in some way involved. I didn't believe in the cutpurse explanation for a second.

"I will come with you, Ralph," Nelly said. "Tell the man, Martha."

"That is out of the question, Madame," said M. Blanchard (for now I must call him that), after I had translated her intention. "You sister's son does not appear to be a minor. He must answer for himself without holding his maman's hand."

"We can make our way to the Prefecture separately and wait for Ralph to be finished," I told her. "But you may not accompany him now."

I omitted to translate M. Hubert's somewhat sneering conclusion, though Ralph of course had understood perfectly. Truly he looked very young and fearful, as if to be led straight to the guillotine, the which I am sure Nelly too was convinced was about to happen.

We all four descended to the hotel entrance hall. Off went Ralph in the police car, Madame Albert agog.

"What has he done?" she asked me.

"Nothing. He is just going to provide information."

It was perhaps not a good choice of words, given her suspected connections.

"There has been a violent death," I added. "Ralph knows the victim."

"A woman?"

"I am sorry, Madame. Just now I am not able to say."

"Where did it happen?"

I looked at her blankly, realising that in my shock I had not thought to ask.

Nelly and I, while not permitted beyond the barrier, into the hallowed sanctum of the Prefecture, were at least allowed to sit in a waiting area. The officer on the desk was not M. Blanchard

214

and I wondered if it were he who was interrogating Ralph. Surely, though, it would be the Prefect himself. As it turned out, Ralph had not been as reticent as I, and, once he understood the matter, had not delayed in pointing the police towards Etienne, revealing all that had happened on the night in question. At that very moment, M. Blanchard was tracking down the volatile artist.

Meanwhile, Nelly and I sat waiting, on a rather hard bench, let it be said. Or rather, I sat, while my sister mostly paced about. She was as restless as a bag of frogs.

"I cannot understand it," Martha," she said over and over. "Why will you not tell me anything? Why should Ralph be suspected?"

"He is not suspected. He knows the victim. That is all."

"And why did they first bring you here? Did you know the victim as well? Please tell me who it is."

Finally I gave in, and she stared at me, speechless. Then sank on to the bench.

"Sylvie," she whispered. "My God, they will fix it on Ralph, for sure."

"Not at all, Nelly. Why ever should they think he killed her?"

Again she was silent. Then she spoke even lower.

"But what if he did, Martha? What if he did?"

Ralph emerged after about an hour. I must say that with his bruises and broken nose he looked very much the criminal. However, he was let go, pending further investigations. I had tried to impress on Nelly the extreme unlikelihood of Ralph's guilt, hoping she would not ask him about it directly, since it would certainly antagonise him further. Just now, he needed our support and belief. All the same, I could not help remembering that in his studio there was a bottle of acid.

Ralph expressing a strong desire for a drink, we found a place nearby that was respectable enough for us two women. Ralph ordered a glass of red wine and a cognac, Nelly refraining for once from comment. I should not have minded a glass of cognac myself, but settled for lemon tea, while Nelly took only plain water.

"Did they tell you where she was found?" I asked.

"In the catacombs."

"The what?"

He shrugged and shook his head. I reached for my Baedeker.

"Here we are," I said. "It's a series of tunnels under Paris, a vast ossuary, lined with bones. Goodness! Whatever was she doing there?"

"I told them," Ralph said, "that I've never been there. I don't even know where it is. But I'm not sure if they believed me." He gulped back his cognac.

"They must," said Nelly, though without a deal of conviction.

"The catacombs," I repeated thoughtfully. "How very extraordinary. If we only knew why she was there, we might find the who as well."

"There you go again, Martha," Nelly said. "Fancying yourself as good a detective as your lodger."

"I most certainly do not," I replied. "Still, I will do my best to endeavour to prove that Ralph is in no way involved."

I regarded my nephew at that point, but he was staring down and did not catch my eye.

216

Chapter Seventeen: Back to the Yellow Dog

"But Garance is still missing! Where is she? Where can she be?"

Dr. Lepine looked at me despairingly.

After returning with Nelly and Ralph from the Prefecture, we had found the doctor awaiting us at the hotel, his pretext being to check on his patients. After we had explained the reason for our absence and he had changed the dressing on Ralph's wound, he instructed the two of them to go to bed and rest from the mental and physical exhaustion of their ordeal. Then he asked me to take a walk with him and we headed towards the Butte of Montmartre. The rain had stopped and a weak sun was turning the streets silver, a pretty sight, though one had to be careful where one stepped to avoid any puddles.

I told my companion about my fears that the body in the morgue might be Poppy's, but he already knew it was not she.

"Do you not imagine, Madame, that I go there constantly to check? Every morning, every evening."

"Well, the fact that she isn't there is good news, is it not?"

"It only tells me that they have not yet found her."

He had not informed where we were going, but I soon guessed our destination. Yet again we were returning to her lodgings, not, I felt now, that he was expecting to find her there, but in order to hunt out any clue as to what had happened to her.

I was a little surprised – perhaps I shouldn't have been – that Dr. Lepine didn't need to ask Mère Angèle to let us in this time, but produced his own key to Poppy's room. Opening the door, he gave a gasp of shock.

"She has been robbed!" he cried.

I looked around. The place was certainly emptier than before. Most of the artwork was gone, including the woodland painting that I had so admired. Clothing and papers were scattered over the floor as if someone had rummaged through them in a hurry. For my part, I could not tell if anything else were missing. Dr. Lepine kicked through the mess with his foot. He bent down and picked up a tiny statuette that the robber, if robber there be, had overlooked. It was exquisite, delicate, a female nude, her arms crossed over her breasts.

He sat down on the bed and started to weep, still clutching the object.

"Garance…"

"Monsieur…" I turned. The old crone stood in the open doorway, sucking in her toothless gums.

"Who did this?" Lepine asked her.

She shook her head, then started to babble something unintelligible to me.

The doctor put his head his hands. When the old woman stopped talking, I asked what she had said.

"They came in the night," he said. "Mère Angèle was terrified. She thought they would cross to her room next and slit her throat, but they did their business and then left."

"She did not think to call the police?"

He almost smiled at the suggestion. "No, Madame Martha, she did not. Up here on the Butte, no one likes the police."

The old woman must have caught the word, which of course sounds similar in both languages. She gabbled some more and spat. No need for a translation of that.

We left the house, both thoughtful.

"Strange," I said at length. "Do you think it was the anarchists? What ever could they have been looking for?"

"Would the anarchists steal her work?"

"They might. As cover for their true intentions."

He shook his head. "Who can say?"

"Maybe," I went on, "they too were looking for her. If that is the case, then she must still be alive and perhaps in hiding."

This at least seemed to cheer him.

"You are right. Yes, indeed."

"In any case, we should endeavour to trace her last known movements. She left Le Chien Jaune, did she not, in the company of Valentin le Désossé?"

The doctor slapped his head. "Of course. I am so stupid. Madame Martha," he stopped in his tracks and seized my hand, "you think as clearly as your associate, Mr. Sherlock Holmes. How lucky that you are here."

More misapprehensions, more undeserved praise. No need for Mr. H. here. Anyone pausing to think objectively and unemotionally might have come to the same conclusion. Indeed, I myself, had I sat down without distraction, should have done so much earlier.

We duly made our way down the hill to the cabaret. By daylight, Le Chien Jaune looked even more tawdry than by night, especially the closed door crudely painted to resemble the teeth of the dog whose open jaws surrounded the entranceway. Although the long day was settling down to evening, it was still too early for the place to open. Nothing daunted, Dr. Lepine hammered with his fist on the dog's teeth. In vain.

"There must surely be a way in round the back," he said. "For deliveries and so on."

Without a passage-way down one side or the other of the club, we made a detour into another street where we found a narrow track leading between the buildings. Now, I am well used to the filth and waste of London, but nothing I have ever seen there was on the scale of this place. Heaps of rotting stinking matter were home to fat rats that proved not shy to shew themselves, so busy were they with their ghastly feast. It even occurred to me, though I would not for the world have expressed the notion to my companion, that if a body were to be dumped here, short work would surely be made of it by these ravenous vermin.

The doctor proved less fastidious than myself – I suppose his occupation regularly brings him to such places – and he strode ahead of me to find the back door of the club. Here too piles of garbage lay strewn, and among the foul mess I recognised the debris of the food served us on the opening night. The nauseating sight convinced me never to eat in that particular establishment again.

The door here was unlocked and, without knocking, Lepine let himself in. I was a little less forward but followed him, not wishing to linger by myself in that rank alleyway. We found ourselves at first in a filthy kitchen area. No one was about and we proceeded into the main hall.

If it were possible, the inside of the club was even less prepossessing than the outside. The dim lighting on the previous occasion had softened the effect but now harsh electric bulbs shewed up the vulgarity of the place. The paintings on those yellow walls looked not decorative but crude and ugly. Moreover, no one had yet cleared away the debris of the night before. Empty and half empty bottles covered tables, where they had not fallen to the floor and smashed. Dirty plates, with the remnants of sausage or bread, seemed to call to the rodents outside to come in and gorge. Looking about myself, I was astonished and dismayed.

Here at least we were not alone. Slumped at one of the tables, snoring, was a mound of flesh I soon recognised, if only by the feathered hat that rested beside him, as M. Renard, the owner of the club. Dr. Lepine did not hesitate to shake the man by the shoulder, to rouse him. The effect was unexpected to say the least. M. Renard leapt to his feet, grabbing his sword and waving it in threatening manner.

"You will get paid when I am good and ready," he shouted.

I supposed he took us for creditors.

Soon realising his error, he calmed down, apologising. However, it took some time for him to discover the purpose of our visit. He appeared groggy, from lack of sleep perhaps, or because an open bottle stood at his elbow beside a glass containing a cloudy liquid, a bowl of sugar and a jug of water.

"Garance?... Gigi?..." He shook his head.

"She made a scene at the table of M. Bourdain," Lepine explained. "Then left with Valentin le Désossé."

Renard scratched his head. "When was this?"

"On the opening night."

"Ah," he smiled. "What a night that was. What a success. What a glittering occasion… Since then… alas." He gave a gesture indicating empty hands.

"But you have such wonderful performers, M. Renard," Lepine said. "Bruant, Guilbert, Satie, La Goulue…"

"Ha!" Renard shook his head. "You think I can afford to pay such people every night. No. Who performs here now?" He reeled off a list of names. "No one wants to see them. No one comes except low-lifes from the far side of the hill. Where are the people of fashion? Where are they?" He hammered with his fist on the table. "Low-lifes and people looking to be paid. No, Monsieur, Madame. I am finished." He seized his glass, downed the contents and then spat on the floor.

"But Monsieur," I said. "You have only been open for a few days. These things take time. You must be patient."

He screwed up his eyes, and stared at me as if seeing me properly for the first time. Then he grabbed my hand.

"Do you think so? Is that what you think?"

"I am certain of it." Nothing of the sort but the man needed encouraging. It is a terrible thing when despair takes over. "But," I went on, "you must pull yourself together, get the place cleaned up. It's a pigsty at the moment. No wonder no one wants to come."

He still had hold of my hand. His was hard and strong and there was no way I could extricate myself.

"Madame, you are an angel, a beacon of hope." He actually pressed my hand to his lips. "Marry me."

I burst out laughing and he had the grace to laugh as well, letting go my hand at the same time, for the which I was most grateful, keeping both those members out of his reach from then on.

"Garance?" Dr. Lepine ventured. "You don't remember what happened to her?"

Renard frowned. "She left with that dancer and neither of them came back."

"And he hasn't been here since?"

"I told you. I can't afford performers like that." He shewed signs of slumping back into despondency. "If you want to talk to him… and mind you, the fellow isn't at all talkative… try the Moulin Rouge." He said the last words with a sneer. "And then," he perked up a little. "Come back here tonight, Monsieur, Madame. I will give you the best seats in the house." He swung his arm around the hall, almost knocking his bottle flying. Shouting an oath, he seized the bottle and poured a splash of green liquid into the glass. He then positioned a slotted spoon over the glass, placed a cube of sugar on top and poured water over the lot. The liquid in the glass turned from green to cloudy white. I was fascinated at the ritual. It was like a magic trick.

He saw me looking. "You want some, Madame." He proffered his glass.

I shook my head.

"Tonight, perhaps." He gave a leering wink. Raising the glass he said, "To the beautiful English lady, my angel."

He was mocking me, of course, but it was nothing to me. I did not seek approval from such as him.

"Absinthe," said Dr. Lepine as we made our way out. "That's what he was drinking. You mustn't mind him, Madame. It twists the mind."

"Absinthe?"

"They call it the green fairy, since it carries those who partake to fantastical worlds. It's much favoured by the bohemian set, you know, your Mr. Oscar Wilde, among them. Artists say it stimulates their creativity."

I now recalled hearing of it before. Something censorious.

"You seem familiar with it yourself," I said.

He smiled just a little. "I have been known to mix with such a set myself from time to time."

"And to drink that drink?"

"Sometimes one needs to escape all this." He gestured at the Paris street we were in. "Just for a little while. But one risks madness."

The madness of obsessive passion, perhaps.

He was all for going straight away to the Moulin Rouge, to track down Valentin le Désossé and find what he had to reveal about that night. Further adventures, however, were beyond my strength. It had been the longest day of my life, and all I wanted to do just then was to eat a simple supper, and then sleep. Sleep and sleep.

I prevailed on the doctor to accompany me to a decent restaurant, although I could see that he was anxious to continue the hunt. Being a gentleman, however, he concurred without an argument. Perhaps he was concerned at my evident fatigue, for veritably I was about to drop. I cannot even remember what I ate except that it was plain and good. Afterwards, he conducted me by cab back to the hotel, and then disappeared off into the night.

I looked in briefly on Nelly. Thankfully there was nothing more to report regarding Ralph. It seemed that the police were leaving him be, at least for the time being, and after dinner he had returned to his studio. She hadn't been too pleased about that.

"He is not well yet, Martha. He needs a mother's care."

He needs a good talking to, I thought, but said nothing.

Now she was escaping into one of the lurid novelettes I had bought for her and she did not ask me about my evening, for which I was grateful.

Chapter Eighteen: Arrested!

The next morning dawned dull and heavy, and I felt the same. It was as if a metal band were clamped around my skull. I idled in bed for a while, wondering about the day ahead, wondering what more could be done in the search for Poppy, wondering if I even had the spirit to continue. After we parted on the previous evening, had Dr. Lepine gone to the Moulin Rouge? Had he discovered anything new? Was Poppy's body even now lying in that terrible morgue? Did I even care anymore? Did I care about anything except this throbbing ache? Perhaps Nelly and I should wash our hands of the whole business and return to England forthwith.

I dragged myself out of bed, automatically performed my ablutions and dressed myself. Then I went in search of my sister who, I thought, looked as wan as I did. Maybe we would both feel better after breakfast, though I craved something more than the rolls and croissants and hot chocolate on offer. Oh, for a strong cup of tea. Some devilled kidneys or a pair of kippers on good brown bread, or a dish of kedgeree. Even eggs alone would do, fried, boiled, poached, scrambled. My mouth watered at the mere thought.

Nelly and I had energy only to take ourselves as far as Le Petit Bonhomme, even though I was not looking forward to another encounter with Laure. However, I need not have feared that she might again make a knowing remark concerning my aptitude in the French language, and, if so, what that might signify. Today she was neither friendly nor hostile – hurrying to fulfil our order and making no attempt at conversation. Perhaps she was too busy, for the café was full, or perhaps she could tell from our expressions that neither of us was in a chatty humour.

My sister seemed conscious that I was not myself, for after a while she asked me, somewhat timidly, what I was planning to do for the day. I shook my head.

"I don't know," I said.

"Where is your Baedeker? That might suggest somewhere interesting."

I had left the book in my room, an indication of my inertia, for usually I had it by me all the time.

"We could go shopping, I suppose," she said.

"Yes, we could," I replied listlessly.

"I need to buy a few presents to take back, you know," she went on. "I haven't had a chance until now."

I roused myself. Really, I was being most selfish. While Nelly had been languishing on her sickbed, I had managed to see a deal of the city. Now I recalled the day – a day which seemed so very far off – when I had visited the Vivienne Gallery in an attempt to shake off my anarchist pursuers. I had thought then to return at my leisure to that most attractive of places, and, though now I had little appetite for the expedition, Nelly would surely like it. I proposed the notion and she agreed gratefully. Although the distance was not so very far, we decided to take a cab.

Nelly was indeed delighted with the place – with its attractive and airy architecture hardly less than the abundance of well-stocked little shops – and all in all displayed more animation exploring it than she had shewn since we first arrived in the city. She bustled from store to store, selecting small gifts for various friends and neighbours, including a couple of fans like the one I had bought for Phoebe.

"So very French!" she said, waving one in front of her face.

As for me, I was pleased to find an herbalist, where I was able to buy an essence of lavender to sprinkle on my handkerchief to soothe my pounding head.

When Nelly was at last satisfied that she had bought trinkets enough, we betook ourselves to the nearby gardens of the Palais-Royal. Clouds still loured ominously, as if about to discharge a weight of water, but we had both come armed with umbrellas. Moreover, if the heavens were to open, we could always retreat back into the shelter of the gallery or to some café, or even take a cab back to the hotel, though this final option was, I think, the least attractive to both of us. There was no great enjoyment to be had in staring at the four walls of our little rooms. For now, anyway, it was pleasant enough to sit ourselves on two of the seats around the basin of a fine fountain that was sending white plumes high into the air. The ensuing spray lessened the oppressive atmosphere around us, and my headache at last started to lift, although my limbs still felt heavy. I hoped I was not about to fall ill.

We could not stay sitting there forever, however – I was conscious that I wasn't a congenial companion, replying in monosyllables to Nelly's chat – so, after taking a turn around the gardens, examining the statuary, the rose-filled flowerbeds and the elegant architecture of the palace itself, we found a café facing the Theatre of French Comedy. Despite my longing for a cooked English breakfast earlier, I found I had little appetite now and ordered a plain omelette. Nelly on the other hand feasted quite lavishly for her, on a plate of chops and boiled potatoes. I wondered somewhat at that and remarked on it.

She regarded me as if making up her mind about something. "Well, you know, Martha," she said at length, "how worried I have been about Ralph."

I nodded. How could I not be?

"Well," she gave a beaming smile. "Last eve he actually expressed the desire to come back to England."

"Indeed?" I confess I was most astonished.

"Yes. He has returned to his studio to sort things out. He can't just leave his art behind, you know. He must make arrangements."

I found this speech vague as to particulars, but agreed with her that it was very good news. But why did she not tell me about it at once?

Nelly gave a little smile. "You know, I am somewhat superstitious, Martha. I rather feared that if I said anything, it would stop it happening." She laughed at herself. "However, I cannot keep silent any longer."

So I was wrong in thinking her as low as I was that morning, my famed powers of observation having let me down for once. Nelly had merely been keeping quiet to stop herself bursting out with her secret.

"The last events have persuaded him that life here is too difficult, too fraught with danger," she went on. "It is not amusing, you know, to be attacked in the streets all the time, let alone be carried off to police stations."

Not to mention being challenged to duels, I thought.

It was therefore in quite a merry mood, at least on Nelly's part, that we made our way back to the hotel.

Alas, joy was to be short-lived, for as soon as we entered the premises, Madame Albert rushed out with horrible news. The police had come looking for Ralph. He was to be arrested. Nelly sank to the floor in a swoon, and immediately I extracted from my reticule the little bottle of sal volatile that I always carry with me for such an occurrence (though on the occasion I myself had fainted in M. Cochot's office, I had, I confess, forgotten all about it). Now I uncorked the bottle and applied it to Nelly's nose, so that she might inhale the salts. It had the desired effect, for she soon came to herself again.

I helped her to her feet.

"How can they arrest him, Martha? How can they think he had anything to do with it?"

"I don't know," I said.

She grabbed my hand. "We must warn him. He must flee."

"Nelly," I said. "That is the very worst thing he could do. It would make him look guilty. No, he must give himself up and we must get him a good lawyer."

As it turned out, if Ralph had even considered flight, it was out of his hands, for the police had already tracked him to his studio. He was being held in custody. This we learned soon enough from a note he had been permitted to send to us.

Madame Albert was all concern. As a mother herself, she said, she was able to feel for Nelly. How distressed she would be if the police ever came for her darling Philippe! Something which, as I reckoned privately, might soon happen unless he changed his associates. Of course, I said nothing of this, just asked if she knew of a good lawyer.

"How ever would I know such a thing, Madame Martha?" she said, a little affronted. "We here have always been a law-abiding family."

Again I did not betray any opposing awareness.

"Dr. Lepine can no doubt advise you," she went on. "He will surely call around later as he usually does, since he seems to like you so much."

She smiled archly. Surely she could not think there was anything between the doctor and myself, he being some twenty years my junior, and a married man to boot. On the other hand, as I was coming to learn, they saw things differently in France.

"If he should arrive," I told Madame Albert, ignoring her insinuations, "perhaps you could explain the matter, as much as we understand it ourselves, and ask about a lawyer. Meanwhile," I turned to Nelly, "we should go to the Prefecture and find out what exactly is going on. It is bound to be some absurd misunderstanding."

I wish I felt as confident of this as I sounded.

"Oh, yes. At once," she replied.

M. Blanchard, installed at his usual desk, shewed himself less than obliging. No sign now of the gallant cavalier who had danced with me at Le Chien Jaune. No, he could tell us nothing, he said, and we would not be permitted, just now, to see Ralph.

"Where is he? Is he here?"

The policeman pressed his lips together.

"I cannot say."

"I should like to see M. Cochot," I said.

"That is not possible."

"Why not? Can you not just ask him?"

He shook his head.

"I am sure he would admit Sherlock Holmes." I said this last in some desperation.

He looked at me coldly. "You keep mentioning that gentleman's name when you want something, Madame. I have to say, I am not convinced that you know him at all."

"What! He lives in my house!"

He shrugged. "So you say. But have you proof?"

"Proof?" I was astonished.

"You claim to be his associate, yet you have no papers establishing this." He leaned forward on his desk and stabbed his finger down on a form in front of him. "In France, Madame, we expect to see papers."

"Oh, Good Lord," I said. "If that is the case, I will send him a wire forthwith, to ask him to reply and prove my credentials."

As the words left my mouth, I remembered that Mr. H., to my most recent knowledge, was not in Baker Street, but somewhere unknown in the west of England. Still, in the face of my confident tones, M. Blanchard looked a little deflated, a little less pompous.

"Well," he said. "I suppose that we shall have to wait and see."

I informed Nelly that there was no hope of visiting Ralph or anyone else at the Prefecture just then.

"So what do we do now?" she asked.

232

"First I will send a wire to Mr. H.," I replied, "in the hope that he is returned. And I have a good idea where we should go next."

Thereupon we swept out of the Prefecture, I hope with some dignity, though inwardly I cursed M. Blanchard and the petty bureaucracy he represented.

The entrance to the catacombs was at a place called the Gate of Hell, not a very auspicious name, it must be said. Moreover, our long journey thither proved to be in vain, for the place was closed, a notice on a heavily barred door informing us that visits were only permitted once a week on a Friday. This being a Tuesday, we should have to return in three days if we wished to see inside.

While I was somewhat curious to view the place, I told a dismayed Nelly that after all a visit might not be necessary.

"You can see how securely it is locked up. That is surely a fact in our favour. How could Ralph have managed to bring Sylvie here to kill her? She was still alive on Friday night, when we saw her at Le Chien Jaune. Unless he had a key, which is so unlikely as to be almost impossible, he could not have attained entrance to commit her murder."

And why, indeed, would he have gone to so much trouble? I simply could not see him committing a cold-blooded murder, which the poor girl's death surely must have been. He might, I supposed, have strangled her in a fit of madness, though even that was surely out of character. But not here, not like that, deliberately bringing acid to fling in her face. No, Ralph would never do such a thing.

Nelly was much cheered by the intelligence regarding the locked door.

"You are right," she said. "He could not have done it. The police will soon realise it, too, and will release him."

I was not so sure, suspecting that the police, in their haste to find someone guilty, would have a quick answer to our objections. However, I did not intend to convey my doubts to my sister.

We made our way to a nearby café in order to rest our feet, have some refreshment, and decide what to do next. The waitress who served us – plump, high-coloured and no longer in her first nor even second youth – proved to be a nosy, chatty sort of woman. Having placed the lemon tea and orange with seltzer water on the table, she asked us directly, arms akimbo, where we were from and, when enlightened, how we liked Paris. I of course told her we loved it, so beautiful – the expected reply, for she nodded and smiled.

"I suppose," said she, "that you were hoping to visit the catacombs."

I replied how disappointed we were that they were closed.

"No, they only open on Fridays. If you wish to see them, you'll have to come back then."

"Yes, we might do that."

"Well, if so, make sure to arrive early. There's bound to be a rush."

"It's a popular place, then, is it?"

"It is now."

She proceeded to inform me, eyes aglow, that a murdered body (her phrase) had been found there just a few days ago.

I expressed shock at the news.

"Yes, a beautiful young girl." She shook her head, and added with some satisfaction. "Horribly mutilated, she was… So, you see, the usual crowd of gawkers will be bound to turn up. That's why you'd better be early."

"Thank you for the hint," I said. "But I am a little confused. The door seems so securely locked. However did the murderer and victim get in there? Are there other entrances?"

"That's the only way in." She paused. "There's a way out, of course, around the corner. But that's well-bolted, too."

A locked room mystery, then, just as in Mr Poe's thrilling story, *The Murder in the Rue Morgue*.

"Well," she went on, "I say two ways in and out, but that's for where all the bones are. What the visitors come to see. But actually, Madame, those tunnels go on for kilometre after kilometre under Paris, and they say there are many other secret entrances. But don't ask *me* where to find them." She crossed her arms over her pigeon chest, "because *I* don't know."

Oh dear, I thought. Many entrances. That makes it all so much more complicated.

"I wonder," I said. "Do you happen to know where the girl's body was found?" In case she wondered at my curiosity, I added with the smile of the avid, "It's so very shocking."

"It is, Madame. The poor creature. However, I happen to know she was found in the ossuary. That's where the bones are."

"Ah."

"See, nowadays," she continued, "they only allow folk to go one way round. In through one door and out the other. In the past people went wandering willy-nilly through the tunnels, getting lost, some of them." She shivered. "Imagine getting stuck down there with all the dead people."

I agreed that it would be ghastly.

"Some have even been known to take a skull home. Imagine that, Madame. Who ever would want someone's skull as a souvenir? I certainly wouldn't."

I agreed, saying such remains should be left in hallowed grounds.

She nodded, but what she told me next undermined my argument regarding the impossibility of Ralph's guilt.

"Of course," she said with a shiver, "there's folk who enjoy that sort of thing… Sometimes they even have parties down there, you know."

"Parties? In the catacombs. Is that allowed?"

She laughed heartily, her ample flesh all a-quiver.

"Bless you, Madame. Of course it's not allowed. But some people… some people manage it anyway." She leaned down and whispered in my ear. "I'm not saying, Madame, that they don't come by the keys in the correct way. Maybe and they do. All I know is that one of the guards, whose name shall never pass my lips, suddenly started spending money like nobody's business. Word was that he had sold duplicates of the keys to various people and received even more of a pay-off for turning a blind eye to the goings-on." She gazed at me with the satisfaction of the impregnably virtuous. "Wild parties, Madame." She pursed her lips and nodded. "Orgies, Madame. I reckon that's how that young one got herself killed. Taking part in a…"

Just then a stern male voice called out, "Berenice!" summoning her back to the bar. She shrugged and, winking knowingly at me, returned to her duties.

"What was all that about?" Nelly asked, huffed at being left out.

"Foolish stuff," I replied. "The woman is just a silly gossip." Though I couldn't help but wonder if there were any truth in what she had said.

Parties in the catacombs! That put a whole new perspective on the matter. What if Ralph..? But I could not believe it.

Just as we were finishing our drinks, the loquacious Berenice approached us again.

"As you plan to visit the catacombs next Friday, Madame, give me your name and I'll have a word with my friend, Denis. He's one of the guards. Not *that* one… He's straight, Denis is. He'll let you in, even if there's a rush."

"That's most kind of you," I said, and supplied the necessary information. I also left the woman a sizeable tip, which was, I suppose, the motive behind her apparent goodwill.

Upon quitting the café, we went in search of the other official means of egress to the tunnels. Finding it easily enough, I noted with some satisfaction that, as Berenice had reported, the door there was as securely fastened as the first. No easy way in there, at least. Having established this, we took a cab back to the hotel.

Perhaps it was too early to hope for a reply from Baker Street. However, I was disappointed to find no message awaiting me, either from Mr. H. (having sent a telegram to him immediately on quitting the Prefecture), or from Dr. Lepine, who had, as

Madame Albert informed me with regretful sympathy, yet to put in an appearance that afternoon.

Chapter Nineteen – A Visit to a Lawyer

So there was I after all, staring at the four walls of my hotel bedroom, feeling helpless and frustrated, no nearer finding out what had happened to Poppy, and no nearer proving Ralph innocent either. Moreover, my headache had returned with a vengeance. I sprinkled some of the lavender essence on my pillow, lay myself down and closed my eyes.

I do not think I slept, yet an hour passed unnoticed before I heard a light tapping on the door. I sat up, and made sure my hair was neat enough before bidding the unknown visitor to enter. It was not, as I had hoped, Dr. Lepine. Just Madame Albert, bearing a telegram addressed to me. At least Mr. H. had replied promptly.

Thanking her, I could not but notice that the good woman yet lingered. I asked if she wanted anything.

"I have been thinking, Madame. About the lawyer, you know."

"Yes?"

"Well, I mentioned it to Philippe and he suggested Maître Loiseau. I had forgotten all about him, but he has successfully defended some people that we know."

"That's very helpful. Thank you, Madame. Where can I reach this person?"

"I have written down his address. It is not far…"

She seemed a little uneasy, however.

"Is there anything wrong?" I asked.

"Not at all, Madame. I am glad to be of help."

She left me then and I tore open the telegram. Alas, it was not from Mr. H. at all, but from Clara, to tell me that my lodger had not yet returned. A step forward, a step back. At least I could approach this Maître Loiseau. Gathering myself together, I crossed to Nelly's room and told her the news. With haste and after getting further directions from Madame Albert regarding the whereabouts of the office, we were soon making our way to the narrow street where it was situated, only to find the lawyer absent. Yet another setback. However, we were politely received by his clerk, an aged, dusty individual, bent near double from a lifetime hunched over large tomes, someone who might, I mused, have stepped from the pages of a novel by Mr Dickens, or perhaps more fittingly from something by M. Balzac or M. Hugo – though I confess that, having read none of the works of those eminent gentlemen, I could not say if they feature personages of this ilk. This old clerk assured us respectfully, on hearing our business, that Maître Loiseau would be able to see us at eight of the following morning, before court was in session. We had to be satisfied with that.

Neither Nelly nor myself having much of an appetite, nor indeed much energy, we bought some rolls and ham and cheese from a grocery on the way back, and picnicked in my room, which according to Nelly, was the more comfortable (to my mind, they were identical). I had recently purchased a pack of cards – the occasional game of solitaire, I find, eases the mind, by distracting from other problems – and we played cribbage for an hour to pass the time before bed. Our hearts were not much in the game, however. I am sure Nelly's thoughts, like mine, were all on Ralph.

I slept badly, afraid perhaps of not waking in time for our appointment with the lawyer. Nelly, I think, was the same, for she came to my room at seven to make sure I was up. We decided not to break our fast until after our consultation with Maître Loiseau.

The little man could almost have been the twin brother of Père Perrot, round and jolly, with a splendid moustache that made up for the hairlessness of his pate. I almost expected him to start rubbing his hands together, saying "Bon, bon, bon." Nothing of the sort, however. He listened with solemn attention while I laid out the charges, as much as I knew them, against poor Ralph, thereafter adding my own feeble arguments as to why he could not have murdered the girl.

"Dear Madame," he said, interrupting me. "Forgive me, but I am not concerned as to whether or not the young man is guilty. Only whether I can persuade the judge that he is not."

I suppose that is the practice of defence lawyers in general. Yet, expressing it baldly like that, the Maître came across as somewhat unprincipled. Without any other options, however, he was all we had, and we soon found ourselves discussing terms. To me they seemed steep, though Nelly was not inclined to argue. She was simply relieved to have found someone to take on the case, Maître Loiseau informing us that he would leave no stone unturned, and that he would visit Ralph as soon as the morning's court adjourned.

"In which commissariat," he asked, "is the young man being held?"

"I don't understand."

"At which police station?"

"Is he not at the Prefecture?"

"No, no. That isn't possible." He observed my downcast expression. "He is in a holding cell somewhere… Dear me, dear me." He frowned, and drummed his fingers on his desk in irritation. "They should have told you where. His next-of-kin has a right to know. But fear not, Madame. If he was arrested in Montmartre, I think I know where he will be. We will soon track him down."

Curses upon M. Hubert Blanchard. At the time I had suspected that the petty official's refusal to pass information to us was based on his own sense of self-importance mixed, for some inexplicable reason, with spite. Now to think of Ralph in some anonymous prison cell, maybe crammed in with violent miscreants, was quite horrible. I decided not to break that particular piece of bad news to Nelly, just yet. She was upset enough.

Satisfied, as far as we could be under trying circumstances, with what had been arranged, we quitted the lawyer's office, intending to go somewhere nearby for breakfast. I was astonished, therefore, to see, waiting outside, none other than Dr. Lepine. He ran towards us.

"Forgive me, Mesdames," he said, "but Madame Albert told me where you would be."

"You have news of Poppy? Garance?"

"Not exactly. But I have news."

242

On hearing that we had not yet breakfasted, he led us to a nearby café. He inquired politely after Ralph and said that Loiseau was known to be a formidable lawyer, who was sure to present a strong case.

"But what have you to tell me?" I asked.

"Puzzling intelligence, indeed... It concerns Valentin le Désossé. The man has not been seen since the night he left Le Chien Jaune with Garance."

I started in surprise.

"He was supposed to perform at the Moulin Rouge the following evening, but did not appear. At first no one thought too much about it: It has happened before, apparently, for one night, or even two in a row. But he always turns up again in due course. Now, however, he is not to be found at his lodgings, not in his usual haunts. La Goulue is raging."

I stared at him. "What can it mean?"

"I don't know. That Garance and he are together perhaps, or that something has happened to the two of them. Who can say?"

He looked distraught.

"What do we know about this Valentin?"

"Not very much. He is something of a mystery man." He leaned forward. "Madame Martha, I propose to seek out La Goulue later – it is far too early for her to be up and about just now. But I want to find out if there is anything more she can tell me."

"An excellent idea."

"I was wondering," he went on, somewhat diffidently, "if you would like to accompany me, since you take such a special interest in Garance." I started to nod. "I should warn you," he

243

went on. "La Goulue does not frequent reputable establishments."

"I should like to come, even so," I said. "I suppose you can chaperon me."

He smiled a little at that. "Of course, Madame Martha. I should be honoured."

Poor Nelly was sitting quietly through all this, as usual in ignorance of our conversation. When I told her that it concerned Poppy, and what I intended to do later, she sniffed in annoyance. Presumably she thought that I should stay by her side and wait for news of Ralph. Well, perhaps I should, and yet I cannot stand inactivity.

"I will only be gone for an hour," I told her.

She sniffed again. "You have said that before. A number of times."

I had the grace to blush at that.

Dr Lepine suggested that he should call for me at five o'clock, when we should be sure to find the Queen of Montmartre holding court in one or other of her usual haunts. I agreed to that and for the time being we went our separate ways.

For now there was nothing to do but to return to the hotel and await news from Maître Loiseau. Nelly installed herself in my room for yet another game of cribbage but nearly drove me to distraction betimes with her constant chant of wonder that we had not yet heard from the lawyer.

"And you know, Martha, if he comes when you are out, I shall not know what he says, for I do not think he speaks any English. Do you really have to go out this evening? Cannot it wait?"

I mumbled a cautious reply but listened out eagerly myself for the arrival of the lawyer, since I did not wish to have to choose between him and Dr. Lepine. Luckily, that particular dilemma was avoided since the Maître arrived in the middle of the afternoon. It not being pleasant to talk business in a bedroom, we were relieved when Madame Albert offered her parlour for our discussion.

The lawyer looked cheerful enough, but I rather think he had the sort of face that always looked that way. Except perhaps when fighting a case in court.

"I have spoken to the young gentleman. He is being held…" and he wrote down the name of the police station for us.

"How is he?" Nelly asked. It turned out that the lawyer in fact understood some English, although he spoke it poorly and with a pronounced French accent. At least I didn't have to work quite so hard at translating.

"Under the circumstances," he replied, "M. Ralph is in fair spirits." I felt he was tempering his response to an anxious mother. "It is a pity he is not more forthcoming," he continued in French.

"In what way?" I asked.

"The police have established that the young woman was murdered sometime during the night of…" He named the date. It was indeed on the night following the opening of Le Chien Jaune, "Unfortunately M. Ralph refuses to say where he was during the hours in question, or where he received those injuries. I should ask you ladies to prevail upon him to tell all. It will go better for him in the end. Unless, of course," he laughed, "it turns out he was busy murdering the young woman."

I didn't translate his joke: Nelly wouldn't see the funny side of it. Instead, I asked him if prison visits were permitted.

"Indeed, they are. Whoever told you the contrary was either misinformed or making mischief. I will write down the hours." The which he proceeded to do, appending a list of items which Ralph had requested brought in.

I conveyed the same to Nelly. She was comforted. Something to do.

"Furthermore," Maître Loiseau went on. "I will apply for bail, although I have to tell you that it is unlikely to be granted, given the heinous nature of the crime. Still, we can but try."

I then asked was not the fact that Sylvie was found in the catacombs powerful proof that Ralph could not have done the deed. The lawyer shrugged. He too, it seemed, was well aware of the sale of keys and the illegal activities that took place in those grisly surroundings.

"At the moment we cannot prove decisively that the young man was not there. Again I would urge you to get him to tell you where he was and what he was doing. You see, Madame, M. Ralph does not seem quite to realise the seriousness of the case. You must make clear to him that unless he tells all, he will certainly face the guillotine."

Thank God, Nelly did not pick up on the word. I assured Maître Loiseau that we would do our very best to make Ralph see sense and tell the truth. How bad could it be, compared to execution?

We thanked him for his efforts so far. As Nelly and I left the parlour, Philippe Albert emerged from the kitchen and greeted the lawyer, the two men embracing in the way of continentals. Evidently they were close, which I found most intriguing.

Back in her room, Nelly, not having understood the dire warnings of the lawyer, was suddenly all optimism.

"He will get him released, I know it," she said, beaming with happiness.

"Let us hope so," I said. "Meanwhile we can visit him tomorrow... But I must get myself ready to go out. You will be all right?"

"Oh yes, Martha. I will be just fine. Now."

Chapter Twenty –Valentin le Désossé

Dr. Lepine was not in error when he said that La Goulue favoured disreputable establishments. We had to visit several sleazy bars before tracking her down at last to a place called Le Souris sans Queue, The Mouse without a Tail, the poor creature perhaps the blind victim of the farmer's wife from the nursery rhyme.

Alone I should certainly never have ventured into such a place. It was poorly lit, with a low ceiling, and not, I think, at all clean, for the floor was sticky beneath my feet. I rather feared that the verminous connection here was not confined to the name. A sickly sweetness lurked unpleasantly beneath the odour of cheap tobacco, while the patrons were decidedly shady, regarding us through the murk with appraising and hostile stares. I clutched my reticule more firmly to my person.

The stout dancer we sought was seated at a table with a tumbler of wine and a half-full bottle of the same beverage in front of her. She looked dishevelled, her face puffy, her eyes bloodshot. Whether this was from emotion at the disappearance of her partner or just a symptom of a general debauchery, I of course could not say. Around her sat a crowd of people, some of whom I recognised, including the strange, dwarfish little man that Dr. Lepine had identified as an important artist. Indeed, a notebook was open in front of him, and between taking frequent sips of his drink, he looked to be working at some sketch or other.

"Hey, Maurice!" called La Goulue, recognising my companion. "Who's that with you? Your old mother?"

Everyone laughed, though I could not imagine what they found so funny.

"Or is it your new sweetheart, now that Gigi has skipped out?"

More raucous laughter.

"Skipped out, taking my Jules with her." She smashed a fat fist on the table, and muttered a word I took to be a profanity.

"Your Jules?" Dr. Lepine asked, puzzled.

Did she mean Bourdain? Had he too disappeared? Surely not.

"That's Désossé's real name, idiot. Jules Etienne Edmé Renaudin, if you please. Not Valentin. That's just his stage name. Like mine is La Goulue! You think I was christened that?" She laughed harshly and nudged the raw-boned woman sitting beside her. "Like she is Grille d'Egout. Ha!"

"You reckon that's what has happened then? That Garance and Valentin have gone away together?"

"Do the sums, doctor. Two minus two makes nothing." She clicked her fingers in the air. "Gone, Pffft." She looked around the table. "So now what am I to do? He's gone and left me." She gulped down the contents of her glass and poured herself another. "Gone."

The woman beside her, with the extraordinarily unpleasant name that translates, unless I am much mistaken, as Sewer Cover, put an emaciated arm around her friend and drew her close, kissing her cheek.

"You don't need him, Louise," she said. "You are a great star. The Queen of Montmartre."

Cries of agreement mixed with calls for more wine.

La Goulue looked up at us, malice in her eyes.

"So what? Are you going to stand there staring forever, Maurice? Either sit down or shove off. You and your fancy-woman."

To my surprise, since it seemed that La Goulue knew no more of the disappearances than we did, Dr. Lepine squeezed himself into a space at the table, and I therefore felt constrained to do likewise. So much for him being my chaperone for the evening.

The little artist made room for me. The very first time I saw him I had taken him for a gentleman, and such he proved to be now, even if he was a gentleman who had a little too much to drink, his breath heavy with wine. He spoke to me in low and beautiful tones, and when he found that I lived in London, clapped his hands in delight and said that it was one of his favourite places in the world.

"But you live in Paris, monsieur. What can be more beautiful than this?"

Though our present surroundings rather gave the lie to my remark.

He informed me that he had been in London very recently, where he had met with poor Mr. Oscar Wilde, out on bail pending the trial which was soon to see the writer incarcerated in jail.

"You know Mr. Wilde!" I exclaimed. "How wonderful! I am a great admirer of his work, if not," I felt constrained to add, "of his way of life."

The little man looked at me quizzically, and shook his head.

"You English, always vaunting your supposed superior morality. Forgive me, Madame, it is nothing but hypocrisy. I have seen what goes on beneath the strait-laces of your oh so tight bodices."

I was deeply shocked, even making allowances for different attitudes. He must have realised he had stepped beyond the bounds of propriety, for he patted my hand.

"My regrets, Madame. I did not mean to cast aspersions on your good self. It is just that the treatment of such a great man makes me angry. It would not happen in France. We are more open here, more tolerant."

I accepted his apology and the subject shifted to less contentious topics. I asked if he knew Valentin well and if so, what he thought might have happened to the man. In reply, he shewed me some of the sketches he had made of the two dancers. I was most impressed. Although the pictures verged on caricature, they undoubtedly captured the feverish energy of the performance.

"I cannot tell you what has happened to him, Madame. All I know is that he is a dilettante. Not a dancer by profession, and not because he needs the money. Indeed, they say he refuses to be paid. He does it simply because he loves it."

"How very unusual!"

"Yes, isn't it? Most of the people here live from hand to mouth." He smiled. I was getting used to his appearance, but to find those big wet red lips of his so close to my face was somewhat disconcerting. "I myself am lucky to have a private income."

I remembered then that Dr. Lepine had told me that the little man was – unlikely as it seemed – of the nobility, a count of somewhere or other, like Etienne.

"So how does Valentin live? Does he too have a private income?"

"I don't think so. They say he comes of a good enough family from the provinces, his father a solicitor. But, as far as I know, he works by day in a wine merchant's establishment."

He raised his glass, obliging me to do likewise, and we clinked and drank.

"He works by day and spends the night dancing!" I said, after sipping at the rather sour beverage. "When ever does he sleep?"

The little artist downed the remainder of his drink and refilled his glass, topping mine up before I could stop him. "When do any of us sleep, Madame?" He chuckled. "There will be time enough for that when we are dead."

Ignoring the grim remark, I asked if the wine merchant had been visited to see if Valentin had turned up to work.

He shrugged, then called across to La Goulue, repeating the question.

"What do you think, idiot!" she replied frowning. "Of course, we have. The damned rat's not been there for days."

I then asked M. Henri – for that was what the little man insisted I should call him – if he knew of Garance Germaine.

"The beauty who shouted at Bourdain the other night? The displaced favourite? Yes, I know her, though I have never used her as a model. She is rather too perfect a specimen for me, Madame." He laughed.

"I am very anxious to find her," I said. "Or at least to know that she is safe. She and Valentin left Le Chien Jaune together. Could she be with him still?"

"Madame, I am very wise, but I don't know everything… I can tell you that Valentin is not a man to chase young girls, but, who knows, perhaps Cupid's arrow has at last pierced even his cold heart. Or perhaps he simply decided to help a damsel in distress. Or perhaps they have nothing to do with each other and their simultaneous disappearances are a simple coincidence."

I wasn't making much progress, and hoped that Dr. Lepine was doing better. I took another sip of wine. It seemed to taste less unpleasant now and, as time went by, I found that the atmosphere in the café, while certainly not to my taste, was become less obnoxious than at the start, and not unconnected, I felt, to the company I was in. I had quite warmed to the ugly little artist. What he made of me – a middle-aged matron – I had no idea, though soon he started asking me about myself.

I told him that I had the honour to be landlady to England's greatest detective, naming Mr. H. To my considerable surprise, M. Henri confessed that he had never heard of him. When I further expounded on my lodger's many achievements, he just shook his head.

"Alas, Madame Martha, his name is not familiar to me. Nevertheless, he sounds like a most interesting man. I should dearly like to make his acquaintance if ever I return to London or if he should chance to come here."

"He might, you know. Because he has assisted the French police on previous occasions."

Henri burst out laughing. "In that case, perhaps I should stay well away from him. We and the flics," he swept his arm around the company, "are not always on the best of terms."

"I know what you mean," I said. "The French police don't impress me at all." Perhaps it was the wine I had drunk, or the kindness of the gentleman, but I proceeded to tell him of Ralph's plight. He nodded sagely.

"To kill someone in the overwhelming throes of passion," he said, "is understandable, even forgivable. We French understand that well, and do not treat it so very seriously. However, to have premeditated such a bizarre murder, well, that speaks of a different mentality altogether. An ugly, vengeful act. Your nephew has not shewn signs of brain disturbance before, has he?"

"No," I said, perhaps a little too quickly. "Even if he did, I do not see how he could have gained entrance to the catacombs by night, when they are securely locked."

"Hmm," M. Henri replied. "As to that…"

"I know certain people have keys," I said, "and that things… parties go on there. But Ralph! M. Henri. He is an innocent, a foolish boy. He could not plan such a horrific deed, I am quite sure of it."

I found that tears were welling up in my eyes, the which was most unlike me. I am usually well able to keep my emotions under check.

"Forgive me," I said. "So many terrible things have happened at once."

The artist patted my hand again, and was so sympathetic that I might even have gone so far as to spill out my involvement with the anarchist plotters – dangerous though that indiscretion would have been – but just in time Dr. Lepine pressed my arm, suggesting we leave.

"Take courage, Madame," my new friend told me. "I am sure all will be well with your nephew. Especially since he has the support of such a fine person as yourself."

"What a nice man he is," I said to Dr. Lepine as we left.

"Hmm, yes, well of course he is from a noble family and is a wonderful artist. On the other hand, he lives in a brothel."

I was shocked and rose to defend my new acquaintance.

"If that is a joke, Doctor, I consider it in very poor taste. M. Henri is most polite and respectable. Surely he would not choose to live in such a place."

"I should not dream of joking about it, Madame Martha. He lives there, or at least he used to, and paints the unfortunate women as they are, without attempting to make them look pretty."

"Goodness!" Looking at the doctor's earnest face, I could not think that he was lying. Mistaken, perhaps. Then I recalled the little man remarking that Poppy was too perfect for him. Could it really be that he dwelt with fallen women, that he was privy to the degrading activities that happened in such places? I shuddered. It was all too much to take in. Perhaps, too, Nelly was right and I should leave Paris as soon as possible, before I became corrupted by its ways, so very different from what I was used to. If travel, as they said, opens the mind to new experiences, the danger was that staying on might open mine a little too much.

Once outside, in the fresher air – though even here it was flavoured with smoke and the grease of cheap restaurants – I asked Dr. Lepine if he believed La Goulue, that Poppy and Valentin had gone away together. "Did they even know each other?"

He shook his head. "As far as I know, only in the way everyone on the Butte knows everyone else. But I suppose it is possible." He paused and looked at me sadly. "I just want to be sure that she is well and happy."

As did I. But I wondered would we ever discover that for sure?

Chapter Twenty-One: Imprisoned

The next morning – I with a somewhat spinning head, and Nelly with her lips pinched tight in disapproval – we took a cab to the police station where Ralph was being held, having first purchased the requested items from his list, which included clean linen, cigarettes and wine. Nelly added bread, cheese and a meat pie to the store, saying she could not imagine the poor boy was being fed properly. When we arrived, the basket was gone through item by item by M. Blanchard's officious and unsmiling twin brother before we were permitted to see Ralph.

He looked miserable, the bruises on his face having turned a sulphurous shade of yellow, his hair and scrubby gingery beard scruffier than ever his clothes creased and crumpled as if he had slept in them, the which he most certainly had.

If he were pleased to see us, he hid it well, except for falling greedily on to the cigarettes and wine.

"Please eat something, Ralph," Nelly pleaded.

"I'm not hungry, mother. They feed us so splendidly here, do you see, sending down to fine restaurants for our meals."

"Really? Thank God for that!"

He looked at her derisively. "As if they would. No, it's thin gruel and yesterday's stale rolls for us. But I don't care, I have quite lost my appetite."

"Well," she said timidly, "maybe you'll fancy something later. You need to keep up your strength."

She urged him again to say where he had been on the night in question, but he shook his head stubbornly.

"Nothing to do with anything. I was attacked. I told you before."

"Unless you can prove it, you know what that will make them think," I said. "That you have something to hide, possibly even the murder of poor Sylvie."

"Well, I didn't kill her," he replied.

"Of course, you didn't," Nelly said. "The poor boy is the victim here. How can you suggest such a thing, Martha?"

"I am not suggesting it. I don't think Ralph capable of it, either. But that's because we know what he is like. The police don't know him from Adam. They simply operate on facts." I paused, then continued. "What I don't understand, Ralph, is why it's you they have arrested rather than Etienne, who would seem to have a much stronger motive."

"I thought it must be Etienne, too. That's why I told them about him. But, you see, Etienne claims to have been out of the city, visiting his parents at their chateau… Probably touching them for money as usual." He sniffed, as if he himself would be incapable of such behaviour. "Anyway, his father confirmed he was with them. And of course, the flics will believe the Comte de Vaude before they believe me."

As he was then, dirty and dishevelled, cigarette stub in hand, drinking wine straight from the bottle, he looked like a caricature of a hardened criminal. I might not have believed his protests either. The whole business, indeed, would have been laughable

258

were it not so serious, and yet the boy did not seem to realise this: ever the sulky spoilt child not getting his way. However, I reckoned he might talk more frankly to me if his mother were absent, and tried to scheme how to get rid of her for a short while. Suddenly I called to mind the trick Mrs. Melrose and I had tried in Ireland, during my adventure there. It might work here too.

"Nelly," I said, feigning a sudden weakness, rolling my eyes and waving a hand limply in front of my face. "I beg of you, go and ask the officer on the desk for a glass of water. It's so hot in here, I think I am going to faint. After last night, you know."

"I knew it," she said severely. "Gadding about like that at your age. Coming back at all hours. Drinking…"

"Please, Nelly…" I slumped down in my seat.

She sniffed, collected her skirts in a self-righteous way and swept out.

"Aunt Martha!" Ralph started, shocked out of his self-centredness, and then astonished at the rapidity of my recovery. I sat up straight.

"No time to explain. Young man, if you don't want your mother to know where you were that night, please at least tell me. Your very life may depend upon it."

"My life? Aunt!.. Really…"

"I am not joking, Ralph. I have been told it will be the guillotine, for you, if you cannot prove you are innocent."

He laughed, though somewhat uncertainly. Then he deflated.

"I cannot. It is so… shameful…"

"It will be more of a shame if they cut off your head."

He reached for his neck. At last, the true nature of his predicament seemed to become clear to him, and he broke down, sobbing.

"It wasn't my fault," he said. "It was the other fellows. They... they wanted to go to this house."

"A house?"

"We had all been drinking. Far too much, you know. I hardly knew what I was doing... It was all a blur..." Suddenly it all burst out of him. "The other fellows were laughing and joking. Good company, you know."

"Hmm." Bad company, I thought.

"So we went off to this house... I promise I have never visited a place like that before, aunt."

"Go on." I tried not to sound judgemental, though I felt I knew what was coming.

"You see, there were all these women, sitting around...undressed... Dogs, the lot of them."

I tried not to wince.

"One of them... well, you know, I didn't want to, Aunt Martha, but she dragged me off to this room." He couldn't catch my eye.

"A bedroom?"

He nodded.

"And then, well, she was so ugly, so old, you know. I really didn't want to but... after... I didn't have enough to pay her what she asked. Anyway, I told her she wasn't worth a sou and then she got really angry and called this man. A great hulk of a man, aunt. And he beat me up and took all my money. That's the truth... Please believe me." He sank back.

I looked at the wretched youth. Yes, I believed him at last.

"Aunt Martha," he went on. "Please don't tell mummy. It would kill her."

"I don't think your mother is quite as fragile as all that, Ralph. However, I agree. Unless it becomes absolutely necessary, we won't say anything to her about the sorry affair."

"You hate me, don't you, aunt?"

Of course, he wanted me to deny it, so I did.

"I just think you have been a very foolish young man. But Ralph, you must promise me you will tell Maître Loiseau what you have told me. As soon as possible. If you can recall the house in question, so much the better."

He shook his head. "I have no idea where it is… Oh, aunt, what will I do?"

"I expect at least one of the young men you were with will know the place. But promise me," I repeated, "that you will tell Maître Loiseau everything the next time he comes to visit."

"Cannot you tell him? Please, aunt. I am so ashamed."

"No, Ralph, you are not a child anymore." Though I rather considered that he was. "You must tell him yourself… I will engage to send him to you at his earliest convenience."

At that moment, Nelly re-entered and I did my best to look in dire need of the water she brought with her. Soon professing myself much recovered, we took our leave, though not without her giving me a sharp glance. I suspected that my ruse to get rid of her had not quite been swallowed whole. Still, she forbore to ask what we had spoken of while she was away, and so I did not have to dissemble.

"I suppose," said she as we made our way back, "you will want to rest after your night out."

Really, I had not stayed so very late, for her to chide me thus.

"Actually," I said. "I should like above all things some fresh air."

The day was become sultry again, and the very last thing I wanted to do was to shut myself away in my room.

"Well then, you can traipse about without me, Martha, as anyway you are wont to do. I am utterly fatigued and heart-broken with this business."

My poor sister. If she but knew all!

"I will return in time for luncheon," I said. "We can go back to that café you liked in Trinity Square."

"Luncheon!" she replied. "Only you could think of food at a time like this, Martha!"

I sighed. Clearly, just then I could do nothing right. However, I was glad that she was giving me some freedom. I should not have to think up an excuse to visit the lawyer.

The cab took us from the police station to the street of our hotel, but since I had no reason to enter, I bade Nelly farewell, and took myself off into the back streets on foot.

Maître Loiseau was out, in court again, but his aged clerk took my message, which I impressed on him was of the utmost urgency and regarded the alibi of his client. He assured me that the lawyer would attend the prisoner at his earliest opportunity, which I hoped meant that very day, for I did not like to think of my poor nephew locked up for any longer, if his innocence could be proved beyond a doubt.

Now, one of the delights for me of the French capital, as I am sure my readers will have gathered, is to sit myself down at an outdoor café and watch the world go by. I resolved to indulge myself once more, particularly because seeing ordinary people go about their business helped take my mind off the concerns weighing me down. I duly repaired to another such establishment, near the lawyer's office, with a view over a picturesque square. Ordering my usual lemon tea, I was surprised when the waiter asked if I wanted it hot or iced. I had not thought to drink cold tea but since the day was become oppressive again, I decided to taste it and I must say it proved most refreshing. Yet, the pleasure I usually enjoyed in such places was elusive here. Try as I might to distract myself by regarding the fashions and characters of the neighbourhood, my thoughts constantly harked back to Ralph, to Sylvie and of course to Poppy. To be honest, one reason I sat like that was the foolish notion that eventually Poppy would prove to be among the throng of passers-by. Of course, nothing of the sort occurred on that day, nor on any other day, so eventually and reluctantly I paid my bill and left.

It was still too early for luncheon and I decided to visit the little park in the square before me. To my amazement, given what I know of French history, it was named for the reviled King Louis XVI and his consort, Queen Marie Antoinette. From an explanatory notice posted at the entrance, I learned that this was originally a cemetery, the burial place of the 3,000 and more victims of the guillotine, including the above-mentioned royal couple. The comforting term "laid to rest" hardly applied here, however. It was simply a mass grave into which all were dumped willy-nilly. On the re-establishment of the monarchy, the new

King, as I now learned, ordered that Louis and Marie-Antoinette be moved to somewhere more fitting, though how anyone could distinguish a king's decapitated corpse from a commoner's under such circumstances, and after such a long time, was beyond me. I did not even like to think about it. Nevertheless, the deed was done – two bodies were moved in state to the Basilica of St Denis – and the place turned into the garden as I now found it, with a pretty chapel built to commemorate the royal victims and others. Only white flowers were planted – to mark, I supposed, the innocence of the dead – and on that day in high summer they were burgeoning gloriously around me as I sat in the shade of graceful willows, cypress and hornbeam. How difficult to imagine in such a peaceful spot the bloody past of the place. Inevitably again the dark thoughts I was trying to banish intruded themselves, and I could not help but wonder what would happen to poor Sylvie's remains. Would her body be placed in a similar pit, a pauper's grave? I should not like to think it. Sighing, I at last made my way back to the hotel to find Nelly.

Luncheon with my sister was, as it turned out, not to be. An impatient officer was awaiting me. I was to be summoned yet again to the Prefecture,

"He has been here for an age. Before even your sister returned," Madame Albert told me, rather annoyed. I sympathised: It cannot be pleasant for a hotel to receive constant visits from the police. "Your sister did not know where you were."

I hastened upstairs to tell Nelly the bad news regarding our meal, but she just lifted a wan face from her book and told me that she wasn't hungry anyway. She hoped, as she said rather pointedly, to see me later. When I urged her at least to go out and read in the fresh air, she just turned away.

M. Blanchard also barely looked at me, saying nothing, blank faced, merely opening the barrier to allow my entrance. The same young officer who had brought me thither, without, needless to say, divulging the reason for my summons, now led me along a corridor that was become disagreeably familiar to me, despite its splendours. He knocked on the Prefect's door before responding to a call of "Enter," opening the door and ushering me inside. M. Cochot was sitting as before, behind his imposing desk. He was frowning. Whatever it was had brought me here did not bode well.

He gestured for me to be seated but said not one word, merely continued staring at me. I refused to be intimidated. As far as I knew, I had done nothing wrong. Indeed, but for me M. Cochot might not now be sitting where he was, behind that great desk, looking cross. He might have been lying in the morgue alongside poor Sylvie.

"Your nephew," he said at last, "is in a lot of trouble, Madame."

"I know it," I replied. "Yet even now I think that his lawyer is gathering evidence that will prove him innocent."

"Is that so? Interesting." He made a steeple of his two hands and tapped the plump fingers of each together. "His lawyer… Yes, his lawyer… Might I ask, Madame, what caused you to select Maître Loiseau over all other lawyers in Paris?"

Aha! Here must be the nub of the matter. I remembered Madame Albert's seeming reluctance to provide the lawyer's name, and decided on the spur of the moment to leave out her involvement.

"It was completely by chance," I said. "My sister and I happened to be passing his offices while in search of someone to represent poor Ralph. The Maître was happy to take on the case."

"You came across him *by chance*?" he repeated. "Down a narrow and unprepossessing side street? Forgive me, but I find that somewhat hard to credit, Madame."

"Are you accusing me of lying, Monsieur?"

He shrugged. "Well, are you lying, Madame?"

"Why should I?"

"Why, indeed? That is what I ask myself." Now he was drumming his fingers on his desk. A distracting and irritating habit. "It is a puzzle."

He stared at me and I stared back. How had I ever thought him in any way like dear Henry? I was puzzled, too, all the same. Whatever was the problem here?

"Why should we not employ Maître Loiseau?"

He leaned forward, pressing a bulging bulk against the edge of the desk. "Are you telling me, Madame, that you are unaware Loiseau is among the foremost counsels for the defence of the anarchist scum who have been terrorising our city over the past years? Indeed, had Leon Garcia not… er… killed himself, I imagine your lawyer would have been only too happy to represent him."

I was dismayed at this intelligence, but attempted to stay calm. "I am most discomforted to hear it, Monsieur, but, I ask you, how ever could I have known such a thing? I have been in Paris for barely two weeks."

"But perhaps you have associates to advise you, Madame. People not unknown to the police, perhaps."

"M. Cochot," I replied. "Have you forgotten so soon that it was I who helped you foil the attempt by those self-same anarchists on your life? Why ever would I associate with them?"

"To inveigle yourself into my confidence. To make sure my guard was down the next time."

I am afraid I burst out laughing at that. "Good heavens, Monsieur. Whom do you take me for? A modern-day Lucrezia Borgia? Look at me. I am what you see, a middle-aged, middle-class English woman, here with her sister in hopes of bringing a nephew home to England. A widow and the mother of two daughters. A grandmother. I assure you, I do not consort with anarchists."

I saw him relax at that, and even smile a little.

"Well, well," he said. "Perhaps it is as you say and that you hired Maître Loiseau purely by chance, although… well, never mind." He leaned back in his chair which creaked somewhat alarmingly under his weight. "Perhaps you would care to share with me the information that will clear your nephew? I should like nothing better than that he should go free."

"He confided in me only this morning," I replied. "And knowing the lad as I do, I believe him utterly. However, his account will, I think, have to be confirmed before it is presented to the authorities."

He thought about this. "You are most discreet, Madame. An excellent quality in a lady." Now he was smiling broadly. "Yet, in the light of our past connection – I remember with great pleasure how we dined together that night, what good company you were, how you relished your lobster." He chuckled. "Perhaps – as a friend – you might inform me unofficially. It might simplify matters for Ralph, you know."

This man was far from being my friend and had lied to me before, the which I still resented deeply. However, I could see no harm in relating what Ralph had told me, and duly did.

M. Cochot stared at me.

"This is the copper-fastened alibi that will prove your nephew innocent?"

"Yes." I regarded him in some alarm. His face had gone quite red and he was quivering all over with mirth as if about to explode.

At last he regained some composure.

"An alibi based on the testimony of those impeccably noble souls who work in a brothel, I suppose," he said, merrily. "Forgive me, Madame, but if he were not your nephew would you believe this fairy story?"

"I am sure he is telling the truth, Monsieur."

M. Cochot shook his head and sighed. "These foolish young men! What scrapes they get themselves into. Preferring to risk prison and perhaps execution rather than upset their poor mothers! Dear me! Whatever next..." He slapped a fat hand on the table, making me jump. "No, my dear Mrs Hudson. It won't do. It won't do at all."

"If the evidence of the brothel owners counts for nothing with you," I said coldly, "the young men who brought him to the place will surely vouch for him."

"Of course. How foolish of me not to think of that! Because they stayed by his side the whole time he was there, didn't they. While they all got up to whatever young men do in such places."

The quivering and chuckling resumed. Then he became thoughtful.

"In fact," he said, "he might well have gone to the brothel, as you say, treated the poor whore with disrespect and received a smack in return. In a fury, then he leaves the establishment and takes out his rage against women on the unfortunate Sylvie."

"Having with him all the time a vial of acid and the keys to the catacombs, I suppose."

"Who knows?"

I was enraged at his pig-headedness. "So you have found an easy suspect to blame for the crime, Monsieur and cannot be bothered to look any further."

The Prefect leaned forward, suddenly serious. "The evidence points to your nephew, Madame."

"Forgive me, Monsieur, but I disagree," I replied. "For instance, why have you not investigated Sylvie's ex-lover Etienne for the deed? The man she threw over for Bourdain. My very brief acquaintance with him revealed him to be a most impetuous and even violent young man."

I did not wish to reveal unless absolutely necessary that, out of jealousy over Sylvie, Etienne had fought a duel with Ralph.

"Ah yes," the Prefect stated. "You were present at the opening night of Le Chien Jaune…" When I looked surprised, he added, "Officer Blanchard told me."

"Then he probably also told you of the scene that ensued between Etienne and Sylvie. The fight with M. Bourdain."

"I am well aware of it, Madame Hudson, and indeed, despite what you think, we investigated him thoroughly. But, you see, Etienne was out of Paris at his parents' chateau on the night in question. He could not have done it."

"You are sure? Parents have been known to lie to protect their children."

"The word of a nobleman like the Comte de Vaude can hardly be doubted."

I must have looked unconvinced, for he added, "I assure you, Madame, Etienne is not the guilty party… If not Ralph, then it is, in fact, much more likely to be your missing protégée, Mlle. Garance Germaine."

I stared at him aghast. "Surely you cannot think Garance could have committed this terrible deed. A woman!"

"Why not?" I could see he was pleased at the effect his words had on me. "You yourself mentioned Lucrezia Borgia. Women can be murderers too, you know. And this Mlle. Germaine is, by all accounts, a young person with a temperament no less passionate than that of the young de Vaude. You yourself witnessed, the same evening at the cabaret, how she too threatened Sylvie. I believe she felt she had been displaced in the affections of M. Bourdain."

"It cannot be. I won't believe it. You might as well look at M. Bourdain himself. Perhaps he tired of his frivolous new mistress. Perhaps she made demands on him that he could not, would not satisfy."

The Prefect's lips curled in an oily smile. "Ah no, Madame. That will not do. Jules Bourdain was very much in love with the young Sylvie. Indeed, he is even now arranging a magnificent funeral for her, and apparently intends to sculpt a memorial over the grave."

"The act of a bad conscience perhaps?" I said, though without conviction. I was quite taken aback by this intelligence.

He shook his head. "No, no. If you continue to insist that your nephew is innocent, then suspicion must fall on the head of Garance Germaine, particularly since she has fled and is now nowhere to be found."

I reeled from shock, though at least this time did not find myself about to faint.

"However," he continued, "as I have stated, your nephew remains the prime suspect. He was in a relationship with the victim who then spurned him for another. His alibi is dubious to say the least. He is covered in unexplained injuries…"

I started to object but he raise a hand.

"No more, Madame," he said, standing up. "This interview is at an end. There is nothing more to be said on the matter."

I was tempted to confront him with lying to me about the death of Leon Garcia. However, he might then ask me how I came to know the truth, which would further arouse his suspicions about my contacts.

"So, Madame, I must wish you adieu. We are unlikely to meet again, I think. In fact, I would very much advise you to return to England before you get caught up in more unsavoury adventures." He made a slight and dismissive bow. "And when you do return there, please be so good as to pass my very best wishes on to your esteemed lodger."

Chapter Twenty-Two – Waiting

My mind was whirling. My first conviction that finding an alibi for Ralph would be enough to result in his immediate release was gone, although I still nurtured hope proof could be found to vindicate him. Surely, someone acceptable to the Prefect would be able to vouch for him, though of course then M. Cochot's purblind eye would be fully turned on Poppy. Dr. Lepine must, I decided, be apprised of the matter as soon as possible. However, I did not know where his home was situated, or his consulting rooms either, or even if they were one and the same. I therefore returned to the hotel and requested the information of Madame Albert.

"Maurice, is it?" she replied, and gave me that knowing smile. "Funnily enough, he was here earlier asking for you. However, this afternoon he told me to tell you that he will not be free. He has to attend a confinement on the Butte." She shook her head. "Some poor woman with too many children already, who probably will not be able to pay him."

"He engages in charity work, then?"

"I don't know about that, Madame. But he is very good and will not refuse to help anyone who needs him, even if they have no money. Unlike some of his sort."

My earliest impressions of the man as grasping were turning out to be utterly misplaced. I supposed he took what he could get from more the prosperous patients to subsidise those who could not otherwise afford his services.

"I will write him a note," I said, "and deliver it myself."

The grin on Madame Albert's face grew broader still.

"It concerns Poppy, Garance Germaine," I said, hoping to wipe off that annoying smile. "The police suspect her for murder."

That certainly had the desired effect. The poor woman was so shocked she had to grip her chair to stop herself from falling.

"Murder!" she exclaimed. "Whose murder?"

"A girl called Sylvie. An artist's model."

"Oh," she said, recovering somewhat, She was even able to laugh. "How absurd."

"Indeed. And yet they suspect her. A crime of jealousy, they think."

She looked thoughtful. "Maurice should certainly hear of this as soon as possible," she said. "I know he takes an interest in Gigi." An interest, I thought: one could call it that! "Victorine can deliver your note if you wish," Madame Albert continued. "She has to do some errands for me in the neighbourhood anyway."

I must have looked doubtful, for she reassured me. "She's a good reliable girl, if a little quiet."

Agreeing finally with this plan of action, for, after all, I did not feel like trailing about further in the heat of the afternoon – and also conscious that I had not eaten since breakfast – I quickly penned a missive to the doctor, informing him that I needed to see him as soon as possible, although omitting to say why. Explanations would come better from a face-to-face meeting.

I then went up Nelly's room, to impart the news about Ralph, choosing my words with care. My sister's face was so wan, so drawn, I am afraid I could not bring myself to tell her that he was still the chief suspect. Instead I told her that new information had come to light which might possibly exonerate him.

She jumped up with excitement.

"Let us wait," I said, "before celebrating too much. There will be time for that soon enough, I hope... But if you have not yet eaten, Nelly, I am ravenous, and should love some company while dining."

To tell the truth, I had little appetite, but, reckoning that we both needed sustenance to prepare us for the ordeals ahead, was happy when she concurred. Straightway, we set off for Le Petit Bonhomme, not to wander too far from the hotel in case the doctor or lawyer arrived in the meantime. Père Perrot himself was on duty in the cafe, but his cheery face fell when he heard our request.

"I am sorry, ladies, but luncheon finished at two o'clock. The chef, alas, has left for the afternoon. However," and he smiled, rubbing his hands together, "if you can be satisfied with a bowl of soup and some bread and cold sausage, I can certainly provide that."

That was all we needed, the thick soup sufficient almost in itself to stay the worst pangs of hunger. Though it quite definitely contained onion, my sister said not a word about it and consumed her entire bowl, without any obvious ill-effects. As we ate, she quizzed me on my visit to the Prefecture. I did not feel the need to reveal the dubious credentials of Maître Loiseau in the eyes of the police. Or that Ralph's alibi was quite different from the one she took it to be.

"Nothing much. More bureaucracy," I said.

After our meal, we betook ourselves to my room to await developments as patiently as we could, Nelly with her novel and I with my knitting. I could not have concentrated on reading, and, as it turned out, neither could Nelly for she constantly paused to wonder aloud when we might hear something, how the police could have got it so wrong when clearly Ralph was incapable of a violent deed, how she rather thought a girl like Sylvie had it coming to her anyway, considering her way of life. To stem these remarks, I asked her to read aloud from her book.

"But Martha, you do not know the beginning."

"It is of no matter."

"Oh, but indeed, you need to understand the story otherwise it will make no sense. I shall start from Chapter One. I don't mind, you know. It is most thrilling."

The book in question was among those that I had purchased for her a few days earlier. It was titled "The Secrets of Montchagrin," a translation from the French, and embodied from the first all the vices, and none of the dubious virtues, of the sensational novel, being crude and ill-written, with an absurd plot. I confess, that while Nelly's voice droned on, I allowed my thoughts to drift, and hardly registered the twists of the story, until my sister broke off her reading with a question.

"I am sorry, dear," I replied. "What did you say?"

"Isn't it exciting? You will never guess what happens to Hortense when she visits the Baron in his lair? I know, of course, for I have read it already. What do you think?"

She looked at me eagerly. I had no notion at all regarding Hortense, whom I took to be the heroine, or the Baron, whom I took to be the villain.

"She will be in peril of her life… or at least of her virtue," I replied, hoping not to have betrayed my inattention.

"Yes, indeed, but you cannot imagine the full horrors of it all. That hellish crypt! Oh, I tremble at the thought of it…" She chuckled with pleasure. "Shall I continue?"

I nodded, but now my thoughts had taken direction. Sylvie's body had been found in the catacombs. Presumably she had gone there willingly, since it would surely have been impossible to convey her thither otherwise, living or already dead. So what made her enter that grisly place? Was she accompanied by her killer or had she gone alone, like Hortense, into the lion's den? I needed to visit the catacombs, to see them for myself, for the sakes of both Ralph and Poppy. The following day was Friday, when they would be open to the public. I resolved to make a visit, reckoning that Nelly, with her ghoulish tastes, might like to accompany me. I looked across at my sister, greedily recounting the fate of the unfortunate heroine, locked in a crypt with only skeletons and spilled blood for company.

The hours passed. Nelly, at last fatigued with reading, went to her room to lie down. I started a second sleeve. At this rate, I should have to buy more wool.

It was as the sun sank behind the houses opposite that I heard a light tapping on my door. It was Dr. Lepine.

"You needed to see me," he said.

"You first. Any news of Poppy?"

He shook his head regretfully.

"Nothing. No trace."

"That is perhaps a good thing, after all," I said, announcing. "The police suspect she might have had a hand in Sylvie's death."

He was not as astonished as I expected he would be. In fact, he sank back in his chair with a despairing groan.

"You thought it too?" I asked.

"Not really, but… well… it occurred to me as a possibility."

"Then you think Poppy capable of such a terrible deed!"

"There is a madness in love, Mrs Hudson. It drives us to acts another might abhor."

I presumed he was also talking of himself, how he had abandoned himself to his passion without thought for his wife and children.

"The fact of her disappearance…" he continued. "You must agree, it does not look like the act of an innocent."

"Unless she too is a victim."

"Ah, do not say that, I beg you."

"You would prefer her to be a murderer?"

He was silent.

"Tomorrow," I told him, "I plan to visit the catacombs."

"To what end? Do you think you will find clues there even now?"

I did not know why I felt such a need to see the place. Were I Mr. H., I should no doubt find some piece of evidence overlooked by the police, enabling me to identify the murderer. But I do not pride myself on such a degree of acuity. Nevertheless, a visit would help me see a part of the picture, the perspective if not the whole panorama.

"And what of Valentin?" I asked.

"Nothing. He too has vanished."

I was reminded then of a conjuring trick I had seen once at the Egyptian Hall in London, as performed by the eminent Mr Nevil Maskelyne. His young lady assistant having entered a box which to all intents and purposes was entirely enclosed, the magician spoke some incantation, waved his wand, and, when he opened the box again, to our great astonishment and satisfaction, the lady had disappeared. In that case, of course, he speedily brought her back again, unharmed.

What sorcery was afoot here, then, to make two people vanish so completely?

The doctor left me soon after, pledging to continue his enquiries. I felt, though, that if he did indeed manage to track the girl down, he would tell her to disappear again, and for good, in case the police should come after her.

I sat for a while as night descended over Paris, the lights of the city sparking into life, while my room plunged further into darkness, reflecting my troubled thoughts. It seemed I sat and sat, though it could not have been so very long, after all, before Madame Albert came to tell Nelly and myself that Maître Loiseau awaited us below. We hastened down, Nelly saying, "Perhaps he has brought Ralph with him."

I could not hope it, since our landlady had not mentioned anything of the sort. And indeed, the rotund little lawyer sat in the parlour with none for company but Philippe Albert, the latter, on our arrival disappearing into the kitchen. Speaking in French – for which I was grateful, since I could then censor his remarks for Nelly's benefit if he should happen to refer to something Ralph did not want her to know – the lawyer stated that he had indeed received from the young man details of where he had spent the evening in question, with whom, as well as the source of his wounds. Although Ralph had not been able to identify the particular "house," it had taken Maître Loiseau no time at all, through his contacts, to find it. Several of the boy's companions had agreed that he was with them that evening, until the early hours of the morning, and even seemed to think it a great joke to have taken him there: "the silly drunken Englishman."

Verifying the full account, particularly with regard to his injuries, had, however, taken rather more cajoling – the woman in question, Cecile, and her protector, Gerard, suspecting at first that Ralph wished to press charges against them.

"They claim that he instigated the fight, which I am sure, comparing his puny frame to that of Gerard, I doubt very much. Even Cecile," he chuckled, "would be a formidable opponent in an altercation. She is a big strong woman, Madame Hudson. However, we will not argue with them over who struck the first blow. The outcome we hoped for has been achieved: We have provided the young man with an alibi and the necessary signed documents have been duly delivered to the Prefecture. As a result, I am confident M. Ralph will be released, though do not expect him tonight. The police here are quick to grab and slow to let go."

Despite my strong doubts, I translated a censored version of his words to Nelly, who clapped her hands in delight.

"I should add," the lawyer added, with a disingenuous expression on his face, "that, in order to obtain the co-operation of the parties involved, a degree of remuneration was required. You understand me, I hope."

He had paid them.

I nodded. "You will add the sum to our account," I said. And then proceeded to tell him of my interview with the Prefect and his dismissal of the alibi, which I felt could only be strengthened should M. Cochot learn of the bribe.

Maître Loiseau shook his head. "It is most unfortunate, Madame, that you informed the Prefect of our new evidence. He will be prepared. However, let us not despair." He glanced at Nelly. "You haven't told her?"

"No."

"Well, no need yet. Let her live in hope."

He bowed and took his leave.

Nelly, all smiles now, wanted to celebrate, and we dined rather more lavishly than usual at Le Petit Bonhomme, Père Perrot bustling about our table, rubbing his hands as we placed our orders, saying, "Bon, bon, bon." While all the time my heart sank within me.

Chapter Twenty-Three: An Attack

Nelly would not go with me to the catacombs.

"I am surprised at you, Martha," she said. "I cannot of course think of going anywhere, but must wait here for news of Ralph. Perhaps even now he is being released. Think how terrible it would be if the poor boy arrived here, only to find that I had gone out gallivanting with you."

Gallivanting seemed to be her favourite word as applied to me these days. I could tell that she was strongly of the opinion that where I went was of no real moment, a self-indulgence, and that if I had any sense of duty I should wait with her. This, however, was something I had no intention of doing. It was on the tip of my tongue to reply that I should not be long, but stopped in time and simply asserted that I should see her, and, with God's grace, Ralph, too, on my return.

Arriving once more at the Gates of Hell, I stood in line with others who wished to enter. Recalling the advice given me by the helpful waitress at the nearby cafe, I asked the burly guard if he were Denis. When he nodded, I gave my name.

"Ah yes, indeed, Madame Hudson. Berenice told me you might be coming. You are most welcome."

He gave a courteous bow, the which married strangely with the man's rough and ready exterior, the ill-fitting and grubby uniform, the ruddy complexion of someone who enjoyed strong liquor.

I led him aside a little to inform him, in a whisper, that I was a friend of the girl who had been found murdered, and should like very much to see the spot where she had been found.

His leathery face creased into a frown.

"It is not part of the tour, Madame."

"I realise that," I said. I had come prepared and pressed some coins into his hand.

He assessed the "pourboire" for a second, and was apparently satisfied.

"It was very sad, very tragic," he said. "Such a young girl. I am sorry for you, to lose your friend like that. Of course, I will shew you where she breathed her last."

He motioned me then into the waiting area, where a group of tourists stood already, chatting eagerly. I wondered if they too knew that this place was the scene of a recent murder, and if it was that had brought them here. Impossible to tell from their demeanour. Meanwhile, in contrast to the rest of the noisy throng, a young woman had followed me in, well-dressed in a drab sort of way – all greys and blacks – and seemingly most respectable. Why ever would a person like that come here on her own? She looked back, perhaps thinking the same of me. I smiled, and after a second, she returned a brief nod.

Soon we were joined by Denis, who led us down a passageway to another heavy door, which he unlocked. So more than one key would have been necessary for the murderer to gain entrance, assuming this was the way they came in. We had then to descend deep into the ground by means of a winding staircase, walking along a narrow and dimly lit passageway of rough gravel until suddenly finding ourselves in a hall with skulls and other bones, arranged, it seemed in artistic patterns. To my mind, most grotesque and inappropriate.

Our guide halted here to inform us of the history of the place. How in the last century the cemeteries of Paris were full to overflowing and a danger to health, especially when the walls of Les Innocents collapsed, spilling out rotting body parts (this Denis told us, I am afraid, with considerable relish, some of the ladies present then shrieking or quailing in delighted abhorrence, and clutching at their male companions). It was thereafter that a part of the limestone quarry, which had existed under the city for centuries was adapted for use as storage for the bones.

"There are 6 million Parisians buried here," Denis said. "If you do not believe me, you can count them for yourselves."

His silly little joke provoked some weak laughter which at least dispelled some of the horror. To me, it was strange and disquieting, looking around, to think that all these bone fragments once belonged to living folk, with thoughts and dreams like we who now gazed upon them. I could not help but think of an inscription on a grave that I had once seen, "As you are now, so once was I. As I am now, so you must be." I have to say that I am content enough to think that when I pass away I shall rejoin dear Henry in our family plot at Highgate cemetery, my bones to be buried deep in the earth, not subjected to idle gaze. However, I suppose these departed care not one way or another: wherever their souls are, it is surely far from here.

We continued on through the bone-lined main passageway, Denis coming to a halt by something he called "The Barrel," a large standing oval built entirely of osseous body parts. Again, I thought that I should not like any part of myself combined with those of others no matter how skilled and artistic the result.

Leaving the rest of the group to ogle, Denis beckoned me to a gloomy side tunnel.

"That is the place, Madame," Denis told me, gesturing into the darkness. "The poor girl was found at the end of the gallery. My God! I cannot tell you how horrid was the sight, how she must have suffered. I think I shall never recover from it."

If I had truly been close to Sylvie, I should hardly have found his words comforting.

"So it was you who found her then, Monsieur?" I asked.

"No. Simon found her first, and came running back for me, crying out in horror." He shook his head. "I shall never forget the sight, Madame, her face. Ravaged. Gone... I suppose she was pretty once."

He looked to me for an answer.

"Yes, she was very lovely... I wonder," I said, as if overcome with emotion, "could you leave me here for a moment or two, Monsieur Denis. I should like to pay my respects."

The coins I had given him had clearly worked their intended magic, for he nodded.

"Take care, Madame. It is damp down there and the ground might be slippery."

He withdrew, back to the group, while I proceeded to the end of the gallery.

Here it was too dark here to see much, inky shadows tempered only by a faint gleam from whence I had come. I could have wished to ask Denis for a light but the request might have seemed strange. Instead, I knelt down. An observer might have thought I was praying, and I did, indeed, say a few words for the repose of the girl's soul. However, my main purpose was to search the ground for something, anything that might help identify her killer. Here at least was smooth, without the grit of the main paths. I removed my gloves in order to run my hands over the damp mud. At first it seemed I must go unrewarded, but then my fingers alighted on something, a hairpin, as I thought. I put it in my reticule, and continued the search, aware that I must soon return to the group to avoid arousing suspicion as to my motives.

So intent was I that I did not hear the approaching steps. Only when the person was almost upon me did I start to turn my head. Too late. Before I could register who was there, a crashing blow felled me, and all was darkness.

How long I lay there, I cannot say. I suppose it must not have been more than a few moments before Denis came looking for me, followed by the others. Perhaps he had called out to me, but I was stunned and heard nothing, only gradually becoming aware of a murmur of concerned voices around me. One thing which I recall even now so clearly was the smell of the damp earth on which I lay, the metallic odour of blood. My own or Sylvie's?

"She must have fainted," I heard someone say.

"Or slipped."

"Overcome with grief." That was Denis.

I shook myself into full consciousness, and allowed myself to be helped to my feet by a kind gentleman, though I then had to lean on him to avoid dropping again. Someone handed me back my hat, which had been knocked off my head by the blow.

"I was attacked," I said. "Someone hit me."

At first, I do not think they were inclined to believe me. My head was indeed bleeding but that could be accounted for by the fall. It was only when someone stumbled over a length of bone, a thigh bone perhaps, snapped in two and lying bloody on the ground nearby, that credit was given to my account.

"You were lucky," said Denis, examining the weapon, "that the bone was brittle. Otherwise, Madame, you might have been killed."

Gasps of horror sounded from the assembled company, mixed perhaps with a fearful pleasure, to think that a woman was almost killed a stone's throw from where they were standing, and in such a place, too.

"But who did it?" The murmur went around, each member of the group looking at the others.

"A ghost, perhaps." That from a plump and silly looking matron, in unsuitably youthful frills.

Then someone said, "The young woman. The young woman who came by herself. Where is she?"

I remembered her then, the way she had looked at me, so gravely. Was she a member of the anarchist group, sent after to injure or even kill me? It seemed absurd, and yet I could not think who else she might be.

"A madwoman," someone opined. "Escaped from Charenton."

"Whoever she is and wherever she is," Denis said, "she cannot go far. All the doors are locked.
And good luck to her if she wanders off into the tunnels. She might never be found then."

We hastened to the exit door, or at least the rest of the group went on ahead, while the same kind gentleman supported me the rest of the way. By the time the two of us arrived, everyone else was standing in a circle around a prostrate figure who proved to be the same young woman, my supposed assailant. She was crouching at the locked door, sobbing, but, on seeing me arrive, alive and apparently barely harmed, she cried out, "Thank God!"

"I will summon the flics, Madame," Denis said.

I, however, asked him to wait, wishing to discover for myself the young woman's motive for what she had done, especially in view of the repentant expression on her face.

He was reluctant. "It is most irregular, Madame. We can't have people attacking others willy-nilly in the catacombs. Furthermore, I would remind you that she stole a bone for the purpose."

"Well, you are hardly short of those," I snapped back, then added in more cajoling tones, "Have you a room where I can talk to her privately? I think she will not try to kill me again."

By now Denis must have thought his tip was well and truly already earned, for he frowned deeply. I made a show of reaching into my reticule, his eyes following my movements, like a dog hoping for a tidbit.

"Or," I went on, pressing a coin into his hand, "we could go to a café. I am in need of a reviving drink, and I am sure this young woman could do with one as well." For she had turned white and looked to be about to faint.

"What if she runs off?" asked the gentleman who had helped me in the tunnel.

"If anyone wants to accompany us, to make sure that she does not," I said. "I shall certainly have no objection."

In the end, a number of the group – clearly most curious about the business and indeed avid with excitement – followed us, much to Berenice's satisfaction, for it was to her establishment that we had repaired. They installed themselves at tables near the door, ready to apprehend the villain if she should try to escape again.

I insisted on sitting with the young woman some way off from the group – this was not to be a public tribunal after all – and ordered for her and myself a cognac and water. I should not normally take such a beverage in the middle of the day, but circumstances would seem to demand it for once. And since Denis was hovering about, I ordered the same for him.

"You are a lady," he said, and sat himself away from us, also near the door.

"So tell me, my girl," I said. "What is this all about?"

My assailant was no anarchist, although who she proved to be was perhaps more astonishing.

"My name," she said, after a pause, "is Françoise Lepine... I see that name means something to you, Madame."

I had started with astonishment.

"You are the wife of the Doctor?"

"I am. And the mother of his children..." Tears welled up in her eyes. "It is too cruel of you, Madame, to try and take him away from me."

I almost laughed. "You cannot believe that, my dear," I said. "I am almost twice his age. Why, I could be his mother."

She made a dismissive gesture. "What is age" she said, raising her voice, "when people are seized by passion?"

People, overhearing, were looking at us now with increased curiosity, the which I found somewhat discommoding, and hushed her.

"I admit," she went on in quieter tones, "you are not quite what I expected." I should think not, indeed. "But so many people have told me of it, that I felt it must be true."

"What people?"

But I knew some of them: there were Madame Albert's smiles and hints, the open insinuations of La Goulue. It was preposterous to think of an amorous relationship between myself and the young doctor, and yet people seemed ready to believe it. Perhaps because they were French.

"Then the urgent note you sent yesterday arrived," she explained, "insisting he call on you at once. I admit I opened it and followed him, Madame, to discover where you were staying."

"And followed me again today, I suppose."

She nodded.

"I knew there was someone." Her voice was breaking with emotion. "His behaviour over the last months. Though I hardly thought…"

"You hardly thought it would be the likes of me. Is that it? Well, my dear, let me reassure you. Whoever it might be, if there is indeed such a person," (I was not about to reveal anything of Poppy, of course, that was for Lepine himself to do) "it is certainly not me. Goodness, I have only been in Paris for two weeks and my acquaintance with your husband is purely that. An acquaintance."

I explained how I had met her husband when he had treated my sister and Ralph for various injuries. He had, I continued, been most solicitous.

"But the urgent note?"

What could I tell her? I decided to embroider the truth.

"You may know by now that a young woman was murdered in the catacombs a few days ago." She nodded. "My nephew has been arrested for her murder. I thought that your husband…"

"Good heavens!" She broke in. "You cannot think that Maurice… That she was the one!.. Oh God! That he killed her because… because…"

I had made matters worse. She was recreating one of Nelly's novels in her imagination.

"No, no, no." I hurried to dispel the notion. "Sylvie was nothing to your husband. I doubt he was even aware of her existence. But think about it for a moment, Madame. My sister and I arrive in Paris, knowing no one, and thus with no one to turn to when faced with this horrid business. Now, your husband, as a solid member of society, was the only person we could think of to advise us. He has proved a rock to my sister and me at this very difficult time." Not entirely untrue, after all.

She sank back. Françoise Lepine was a pretty enough woman, though past her very first youth, and worn down with present cares. She lacked all the fire and sparkle of Poppy, and yet I could see that she had qualities the other would never have. Despite her recent blundering resort to violence, there was a gentleness about her, the air of a Raphael Madonna, if the comparison is not too far-fetched. I was sure she made a wonderful mother, and that alone was the reason – the desire to protect her children – which had driven her to take desperate steps.

"I cannot begin to express how sorry I am, Madame," she said, bowing her head. "I have been at my wit's end this last while. Perhaps I am going mad. You are not too badly hurt at any rate, I hope."

My head was throbbing and I should require a doctor to take a look at it, though, under the circumstances, not Lepine. However, I told the young woman that I would live, the which I sincerely hoped to be the case.

"You know," I said, "your husband is a very good man. A kind man. I am sure that his sense of duty would never permit him to leave you and the children." (Though, having seen the degree of his obsession, I was sure of no such thing.) "He loves you very much. Indeed, he told me so." (Which he had, with reservations) "He has been working very hard of late and it is perhaps that, because he seemed so distracted, which led you to fear that his affections were turned elsewhere. My dear," I took her hand. "The attack on me. Whatever were you thinking?"

She broke down entirely at that.

"I had to believe that if you were out of the way, he would come back to me. The thought obsessed me, night and day, taking away my reason. The moment I struck you, it was as if I came to myself again. I couldn't believe what I had done. I am so, so sorry."

What the people present thought about the little drama taking place in the corner, I can only imagine. And when Françoise

Lepine and I stood together to leave, arm-in-arm, jaws quite dropped around us in astonishment.

On the way out, I paused only to tell Denis that the young woman had suffered a bout of hysteria, as women are prone to do, and that I was taking her home. I slipped a few more francs on to his table and said that I hoped this would compensate for the disturbance and damage. Perhaps he was hoping for more – such people usually do, in my experience – but he nodded finally.

We took a cab and drove her home first. I waited for her to go safely in, having impressed on her the need for rest.

"Rest! No, I will only be thinking of all this. The children will distract me." She smiled wanly.

I then asked the cab driver if he knew of a doctor, and he looked at me sideways.

"The place you have just come from," he said.

"Another doctor, if you please." I said, adding as an excuse. "That one is out."

To my great relief, the elderly physician I subsequently consulted proclaimed me not to be in need of stitches. He applied some stinging iodine and gave me a little bottle of that substance, instructing me to apply it regularly for a day or two, to avoid infection. He also gave me some morphine to take if the pain became too bad. I accepted it, although in general I prefer not to dull my senses with such drugs unless absolutely necessary, having too often seen the state of Mr. H. when he has indulged.

Back at the hotel at last, I learnt from Madame Albert that Ralph had not yet returned, and that my sister was up and down the stairs all the time in case there was news. However, I could not face Nelly just then and used the excuse of my accident to postpone the meeting.

The landlady must have noticed the yellow discoloration on my temple, caused by the iodine for she asked if I were all right.

"I had a fall," I told her. "Nothing to worry about, but I should like to rest."

"Of course. Let me know if you need anything."

She gave me an odd look, but that was perhaps because I looked a little odd myself, my hat set askew, not to press down too much on the wound.

Having reached my room, I sank gratefully on to my bed for a few moments. Then I rummaged in my reticule to remove the two bottles given me by the doctor. Everything would be ruined if either of them should leak. As I felt around for them, my fingers alighted on something else. The item found at the place where Sylvie had been murdered. I drew it out. It was, as I had thought, a hairpin. Perhaps fallen from the head of the poor girl herself. Or maybe it was there quite by chance and unconnected to the crime. It could, after all, have been there for years, a century even. But something else suddenly occurred to me. Something which gave me cause to wonder, and when I laid myself down again, my thoughts took an entirely new direction.

Chapter Twenty-Four – Despair

After an hour in which I hardly rested, for my mind was buzzing too much, I roused myself and went to find Nelly. All her good humour had evaporated. My sister was sitting, head bowed, hands folded on her lap.

"Oh, Martha, you are back," she said, looking up.

Her voice was flat, and she looked grey and haggard.

"Has something happened?" I asked.

"Where were you, Martha?"

"You know where I was. I told you. I went to the catacombs."

She didn't ask about my wounded head with its conspicuous iodine stain. Maybe she was too wrapped up in her own concerns to notice, for the which, indeed, I was grateful. I did not feel like telling her what had actually transpired, even less inventing a convincing explanation. There are only so many attacks by cutpurses that can be credited.

"No news then?" I said.

"Oh yes. There's news all right."

I waited.

"Some man was here just now."

"What man?"

"From the lawyer. An old man. We met him before, I think."

Maître Loiseau's clerk.

"And?" I asked. She just stared at me blankly. "Tell me, Nelly. Please. What did he say?"

"Where were you, Martha? You should have been here. I couldn't understand him properly."

"He had news of Ralph, I suppose."

"Yes." She extended a piece of paper to me, crushed into a ball she had clenched it so tightly in her fist.

I smoothed it out. The letter heading indicated that the document indeed came from the lawyer. It contained the worst of news. Ralph had been transferred to La Santé prison to await trial for murder, the alibi evidence presented being insufficient to convince the police of the young man's innocence. The maître urged us not to despair, however, and assured us that he was on the case. As soon as he had further information, he would, of course, let us know, and meanwhile would arrange to bring us to visit the boy.

"You've understood enough of this?" I asked Nelly.

"That my poor boy has been sent to some horrible prison. Oh yes, Martha. I understand that well enough." She paused. "What I don't understand is what went wrong. You told me he would be set free. That's what you said." Her face was full of accusations.

"I thought he would be. Oh Nelly, I'm so very sorry."

We clasped each other in a tight embrace.

"They will guillotine him for sure," she said, breaking away at last. "He is lost."

"No, no, no. That won't happen." Perhaps I sounded surer than I felt, for she grabbed my hand and pressed it to her breast.

"Promise me you do all you can to save him," she said.

What could I say?

"I'll do my utmost, my dear."

But truth to tell, I had not an idea how to proceed.

The following morning, Maître Loiseau undertook to bring us to visit Ralph. La Santé prison proved to be as terrible as anticipated, a great looming edifice, the grey stone of which was covered in a green lichen as if rotting before our eyes. As we made our way through the great doors and into the hellish place, Maître Loiseau told us to be of good cheer, though, if such were impossible for me, how much more for Nelly, who was looking about herself with wild eyes, gripping my hand.

"Ralph will not be here for long, dear ladies," he said, observing our agitation. "I am sure of it."

I dearly wished I could have shared his optimism.

He was evidently well acquainted with the establishment, and spoke of it almost as if we were tourists.

"La Santé is constructed," he explained, "in different wings like the spokes of a wheel round a central hub. It has been described as the best and most beautiful prison in Europe." He paused and winked. "Though I think the person who said that must either have a strange notion of beauty or else a most peculiar sense of humour."

He babbled on, indicating the exercise courtyard.

"It's called La Fromage," he said, "because, like a wheel of cheese, do you see, it's divided into wedges." He chuckled. "So that prisoners can be kept separate from each other."

I understood his well-meaning, if misplaced intentions, to try to distract us from the grim sights around us.

"Unfortunately," he went on, "there are so many inmates now that the wedges are packed too tight for them to do more than wriggle. Maggots in the cheese."

He chortled at his joke. I didn't translate it for Nelly. A peculiar sense of humour indeed.

We found ourselves conducted through the long corridors of one of the wings, cell doors on each side from which distressing moans, shouts and screams emitted, as well sometimes as threatening rumbles. Every few yards stood iron gates that had to be unlocked each time by the grim gaoler accompanying us, and locked by him again behind us. Nelly clung to my arm, perhaps in fear that we would never get out of this labyrinth again. As if reading our minds, Maître Loiseau informed us that escape from the prison was almost impossible.

"It has happened, Mesdames, but too rarely."

At last the gaoler stopped in front of a cell door, and I saw the lawyer slip something into his hand, a bribe presumably. The man unlocked the door then, and stood aside to let us enter. More horrors within. The narrow room was dark, stained plaster peeling from the walls, cobwebs hanging down like a rotting net curtain, a horrid and unwholesome stench pervading all. A man was lying on a plank bed, his back to us. Ralph.

Nelly rushed forward, crying out his name, and he jumped up as if stung. Then fell into his mother's arms. He looked terrible, filthy and bruised. I could not but wonder if he had been beaten, or if the bruises dated from his earlier injuries.

"My poor boy." Nelly was weeping. "My poor, poor boy."

"Have you come to take me home?" he asked pathetically, like a small child. My heart went out to him.

"Not yet, M. Ralph," Maître Loiseau answered.

"I can't stay here." He held tight to his mother. "I can't. I'll die."

"Patience, young man," the lawyer said. "I know it's hard but we your friends are all working for your release. Just be patient a little longer."

He sounded so sure that Ralph relaxed somewhat.

"Can I not be moved to a better cell at least? You have no idea, mummy," he said. "I have to beat off the rats at night, stamp on the cockroaches. It's disgusting. And I am so very hungry. The gruel they give us is made of potato peelings."

"That at least we can remedy," I replied, indicating the basket I was carrying. It had been searched on the way in, of course, and the bottle of cognac confiscated, but luckily the remainder had been passed for delivery to the prisoner.

Now the boy fell on the victuals, cramming a whole pie into his mouth.

"Don't eat too quickly, Ralph," Nelly said. "It'll upset your stomach."

He just gave her a look and continued to gorge.

Maître Loiseau pulled me aside. "It may seem bad here," he muttered. "But in fact, M. Ralph is lucky to have a cell by himself. Very lucky. The other prisoners... well... you understand me, I think."

"I assume you will add to our bill what it cost to arrange this," I replied, and he inclined his head.

We watched Ralph eat for a while longer, listening to more of his woes, trying to comfort him. But all too soon we had to leave, though, in any case, there was nothing more to do here for now, Maître Loiseau engaging to visit Ralph again the following day.

"When I hope to have better news for you," he said.

"Get me out of here, Maître," the boy begged.

"We will do our best. I promise," he said, and I nodded reassuringly.

Nelly had to be dragged away, weeping copiously. I think she would have stayed with her son, if allowed to do so. Ralph, resigned at last, resumed his place on the hard bed, his back to us again.

The gaoler, as hatchet-faced as ever, was standing outside the door. Maître Loiseau whispered something to him, perhaps telling him to keep an eye on the boy. The man nodded, though he didn't strike me as a kind person. Still, kindness can be bought.

Again we endured the long walk through the dingy corridor, the cries of the prisoners, the clanging iron gates.

"Where is the guillotine?" asked Nelly of the lawyer.

He looked at her aghast.

"Do not think of such a thing, Madame."

"Where is it?"

"Not here," he replied. "It is at La Grande Roquette."

"Thank God," she replied, a pleading expression on her face. "He is not to be executed, then."

Maître Loiseau remained silent. He did not say it, but of course nothing could be simpler, if the judge found Ralph guilty, than to toss him in a cart and drive across the city to the place of execution.

Nelly was in such a state of nervous exhaustion when we returned to the hotel, that I prevailed on her to take some cognac in milk to help her rest.

"You need to look after yourself for Ralph's sake," I said, the which seemed to convince her for she swallowed the beverage like an obedient child. Indeed, I was almost as worried about her as I was about Ralph, for she looked so ill. I stayed with her then, sitting by her bed, listening to her lamentations, until at last her eyes closed. Then I went to my own room and sat gazing out of the window, thinking of poor Ralph with only rats and cockroaches for company. Could I keep my promise to help him? How?

I must have dozed off, and only awoke to raised voices outside. A young woman was shouting raucous curses and pulling at the arm of her companion. I watched them for a few moments. The man was respectably dressed in a dark suit with a top hat, while the girl's skimpy gown was tawdry and her furs moth-eaten. A silly beribboned little bonnet was balanced on her dishevelled curls. It was impossible to doubt her calling, a woman of the streets.

It came to me then: the brothel. There had to be more evidence there. On the other hand, how could I, Mrs Martha Hudson, respectable widow, visit such a place? And there was another problem: apart from the unseemliness of the enterprise – the which under the circumstances I was prepared to countenance – I had no idea where the house was. As a plan took shape in my head, the man brutally flung off the girl's hold, and dashed some coins after her into the gutter. As she paused to scoop them up, he strode away. She stood up to watch him. Then, after spitting at his retreating back, she went off in the opposite direction.

Chapter Twenty-five – Dawn

The elderly clerk in the lawyer's office, more dusty and bent than ever, shewed no surprise at my query, which he was soon able to answer: I supposed that in his long life he must have received all sorts of unusual requests. The driver of the cab I subsequently hired, however, was most taken aback, at the address I gave. Perhaps he took me for one of the older women who run such places. In any case, his manner was not respectful when he set me down, not, as I had expected, in an unwholesome part of town with sinister characters lurking in shadowy doorways, but in the rue des Moulins, a narrow, but attractive street lined with high buildings of yellow stone. Indeed, it was situated near the Palais-Royal in whose lovely gardens Nelly and I had so recently walked. The *maison de tolérance*, as such places are euphemistically called, came as another surprise, from the outside it looked to be an ordinary town house. Then, having rung the bell, I was admitted by a very young girl, in the neat black dress of a maidservant, into a hallway elegantly decorated in a style reminiscent of the last century. It was all most strange. I had anticipated something quite different, something shocking, and, if I can admit such a thing, was rather pleasantly surprised. So far I did not feel uncomfortable at all.

The young girl then led me up a flight of stairs – the thick red carpet sinking luxuriously as I stepped upon it – and shewed me into a room with padded couches on which reclined women in various states of undress, some playing cards, some reading, one trying to pick out a tune on an upright piano. This was more what I expected, although there was as yet little flavour of vice here, the women regarding me with a listless lack of interest, the way cows in a field might gaze at people walking by them. Above them, round the walls, hung portraits garlanded with flowers – seeming to be of these same women but rendered prettier, livelier. The whole scene reminded me more of something from Greek mythology, nymphs at rest, rather than a place of depravity. However, this was afternoon. I imagined it to be quite different at night.

A large woman soon bustled in, voluminous brown silks rustling, a big smile on her face. All the girls instantly stood up.

"Welcome, Madame, welcome. What can I do for you?" She waved a heavily be-ringed hand at her charges. "You like my beauties…"

Good heavens! Surely she could not suppose that I had come looking for company. I have heard that such things take place, of course, though I cannot imagine what occurs during such encounters. I soon forestalled her, telling her who I was and what I wanted.

Her face hardened then. She waved at the girls to sit down, and they subsided into boredom once more.

"We have already told Maître Loiseau what happened," she said. "How the boy was here. How he went with Cecile. How he refused to pay. How Gerard made him leave. We signed a paper."

"I know that, Madame," I replied. "And I am most grateful for your assistance after Ralph's bad behaviour here. But now the poor boy has been taken to La Santé, accused of murder, and we have to prove that, because he was here at the time, he couldn't have done it."

The woman made the sign of the cross. A pious Catholic in such an occupation!

"Is there anything else you can think of that might save him?" I continued.

She shook her head.

"I regret it, Madame. What more can I say? He was here. He was very drunk. We threw him out. Who knows where he went after or what he did?"

"What time was that?"

She shrugged. "I didn't look at the clock."

"It was late," one of the women said. She was older than the others, fleshy. Perhaps she was Cecile, the one Ralph had refused to pay. "It was nearly morning."

"Good," I said. "That helps."

"I don't think he was in a fit state to kill anyone," she went on. "Not the way he was."

I smiled encouragingly at her, but thought, such a woman's opinion will hardly change the Prefect's mind.

"Was there anyone else here who might have seen him?" I persisted.

The maîtresse laughed. "You mean not one of us? Someone respectable?... Oh, it's all right, Madame. I know what the flics are like." She shook her head. "But the gentlemen who visit here have other things on their minds. And in any case, they wouldn't wish to get mixed up in a murder. I'm sorry."

I thanked her again. For nothing.

"Before you go, would you like a tour of the premises, Madame?" she asked. "We cater here to every desire, you know. Maybe something will take your fancy. The Chinese den, the bed of Marie Antoinette with its many well-positioned mirrors, the Moorish room... Maybe," she whispered, "the torture chamber."

She burst into a cackle of laughter and the girls laughed with her. I shivered and took my leave. So, after all, horrors lurked beneath the air of almost propriety.

The little maid led me out again, but before I left, she whispered, "Come back in the morning, early, Madame. There might be someone who can help you."

It was the only gleam of hope in the darkness.

That evening must have been the lowest of my life, sitting with Nelly, contemplating Ralph's fate. She said little, but every so often raised a despairing face to mine.

"Is it quick? Does it hurt?" she asked.

"What?"

"The guillotine."

"Don't think of it," I replied, then added. "I am sure it's quick."

The actual moment, yes, but what of the agonies of anticipation beforehand. No need to say as much. Nelly must have thought of that, too.

We didn't have the heart to do anything to distract ourselves. I tried to knit, but cast the work away from me after a few rows. Outside, night came, but we lit no lamps.

At last Madame Albert knocked on the door and told us that the maître awaited us below. We hurried down, but one look at him convinced us that the news wasn't good. All his usual ebullience had evaporated. Even his moustache drooped. He tried to tell us that Ralph was in good spirits, but Nelly shook her head. She could not believe him.

"Is there no chance of bail?" I asked. "We would pay any amount."

What I meant was, we would pay a bribe if necessary.

"Out of the question," Maître Loiseau replied. "They know Ralph would escape to England. They are determined he shall stand trial."

"So much fuss over a worthless girl that no one will miss," Nelly snapped.

The lawyer looked at her gravely. He had understood her words.

"She was someone's daughter, Madame. She had her life ahead of her, just like your son. No one is worthless."

"My sister is very upset," I said to him in French. "Please forgive her."

He bowed his head in acknowledgement.

I told him then of my visit to the Rue des Moulins.

He was shocked. The elderly clerk must not have told him I had come looking for the address. "You shouldn't have gone there, Madame. It's no place for a lady."

It was my turn to snap.

"So I must remain ladylike, even at the expense of my nephew's life."

He had the grace to smile at that. "I see you are not to be stopped, Madame Hudson."

"No, and I shall return to the brothel tomorrow in the hope of some good news."

He shook his head. "I wish you well, but can assure you that I have already explored every avenue there. Marie-Victoire, the maîtresse, was paid handsomely to tell me all she knew."

I did not doubt it. Still, I thought of the little maid and her "someone."

"All the same, Mesdames," he continued. "Do not give up. Ralph has not yet been found guilty. There is no firm evidence against him. It is all circumstantial. The judge may well rule that the case against him is not proved."

He caught my eye as he spoke. I could not see any cause for hope in his expression.

After he left, I prevailed on Nelly to take another glass of cognac, diluted this time with hot water to help her sleep. For myself, I lay on my bed, staring at the ceiling, waiting for the morning.

Light passing through the thin curtains woke me. For a moment I thought I had slept late but was reassured to find, from my pocket watch, that it was not yet seven of the clock. I was not sure what the little maid had meant by "early," but decided to make my way to the Rue des Moulins as soon as I was dressed.

It was a grey morning, with a fine lace curtain of rain drifting across the streets. At least I had the protection of my umbrella. At another time, it had served me as a weapon, but I trusted that today I should not need it for any such purpose.

My destination was not so distant that I needed to take a cab, and I walked through the almost empty quarter, wondering if the effort would prove worth it. In the narrow street, the house looked closed, asleep. Would anyone be about at this hour?

Somewhat diffidently, I knocked on the door, and was relieved when it was opened by the same little maid as before. She smiled at me.

"Ah, Madame, good morning," she said. "Come in. Monsieur is here."

Monsieur? I thought. A client after all, perhaps, and one who had his wits about him.

The maid led me down the hallway, to a room at the back of the house. She tapped gently on the door and on receiving a mumbled answer, opened it, saying, "I have brought the lady to see you, M. Henri. May I bring her in?"

I heard a gruff "yes" and was admitted.

Imagine my surprise to find there none other than my acquaintance of a few days previously, the little painter, the Comte de Toulouse Lautrec. He was sitting on his bed, wearing a robe of purple and red, tattered and stained, but of good quality silk. I recalled then what Dr. Lepine had told me, the strange rooming arrangements of the man, how he lived in a brothel.

"Madame!" he said, getting up on his short legs with some difficulty. "What an unexpected pleasure to see you again."

"I am sorry if I woke you up, Monsieur," I said.

"No, no. I am just returned. I haven't been to sleep yet." He turned to the maid. "*Chérie*, some coffee if you please."

She nodded and left us. He sat down again on the bed, and gestured to me to take the one chair in the room.

"So, why are you here?" he asked. "Perhaps you wish me to paint your portrait?"

"That would be an honour," I replied, "but, alas, no. It is something far more serious."

"More serious than art," he said with a smile. "Then it is a weighty matter indeed."

While I explained all, he stared at me with his beautiful eyes. After I finished, he sat silent for a while. I waited. He looked to be in a daze after his night out.

"Interesting," he said, at last. "Most interesting."

Not the answer I had been hoping for.

"I don't know how you can help," I said. "Just that the maid thought so."

At that moment, the girl herself entered with the coffee.

"Thank you, my love," he said. She curtsied, and left, smiling.

"The poor little one," he said. "I suppose she is destined for the same fate as her sisters. Still, Marie-Victoire isn't the worst of the brothel-owners. *Chérie* could do much worse. It's better than being on the street."

While he poured the drinks, I considered the sweet child we had just seen. How she too would sit upstairs one day with nothing to do but wait for a client. What a world we live in, I thought to myself, when even the children aren't safe.

The coffee was the same strong brew that Ralph had served us on the first day of our visit. This time I copied my host and added in several spoonfuls of sugar, which made the beverage more palatable.

"I think maybe I can help you," the artist said at last. The coffee seemed to have revived him.

"Really?" It seemed too good to be true.

"Yes, you see, I returned that evening quite early and sat with the girls, doing some sketching. I well remember the fracas with the young man. Wait…" he stood up and stumbled over to a table on which lay some albums. He flipped through the pages.

"Is this your nephew?" he asked, shewing me a sketch.

It was Ralph to the life, sitting at a table, staring at a glass in front of him, a roughly drawn naked woman beside him.

"That was before the fight," the artist told me. "I could see the boy was far gone even then. He hardly knew where he was or what was happening. His friends were all laughing at him. But later I am afraid he wasn't very kind to Cecile."

"So was he here all night?" I asked. This was important.

"It was dawn when they threw him out. I think he lay in the doorway for a while, because I heard cursing when the baker arrived with the morning bread. He had to step over him."

"The baker?"

"Yes, there's a delivery at around six. It saves the little one having to go out to the shops."

The Comte Henri de Toulouse Lautrec. A baker. The new witnesses for Ralph were respectable people. It was more than I could ever have hoped for.

"And you are willing to tell all this to the police?"

"Of course, Madame. Why would I want an innocent man to suffer?"

"I cannot tell you what this means to me, "I said, and added in sudden wave of emotion. "I should like to kiss you, Monsieur."

"Please do." He lifted his face towards me. "And remember, it is always Henri, to you."

I planted a little kiss on his cheek, his beard brushing my chin. By now, I didn't find him ugly or freakish at all.

"Now you have kissed a man in a Paris brothel," he said. "Something to tell your children and grandchildren, I think."

"Or perhaps not," I replied.

His smile lit up his face.

"More coffee?" he asked.

"Yes, I think I will. Thank-you," I said.

Chapter Twenty-Six – Lobster Again

"I don't know how you managed it, Madame," Maître Loiseau was saying. "You must have magic powers."

This was the evening of the same day, Nelly and I sitting in Madame Albert's parlour with the lawyer. After quitting the house in Rue des Moulins, I had hastened to his offices, where I had to wait a good while until the gentleman himself put in an appearance. I then explained all to him, the new supporting evidence, and left it in his capable hands to inform the authorities. I could just imagine the expression M. Cochot's face – to receive such news and from a man he despised! Indeed, as the Maître told us, the Prefect was at first loath to admit that the alibi was now unimpeachable. However, he could not ignore the statements of both the Comte de Toulouse Lautrec and, in particular, of the baker, a gruff individual who instantly recognised Ralph as the vagrant lying outside the brothel in the early hours of the morning. He was unimpressed with the police disturbing him over the matter.

"As if," he had said, "I don't have better things to do with my time than be dragged off to La Santé. Of course, it's the same one I tripped over, damn his worthless hide."

"So now," Maître Loiseau told Nelly. "It can only be a matter of time before your son is back with you, although don't expect it to be instant. As I have said before, the police here are quick to lock up and slow to release. My God!" He threw up his hands. "The paperwork ahead of me. But be of good cheer. Your sister has worked a little miracle."

Nelly – who remained ignorant of the full details – was somewhat less grateful than she might have been.

"I always knew he would get off," she said. "The whole business was perfectly ridiculous."

My worries, however, were not over. I now feared greatly for Poppy and hoped to God that she was somewhere well beyond the reach of M. Cochot. If not, as I informed Maître Loiseau, his services might be needed again, to defend the young woman.

"I am sure you will be able to prove her innocence too, Madame Hudson," he replied jovially.

I wished I could be so sanguine.

The following morning, after a restless night (Nelly had slept very soundly, as she informed me), I decided to try one last time to visit Poppy's apartment, in the unlikely event that she had returned there or at least sent word of her whereabouts. It was damp again, with that deceptively thin rain that seems to soak one to the very bones. However, I needed air so I took my trusty umbrella and walked up the hill to the now familiar little set of rooms.

Of course, it was a wasted journey. Mère Angèle waved skinny hands in the air and shook her head, mumbling incomprehensibly. Thereupon, I made my way to the Place du Tertre to ask the artists I recognised if they had seen the model recently. None of them could help me.

"The flics have also been asking," one said, confirming my fears.

Perhaps her continuing absence should have reassured me that she was safe from them. Unless of course, she too was dead. No, there was no room for complacency.

Of Etienne de Vaude, too, there was still no sign. Hiding out with his illustrious family perhaps. I had not completely given up on him as a suspect for he was evidently perfectly capable of extreme violence. Yes, Etienne was one to consider, despite his supposed alibi.

I stopped for a cup of lemon tea under the canopy of a café on the square and watched the artists at work, none of them in my opinion, displaying any of Poppy's skill and flair. As I sat there, one of those poor lost souls who live rough on the streets approached me looking for a coin or two. I rummaged in my reticule and gave him a few sous. He screwed his frightful visage into what could pass for a smile, or equally for a curse, and then went on his way. It was not inconceivable, I suddenly thought, that Sylvie's killer might simply be some evil madman, like the one they sensationally called Jack the Ripper. He it was had roamed the streets of Whitechapel in London some years before, searching for victims, defenceless young women. Had the Prefect considered that, I wondered? A man who liked to kill simply for the sake of it. Oh dear, I thought, watching the beggar limp from table to table, I am no nearer solving this mystery than I ever was.

At least there was some truly excellent news back at the hotel. In the time I was away, Ralph had returned and left again.

"So where is he now?" I asked.

"He has returned to his studio to pack up. He is very badly shaken. It was a terrible experience for the poor dear child."

"To pack up?"

"Yes, he has had enough of Paris. He is coming back to England with us." She smiled broadly.

I congratulated her and gave her a hug. She did not add that it was thanks to my efforts, but never mind.

"I doubted he was strong enough, after what he's been through," she went on, "so I offered to accompany him to his studio. But he said I would only be in the way." She laughed. "He was joking, of course."

"He is definitely coming home with you?"

"Oh yes. We leave tomorrow."

Tomorrow! I thought. With so much as yet unexplained. I did not think that I could, in all conscience, leave so soon. I started to explain this to Nelly.

"Well, Martha, you can stay on if you want," she broke in tartly. "I won't even ask why, though I think I know… At your age, really!"

Good heavens! Did she too imagine that I was enamoured of the doctor? Or maybe of someone else, the beau who sent the flowers perhaps?

"You are content to travel back without me?" I asked.

"Why not? I shall have Ralph, won't I?" The triumph in her voice was unmistakeable. It was all she had ever wanted, and I felt a sudden nudge of pity for the boy. Would he ever be allowed to grow up?

She did not bother to ask if I would be able or content to journey alone.

315

"Might we at least have a celebration dinner out tonight?" I asked. "Before you go."

Ah, I had misjudged her somewhat. Her expression at my last words told me how astounded she was that I actually intended to stay on by myself.

"Well," she said uncertainly, "I suppose that would be pleasant, although I shall have to see if Ralph has other plans." Victorious, she was graciously able to concede the point. "He might wish to go out with his friends, to say goodbye, you know."

Given what had happened the last time he went out with friends, I doubted that very much. In the end, we left it that Nelly and I would pick a good restaurant for our final meal together, and, if Ralph wished to join us, so much the better.

"Perhaps," Nelly ventured, "we might return to that very nice place Ralph took us. Remember, Martha."

The Rabbit's Burrow where we had encountered the anarchist Fénéon.

"Yes, indeed. That is possible." Although for myself I had in mind the fish restaurant where M. Cochot had taken me. I rather fancied indulging in lobster thermidor again, and mischievously imagined Nelly's shock at the sight of me dismembering the creature. It had seemed a very expensive place, but for once I felt that we deserved to treat ourselves.

The rain had stopped and the sun come out, so I left Nelly to do her packing and took myself off for a walk to Trinity Square, which was as far as I could manage, fatigued as I was both mentally and physically. Strolling under the trees, I asked myself if, after all, it was worth staying on. Could I hope to progress my investigations any further? All I had were vague, and possibly misplaced suspicions, and, lacking the resources to pursue them, there was nothing I could take to the authorities except intuitions. I could well imagine how instantly they would dismiss those. Moreover, any faith I might ever have placed in the competence and integrity of the French police had been sorely tried of late. After a while in which nothing at all was resolved, I went into the church. Perhaps divine inspiration could assist me.

Seated at one of the pews, gazing up at the soaring vaults, I indeed felt a lightening of my spirits. It was not so much that things suddenly made sense to me, but more the admission that here on Earth all is vanity, that all this will pass and that our petty human cares mean so little in the face of eternity. There was, I suppose, some comfort to be had in that.

At the same time, I observed an old woman shuffling into a confession box, and for once I envied her the possibility of talking things over with another, a sympathetic ear. No priest would do for me, of course, but perhaps if I explained all to Mr. H., he would be able to reveal the elusive pattern I was seeking. I closed my eyes, and imagined myself back in Baker Street, Mr. H. stretched out on his favourite chair, smoking his pipe, dear Dr. Watson seated discreetly at a distance.

"Mrs Hudson," I heard my lodger saying. "It is quite elementary, you know. In this case it all comes down to motive and method. Identify the motive and method, and you will discover the murderer. And never ever forget to use your powers of observation. They are your strongest weapon."

By the time I had risen from the pew, having followed Mr. H.'s advice, I was persuaded that one of the threads I had been following was more likely to lead to the centre of the labyrinth, so to speak, than any of the others, though I still needed confirmation regarding opportunity. It would not be simple but I thought I knew how to discover that as well.

Somewhat more satisfied than when I had set out, I went back to the hotel.

Having anticipated an argument, I was somewhat astonished, then, that both Nelly and Ralph, whom I found with his mother, concurred with my suggestion regarding the restaurant for the evening. He looked paler than usual, but, otherwise, cleaned up, seemed not to have suffered too much from his ordeal.

"I knew the flics would recognise they had made a mistake sooner or later," he said with a touch of bravado.

Sooner rather than later, or too late, is to be preferred, I thought.

"Great that old Loiseau found those other witnesses," he went on.

I was astonished. "*I* found them, Ralph," I said.

"Oh, did you? Well then, thanks, aunt."

It was as much as I could expect.

"About that restaurant," he said. "If it's a very fashionable place, we should let them know we are coming. You know, so that they can hold a table for us."

At last the boy was saying something sensible. I had not thought of it myself and questioned Madame Albert on the subject. She engaged to send Victorine or Philippe on our behalf, whichever of the two was free, I promising a few francs in exchange for the service.

"A very chic restaurant!" she said. "A place frequented, as I understand it, by people of influence."

"Is that so?" I replied coolly, returning her gaze.

She smiled then. "So Madame Nelly is going tomorrow, but you are staying. Very good!"

If she thought it queer, she did not say so.

"Oh, I will be gone too, soon enough," I replied. "But there are a few more things I wish to do."

She agreed. "There is so much here to see in Paris, Madame Martha. A lifetime is hardly enough."

"That is true. I shall be sorry to leave."

I returned upstairs to my sister and nephew. Ralph was dashing off again, to finish sorting out his affairs. He would return, he promised, in time to go to the restaurant, a promise we hoped, given his poor record on punctuality, he would fulfil. Meanwhile, Nelly and I went to purchase return travel tickets for herself and her son, and to have ourselves a light luncheon. She chattered on, thankfully not seeming to notice that I paid little attention, being wrapped up in my own thoughts.

For once, Ralph was as good at his word, and returned before Nelly could start worrying. He was in buoyant mood, and could not now be stopped from talking. Though his room, as he told us, was paid for till the end of the month, he had been lucky enough to find someone to take it over from him, another artist, who, moreover, had purchased his paints, easels and other equipment. In addition, he had sold most of his paintings, and would only be bringing a few favourites home with him.

"That is wonderful news," said Nelly, clapping her hands. "Your talents are appreciated at last. I just hope you got a good price for everything. You are so impractical, you know. I should have come with you, to make sure."

If Ralph gave his mother a strange look, I did not think much of it at the time.

"The price was as good as I could hope for," was his only reply.

I wondered if, on the basis on his new wealth, he would treat us to dinner, since we had treated him so many times before. Somehow I doubted it.

For the occasion I decided once more to cheer myself up by sporting my cerise silk, while Nelly wore her grey broadcloth, the best she had with her. At least her shawl had some colour in it, blue and purple, though it was mostly black. Even Ralph made an effort. His hair was flattened and he had got his beard trimmed. His suit was almost respectable. Only the bruises on his face, turning yellow now, gave him a somewhat disreputable air.

They were both most impressed with the restaurant, a far fancier place than those in which they had been accustomed to eat. Indeed, Nelly seemed quite intimidated by it all, the oak panelled walls, the meticulously detailed seascape paintings so unlike anything Ralph might produce, the velvet and the damask, our booth, intimate and discreetly lit, the attentive waiters. I could not think that I was recognised from my earlier visit, although the man serving us seemed particularly friendly to me.

Of course, I ordered the lobster thermidor, as did Ralph, much to Nelly's disapproval, partly because it was the most expensive dish on the menu and partly because the creatures we were to eat were plucked live from a tank and shewn to us, before their removal to the kitchen to be plunged into boiling water for our pleasure.

To be honest, I was rather shocked myself.

"That did not happen before," I said, though thinking back I realised M. Cochot had dealt with that aspect of the meal.

"Hmm," said Nelly, and sniffed. She scrutinised the menu which, for all she could understand of it, might be in double Dutch.

Ralph ordered snails for his starter, but I balked at that and decided on a salmon paste. Nelly was still frowning, indecisive, even though her son had translated the entire menu for her, twice already.

"It all sounds very rich," she said. "I wonder will my digestion bear it."

The waiter was hovering, and we asked him what would be the lightest dishes. He recommended a chicken consommé followed by poached sea bass in a white sauce.

"Very delicate for Madame," he assured her.

"Good," said Ralph, replying for her. "That will do perfectly. And some wine. What would you suggest?"

"I shall send the sommelier to you at once, sir," the waiter said bowing. Ralph crimsoned at his faux pas and I smiled sympathetically.

"It's that sort of place," I said. "Do not let it concern you."

"They will be laughing at me."

"Let them."

The poor boy was so intimidated, however, that he accepted the first, and most expensive recommendation of the wine waiter. For my part, I could not tell you what we drank, only that it was white and fresh tasting, though Nelly, having sipped it, pulled a face and pronounced it too sour.

"Then why don't you put some sugar in it?" asked Ralph snappily.

"A good idea," replied Nelly. "Could you ask for some?"

"No," said Ralph. "They would be horrified." Another unforgivable faux pas.

I was glad not to be travelling back with the two of them.

It was while we were finishing our main course that the first waiter came up to me.

"The gentleman sends his compliments," he said.

I looked where he was indicating, and to my immense surprise – nay, shock – saw none other than the Prefect himself seated at a table with a lady of a similar age to himself, rake-like where he was portly, with stern features. I supposed she was his wife, for – and here I am displaying the corrupting influence of Paris upon me – she hardly looked to be his mistress. Perhaps I should not have been so taken aback, since he had told me he visited the place often. Yet to be there at precisely the same time as myself was somewhat astonishing. He waved over at me and then got to his feet, clearly intending to come and talk to us. This was a little embarrassing, particularly given the presence of his erstwhile prisoner. That M Cochot had not yet seen the young man was certain, for Ralph was tucked into the corner of the booth.

"Madame Hudson," he said, "what a most delightful surprise." The coolness – nay hostility – of our last encounter, on his side at least, was quite gone. "Ah," he went on, "and M. Ralph too, the naughty boy." He waved a chubby finger in admonishment at the young man. "No more visits to houses of…"

322

I interrupted, "Let me present Ralph's mother, my sister Madame Eleanor Morris, Monsieur."

"Ah, the lovely mother. Enchanted, Madame." He kissed his fingers at Nelly, who was staring at him, wide-eyed.

"Nelly," I explained. "This is M. Cochot. The Prefect."

"Goodness," she said, shrinking a little, while Ralph for his part did not know where to look.

Our visitor, however, ignored or was ignorant of their reaction. He was all geniality, boosted, I rather suspected, by a free indulgence in wine.

"I see you are eating lobster again, Madame Hudson." He smiled. "I trust you are enjoying it as much as before."

"It is very good."

"I can only persuade my wife..." He gestured back to his table, where the woman in question was staring fiercely at us, "to have a little poached fish... Like yourself, Madame." He nodded at the uncomprehending Nelly. "To keep your svelte figure, no doubt." He laughed. "Madame Hudson has no such inhibitions."

"Your meal will be getting cold," I said, hoping he would leave us in peace.

"Actually, Madame," he said, more seriously, "I wished to inform you, in case you were unaware of it, that the funeral of Mlle. Sylvie will take place tomorrow in Père Lachaise cemetery. It occurred to me that you might like to be present."

"Indeed, I would," I replied. "At what time is it?"

"At two o'clock. I shall be going myself, to pay my respects." My surprise must have shewn on my face, for he went on. "You never know who will turn up at the graveside, Madame. The true murderer, perhaps." He glanced at Ralph.

He stood for a moment, uncertainly. Were we about to receive an apology?

"Bon appetite!" he said, chuckling. "The food here is rather better, heh Ralph, than what you get in La Santé."

No one laughed. Nelly because she didn't understand, and I because I didn't think it funny. Ralph made an attempt, but it came out as a strangled squeak.

M. Cochot bowed to us then, and made to leave, "By the way, Ralph," he called over his shoulder, "did your aunt ever tell you how she saved my life?" Chortling to himself, and swaying just a little, he returned to his wife.

We looked at each other. Then "Whatever was all that about?" asked Nelly. "Who in heaven's name was that dreadful man?"

"I told you," I said. "The Prefect."

That meant nothing to her.

"The chief of police," Ralph muttered. "The one who locked me up. Aunt Martha's special friend, apparently."

"Oh!"

"No friend of mine," I said.

"Oh no? Didn't you save his life? Didn't he bring you here, to wine and dine you? Didn't he send that bouquet of lilies?"

Who would have thought Ralph so sharp?

"I remembered how you asked me about him," he went on, since I remained silent. "How you asked about the Prefecture and then went rushing off to it, leaving me sitting with mummy." He pouted. "I had plenty of time in prison to think about things."

What should I tell them? Not the whole truth anyway.

"I overheard something I thought the authorities should know. As for saving his life, that's an absurd exaggeration. I did him a favour, that's all. He was perhaps a little too ostentatious in his gratitude."

"It all sounds very strange to me," Nelly said and sniffed. "It's beyond me how you get yourself into such scrapes, Martha."

"Well anyway," I turned to Ralph. "Will you not now wish to delay your departure in order to come with me to poor Sylvie's funeral?"

"Absolutely not," he said with a shudder. "I want to put all that behind me."

"I cannot believe you would even suggest it, Martha," Nelly added.

It was hard, after that, to enjoy the rest of the meal. None of us felt like indulging in a dessert. Ralph finished the wine and the two of us took a cognac, while Nelly condescended to try a sweet liqueur as suggested by the waiter. A Benedictine, as made by the monks of that order, he said.

Ralph and I watched while she sipped it. "It quite warms you up," she said, appreciatively at last. "Those monks know what they are doing."

It was a welcome concession and we raised our glasses in a toast, though to what exactly I am not sure. Ralph's release? Nelly's victory?

When we requested the bill, we were astonished to be informed that M. Cochot had already taken care of it. Looking over to where he had been sitting with his wife, I saw that in their place a different couple were now seated. The Prefect and his wife had left. My companions were elated, for we had not stinted and the sum must have been steep, while I wondered if after all it was M. Cochot's way of saying sorry.

Chapter Twenty-Seven – A Burial

The next morning, Nelly woke me a little after sunrise. She was so anxious to be in time for the train to Dunkirk that she had begun her preparations absurdly early. Ralph had stayed for the last night in his studio, and of course she was worried that he would be late. In the end, however, all was well. Once again, Ralph was early, in haste, perhaps, to leave a city which had proved so ill-starred for him. I was surprised at the paucity of his luggage, just a small enough suitcase and an oblong package wrapped in brown paper that must contain the few paintings he was bringing home with him. My sister and I, for the short while we were in the city, had many more bags. But that I suppose is the difference between men and women. Dear Henry, too, always used to like to travel light.

I insisted on accompanying them to the station even though Nelly assured me that it was quite unnecessary.

"We can manage by ourselves, Martha, especially since you must surely have lots of other things to do."

Ignoring the reproving tones in which she spoke to me, I said that of course I wanted to see them safely on to the train.

"I shan't be sorry to say goodbye to this place," Nelly remarked as we trundled to the Gare du Nord in our cab. "Undeniably beautiful though it is there is something... evil, rotten, decadent here. Don't you agree?"

"No more than any other big city," I replied, thinking once more how my sister's outlook on life was coloured by her lurid reading matter. "The same thing could equally be said of London."

"Oh well, London..." She sniffed and gazed out of the window.

Ralph was silent, and I wondered if, after all, he were having second thoughts. It was strange, I thought, that none of those very good friends we had met had rallied round him in his time of trouble, or even now come to say goodbye to him. But then it was probably too early in the morning for those nocturnal revellers.

I waved my sister and nephew off, the monstrous machine that was to take them away belching foul smoke as it steamed out of the station, causing them soon to vanish. They were gone.

As I headed back into the city, I wondered what the day ahead would hold. Sylvie's funeral and perhaps confirmation of my suspicions.

Unencumbered by luggage, I was happy to walk for a while. At that early hour, the air was almost fresh, with a blue sky in which a few yellow clouds were only now starting to mass. Still, the area around the station was rough enough, and I was conscious of low-life individuals loitering in doorways, watching me as I passed. On top of that, my head had started to throb again from my wound. Still, I kept going, by no means in a mood to return to the hotel, which, despite everything that annoyed me about Nelly, I felt would now seem bereft.

Eventually I came to a leafy canal which provided a pleasant change from the high buildings of the boulevards. At intervals, benches had been placed along the path, and I took advantage of

327

one of these, seating myself for a while to watch the barges pass by, waving to the children on board, and, when they were gone, observing the activities of the water birds, gliding and diving, or hopping up on to the bank, an eye open for any crumbs they might find. It was so wonderfully peaceful that only then I realised how much I dreaded what lay ahead of me.

I walked on until I came to a charming canal-bank establishment named the Hotel du Nord. What a delightful place to stay, if rather far from the centre. By means of an arched metal footbridge, I crossed over to it, and sat myself at one of their little tables to enjoy a chilled lemon tea, conscious I was only delaying the moment when I must return to the hotel.

Madame Albert had already informed me that the Père Lachaise cemetery was on the outskirts of the city, in a suburb named Belleville.

"That sounds nice," I said. "Beautiful town."

She laughed. "You will see how beautiful it is when you get there." Then added, "but the cemetery itself is impressive. And historic. Near enough two hundred Communards were shot there, you know. You can see the wall. Their bodies were then thrown in a pit below it, like animals."

"The Communards?"

"Members of the Paris Commune of 1871, who were holding out against the Prussians and the Versailles mob. It was a glorious few months but it ended in tragedy, Madame Martha."

Tears had come to the woman's eyes.

"I was a young woman then, only recently come to Paris with my husband. They killed him too."

"I am very sorry to hear that," I said, conscious of the inadequacy of my words.

"Yes, well, but the dream itself will never die."

She looked at me defiantly and, once again, I wondered if she were attached to the anarchists in some way and, moreover, if she indeed suspected me of involvement in the death of Leon Garcia. Surely not, or she would not have spoken thus to me. However, I felt uncomfortable and guilty, and, wishing to change the subject, asked how best to travel to the cemetery. There were buses and trams that could bring me near, she said. However, it might be easier to take a cab. I sighed. My purse was emptying again.

"You are not going to the church, then, Madame, for the mass?"

I stared at her. How foolish was I! It would of course be the appropriate – and useful – thing to do. However, M. Cochot had not informed me where the service was taking place and now it would be too late to find out.

I donned my good black bombazine, too heavy for the weather which had turned sultry again, but suitable for the occasion. Fearing to be late, I left in good time, though not as early as Nelly would have done. The cab made speedy enough progress through the city, arriving at the cemetery gates a good forty minutes before the cortege was due to arrive. On the way I viewed how the fashionable boulevards gave way to the poverty-stricken district of working people that was Belleville. What ironist had given it the name, I wondered? With time to spare, I decided to visit some of the eminent dead, as indicated on the map I purchased at the gate from a crabbed old man with an impenetrable accent.

Père Lachaise resembled the cemetery at Montmartre though on a much grander scale. Cobbled streets of this city of the dead, with the little palaces that were family mausoleums, stretched up and down and round the hill in dizzying directions, flat gravestones and other monuments seemingly heaped haphazardly between them. Here was M. Frédéric Chopin, the composer and pianist, his tomb a mass of red roses. Another musician, M. Bizet, author of that marvellous opera "Carmen," the writers Molière and Honoré de Balzac, were all laid to rest here. Sylvie would be taking her modest place among the greats.

My map indicated the Wall of the Communards mentioned by Madame Albert, but it was to be found at the far end of the cemetery, and I did not have time to visit it, even if I'd had a mind to do so. Returning instead to the gate, I purchased some white lilies from a flower seller there. Not because Sylvie was an innocent but because, whatever she had done in her short life, she did not deserve such a terrible end.

A small group was already assembling, among them some artists I recognised, including, to my surprise, the impetuous Etienne, with his thick black beard. Although my new suspicions had more or less ruled him out as the murderer – a man like him would not have constructed such an elaborate trap but would simply have strangled or stabbed his lover in a fit of jealous rage – I reckoned that the alibi he offered was baseless: his illustrious family relying on their name and influence to avoid further embarrassing questions. Still, he might have some useful information for me. I approached him and introduced myself as Ralph's aunt.

"Of course, Madame, I remember you very well." He looked around. "Ralph is not here?"

"He and his mother returned to England this morning," I replied.

He laughed, "Ah, I see. The Paris art world will be lost without him."

"I did not think he had a great talent," I said, slightly affronted at his mocking tone. "But at least he managed to sell most of his paintings before he left, so someone must appreciate his gift."

Etienne laughed even more heartily at that. Then apologised. "I am sorry, Madame, but since you found his work lacking in genius and therefore must be a woman of taste, I will explain the joke. Yes, Ralph sold his pictures. In fact I bought two myself. But for the canvases, you understand."

I did not, and looked at him puzzled.

"Good canvases from a dealer are expensive," he explained. "Ralph sold us his pictures at a knock-down price, so now we can scrape off his daubs and paint our own masterpieces on top of them."

No wonder my nephew had looked sheepish when his mother congratulated him on his sales.

"Poor Ralph," I said.

"No, Madame, he will be better off back in England, in some clerical job. As an assistant in a draper's shop, perhaps."

The scorn and snobbery riled me.

"I am surprised to see you here, M. Etienne," I said coldly, "after your history with Mlle. Sylvie and the row you had with her at Le Chien Jaune."

"Oh," he said and reddened. "Of course, you were there. Well, I admit I was foolishly infatuated with the girl for a while. I didn't like to see anyone steal her away from me. Certainly not that old degenerate, Bourdain."

Not Ralph either, I thought, though I considered it prudent not to rake that up.

"I only saw poor Sylvie a few times," I said, "and, to be frank, she didn't strike me as particularly special. Pretty girls are two a penny in this city, and she seemed rather silly and vain. Yet she must have had something that set her apart, for you and Jules Bourdain both to fall for her."

He looked at me in surprise. If I was perhaps somewhat inappropriately forward in my remarks, it was because I thought the youth might be able to explain her particular attractions to me.

"Well, Madame. She did. But I hardly think it is something I can talk about with Ralph's most respectable aunt."

It was my turn to blush.

"I see," I said. And thought, Heavens! to myself.

"Though," Etienne continued. "The degree of Bourdain's infatuation did, I admit, surprise me. The old fool was talking of marriage, you know. The first time he has done that with any of his... er... conquests."

"Marriage?"

"The ambition of senility, Madame. To try to renew oneself through mating with some young nymph. It's quite pathetic, don't you agree."

"If he had that in mind, I should have thought Poppy a more suitable partner." I was treading very carefully here.

332

"Poupée? No. She was too much of an equal. A threat, even. Have you seen the work she did with him? It is stupendous. She has a great talent."

So, after all, Etienne was capable of generosity when it came to matters of true art.

"But where is Poppy now? Do you know?"

"What? She is missing?"

"Since that night at Le Chien Jaune."

I was astonished that he had not heard.

"Oh, I expect she'll turn up again," he said. "Probably gone off somewhere to sulk … But look. Here comes the cortege."

A horse-drawn carriage bearing the coffin was entering the gate. It was an elaborate affair, bedecked with black feathers, the coffin itself covered in white flowers. I had judged that right, at least. Behind, now on foot, trudged the mighty figure of the sculptor, with his long hair and grey beard, for all the world like some ancient god. Beside him a tiny woman I did not recognise, with the look of a laundress.

"I think that must be Sylvie's mother," whispered Etienne. So the girl had family after all.

Among those who followed behind, I recognised a few familiar faces. Jean Renard from Le Chien Jaune, swaggered by, still wearing that eye-catching yellow-feathered hat, so unsuitable for the occasion. With him were many artists, including my old friend M. Henri who limped along with the assistance of a walking stick. I tried to catch his eye, unsuccessfully: he was too busy chatting. La Goulue was there, too, but no Valentin. Instead the dancer was clinging to the arm of her friend Grille d'Egouts. Thérèse came behind them all, head down, dressed in a black that did not suit her muddy complexion.

"Madame Hudson." It was M. Cochot, in full uniform, his medals glittering in the sun.

"You make a good target, Monsieur," I couldn't help myself saying.

"I am well-protected. In any case, I believe in living dangerously, as you do yourself."

"I?"

He smiled and took my arm, whether I wanted him to nor not, and we joined the procession.

"I trust your sister and young Ralph have left safely."

"Yes, Monsieur, I saw them off myself."

He squeezed my arm.

"It was very generous of you, Monsieur," I said, affecting not to notice the gesture, "to pay for our meal last night. I was astonished."

"It was nothing."

"Hardly that."

"Let me tell you a secret, Madame Martha. I have – let us say – an arrangement with that particular establishment." He chuckled and his chins shook. "I do them favours and they gratefully reciprocate."

"I see." Bribery and corruption. I tried to shake my arm free, but he just grinned and held on all the more tightly.

By now we had reached the graveside. Delivering his eulogy, M. Bourdain broke down utterly. He made no reference to Etienne's claim that he had intended to marry the girl. Instead, he said, weeping and clutching his breast, that she was become a

334

daughter to him, the which, I am afraid, provoked a few sniggers and sidelong glances. He added that every night he prayed that the perpetrator of the foul crime be brought to justice, striking the balled fist of one hand into the palm of the other.

"I would like to do to him what he did to my darling girl."

If this aspiration was rather less than Christian, the priest made no comment but instead proceeded with the service.

"Dust to dust," he intoned, "ashes to ashes."

As flowers were thrown into the grave, M. Bourdain fell to his knees as if to join Sylvie in her resting place. La Goulue and others joined him, emitting loud sobs, though the poor mother stood by, quiet and dry-faced, as if perplexed by the whole business.

"I shall erect a monument on this tomb that will astonish the world," the sculptor shouted, rising to his feet, towering over the assembled company. "I, Jules Bourdain."

"What do you see?" M. Cochot whispered into my ear. "Landlady of Mr Sherlock Holmes."

What did I see? I saw a man who to my restrained English nature and, in the words of the Bard of Avon, doth protest too much. I saw Etienne pulling at his beard with a cynical expression on his face. There was no sign of Poppy, but I had not expected her to be present, even if the Prefect were hoping so. But I saw other something else, and told of it in lowered tones to M. Cochot.

He looked at me in astonishment.

"Think about it, Monsieur," I whispered back. "There is motive certainly, and the method fits, too."

"We must talk later," he said, looking about, I suppose in case anyone was listening in to our conversation.

It was later that afternoon, after reviving myself with an omelette lunch, that I rejoined M. Cochot at the Prefecture and told him in detail of my suspicions.

"That is all they are, Monsieur. Suspicions. I have no firm evidence, just intuition based on my knowledge of human nature, as well as certain observations of the behaviour of the person in question. Nevertheless, if we can possibly get a confession…" I explained my plan.

"I have to say, Madame," the Prefect replied, "it is almost beyond belief that such a one could be guilty of the crime. However, for the sake of Mr. Sherlock Holmes, I am willing to humour you, and see what transpires. God knows, we have no other leads right now."

While grateful for the accommodating influence of my lodger, I was somewhat piqued by the fact that M. Cochot did not take my plan on its own merits. On my own merits.

"You realise that your proposition is not without risk to yourself, Madame," he added.

"Oh you know me, Monsieur," I replied. "I like to live dangerously."

He laughed. "Touché," he said. I believe it is a word from the world of duelling.

Preparations were made. The trap was to be set for the following morning.

Chapter Twenty-Eight – An Invitation to Dinner

When I at last returned to the hotel it was to find a message awaiting me from Dr. Lepine. I had almost expected to see him at the funeral, but then reconsidered. Why ever would he be there? He didn't know the girl, after all. I opened the note straight away, standing in the entrance hall, Madame Albert smiling knowingly (as she thought) beside me. What I found inside the envelope was, to my considerable surprise, an invitation to dine with the doctor and his wife that evening.

I decided to amaze our landlady, too, and wipe that silly smile from her face into the bargain.

"Dinner! All three of you," she exclaimed. "So will you go, Madame?"

What she had taken to be an intimate tête-à-tête, had turned out to be nothing of the sort.

There was, I supposed, no real reason not to accept. It would avoid a solitary evening and the troubled thoughts that might accompany it. On the other hand, the atmosphere would surely be strained, each Lepine having secrets of which I was aware, but of which their spouse was ignorant. Nevertheless, I decided to accept.

"I'll go gladly," I said. "Would Victorine or Philippe be free to convey my reply to the Doctor?"

"That won't be necessary, Madame. Maurice said that he would call for you at eight, unless he heard to the contrary."

So my acceptance was understood. A little cheekily, I thought.

There was plenty of time, to rest, to change, although first the landlady detained me a while, to hear all about the funeral.

"Her poor mother," she said.

Yes, I thought. Pushed to the side of the show. For something of a circus it had certainly been. I told her of the elaborate cortege, the carriage with its feathers, Bourdain's fervent eulogy, his behaviour, falling to his knees. She shook her head.

"These artists!" she said, adding slightly mysteriously. "Well, you know all about them by now, Madame."

Permitted at last to withdraw to my room I removed with some relief my good bombazine and lay on my bed for a while in my shift, watching the flickering patterns of light on the ceiling, as that relentless sun penetrated the light curtains. The sun. Would it never stop burning down on the city? How I longed for the pearly grey skies of England.

I must have dozed off, for, when I opened my eyes, the light in the room had changed to the blue of early evening. Rousing myself a little reluctantly and splashing water on my face, I decided against my cerise silk, which was a little too frivolous for the occasion. Instead, I chose to wear a light gown of grey moire, better than everyday wear, but not overly so. In case the evening was chill – most unlikely – my black shawl would suffice to protect me, the whole ensemble topped by my black straw hat, with the little red cherries.

There came a tap on the door. It was Madame Albert.

"Is the doctor here already?" I asked, consulting my pocket watch. It read only twenty minutes to the hour of eight.

"No, it is another gentleman." Her expression was queer.

I followed her down the stairs, only to find M. Cochot of all people standing in the hallway. Possibly the last person on earth I wished to see in that particular spot for a multitude of reasons. At least he was no longer in uniform.

"Madame Hudson," he said, glancing severely at the landlady, who seemed inclined to remain. She took the hint and disappeared into the parlour, though without, I noticed, closing the door, "How very charming you look. I see that you are preparing to go out and apologise for arriving unannounced, but I was hoping to discuss further with you the matter we touched on earlier." He glanced at the open parlour door. "Perhaps over a dinner."

He assumed I was going out alone, so I explained – in some confusion, aware of listening ears – that I had another invitation for the evening.

"Surely," I said, "we have already settled the arrangements you speak of."

"Well, yes. I suppose we have." He paused. "Is it "Hubert" who is calling for you?"

I looked at him in astonishment.

"No, Monsieur. Not M. Blanchard."

"Ah well." He looked most discommoded, the which puzzled me greatly. "Then perhaps you would do me the honour of an engagement, after the business is settled. Always assuming of course that you are correct in your suspicions… We can again talk of Mr. Holmes."

"M. Cochot," I replied. "Although it is most kind of you to invite me, it would not be, I feel, at all appropriate. In any case, I consider that we have by now quite exhausted the subject of my lodger."

In refusing his offer, I was thinking particularly of his wife, not wishing to be attacked by any more jealous spouses. Madame Cochot, from the brief sighting I had of her, would appear to be a much more formidable rival than poor Françoise Lepine.

"Alas, I am devastated, Madame," he said. "Though perhaps you will change your mind. I live in hope."

He bowed and made as dignified an exit as he could.

I was sorely embarrassed. More than that. I was sure Madame Albert knew exactly who my visitor was, and even now might be putting two and two together, as they say. The same lady emerged from the parlour and her expression, indeed, was by no means friendly.

"The Prefect!" she said. "I see you are on good terms with the Prefect, Madame."

"Hardly," I replied carelessly. "I petitioned him on behalf of Ralph and he discovered that my lodger in London was known to him, a man he very much admires."

I explained about Mr. H., but Madame Albert had, it seemed, had never heard of him and was even less interested. However, that icy look had melted somewhat.

"Could you explain something to me?" I said, trying to appear disingenuous. "I am a middle-aged woman, very far from the bloom or shapeliness of youth. And yet I have found myself not exactly pursued but at least sought after by several gentlemen. That would never have happened in England, you know."

She laughed heartily.

"We French do not consider age a barrier, Madame. Clearly you possess a certain something. A certain "je ne said quoi" which turns men's heads. You should be glad of it."

I disagreed. "It just seems to make life more complicated."

"Anyway," she went on, "here comes another of your admirers."

The doctor had just entered, rather puzzled by our merriment. Meanwhile, I hoped I had satisfactorily dispelled her suspicions.

The conversation during the short walk to the doctor's apartment was somewhat strained, and even monosyllabic on his part. No, he had no further news of Garance. Yes, the weather was unpleasantly hot. Yes, it became pleasanter in the evenings. In the end, I felt constrained to babble on about Sylvie's funeral, in which, it seemed, he had no interest, just walking with his head bowed down. At least my chit-chat filled a silence which otherwise might have seemed oppressive. I anticipated a dreary evening if both spouses were equally uncommunicative.

It seemed at first as if this would be so. I was greeted with a timid self-consciousness by Madame Lepine. However, the presence of two delightful children, Jacques and Charlotte, a boy and a girl – aged six and five, as they soon proudly informed me – eased the atmosphere. I always get on well with little folk. They laughed at my English accent as I endeavoured to speak their language, the boy even correcting my mistakes, until told by his mother that he was being most impolite.

"Not at all," I said laughing. "I am delighted that Jacques can help me improve my French."

The children were not to stay with us long, however, and soon their nurse took them, protesting somewhat, to their bath.

The Lepines' apartment was comfortable without any signs of great prosperity. Françoise (for that was what she insisted I call her) displayed taste and discernment in eschewing the heavy dark furniture so beloved by earlier generations, those thick drapes that attract so much dust. All was light and fresh, and the pale wallpaper, with its pattern of stylised flowers, rather reminded me of the productions of Mr. William Morris. In fact, as Françoise informed me when I admired the disposition of the room, she had studied design before her marriage.

"It's a style called Art Nouveau, Martha." (I had of course insisted that she call me by my first name as well.) "In fact, it owes its origins partly to your own Arts and Crafts movement."

I nodded wisely, though my knowledge of such things was slight.

Dr. Lepine still appeared preoccupied, or at least shewed little interest in that particular topic of conversation. He simply remarked that he left all that side of things to his wife. I added then that I thought it a pity she had abandoned her studies, seeing that she was evidently very talented. But she just smiled and shrugged.

"The children take up all of my time, Martha."

I nodded. That is the way of the world for us women.

We were soon summoned to dinner, which proved to be plain but tasty fare. A soup of some sort, was followed by a chicken in sauce and a plum tart, I think, to finish. For once, I have to say, I paid little heed to what I was eating, since the conversation very soon turned into an intense confessional. The couple took it in turns to enlighten me, Françoise first.

When she had returned home after her attack on myself in the catacombs, it seems she had broken down in nervous hysteria, feverish and unable to stop sobbing. The affrighted servants had summoned her husband home, whereupon she, recovered enough to speak, had revealed all to him, her suspicions, her jealousy, and her mad endeavour to do away with the person she had thought had displaced herself in his affections.

Now it was the doctor's turn. Of course, he said, only someone whose wits were wandering could have believed that Madame Hudson might be the object of his desires – apologising to me immediately after asserting this, in case I should be offended by his unflattering words. I made a dismissive gesture, saying that I also had found it absurd. Nevertheless, I rather felt that, out of common courtesy, he might have tempered his rejection of the possibility.

He continued: the extremity of his wife's reaction to his infidelity had struck him like a blow. (I knew how that felt, quite literally, still experiencing, as I did, an occasional twinge from her attempt to crack open my skull.) His own behaviour, he now realised, had almost broken the wife he loved dearly and his affair, with Garance was a horrible aberration, nothing but a temporary madness. He had fallen to his knees before her and confessed all, and Françoise, relieved at last to discover the truth of the matter, forgave him and they fell into each other's arms.

"Our marriage has been strengthened by this," she told me, eyes shining.

Dr. Lepine concurred, and took his wife's hand.

343

I smiled back and congratulated them, although in my heart I was rather less enthusiastic about this most touching reconciliation, and not at all sure if I would have been so forgiving under the circumstances. It seemed to me that Dr. Lepine had extracted himself from the situation rather neatly. For the sake of this particular marriage, at least, I reckoned that it was lucky Poppy had vanished so completely from the scene. However, as I have observed before, the French quite clearly see these things differently, and if Françoise were content to let the matter rest, then who was I to object.

"Maurice tells me that this Garance person has gone away," she said. "Does anyone know where she is?"

"It seems not. She has completely disappeared." I had my own ideas and fears on that subject, the which I was not prepared to share.

"Just as well," she replied, so perhaps she was not quite as sanguine as she claimed.

After the conclusion of the meal, I was not inclined to extend the evening, and I think the Lepines felt the same. Their wanting to share their reconciliation with me was, I suppose, something they needed to do, and I was happy for them and for their lovely children. Nevertheless, given the doctor's impressionable and passionate nature, I wondered if it would be the last time that his head was turned by a pretty face.

He asked if I wished him to call me a cab, but the distance was so short that I insisted I was happy to walk back. Françoise and I embraced, and promised to keep in touch, although I doubted that we would. The doctor accompanied me, since Paris by night is not the safest of places. On the way, he was, in contrast to our earlier walk, much more garrulous, full of the virtues of his wife and speculating how he could have ever been tempted to stray. I broke into this eulogy by informing him that I was still worried for Garance's safety.

"Oh, she is in no danger from the anarchists," he said. "They don't think it was she who betrayed them."

I stopped in my tracks.

"How do you know that?" I asked.

"Madame Hudson," he said, smiling just a little. "You should be more careful in whom you confide. But don't worry. Your secret is safe with me."

"You must explain."

He looked me in the eye.

"Well, you see," he said, "I was able to convince certain persons that their suspicions regarding Garance and yourself were unfounded."

"Garance and myself? So I am suspected." A shiver ran through me.

"Not any more. I have pointed them in a different direction."

"What does that mean? You have not implicated a blameless person, I trust."

"No. Not that. An agent provocateur. Someone, indeed, working for both sides and loyal to neither. Only to himself."

His smile broadened, and, under the dim lamplight of the street, his thin face, with that long nose, looked positively sinister. The face of a fanatic. "That was how I met Garance, and indeed others that you know. In the Cause, all of us wishing to strive towards a better, more equal society."

Lepine an anarchist sympathiser! Poppy also! Who else, then?

"But to use such means," I protested. "Bombs, bullets, innocents dying."

"Neither Garance nor I are in favour of the Propaganda of the Deed, Madame. We are both of the opinion that minds can be changed by rational argument, not violence."

"Yet now you have falsely accused someone."

"The person in question is not innocent, Madame, even if on this occasion it was not he who betrayed the Cause. Let us admit he would have if he could."

We had reached my hotel. Whatever was I to make of his words? I bade him farewell in some confusion, and watched him walk away from me. I was never to see him again.

Chapter Twenty-Nine – The Trap

"He's not here."

She was about to shut the door in my face again.

"No matter. Perhaps you can help me, Madame."

She scowled. "What is it?"

"I should like, if possible, to buy something."

Her eyes narrowed. "To buy something?"

"Yes. I am going home to England very soon, and would so like to have something small by M. Bourdain to take back with me."

"M. Bourdain doesn't do small."

She was trying to shut the door again, but I had placed a foot over the threshold.

"Ah, but when I was here before." I said, "I saw some little pieces, probably models for the big sculptures."

"Well, yes. That's true." She was wavering just a little. Suspicion fighting with greed. She stood aside to let me enter.

"A pity M. Bourdain isn't here," I said. "I was much moved by his speech at Mlle. Sylvie's graveside."

She didn't say a word.

"So touching. He looked upon her as a daughter, he said."

She shot me a glance. "That's what he said… Please look around, Madame, and tell me if anything catches your eye."

I went over to a table where some small figures were standing. I picked one up. The twisted torso of a female nude.

"But surely this is by Garance Germaine," I said.

"No."

"That's strange. It is exactly like a drawing in her sketchbook. Like the figure in the Last Judgment she was working on with M. Bourdain." I glanced across to where the massive piece stood, still unfinished.

She almost snatched the figure from me.

"Gigi must have copied it."

"Hmm. Well, I like it. How much is it?"

She thrust it back at me, naming an absurd price.

I laughed. "Perhaps I might consider that sort of sum were it by Jules Bourdain. But I am sure it is Gigi's, as you call her. Where is she, by the way? Perhaps we can ask her. Or ask M. Bourdain."

She stared at me for a few moments.

"Just take it and go," she said finally.

"Thérèse," I said softly. "I know what you did. And why you did it."

She clenched her large hands into fists, as if keeping herself in check with difficulty. Hate radiated from her. This woman is capable of anything, I thought, and felt a sudden chill. Then she started to laugh. It was almost more terrifying than her hostility.

"What do you think you know, Madame?"

"I know you killed them both, Sylvie and Gigi."

"You know nothing. I never laid a finger on Gigi."

"But on Sylvie? You laid a finger on her, all right. You threw acid in her face and then stabbed her to death."

"No. Not me. You can't prove that." The answer was too quick, too defensive. "Though that slut got what she deserved…" adding with a sly look at me, "whoever it was did it."

"Come now, Thérèse. Everyone knows by now that Jules was planning to marry Sylvie. What would have happened to you then? Cast out after so many faithful years. Where could you have gone? What could you have done?"

"You are so clever, Madame. You have worked it all out. Except that I didn't do it."

"How did you persuade her to go down there, to the catacombs? Did you tell her there was a party? Maybe a private party?"

"You think she would deign to listen to the likes of me. Never. She never even spoke to me, that one. Thought she was far too high and mighty. I was dirt, in her eyes. I, who, as you say, remained faithful to Jules all through the years. Through bad times and good. And, Madame, I too was beautiful once, although you wouldn't think it now."

She reared up proudly, remembering. No, there was nothing left of any past beauty and I almost felt sorry for her. But then that harsh and bitter laugh sounded out again.

"Ha! The silly trollop thought she had him wrapped around her little finger…" She shook her head. "I've seen it so many times before. She might have thought she was different but she was like all the others. Just another silly little bit of amusement for him. No, Madame. I had nothing to fear from Mlle. Sylvie. He'd never have married her."

"But could you be sure this time? I'm told he was utterly bewitched."

"Bewitched, yes, that's a good word. Yes, she was a witch, all right. Or tried to be."

No, I thought. Sylvie was no witch. But you…

"Semele," I said. "Remember her?"

"What?"

"I've read the full story, Thérèse. How Hera, Zeus's wife, maddened with jealousy, causes her rival to be killed. Disguised as an old crone, she inveigles her way into Semele's confidence, and convinces her that Zeus must prove his love by swearing to grant whatever she asks him. Knowing it will destroy the girl, Hera then urges her to ask Zeus to shew himself to her in his full glory, as King of the Gods. Zeus will be bound by his sworn promise to fulfil the request, even though he too knows what will happen. That, being mortal, Semele will not survive the manifestation."

"What a charming tale," she sneered.

"As you well know, Jules Bourdain made a sculpture of Semele in the split second before she is reduced to a pile of ashes. I saw it in the Louvre. Was it that gave you the idea? Did you make Sylvie your friend with a view to disposing of your rival?"

"You are quite mad, Madame. In any case, the model for Semele was your Gigi. Not Mlle. Sylvie."

"Which brings me back to my earlier point. What have you done with Gigi? Where is she? Is she also lying dead in the catacombs?"

Her pale eyes glinted malevolently. "You must be deaf, Madame. I already told you, I have done nothing to Gigi. I have no idea where she is."

"So it is only Sylvie you admit to killing…" She was about to protest again but I continued, suddenly understanding. "In the myth, Semele was expecting a child by Zeus. Was Sylvie in the same condition? Is that why he wanted to marry her? Is that why you felt you had to kill her?"

"She wasn't pregnant."

"Did you murder Bourdain's unborn child along with that poor girl?"

"Poor girl! Poor girl!" Something broke in her. The woman was raging now. "There was nothing poor about her. You yourself called her a witch!"

She started pushing me.

"He was so pleased, the old fool. To think that at last he would be a father. Ha!" With each phrase she pushed me harder. Oh, she was strong. "I could have given him a child back then, but back then he hadn't wanted one…"

I wasn't expecting what happened next, although perhaps I should have. With that surprising strength of hers, she had driven me towards the massive marble sculpture of the Last Judgment.

"How tragic when you are found crushed beneath it," she said. "And I only left you for a moment to fetch something. You shouldn't have touched it, Madame. I told you not to touch anything."

She knocked me to the floor under the writhing figures. Then grabbed a corner of the huge piece, quite intending to pull it down on top of me. But, though she was strong, it was more difficult than she expected, and I had time to roll away. The sculpture crashed down, just missing me.

She came at me again, eyes wild, hair hanging down. I was still grasping Poppy's little figurine, and in desperation smashed it into her face. She fell back, screeching curses, blood pouring from her cheek and forehead. But before I could get up she was on me again, tearing at me with her nails, punching me, trying to throttle me. A blackness was engulfing me.

"Thérèse! Stop! Stop!"

Someone pulled her away. Blessedly I gulped for breath, and gradually became conscious of several figures standing around us. A uniformed officer was restraining the still struggling woman, while Jules Bourdain himself, haggard and bent, extended a hand to me to help me to my feet. Beside him, stood the familiar rotund form of the Prefect.

"You took your time, Monsieur," I said to him.

"We had to be sure. She kept denying it."

"For goodness sake. Was nearly killing me not good enough for you?"

Meanwhile the sculptor addressed himself to the wild Maenad that was his erstwhile companion.

"Why did you do it, Thérèse?" he said, gently and sadly. "Didn't you know I would always have looked after you?"

"She wouldn't have let you. That witch would have driven me out and you would have let her."

"So you admit to the murder of Mlle. Sylvie Ledoux," M. Cochot said, become all official.

She laughed that terrible laugh again. "It was so easy. I sent her a note from you, Jules, with copies of the keys. She thought it was a romantic rendez-vous… That you had a lovely surprise for her. Well, there was a surprise all right." Now it was in the open, she had turned boastful, proud now of what she had done. "I took the acid. I took that lovely sharp dagger you brought back from the cabaret. Then I let her wait. There in the damp dark, with the bones of the dead all around her. It's said that at night they speak. But she was too stupid to be scared."

M. Bourdain slumped to the floor his head in his hands. "You had to destroy her beauty, too. The acid! How she must have suffered!"

"Not really, Jules. It was quick. Too quick for me."

"My child, too." He raised an anguished face towards her. "You had to kill my child."

"*Your* brat! It could have been anyone's. Anyone's. How could you tell with a whore like that?"

She started to say more on the subject, in terms which I blush now to recall. It was all too much for Bourdain. He jumped to his feet and seized her by the neck, intending I am sure to squeeze the life out of her in front of us. It was all the two officers could do to hold him back.

And then of a sudden, the energy went out of Thérèse. It was her turn to sink to the floor. "You should have let him kill me," she said in a low voice. "My life is nothing to me now."

By now, my readers are perhaps wondering exactly how we arrived at this point, so I must explain a few things – in the first place, how I became convinced that Thérèse was the murderess. Acting on Mr. H.'s (imagined) advice regarding motive and method, I sat myself down to analyse the case. Since the murder itself seemed to me very much a crime of jealousy and revenge, I asked myself was the perpetrator indeed a lover? Etienne, M.

Bourdain himself, even Ralph, or someone else unknown? One thing that had puzzled me all along was why the acid? Not content to kill, the murderer had also to destroy the girl's beauty. Did that not then point to a green-eyed woman, rather than a man? Acid would of course be readily available to any artist – Ralph had some – but also to anyone close to an artist. The story of Semele, in the little book of Greek myths I had previously purchased, almost seemed to foreshadow the motive and to some extent the method of Sylvie's demise, and that brought me to consider Thérèse. She had shewn herself at the very least deeply resentful of M. Bourdain's pretty young models and assistants. In addition, she would surely have known the fate of Zeus's lover from Bourdain's work on the statue.

Use your powers of observation, urged Mr. H. in my imagination. I therefore made it my business to study the woman's demeanour at the funeral. It was most revealing. While everyone else was solemnly concentrating on the burial rites, Thérèse could hardly stop herself from smirking, so satisfied was she with the fate of her rival, something in itself, of course, that did not necessarily indicate guilt. Nevertheless, I was sure I was on the right track.

When I explained all this to the Prefect, he was at first unconvinced.

"No woman could have committed such a terrible murder," he said, shocked at the very notion, conveniently forgetting he had already suggested that Poppy might be guilty.

"On the contrary, Monsieur," I replied. "I have come to the conclusion that only a woman would have done it that way."

I am afraid that I again invoked the name of my lodger to back up my reasoning. The practice was losing its efficacy, yet it still counted for something. At last, perhaps more to humour me, M Cochot agreed to take part in my attempt to get Thérèse to confess.

"I doubt anything will come of it, Madame Hudson," he said. "Except that you will have vilified a guiltless woman. Still, no stone left unturned, and all that."

As we planned the undertaking, M. Cochot insisted, against my better judgment, on involving the sculptor himself. I argued in vain that it would be terrible for him to hear his faithful companion accused, if she indeed turned out to be innocent. Yet, undeniably, we needed a covert listening place within the studio, and, since only M. Bourdain himself could arrange that, in the end I had to agree. Without informing him exactly what was afoot, the Prefect took M. Bourdain into his confidence to the extent that, before my arrival at the studio, the sculptor and the police had installed themselves in a storage room that Thérèse would have no reason to enter.

As M. Cochot told me subsequently, when I started making my accusations, it was all he could do to prevent the sculptor bursting in on us in a blind fury. But as the horrifying realisation dawned, as Thérèse implicated herself more and more, the man started to break down.

Now that the business was over and Sylvie's killer under the very heavy locks and keys of St Lazare women's prison, there was nothing more to keep me in Paris, and I prepared, with some considerable relief, to return home at last. Still, M. Cochot was insistent that we have a final meeting. In any case, I was curious to discover what had transpired when Thérèse was properly interrogated. Because I refused another intimate dinner with him, we met on the afternoon before I was leaving in a pretty garden café on the same St Martin's canal I had discovered by chance on an earlier walk. Some of the single men at other tables were evidently police officers, there to protect my companion from attack, for I recognised a few faces from the Prefecture. They were discreet, however, and sat at a distance.

At first we quietly sipped at our drinks, watching the passing barges, heading with their loads down the canal. Yet again I was struck by the peacefulness of ordinary life that they represented, in contrast to the horrors of the past weeks. I could hardly wait to put all that behind me. However, here the air was fresh and sweet – a thunderous storm had passed over in the night – and I confess I had a few regrets at leaving the beautiful city I should probably never visit again.

M. Cochot, overly gallant as ever, also deplored my departure.

"You will be sorely missed, Madame. If only women were permitted to join the police force," he laughed merrily at the thought, "you would be the first I should like to appoint."

Eventually conversation turned to the matter in hand. The Prefect informed me that Thérèse, while very open about her plan to get rid of Sylvie, continued to deny she had any hand in the disappearance of Poppy, and, since a careful search of the catacombs had uncovered no further bodies apart from the remains that were supposed to be there, he had to conclude that she was speaking the truth. Poppy's vanishing, and also that of Valentin le Désossé, remained a mystery.

"You can be proud of yourself, Madame Hudson," he remarked. "I doubt that without your help we could have arrived at the truth quite so quickly."

If you ever did, I thought.

"You are a true disciple of Mr. Holmes," he continued, and I think he would have patted my hand, had I not hastily withdrawn it.

For myself, I cannot say that the unmasking of the murderer caused me any great satisfaction. It was all so very sad. So many lives broken by Thérèse's jealous act, including her own.

"What will happen to her?" I asked.

"The judge may look kindly upon her. A crime of passion, you know, is often pardoned here in France."

"But it was carefully planned. And so cruel."

"Yes, indeed. Her better course would be to plead insanity. Women of a certain age go a little mad sometimes, do they not, Madame?"

"I wouldn't know anything about that," I replied coldly.

"Oh, I didn't mean you, Madame. You are still young. Young at heart, at least."

I pursed my lips. It was quite definitely time to go, but before I could rise, an officer came rushing up to M. Cochot, and whispered something into his ear. The Prefect's face turned grave.

"My God!" he said, and looked at me. "Madame Hudson, I have to go at once. Something terrible has happened."

"I am sorry to hear it," I replied.

"Yes indeed. In fact, you know the person involved."

"I do?"

"It is M. Blanchard... He has..." he paused, perhaps thinking to spare me, but continued. "He has been shot."

"Not dead, I hope?" Shocking news indeed.

"They have rushed him to the hospital of Salpetrière, but the worst is feared... Those damned anarchists, again..."

"They are behind it?"

"It is certain. The assassin was heard to cry out "Death to traitors of the Cause" before firing the fatal blast... I am sorry, Madame."

"But M. Blanchard was surely no anarchist."

M. Cochot shrugged. "I cannot explain now, Madame. Let me just say that poor Blanchard had connections, and proved most useful to us in providing... certain information."

He rose, kissed his fingers at me and was gone, whereupon all those single men from the surrounding tables left too.

I decided to stay put for a while longer. It was so pleasant, so peaceful there. I ordered another iced lemon tea and a madeleine, and stared at the rippling waters of the canal.

Hubert Blanchard dead! That officious little man. I could hardly believe at first that he was the treacherous agent provocateur described by Dr. Lepine, and yet it could be. He was well-placed after all, working for the police – who believed him loyal to them – to spy on the anarchists, who in turn thought that he supported their Cause. He had turned up that night at Le Chien Jaune, a strange enough spot for a policeman to frequent, but perfect for meeting shady individuals in order covertly to exchange information. If that were so, and if Dr Lepine had accused him to his friends, then I was indirectly responsible for yet another death: a truly distressing prospect. Yes, Paris and all it contained must be put behind me and forgotten, if that were possible.

I bit into my cake. It was delicious.

Epilogue

I am back in London, ensconced in the comfortable familiarity of Baker Street. Clara and Phoebe are delighted with their little gifts and have asked if I enjoyed myself in Paris. What to reply, except that I did? Mr. H. and the Doctor are also returned from their travels, and full of some case they solved in the West Country. They are not at all interested in my adventures, and when I told of greetings from M. Cochot, the fact hardly registered.

"Oh yes, I did the French police some service a while ago," Mr. H. said carelessly. "I must confess, I was not very impressed with their efficiency."

"Nor was I," I said, but already Mr. H. and the Doctor were discussing another matter.

That was that, then, and almost the end of the story.

In due course I heard from Nelly that Ralph had settled into a post as clerk in a shipping firm, almost as predicted by Etienne. My sister expressed herself delighted to have him back home, but I wondered how long he would put up with that. I should not be at all surprised to hear that he is off again sometime soon. Maybe hopping on to one of those very ships with which he has dealings.

One other unforeseen but most delightful happening: the arrival of a large package posted in France, forwarded on by the good Madame Albert. On opening it, what did I discover only the very same painting by Poppy which I had liked so much. A woodland scene in the Impressionist manner, sunlight glancing through the leaves. I gazed at it in puzzlement. What did it mean? There was no accompanying letter or return address. Studying it more closely, I noticed something different about it. Where the path disappeared off into the forest, the shadowy figure of a woman had been added in a few telling strokes. She was walking away, her head turned to look back, a little smile on her face. Turning the painting, I saw a title inscribed on the back: "*Adieu,*" it read.

I smiled broadly. I could not doubt now but that Poppy had returned to the countryside she had so much missed, throwing off the distractions and torments of Paris. There to live happily, maybe with Valentin, maybe alone, maybe with someone else unknown to me, free to paint as much as she wanted, and to realise the great talent that she had. I resolved to look out for her work in the future, anything signed with that distinctive "GG".

Her painting now hangs in my parlour, next to the little sketch of myself that she had made and above the figurine from the studio of Jules Bourdain he insisted I keep. All of them are much admired by visitors.

"But is that not blood on the statue?" Dr. Watson asked one time, picking it up and examining it.

I thought I had cleaned it all off.

"It's a long story," I said.

NOTES AND ACKNOWLEDGEMENTS

The novel is set in Paris around the year 1895. I have endeavoured to be as accurate as possible. However, for literary purposes I have been a little free and easy regarding dates and events. Certain historical people have walk-on parts, such as the artist Henri de Toulouse Lautrec, the anarchist Fénéon, the singers, Aristide Bruant and Yvette Guilbert, the composer Erik Satie. Valentin le Désossé, partner of the dancer La Goulue, both immortalised in the well-known poster by Lautrec, did indeed mysteriously disappear one night in 1895. Some say he returned to Paris a few years later, some say he was never seen again.

Any resemblance between the fictional sculptor Jules Bourdain and Auguste Rodin is purely coincidental.

The Paris Morgue was a tourist attraction in the nineteenth century. The writer Thomas Hardy even took his wife, Emma, there on their honeymoon.

A female toreador named Marie Genty did indeed perform at the Bois de Boulogne in 1895.

I should like to acknowledge the helpful advice of my readers, Ann O'Kelly, Phyl Herbert, Patricia McCarthy, and in particular of Peter Morriss, who spotted a flaw in the plot which I hope I have been able to correct. As ever grateful thanks to Steve Emecz and the team at MX Publishing for their continuing encouragement and support. Brian Belanger for his great covers.

Also from Susan Knight

Mrs Hudson Investigates
A triumph
> Mark Mower, *The Sherlock Holmes Journal*

Mrs Hudson Goes To Ireland
Rarely do I finish a book in one sitting; on this occasion I had to burn the midnight oil to find out what happened in the end. If Mr Holmes ever worried about his competition, he need only look under his own roof; in Mrs Hudson, he may have well and truly met his match in terms of her investigating skills!
> Sarah Obermuller-Bennett, *The Sherlock Holmes Journal*

Lightning Source UK Ltd.
Milton Keynes UK
UKHW022030130222
398617UK00003B/23